DESTINY'S ECHO

A novel by Dale A. Carswell

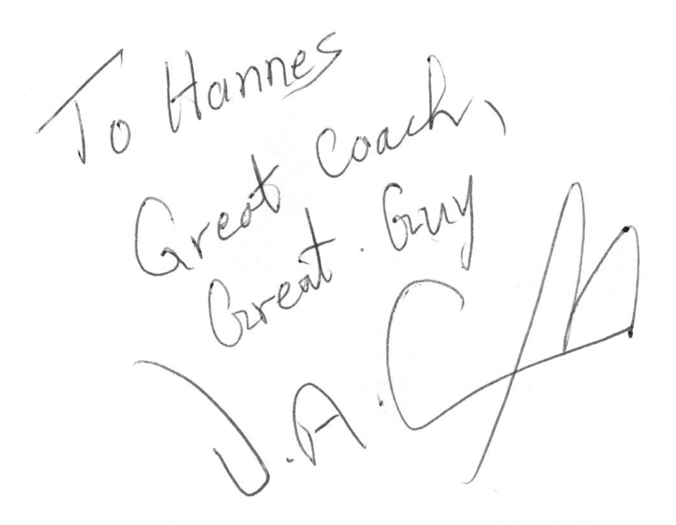

- where Indiana Jones meets Joan of Arc -

Order this book online at www.trafford.com/07-1021
or email orders@trafford.com

Most Trafford titles are also available at major online book retailers.

Note for Librarians: A cataloguing record for this book is available from Library and Archives Canada at www.collectionscanada.ca/amicus/index-e.html

Printed in Victoria, BC, Canada.

ISBN: 978-1-4251-2909-5

www.trafford.com

North America & international
toll-free: 1 888 232 4444 (USA & Canada)
phone: 250 383 6864 • fax: 250 383 6804 • email: info@trafford.com

The United Kingdom & Europe
phone: +44 (0)1865 722 113 • local rate: 0845 230 9601
facsimile: +44 (0)1865 722 868 • email: info.uk@trafford.com

10 9 8 7 6 5 4 3

Dedication

For my Family
(and particularly Tanya's nimble fingers)

Destiny's Echo

Table Of Contents

PROLOGUE

JOURNAL ENTRY NOVEMBER 11

FROM GOOD to evil is but a twitch; a morbid thought jolted to action by careless whim; a renegade micro-neuron skewing some molecular structure in a previously untainted mind. It is said that evil is a perversity, yet what is perverse? Is it immoral? And is not morality but a subjective allegory? What shade of black is definitive evil? Good and evil may be two different paths, but both are always shades of gray. We need only to observe mankind's history to bear this out.

Just what was it that was great about Alexander the Great? He was but a youth committed to megalomania. His birthright permitted him unfettered power and privilege to act out his fantasies of conquest. Such conquest included subjugation of independent peoples, pillaging, murder, rape and destruction of culture. For what? The greater glory of Greece? Perhaps, but without doubt this was for the greater glory and unquenchable egoism of young Alex. Greece was the coincidental beneficiary. Such has it ever been.

Fast forward—past the Romans, the Huns, and the Mayans. In the seventeenth century young Charles the XII of Sweden burst upon the European stage. This proficient warrior was a ravaging storm throughout eastern Europe for many years, rarely returning to his homeland. He lived off the generosity of those under heel and the homeland taxpayers to satisfy his adventurous soul. Like Alexander he was revered and iconized by his people and historians. But what grand contributions had he made to mankind and culture? Perhaps we could consider the fair-haired and blue-eyed scions of northern Italy and eastern Europe as his offering.

Fast forward once again. Now in the twentieth century, where finally, man has evolved. Alas, if it was only true.

Many have simply slipped on a different slicker and ply the ship of avarice on a different tack, attempting to harness the winds of destiny. But destiny will not be harnessed and grave consequences inevitably result—especially for the meek and underprivileged. Man's conscience has evolved, but for the more cynical and wicked it seems only as a hiccup to be handled with discretionary diplomacy. Hence the Hitlers, the Pol Pots, the Mengeles'—angels of death all. And what of God's angels? Did they ride with the conquistadors, or the Pope's many Mussolinis? Did they twitch?

I, for one, am no innocent. At least so far as my contributions to society, for I have taken much and returned little. The potential squandered, the responsibilities I have shirked, the tactless decisions uncaring of consequences. And I have seen my blackness in adversity. It is time—I must not flinch from change, from redemption—I must not twitch.

These moribund thoughts ricocheted through my mind as I prepared the eulogy. I must heal myself. My soul has been slowly ebbing away and I am afraid I will be left with only a shell of this once bonny heart. I must write of my experiences if I am to survive—and I am a survivor, for I am a member of mankind. My love of loves would accept no less. Tomorrow I will begin to transcribe an incredible tale from my journal. It shall be a culmination of the eulogy. I look forward to recounting the triumphs, the joys, the blessings, and I shall deal with the rest.

Jackson Malcolm Maxwell

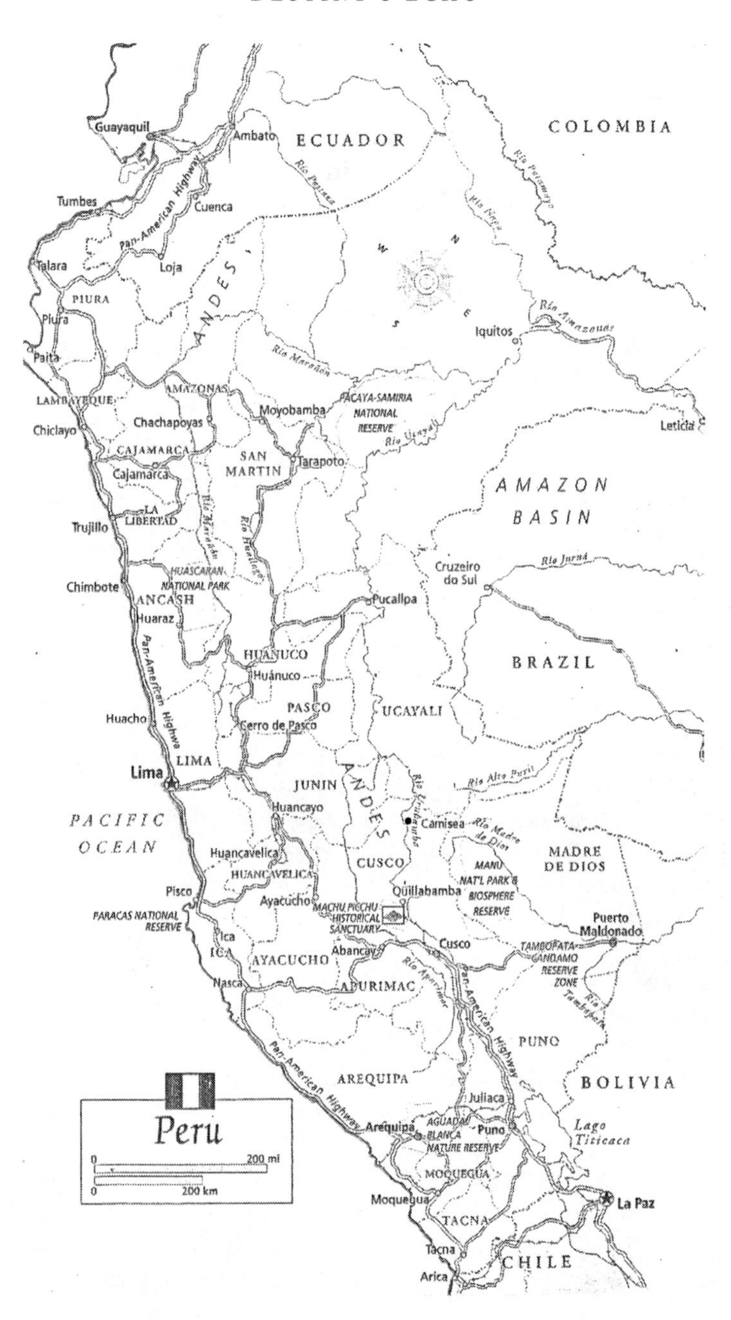

COLOMBIA
ECUADOR
Guayaquil
Ambato
Cuenca
Tumbes
Pan-American Highway
Loja
Talara
PIURA
Piura
Paita
ANDES
Iquitos
Río Amazonas
Río Marañón
AMAZONAS
LAMBAYEQUE
Chachapoyas
Chiclayo
Moyobamba
PACAYA-SAMIRIA NATIONAL RESERVE
Río Ucayali
Leticia
CAJAMARCA
Cajamarca
SAN MARTIN
Tarapoto
AMAZON BASIN
LA LIBERTAD
Trujillo
Río Marañón
Río Huallaga
Cruzeiro do Sul
Río Juruá
Chimbote
HUASCARAN NATIONAL PARK
ANCASH
Huaraz
Pucallpa
BRAZIL
HUANUCO
Huánuco
PASCO
Cerro de Pasco
UCAYALI
Huacho
LIMA
Lima
JUNIN
Río Alto Purús
Huancayo
Camisea
Río Madre de Dios
PACIFIC OCEAN
Huancavelica
HUANCAVELICA
CUSCO
MADRE DE DIOS
MANU NAT'L PARK & BIOSPHERE RESERVE
Quillabamba
Pisco
Ayacucho
MACHU PICCHU HISTORICAL SANCTUARY
PARACAS NATIONAL RESERVE
Puerto Maldonado
Ica
ICA
AYACUCHO
Abancay
Cusco
TAMBOPATA-CANDAMO RESERVE ZONE
Nasca
APURIMAC
Río Apurímac
Río Tambopata
PUNO
AREQUIPA
BOLIVIA
Juliaca
Peru
Arequipa
AGUADA BLANCA NATURE RESERVE
Puno
Lago Titicaca
0 200 mi
0 200 km
MOQUEGUA
Moquegua
La Paz
TACNA
Tacna
CHILE
Arica

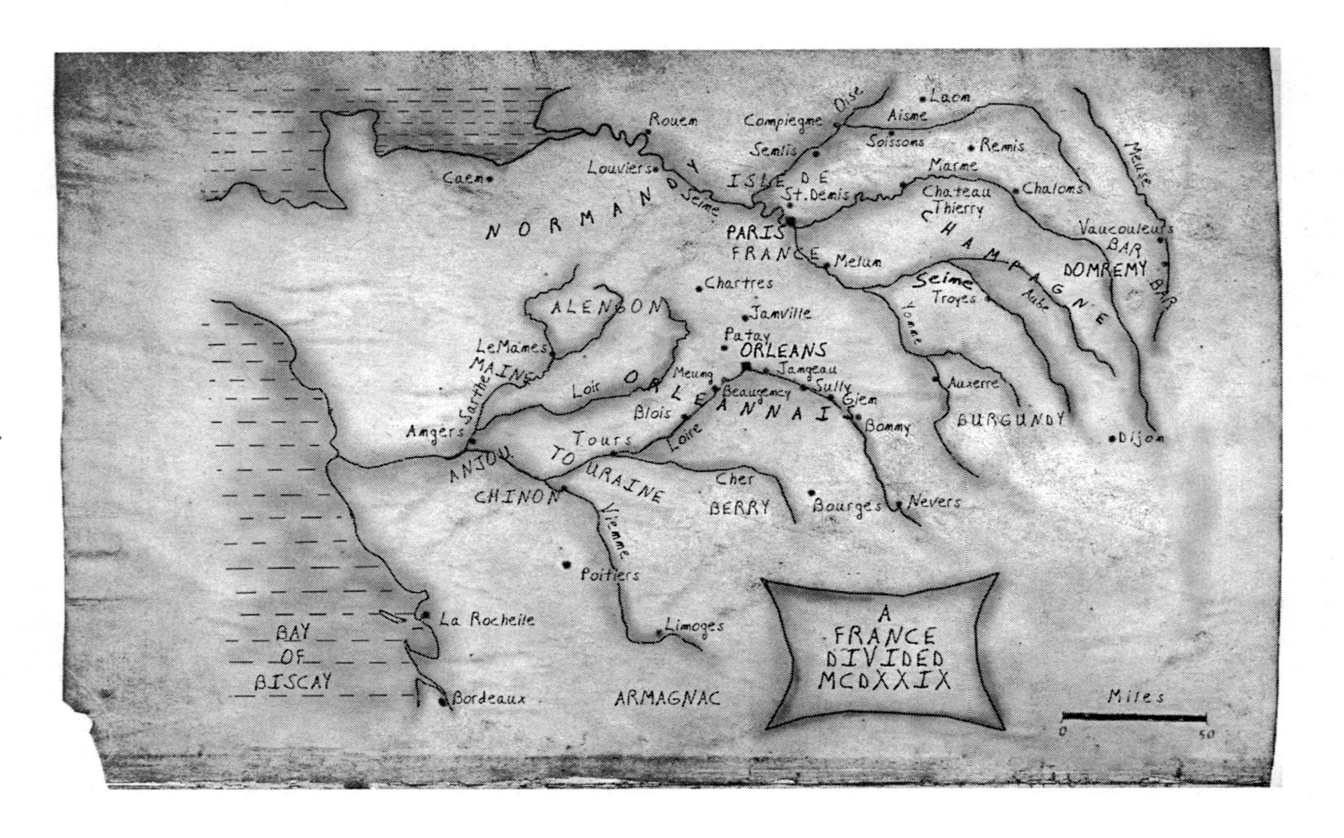
A
FRANCE
DIVIDED
MCDXXIX
Miles
0
50
Laon
Oise
Aisme
Compiegne
Rouem
Soissons
Remis
Semlis
Marne
Louviers
Caen
ISLE DE
St. Demis
Chateau
Thierry
Chaloms
Meuse
Seime
NORMANDY
PARIS
FRANCE
Melun
CHAMPAGNE
Vaucouleurs
BAR
DOMREMY
BAR
Seime
Troyes
Aube
Yonne
Chartres
ALENSON
Jamville
Patay
ORLEANS
LeMaimes
MAINE
Sarthe
Loir
Meung
Jamgeau
Beaugency
Sully
Giem
ORLEANNAIS
Blois
Bommy
Auxerre
BURGUNDY
Dijon
Angers
Tours
Loire
ANJOU
TOURAINE
Cher
CHINON
BERRY
Bourges
Nevers
Viemme
Poitiers
La Rochelle
Limoges
BAY
OF
BISCAY
Bordeaux
ARMAGNAC

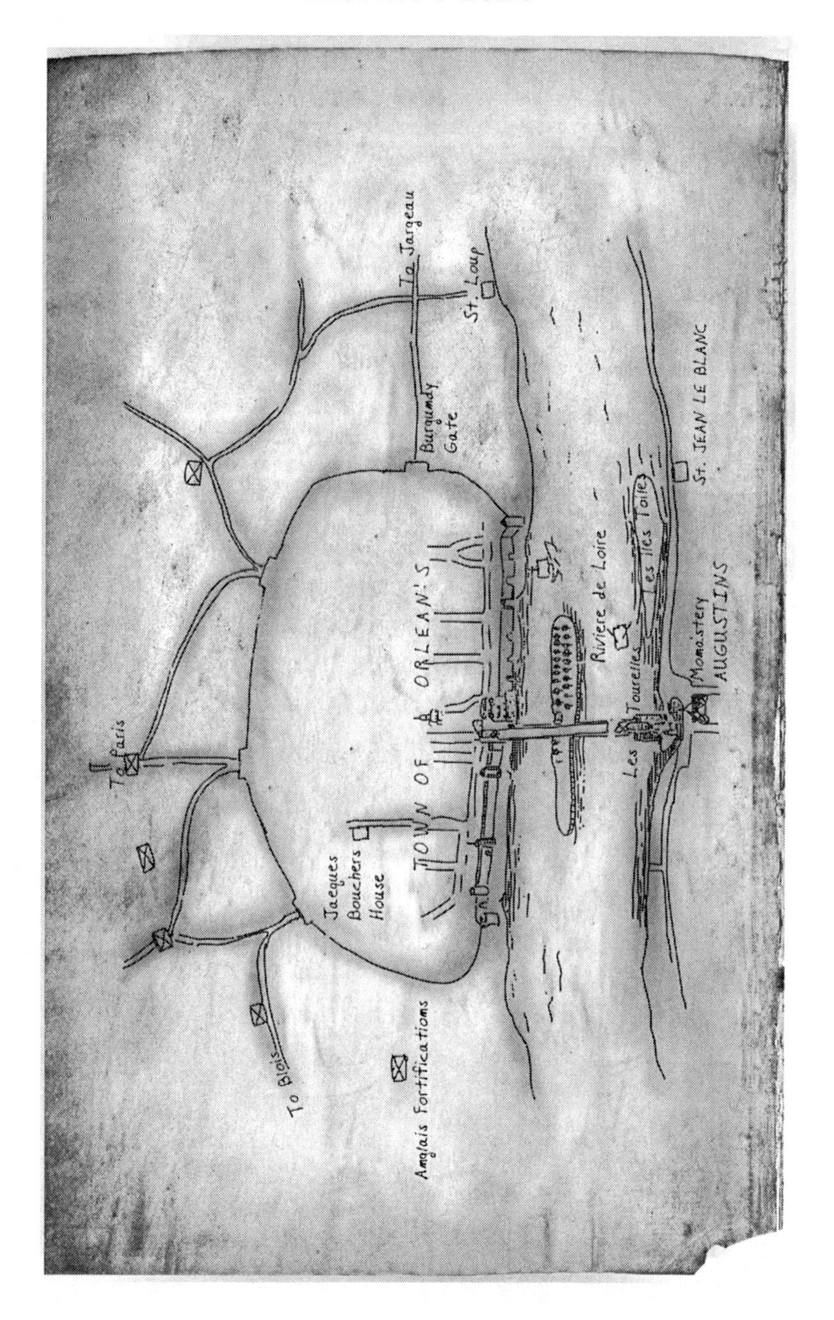
To Paris
To Jargeau
St. Loup
Burgumdy Gate
St. JEAN LE BLANC
TOWN OF ORLEAN'S
Riviere de Loire
Les Iles Toile
Les Tourelles
Momastery AUGUSTINS
Jaeques Bouchers House
To Blois
Amglais Fortificatioms

PART I

Chapter One

Journal Within a Journal

'Like love and hate, heat is a four letter word,' I doodled in a tattered page corner of my journal. This combination of sun and altitude slow-cooks your senses and saps your energy.

My eyes were beginning to sting from the sweat and dust. I raised my hand to rub them. What was that? A reflection had caught my eye as I moved my head. After soothing my tired eyes with a good rub, I searched the far wall of this Peruvian excavation for whatever had winked at me.

There, just over halfway up, maybe four feet above the base. How in the hell did that get missed? Rising from my crouch, I was startled by a scratching behind me. I turned just in time to see a scorpion skittering off into a tiny crevice. Little bastards—got stung by one last week. They're not as bad as spiders though. Only two things scare the hell out of me—women and spiders, in no particular order.

Using the journal to shade my eyes, I reached out with my other hand to brush dust off the barely exposed object. I froze with arm partially extended. The sweat trickling down my spine turned icy cold. Shuddering, I took a slow step back. The large, hairy creature emerged from a crevice above the gap and confirmed the reality of my worst nightmare.

Spider! Oh God, BIG spider! "FUCKING, LEAPING SPIDER!" I shrieked, as it sprang at me. This brown-black nightmare incarnate was as big across as my hand and had an abnormally fat body. I barely had time to wield my journal in self-defense, but it was enough to deflect the creature away. In the same motion the journal slipped from my sweaty grasp, luckily landing on top of the aggressive arachnid.

To my horror, the spider then scratched and clawed its way from under the journal. As it limped away toward the shady corner I grabbed a wooden survey stake and forced myself to pursue it, though my bowels were quaking. I got there just before it escaped into another crevice and plunged the blunt end of the stake down, just missing the fat furry body. Three of its legs were pinned by the stake. It clawed at the dirt with the other five—audibly, like rustling branches on a brick wall. I was paralyzed and could not tear my eyes from this horror. I knew tarantulas to have eight eyes and I could feel them, rather than see them—as if they were crawling across my skin. Its two vertical, black, venom injectors over its mandible were like serrated knives. They appeared to be grinding, threatening, defiant. The long brown and black hairs on its body and legs were standing straight out, vibrating. So also was my body hair standing at attention, but rather from transcendent fear than defiance.

I swallowed back a wave of nausea. What courage I had was ebbing. I must do it, I must, and I raised my foot. I crushed it almost hesitantly, feeling the crunch under my boot. And then, oh God, and then my eyes could not comprehend what they saw. Tiny yellow spiders. They started coming from under my boot. Just a few, and then a few more. Sweet Jesus, there were dozens of them. They were fast and they were spilling out in every direction. They were crawling on my BOOT.

My throat was drier than any desert. I could taste sand. I tried to scream, but it only came out as a hoarse croak. A worse nightmare I could not have conceived. My world had ground down to slow motion, as I tried to move. The tiny spiders, however, were moving ever faster—surrounding me.

Stomping my feet, as I ran for the ladder, my terror was complete. My chest was tightening as if in a vice and I could not breathe. Scrambling up the ladder out of the excavation my boot slipped, skinning my bare knees, but the pain didn't register. I started to run, but soon realized I needed to breathe. Forcing myself to stop, I was able to get enough of a grip to realize that I was having an anxiety attack. This had never happened to me before, but neither had I ever encountered Lucifer's Legion before.

The water saved my life, or maybe it was the water container. I saw our five-gallon container in the shade of a low adobe wall and staggered over to it. I remembered a friend who had asthma, and when she had an attack, she would breathe into a paper bag. Carbon dioxide was the key she said. I tried breathing into the wide-mouthed container. That and little sips seemed to allow air into my lungs again.

Maybe it was time to call it a day. The laborers had already gone and there was only Janeen left, working in another section about a hundred yards away. I was drained, overheated, and my head was throbbing.

I wanted to forget the leaping spider incident, but it was an odd occurrence to find such a creature up on the plateau. Thinking about it now though, I could at least make some sense of the encounter. My leaping foe was so fat, because she was carrying her cocooned brood with her. They were obviously ready to hatch. She must have crawled into the excavation in search of a shady crevice for her brood.

Though I am not superstitious by nature, poking around ancient bones and dwellings can be an unsettling experience, and a hairy harbinger like this did not seem to bode well. Curses were the fodder of plebeians I had to remind myself, though without conviction.

But then I remembered that something extraordinary had caught my attention in the excavation. Curiosity, that old cat killer, got the better of me, so warily was I drawn back to my pit of horrors. I was taught early on that there's only one way to handle a problem—be proactive, just deal with it.

The excavation of this Chimu/Inca habitat was about fifteen feet square and the autochthonous level had not been reached yet. The spot that had caught my eye may have originally been mistaken for stone, but the hard-packed mud had deteriorated after being exposed for a few weeks. Stone structures such as this exhibited wonderful masonry by the Incas, thereby rendering mud cement unnecessary. Because of that, I reasoned, the mud-casted alcove could be some sort of hiding place.

Scanning the pit, I could see no sign of the tiny yellow spiders. My knees were a bit shaky climbing down, but I was able to keep my breathing under control. So far, so good. Cautiously approaching the wall of interest, I noticed that the dead spider was being cannibalized by some of its offspring. Oh well, not so different from a couple of my mate's families back in Aberdeen.

I used my brush to delicately clear away some of the deteriorating mud cement around the object. I could now clearly see that there was something metallic and leathery wedged into this alcove. My concentration was suddenly shattered by a loud voice above me.

"Hey, Jungle Jim." Though familiar, Janeen's husky voice still caused me a start.

"Dammit, Janeen, you scared the piss out of me—if I had any in this heat, that is. And by the way, it's Jungle Jack, if you don't mind."

"Ah hell, Jungle Jim has a more famous ring to it. Just be thankful I don't call you Jungle Jack-ass," she quipped. "Geez, I'm whipped. It's after four, and ten hours is more than enough in this climate, MISTER Jack Maxwell." She brushed back a long lock of brown hair and added with a weary sigh, "Hell, I could sure use a beer, a bath and a good meal."

"Aye, lass, I'll drink to that. Why don't you get your gear together and I'll be right there."

She turned and shuffled off, her full, but well proportioned form moving with an exhausted gait.

For some peculiar reason I had not mentioned to Janeen the oddity I was investigating, nor even my encounter with its arachnid guardian. Perhaps it was my ignominious reaction to the creature, I temporized.

Returning to my scrutiny, I immediately noticed something odd on the inside of the mud cement cast. Scratching and brushing at the area around it, more of the desiccated mud fell away. It revealed what looked like a metallic object encased in a badly decomposed leathery hide. The metal sticking out of the leather had been the glint that had caught my eye. Very gently, I continued to brush and chip away at the mud to liberate what was starting to look like a box. Finally, it became loose enough, and taking great care, I was able to slide it out.

At that moment a shadow fell across me and I heard Janeen shout something unintelligible. As if caught with my hand in the cookie jar, I flinched guiltily and lost my grip. The object landed flat on the ground with a dull metallic thud. As I looked up, the brilliant sun streaming in over the dig edge blinded me. Pulling down my hat brim I blinked to gain focus. The shadow was not Janeen's, but rather that of a rugged looking local Indian.

The stranger had an alpaca manta over his left shoulder and stocky bowlegs sticking out of his ragged dirty cutoffs. A long scar ran down the side of his nut-brown face, extending from just above his right eye to the corner of his mouth. This disfigurement left him with an unnatural, lopsided smile under his broad nose and a perpetual half-wink. The pinkness of the cicatrix glinted glossy in the sun.

"What the hell do you want sneaking around here?" Janeen snapped at the Indian, as she strode into view. His expression seemed puzzled, yet menacing. She repeated her question in Spanish. At that, he smiled a mostly toothless, crooked grin and turned to me. Raising his right hand, he used his fingers to make spider-like prancing motions. He then laughed hysterically, until the alpaca blanket fell off his shoulder. Quickly, he replaced it, but not before I noticed a large tattoo on his left breast and a gun in a shoulder harness.

He turned on his heel and loped toward the distant jungle edge with a slow, efficient stride. Janeen yelled after him in Spanish, something that sounded like, "Who the hell are you? What are you doing here?"

I was just happy to see him go. I seized the moment to scoop up my *prize* and stuff it into my pack. I had no idea why I was being so secretive with it.

Rattling along the slightly widened llama track in the agency's battered old Rover, my mind was decidedly active. However, my body was somewhat enervated by this still unfamiliar climate. It was slowly dawning on me that the Indian must have seen my clash with the spider. That being the case, I was particularly disturbed by his mocking attitude and stealthy disposition. Janeen was excitedly prattling away about uncovering an intricately cut stone assemblage, while I cautiously negotiated our way down off the plateau. Maybe, just maybe, what was secreted in my pack was also a significant find. I was almost embarrassed about keeping it hidden—especially from Janeen, the consummate professional.

Janeen was a special person in my life. I guess that was why I was here, chasing my elusive dreams and schemes—an archaeologist wannabe, you might say. My passion for archaeology originated with Janeen. She was on a scholarship at Cambridge and we met in a lecture hall. We became lovers and it seems one passion led to another. She was the serious and brilliant young Canadian of Dutch heritage with a temperament to match. I, on the other hand, was the rich Scottish brat, bent on hedonistic pursuits.

My family had done well in the North Sea oil game. Uncle Malcolm and my father supplied specialized rental equipment to drilling rigs. They were in at the beginning of the North Sea boom, having worked offshore for drilling contractors around the world. 'Get the MAX' from Maxwell Oilfield Supply was a catch phrase known throughout the industry. They encouraged me to take the educated route, so I decided geology with a linguistics minor might be my ticket, and boarding away from parental influence was just my style. A dozen years since graduation and I still haven't figured out how I got through. Never an academic, it even took me an extra year to complete a basic degree. My party-hardy attitude certainly didn't help. I spent more time at the rugby pitch and pubs than on any studies, leading to my well-earned nickname, '*Mad Max*'.

Standing just over six foot and weighing in at fifteen stone I had no trouble holding my own on the rugby pitch or in a pub brawl. Fortunately, I also had sufficient intellect to see me through despite my lifestyle.

Janeen Evers loved my wild side. For her it was a new elixir that offset her intense studies. She was driven and I was driverless. Oh well, the sex was certainly worth the eventual heartache. What a body she had then. Not that there's anything wrong with it now. I still dream of those marvelous thimble-like nipples and large pink aureoles. Her breasts seem more pendulous now, but that only serves to excite me all the more. She never had a drop-dead, knockout figure, but she has that classic Rubenesque wide bottomed, full-figured beauty. She never uses makeup and her light olive complexion, unlike mine, makes working in the tropics tolerable. Long light brown hair, crystal blue eyes, and saucy full lips give her a distinctive sensuality. She has always been totally unaware of her sensuality, being immersed in her one true love, archaeology. This total dedication tended to arouse the jealous side of my nature and that is likely why our relationship never got much further than sex. I could not help wondering, with some compunction, if this puerile jealousy could be the reason for my clandestine reaction to my little discovery today.

Negotiating the last hairpin turn, I could see our camp beneath us, the small clearing a haven amongst the dense, forbidding greenery. The tents and equipment appeared Lilliputian from here and neatly arranged like a military bivouac—five sleeping tents with planked bases, one large cook tent, a canvassed wash up with rudimentary shower, and a canvassed latrine.

Bouncing into the clearing we were greeted by Raul, our rotund cook. Raul was as wide as he was tall, which wasn't very. In a good-natured way, he chided Janeen for being late, though we were actually back at our normal time. It was his joy to tease Janeen at every opportunity. As he waddled away one could only liken his gait to that of a bowling ball encumbered by two pegs.

As was usually the case, this archaeological project was very cost sensitive. The camp facilities were Spartan, but acceptable. Besides Janeen and myself, our party consisted of two postgraduate students, an excavation site laborer, Raul, and the obligatory two armed guards. Our party of eight had four fully loaded jeeps when on the move, but the sites we were investigating were of fairly close proximity to our base camp. Save for Raul and one guard, we were gone with three of the jeeps to the current dig ten or more hours per day. It was a fairly safe, yet remote region.

Safety from pilfering by indigenous recalcitrants was always a factor, but the *Brillante Sendero*, the *Shining Path,* was our main concern. Though they were not active in this area, they were an unpredictable lot that could show up anywhere, anytime, and were not to be treated lightly. As well, there were always the inherent dangers posed by non-human creatures of the wild. Thus, the research agency considered a certain amount of caution and an armed escort mandatory.

After cleaning up and sating our appetite on Raul's hearty, but definitely non-dietary fare, I told Janeen and our helpers that I was turning in—insisting I was too tired, even for chitchat and cribbage. Raul, my cribbage nemesis, would not let this go without comment.

"But Senor Jack, I would think you might like some sweet revenge after such the *skaunking* I give you last night." He said with his wide-set, round, Peruvian eyes hinting at mockery.

"Achh Raul, my friend, these weary bones dictate salvation for you, for I would surely otherwise administer a severe thrashing to your cribbage ego."

Good-humored derision was dealt to me by all present.

Replying to their quips with an unforced yawn, I begged pardon and escaped the smoky cook tent into the encroaching darkness.

The mosquitoes and other insect flying machines were particularly insufferable in the evening, so I wasted no time in getting to the sanctuary of my tent. The tent was a sturdy, prefabricated canvas material with a wood frame and base—easy to erect and break down. The ten-by-twelve-foot square structure afforded me plenty of room for a small portable desk and chair, besides my cot and stow space. Janeen and I had our own tents while the others shared two larger tents. All were fumigated daily to combat the undesirables of the insect world.

Sitting down at the desk, I excitedly removed the prize from my pack and carefully placed it before me. I made sure the Coleman lamp was not so bright as to illuminate my activities through the canvas walls. There was indeed some kind of leather hide covering. The hide was tattered, as one would expect if it were of antiquity. Its exterior was gray-brown, partly a coating of encrusted mud. As I turned it over in my hands, there was a metallic blue-gray section exposed which must have been the glint that caught my eye in the excavation.

I hefted it—perhaps two kilograms I estimated. It was the size of a thick bible or a sizeable library reference text. I recorded this information and measured it accurately, as would a trained archaeologist. Carefully peeling away the ragged leather encasement, the blue-gray interior appeared to be a metal box. The bluish tinge was telltale of its copper nature. It was a rectangular box and again I recorded its dimensions precisely. It had no hinges and its cap seemed to be sealed with a cement-like material that may have been some type of mortar and tree gum. Much of the cement material had disintegrated. On each side, however, were clasps of the same metal keeping the seal intact. The clasps were not difficult to pry loose and as I cautiously attempted to remove the cap, some of the remaining cement seal fell away from the slightly overlapping edge. I used a pair of tweezers to assist and picked away at the seal for a considerable time.

Finally, I was able to lift away the snug-fitting cap. The interior of the box glittered copper, with abundant blue-green oxidized patches. It looked as if it had not been exposed to air for centuries. The box contained a stuffed leather pouch that was in much better condition than its outer-most cover. Scarcely breathing and with trembling fingers, I delicately peeled back its flaps. My eyes grew wide in amazement. What I found were innumerable, mostly well preserved, sheaves of inscribed, parchment-like paper.

Chapter Two

Alex del Aries

IN THE year of Our Lord MCDXXXI, I, Alex del Aries, begin these chronicles of my humble life. Here in this land far from home, I must do so to preserve my past and soothe my sanity. I have lived among the pious and I have marched with armies, fighting fierce battles against the civilized and the philistine. I have loved a Saint and I have loved a sinner. Torn between them, it seems I am banished to wander the earth and thus find myself in this strange land.

Perhaps my destiny is preordained, as foretold by Marie Robine. If so, these chronicles could prove most interesting, for already has my life been eventful. For every joy there has been a crushing sorrow, for every triumph a devastating defeat, and for every success, sardonic failure. Must it always be so? For those who would read this, forgive my lament, for I am lonely. Perhaps the loneliness will abate if I proceed with my recollections.

I sit shaded from the sweltering tropical sun and thank my one true God for such tall, broad-leafed trees and their nut-like fruit of sustenance. It was after the second storm that our ship foundered upon the three treacherous sister islets. Most of the remaining provisions were cast asunder in the briny deep as our ship broke up. Soon after leaving the Santa Maria Islands, a man-eating, devil-storm was upon us. It battered us westward for what seemed a fortnight. I was exhausted and at the end of my tether. It seemed God was punishing us for our evil ways and would shake us in the teeth of his fury until dead.

After the storm finally abated we were adrift for another fortnight, wallowing with no useable rigging and a damaged rudder. The rudder was reparable and we carried spare canvas, but it would be of little use without masts. The storm had come upon us so rapidly that we had not time to make fast the rigging. It was truly miraculous that we were still afloat. Five sailors perished in the storm, washed overboard by towering swells while attempting to secure the rigging. There were quiet grumblings among the survivors that the captain, in his zeal to make headway, had sacrificed safety. The captain, Eduardo, the first mate Emanuel, the helmsman, Santiago, and myself survived with only minor afflictions. The other four survivors were less fortunate.

Captain Eduardo was a tyrant. Among his superiors he was as smooth as fashionable silk, but with his underlings he was rough and treacherous, like barnacles upon jagged rock. Emanuel called him *the fish*, for he was slippery and shed scales of deceit. If not for him, more might have survived the ordeal. It was he who hoarded the food and water. Santiago was his accomplice in this foul plot, contrived after the storm.

The four disabled survivors were in wretched condition with broken bones and festering lacerations. Eduardo dispensed only minimal food and water, claiming such was all that could be allotted. One by one the four enfeebled perished.

Just before the second storm descended upon us, Santiago seemed to lose his senses. It started as a quiet discussion between Santiago and the captain. Slowly, it escalated into a vehement argument with Santiago demanding an increased allotment of provisions, now that there were only four of us. Emanuel and I were shocked to hear of their hoarding arrangement.

Enraged, Eduardo drew his sword to slay Santiago, but the little helmsman was swift. He caught Eduardo's wrist and held on for his life. They spun across the breadth of the ship in a dance of death, before teetering over the gunwale. It was then I saw Eduardo free his left hand and draw a dagger from his belt. Too late I moved to intervene. Santiago's narrow eyes widened, as Eduardo, with deliberate slowness, slid the blade into his side, twisting and turning it.

The moment seemed frozen. Eduardo had Santiago bent backward over the gunwale, their noses almost touching, inhaling each other's sour breath. There was a thin, quivering smile upon the captain's face, but then, it became a mask of shock. Eduardo's thick, black eyebrows arched high and his smile rounded into an open-mouthed scream. Emanuel and I stared transfixed, as Santiago had wrapped his arms around Eduardo, embracing death, and with a backward lunge carried them both over the side.

We rushed to the gunwale and saw naught but many bubbles rising from the becalmed sea. Then there was a shape and Eduardo surfaced, coughing and cursing. There was no sign of Santiago.

"My, my good compadres. Throw old Eduardo a line, for I fear this sea wishes me ill will," he sputtered, between coughing fits.

I looked at Emanuel who, after a pensive moment, said, "I am sorry my captain, for it seems we can find no available rope to offer you."

I was astonished, dumbfounded. Emanuel had sailed with Eduardo many times, always enduring his foul nature, but it seemed that Eduardo had finally gone too far. Perhaps it was the severe tribulations we had endured which this time made Eduardo's deprivations particularly heinous and reprehensible.

He cursed loudly, trying to grasp anything along the caravelle's side, but there was nothing within reach save for the slimy, wormy crust left by the sea. Rapidly, his efforts exhausted what strength he had left. He began to spend more time under the water than above, and his pitiful pleas became barely more than gasps.

"… the name of God … Have mercy on… "

"Si, have mercy—just as you did on our other brothers and the sadly misguided Santiago. Too many years—too much treachery. It is your time. May God have mercy on you—and on me," Emanuel said, in a listless whisper. Then he sat upon the deck, with his face in his hands, and remained so for a very long time.

Once more we encountered a man-eating devil-storm and were blessed that it did not entirely consume us. It had splintered what remained of our two masts and devoured our repaired rudder. We rode the cusp of its frenzy to these strange shores, and now, so close to possible salvation, it threatened to hurl us upon jagged rock.

Emanuel, that indomitable Taurus had cut the last tangled line and with a mighty heave of legs and arms seemed to push the shore-boat clear of the ship. In doing so, he became submerged in the torrential sea, as he had lost his grip on the gunwale. I desperately tried to fasten the oarlocks to get oar to water. Suddenly, as Emanuel surfaced, gasping for air, another huge wave engulfed the boat crashing it back into the side of the caravelle. As I was catapulted sideways, almost out of the boat, I glimpsed Emanuel being crushed between them. Desperately trying to bail one-handed with a pail and at the same time stretching overboard to reach Emanuel, I shrieked his name. Frantically did I plead aloud for God's mercy. Incredibly, I felt a familiar powerful hand grasp mine from the depths of Satan's sea. I pulled with every reserve I possessed, for to this man, I owed my life. He was semi-conscious and it was a great struggle to get him in the boat, but I would not be denied.

A backwash miraculously swept us away from the caravelle to a gap between the islets. With Emanuel insensible, I bailed frantically and locked the oars in place. My chance was now, and I pulled on the oars like a madman to row us through the islets. My bones and flesh ached with every stroke, but I knew death and Satan were staring me in the face, smirking, waiting. There was land not far, we had seen it just before the storm had tossed us upon the jagged islets. There lay our only salvation—that or a watery death.

Soon my strength was sapped and my efforts disjointed. Suddenly, my oars stroked nothing but air and, unbalanced, I toppled backwards into the bottom of the boat. Then I was flying, like a bird, weightless, helpless. An enormous breaker wave had picked the boat out of the water and tossed us like chaff in the wind. Hurtling through the air I hit the water hard. My head and shoulder slammed painfully into a shallow sandbar. Stunned by the blow, I fought to gain some footing against the water's force. I found myself in waist deep, turbulent water.

The huge breaker wave must have tossed me a very long way. As I tried to get my bearings and maintain my footing I was being sucked back by the backwash. I struggled against it and at that moment heard a thunderous crashing and creaking of wood above the din of the waves. Looking toward the malevolent three-sisters islets, I saw our caravelle being impaled upon one of them—splintering apart as if it were made of sapling twigs. There was no time to grieve, for the monstrous wave, which destroyed the ship, was now upon me. I had only time for another gasp of air before it engulfed and hurled me like so much flotsam.

I must have lost consciousness, for I next recall finding myself blessedly alive on a sandy beach. Uncontrollably did I cough while vomiting copious amounts of salt water and sand. The wind was still howling, but the sea had subsided somewhat. I remembered it had just begun to dawn as our ship foundered upon the islets. According to the sun, now peaking through the dark clouds, it must be mid-morning. My senses were slowly returning and I rose upon my knees to yell out for Emanuel, but it came out as a weak croak. I could see our shore-boat perhaps fifty paces away. Too weak to stand, I crawled along the shore with the waves lapping at me.

On the other side of our overturned boat lay Emanuel. Sobbing with relief, I tried to raise him to a sitting position. He coughed and vomited and I thanked God that he still lived. Holding him upright in my arms, I saw a terrible gash on the side of his head. He was losing little of his precious rouge inner soul, but there was a fearful yellowish substance oozing from his head wound. He coughed again and this time his spittle ran bright rouge.

"Dearest mostly Holy Mother of God, why have you deserted us?" I remember wailing. A short while later as we rested against the boat, Emanuel's eyes fluttered open. His black grizzled beard became further streaked with blood every time he coughed. His eyes were glazed as he spoke in his native Portuguese tongue.

"Alex, my compadre, you're alive!"

"Yes, my friend, but is this Hell or just Purgatory?" I replied in French. His understanding of French was always better than my spoken Portuguese.

"For you I do not know, but for me I am nearing Purgatory. You must hear my confession," he gasped.

"Do not be the jester Emanuel—you are too tough and hardened to be ready for Purgatory."

"I remember being crushed against our ship. I think my insides have been all rearranged. Dear God, my head throbs so. The pain in my body and head was not meant for mortal man." As he rasped these words between grimaces, I lifted his tattered tunic from his torso. What I saw seemed inconceivable. His once powerful chest was almost collapsed, while his belly and lower ribs were bloated and covered with purple blotches.

"My breath is leaving this body, good Alex del Aries. I know not where we are … perhaps Polo's China." He seemed to find this amusing, but a laugh turned into a painful cough.

"Alex, the Captain's sea chest, you must try and salvage it. It likely contains riches and you will live to see many more sunsets, such as this." Strange, I thought, mid-morning must seem like sunset to him.

"Judgment awaits me, my learned friend. I fear my time is short, so listen closely to what I say." I started to shake my head in protest, but then simply nodded and listened.

"Our so-called captain, Eduardo, was Enrique's bastard cousin and few people knew of this. Enrique trusted him more than most other captains." Emanuel tried to chuckle but succumbed to another coughing fit. Blood spewed with the spittle and I felt that I should immediately clear his throat to allow him breath. He pushed my hands away, telling me he needed no attendant.

"The sea chest may be of great value, as we were to use it for trading purposes if we found natives in the Santa Maria Islands. Who knows what it might contain. Since losing his brother to the Moorish jails, Enrique has not been the same man. I believe that is how he came to trust flotsam such as Eduardo. Captain, hah, I spit on his grave." Attempting to spit caused more coughing and then his eyes rolled back from sight. He began to mumble incoherently. I frantically looked about, thinking that maybe some water might ease his suffering. I could see a barrel with waves lapping on it about ten long lances down the shore. I rose, and then fell. On hands and knees I crawled to it. Twas the last of the ship's water barrels, and we had tapped it but three days previous. If not fouled by the sea, the double hogshead should still contain almost one hundred *setiers*. It took great effort, but I managed to roll it back to Emanuel.

"At least we will have water, my friend," I panted, as I heaved the hogshead upright beside him.

To my horror I saw Emanuel's neck had become very swollen and purple. His eyes were wide open, but it was apparent Emanuel no longer saw anything in this world. Choking back my sorrow and anger I made the cross upon his earthly body. I remembered little of the last rites ceremony, but I conducted such as I could for his anguished soul.

In the Year of Our Lord MCDXCII.

Oh, to once again hold a quill in my hand, tis more peculiar than familiar. For many years have I carried these writing materials with me on my travels. When I was forlorn and lonely on a strange island I began a chronicle in an effort to quell my anguish.

Upon first showing such writing methods to the savages, I was met with ignorance and a hostile response. Their *Barbers* felt I would anger their Gods. I say *Barbers*, but they were a strange, primitive lot who attempted to divine, as well as heal, by means most foreign. I feel those first *Barbers* I encountered were simply envious of my scribing and tools, for their elementary scratchings on rock were most crude. Hence, I have kept them secreted these many years.

Recently my grandchildren have discovered them and I was made to explain of such things (as children do have their convincing ways). This elicited such a melancholy for my distant past that I find myself once again putting quill to parchment. It seems I must learn scribing all over again and accordingly I may use Latin, French, Gaelic, or Portuguese to relate my story. Someday, I would expect my long-ago countrymen to visit these lands. If so, perhaps this humble chronicle may be of some interest. But readers beware, lest your destiny become entwined with mine.

True, I have been blessed and drank of God's chalice, but my curse was to also drink of the Devil's cauldron. As I alluded to when I initially began this chronicle so many years past, for every radiant light in my life there came a damning darkness. Nothing has changed. In this land I have found a perverse worship of the carnal, but I have also found that love abounds. I have wrestled with that ultimate obscenity called war and I have seen whole peoples swallowed up by the perverse winds of hate. Therefore, I must rightly ask, what is perverse?

My life has been a delicious madness and I have drunk fully from its cup. I believe I am in my eightieth year as I begin these recollections.

I had the Coleman lamp turned down as much as practical, yet the nighttime flying machines pecked incessantly and noisily at my tent. It wasn't even a buzz, it was more of a zzzz, as if they were trying to saw their way through. The deciphering was difficult in this light, but I did not want anyone to know of my discovery just yet.

There was an obvious difference in the condition of the parchment recording the shipwreck, and the second section by the older author dated MCDXCII. How could such a manuscript be here in the ruins of a Chimu/Inca dig site, likely abandoned fifty years before the Spaniards even arrived? I was finding this script to be incredibly heady stuff, though I could not comprehend its relevance to this Chimu/Inca time period. I tried to tone myself down, but this manuscript seemed authentic, and most of all, understandable. How could this be? The date recorded on the first sheaf was in roman numerals, MCDXXXI. And how had it come to be written in a Gaelic/Latin/French dialect mostly decipherable even to a linguistics minor such as myself? Shite—I must really be losing it.

Carefully replacing the first few sheaves I had deciphered back into the copper receptacle, I glanced at my watch and realized it was already two in the morning. Bloody hell, I had to get some sleep! Extinguishing the lamp and doffing all but my shorts, I scooted under the bed netting. I lay exhausted on my cot, but my mind was still racing with the possibilities. My skeptical side insisted that this must bc a clever hoax—but if it wasn't ... Skepticism and prudence prevailed for now, so soundly did I sleep.

Chapter Three

AWAKENING AT THE FAIRY TREE

THE SUN was at its apex and it was one of those indelibly bright summer days. Climbing up into the shaded limbs of the dome-like Fairy tree, I pretended I was a wild bird. It was a high refuge, a secure spot, a safe and magical place for this orphan. No sooner had I attained my perch, than I heard the crunch of footsteps upon the path leading to this sacred tree and was surprised to see a somewhat familiar figure. By the blessed Saint Christopher, if I had only known then that this girl, this vision, was to be the shaper of my life.

I knew little of my mother and father, but I knew my father had been a secret member of the Order of the Templars. This Order was ostensibly expunged, its followers cast asunder, but Marie Robine had made me aware of their covert existence. I had come to the Fairy tree to ponder these things, but was now interrupted, to be set upon a course that could only be termed *destiny.*

Jeanne, whom I had admired from afar, was a very pious girl and I felt a certain admiration and affection for her. She exuded a confident air, which made others revere her more than her age or stature warranted. Content to gaze upon her I made no sound to disturb her, as she knelt under the Beau Mai tree. I was not very surprised to see someone else here, as the revered old Beau Mai, with its broad drooping branches almost touching the ground, was a special place. She was obviously here to meditate and pray to the One True God. She knelt, her hands tightly folded in her lap, her head bowed. The sun had slipped behind a fluffy cloud and I briefly lost interest in Jeanne while pondering my own predicament.

Friar Clement was my overseer, and I still quail and quake at that execrable memory. An orphan left under the auspices of a monastery has little to say about his guardians or pedagogues. Collecting and spreading the cow dung and chicken fodder in the fields is but normal. A step up in this world would be to clean the friar's eating bowls and chamber pots. Perhaps it was due to Marie Robine's influence that I was accorded this latter dubious privilege at the Coussey Monastery. My duties certainly did not end there, but my lot did not worsen either—at least for a time.

The monastery itself was reliant on the Lord of Bourlemont-Domremy in the province of Lorraine. The relatively new Bourlemont castle was situated on the commanding hill above the monastery. I will relate further on my history and circumstance, but suffice to say I was in servitude with minimal freedom at the time of my Fairy tree experience.

I was once again be-dazzled as the sun came forth from the passing cloud. Looking down upon Jeanne, I noticed that she now sat upon her posterior with feet tucked under and knees apart. Her hands in apparent supplicant prayer were now hooked under the hem of her skirt between her legs. Her face, made radiant by the sun, seemed to be looking directly into its brilliance. She began to gently rock back and forth upon her derriere. The rocking motion was rhythmic and seemed to have an up and down gait to it, as if she rode a horse. Perplexed by this form of worship I began to pay closer attention. The whispering breezes did not entirely mask her occasional whimpering sigh. She seemed to lose her breath and then gasp as if in pain. I found this most distressing for I thought the maiden must be in some physical distress. Like a cat, I scampered down and alighted almost within touching distance of her. Jeanne had rolled on to her side and seemed unaware of my presence. At first, I wondered if this might be just a bad dream. Here was my angelic damsel in some form of distress I did not understand. I must help. I must be her crusader, but I knew not what to do. I noticed her eyes were glazed and partly rolled back into their sockets. She appeared oblivious to all about her. It was then I became aware that her chemise was gathered about her hips. I was stupefied, seeing her on her side with knees drawn up and her nether region exposed through her tattered undergarment. Her hands down between her legs, in apparent prayer, were actually....

I was unable to divert my gaze. I was mortified, captivated and confused by this sight. Prior to this I had only heard vulgar rumors and embellishments from older pauper boys and ruffians regarding the female form. It must be understood that my partial Templar upbringing had left me sexually pure and uninitiated, except for one perverse experience. Yet, what is perverse?

She suddenly convulsed. Her middle finger, I could clearly see through her ragged undergarment, was nestled between two lips, which were lightly covered with a dark, curly down. She had a round, creamy white bottom not much larger than my own and I felt most desirous to touch it. I could not understand these intense feelings that suddenly rushed through me like a pitch-fire.

Instinctively, my right hand moved under my robe and apron to discover my member had grown far larger than its normal size. I had occasionally experienced this when I awoke in the early morning with an urgent need to pass water, but I had no inclination to pass water at this time. Scarcely was I breathing, for I realized she was not aware of my presence due to her own intense reverie. I sensed I should not be privy to this scene, but I was spellbound. Without realizing why, I began to stroke my quill, and the pleasure of it was indescribable. Jeanne then seemed to be coming out of her trance-like state. At that moment, I became dizzy and an intense, but pleasurable sensation rapidly arose from my loins. Groaning and slumping backwards, my member gushed an odd creamy substance, as if shot from a siege catapult. Confused, I lay prostrate on my back, gripping my throbbing self and succumbing to the wonderful pleasure it purveyed.

Jeanne sat upright and as her eyes focused, they grew wide with shock.

"You foul, foul, despicable boy," she remonstrated, but with just a touch of curiosity I fancied, as she stared wide-eyed at what my hand still gripped. Embarrassed, I struggled to rise on wobbly legs while pulling down my apron and robe. Jeanne leapt to her feet, straightened her garments, and bolted to the other side of the Fairy tree.

"What devilment are you up to Alex del Aries de Coussey? You, you have befouled my vision."

"You had a v, vision?" I asked.

I was barely regaining my senses and her agitation now erupted into a tirade.

"You are a disgusting boy and I will not share my holy reverence with you. You disturbed my vision and degraded it with your foul maleness."

Ahh, such bittersweet memories I must record. She always had a tongue, this fine young maiden—one that could cut like a sharply honed short-sword, even under awkward or tense situations. Yes, she was a maiden for all of Gaul.

"Oh most reverent maiden, please do not think of me so. I do not understand these things that have happened here. Please, please tell me of your vision."

There was a long pause as Jeanne considered the situation. "How many summers since the birth date of your sorry self?" she finally spat at me.

Proudly I stated, "I was born on a portentous date, that of Epiphany, fourteen summers past. I know this to be so, as my guardian who attended my birth told me of such things before she left me at Coussey one summer past."

At this, to my dismay, she burst into laughter.

"I doubt such a claim, you jesting, mendacious brat, as that is exactly my birth date. And besides that, you appear much too slight to be fourteen summers."

"Not so maiden. I may be slight, but it is true. And I also bear a portentous sign upon my body", I said, in an attempt to impress her.

Turning my head to the left I showed her the red, star-like mark behind my right ear. At once, her demeanor changed from mirth to shock.

"What … how can this be? No one knows but my mother, that I have the very same mark behind my right ear." And it was true, for she showed me the star-like red sign behind her right ear.

After a period of contemplation, she said, "Very well, Alex, I believe you, and this is an amazing blessed coincidence. I may tell you of my vision, but you must promise never to tell anyone else."

"But of course, honorable maiden, I am at your service and I apologize for my reprehensible behavior." At this reply she seemed visibly relieved.

"You did not know any better, poor Alex. You must never again use such furtive manners around maidens or reduce yourself to such base male desires," she admonished gently.

Feeling great remorse at my sinful ways, I said, "Yes, Jeanne, truly I beg your forgiveness and indulgence. How may I make amends?"

After a few moments of quiet thought, she said, "Fear not Alex, you are forgiven—IF, you keep my trust. One day, perhaps soon, I will make my visions known. But for now I will tell you that Saint Michael, Saint Margaret and Saint Catherine came to me today. I have had other visions of them individually, but today I saw all three in a most brilliant and radiant light. They had said God would have a mission for me, and today they told me of that mission."

She grew silent and I was too dumbfounded to speak. She raised her eyes to mine, looking deeply into them for what seemed a long time. "That is all I can tell you for now, Alex, for I must meditate further on my task." Not knowing how to respond, I simply nodded and she asked, "Do you believe in my visions, Alex?"

Stammering slightly, I said, "Yes, yes of course Jeanne—why should I not! You need only to tell me how I might assist you in your mission."

"For now you must simply be silent about it and when the time comes I may ask of your help." Rising and appearing much more at ease, she said, "I must hurry on to meet Hauviette and Mengette at Bourlemont, as we are helping Father Frederic in preparations for the summer-rites fete."

As she strode confidently away, I called after her, "Thank you, maid Jeanne, I shall be at your service whenever needed and I… " My voice trailed away, as she was already gone, gone as a wisp of smoke upon the wind.

Hurrying along the ox-cart path through the Bois Chenu forest, my mind was assailed with the day's amazing events. It seemed that Jeanne must have experienced something similar to me under the Fairy tree, so maybe I also was prone to visions. Yet, I saw nothing while experiencing that euphoria. Sometime later, I came to understand these events and such sexual awakenings, but for a young orphan it was all most confusing.

I knew Jeanne from church events and related children's games, but she only occasionally participated. She was very devout and aloof. I had arrived in the Meuse valley one summer previous, to the sanctuary of the Coussey monastery.

My guardian, Marie Robine, told me that my father had been killed in the Holy Land. He had been gone seven Epiphanies and this being half of my born years, my memory of him had grown dim. Marie raised me for those seven summers and I would travel with her as she prophesized for rich nobles. She claimed not to be my mother, but offered no explanation as to my maternal parentage. She did, however, insist that my destiny would be even greater than my eminent heritage. Marie said I was from a long line of Templar warriors who were crushed exactly one hundred summers before my birth. The infamy by which they were betrayed had only partially been avenged. She knew not my role in the scope of the Templar future; only that God physically marked me. She portended through these bodily markings and the timing of my birth, that I would have a most propitious and peregrinate destiny. She said I was marked—marked to be among *the Destined.*

Marie had tutored me well in the arts of writing and reading. What she could not teach me, she inveigled the scholars of the various courts to instruct me. I became at least familiar with, if not proficient in, the languages of Latin, Portuguese, Gaelic and Anglais. Marie also insisted that I know something of history, especially that which was pertaining to my heritage. Fortunately, I have always had the ability to quickly absorb and retain the many things taught me.

My father, Miguel del Aries de Setubal, was Portuguese paternally. However, his mother, Erika de Molay, was of Gaelic and French heritage. She was reputed to be a most beautiful redhead with a fiery disposition. She was feared, as well as respected, by reason of her temperament and heritage.

My paternal grandfather had been murdered in France on his journey back from fighting in the Holy Land. It was said he admitted to someone he should not have trusted, that he was a Templar in the Portuguese Order of Christ. When news of her husband's death reached Erika, it set her upon a vengeful course to placate her great sorrow. Her Grandfather had been Jacques de Molay, the Grandmaster of the powerful French Templars. The treacherous King Phillip of France and Pope Clement V had betrayed him. Jacques was burnt at the stake under contrived heresy and idolatry charges. Erika had been eternally bitter about this, and as well she had to bear the loss of her beloved. According to Marie, it was Erika's insistence that one day retribution would be served, which gave the Templars incentive to carry on covertly in Portugal. Erika could never take part in Templar rites, but she could wield considerable influence. Often, Templar detractors would find themselves discredited, or worse.

The various *Orders of the Templar* had become quite wealthy during de Molay's time. They had been bestowed significant tracts of land for their laudable exploits in the Holy Land. So much so that, King Phillip had coveted their possessions to further his personal warring efforts. Hundreds of Templars were burnt at the stake or otherwise murdered, causing the remainder to either denounce their beliefs, or go into hiding.

According to the history as related to me by Marie Robine, my ancestor Jacques de Molay swore an ominous curse as the flames licked the flesh from his body. There pervaded a deathly silence from the crowd of onlookers and above the crackle of the fire he was heard to exclaim, "Ohh … perfidious Pope in Rome—you foul collaborator—I invoke our One True God to summon you within forty days hence and make judgement according to your treachery. May your flesh feel the searing sting of hell's flames to eternity. And the wickedness of King Phillip, a king in name only, I avow this curse. May you and your Capetian family suffer ill-fate and be wrought with internecide—such that you may never see the profit of this treachery, or another spring as King."

It makes my eyes brim and my body shudder as I imagine how his flesh would have crackled and charred till the blood began to boil. Hot bubbles would course through the veins reaching the heart. Only when the heart became poached would the life and soul leave the body. But they could never char his faith. The faith could never leave—it never has, for he was a Templar.

History records that Pope Clement V died thirty-three days after Jacque de Molay was put to the stake. History also records that King Phillip died one cycle of the moon prior to the Mass of Christ after that spring. Not many summers after Phillip's death, his Capetian dynasty crumbled, as his sons' bickering and incompetence led to an English invasion. What followed was one hundred summers of a divided and despoiled Gaul.

There were parts of the script I had trouble interpreting for transcription. Other parts I found most readable, almost like a book-journal. Linguistics courses at Cambridge had never been one of my problems and my memory was serving me well. Yet, I could not help but feel I might be deluding myself. Perhaps this was a professionally done fake manuscript. I had been working on it at night for almost two weeks. Janeen was getting a little suspicious of early exits to my tent from which I emerged in the morning only to drag my butt around the excavation during the day. She had commented that too much downtime and nighttime reading were making me lethargic during the day. Of course, the unusual heat-wave in this high country wasn't helping our mood either.

I was making less and less headway with the scripts, partly because the late nights were draining, and partly because difficult passages were bogging me down. I was still not fully convinced of its authenticity, but was so excited by the possibilities I could scarcely contain myself. How could the recordings of a European possibly be here during this era? I went back to the same excavated dwelling many times. It seemed irrefutable that the level of the discovered alcove must be dated to a late-Chimu or early-Inca period. Cautious queries to Janeen, who was the foremost archaeologist on this area and period, left little doubt for me as to the time epoch.

Tomorrow our six week stint will be up, so we will be heading back to Lima for a bit of rest, but not much recreation. We still had to tie together the grid mapping and cataloguing details. Sorting out all the fragmentary evidence collected from the site was like dealing with one monstrous jigsaw puzzle. In but two weeks we must give our presentation to the Peruvian authorities. I know also that I must soon come clean with Janeen on my potentially amazing find.

Chapter Four

THE FALCON

COMING DOWN off the plateau both Janeen and I were a bubbly, giddy pair; anticipating a hot bath, a soft bed, a good meal and a few beers. Getting back to civilization involved a five-hour jeep trek and the fording of a river, just to get to the nearest village that had an airstrip. Once there, at Camisea, it was a one hour flight in a De Havilland single Otter aircraft to reap all the modern comforts of Lima we could handle. As Janeen described to me in delicious detail how her first beer would taste, I pondered how I might reveal to her my discovery without incurring her wrath. What I had done by removing it and not telling her amounted to sacrilege. More than that, it was illegal.

She was now saying, "You know that strange Indio that startled us two weeks ago, I saw him prowling around today."

"Oh, really? I had forgot about that sneaky bugger. What the hell was he up to?"

"I thought I heard some voices, so I went around the *Meeting Hall* ruins and saw him skulking around one of our debris piles. Old Scarface just smiled, when he spotted me. If you could call that toothless smirk a smile. I was going to call for the guard, but then he stuck his tongue out between those missing teeth and seemed to be doing lewd things with it. That caught me of guard—it was kinda comical. You know me; I'm rarely at a loss for words, but his actions ... Anyway, he slithered away into the bush. Looking around to see if there were any others around, I thought I saw Juan, our guard, slip past the court wall. I called after him, but there was no response. I guess I must have been mistaken, and that Scarface pervert was gone, so I just went back to work. I was going to ask Juan about it at lunch break, but forgot. Juan and his brother are pretty decent sorts, eh."

"Where the hell were the rest of us?" I asked.

"Oh, you were all down on the lower level. I had gone up to the *Meeting Hall* ruins to check the stone placement in the entry arch."

"Jesus Christ, Janeen, you should have told me right away."

"Don't be such a worry wart, Jack. Just think, this time tomorrow we'll be sucking back some cold suds in Lima, or maybe even a good single-malt."

Peru is about ten degrees south of the equator. The climate along the coast is ruled by the warm and cold ocean currents, which circulate up and down it. The jungle interior, however, changes little. At this time of year the high-sierra is just coming out of its hot, dry season. We felt the river ford should not be a problem on our descent into the jungle and selva. The only possible glitches there would be heavy rains upstream or some uncommon thawing from the Andes.

We headed out at 0800 hours that late September morning. Our rendezvous was set for 1600 hours, leaving ample time for the five to six hour journey. If we were late the pilot could still hang around till 1800 hours and be safe for a dusk takeoff. That was the usual cutoff, for when dark comes to the edge of the Andean Selva, it comes quickly. Not having the finances to afford a satellite dish on this project, we had made all the arrangements on the camp's antiquated two-way radio.

With Janeen and me in one jeep and the guards, Juan and Jesus in the other, we traversed the precipitous route in less than the usual four hours to the river-ford. The other four workers were left behind to wrap up some site details and close down the main camp, which would take a couple of days.

The trail was fraught with switchbacks along loose talus slopes.

The view from the upper slopes was spectacular—if one dared look. As far as the eye could see there was verdant rainforest laid out beneath us. Occasional thin snake-like veins etched the landscape where the lush foliage could not quite close its inexorable fingers. These watercourses stood out red with iron-rich silt washed down from the Andes. Coming down the last bit of steep switchback, the Picha River was a little higher and faster than we had anticipated.

Reconnoitering, our crossing point looked to be about sixty feet wide and Janeen said, "Shouldn't be a problem unless some of the gravel bedding has been washed away."

"I'm going to wade out and check it," I replied, above the din of the rushing water.

Up to the bottom of my khaki shorts and leaning into the strong current, I realized that part of the base had indeed been washed away. I turned to holler at Janeen and was startled to find her right on my tail.

"What're you doing out here lass? This is a wee bit dangerous."

"Since when did that ever mean dick-shit to me, you weasel," she said smiling, while prodding me forward.

"Don't be a smart-ass, this is going to be a tricky crossing. We'd better see if the winches can reach the other side."

She nodded and we headed back to confer with Juan and Jesus. It was decided to drive one unit out as far as was safe and then hook the other jeep to its tail with the winch cable. Jesus would cross with the winch cable from the front jeep to secure it on the other side. I was mildly surprised that he made it across with little difficulty, for it required considerable agility in this fast rushing water. He secured the cable to the nearest thick tree trunk and we were ready to roll.

We were progressing across the river smoothly, even though the fast rushing water was threatening to spill into our jeep. It was a bit nerve-wracking, as I tried to keep the four wheels churning through the rocky gravel while maintaining tautness on the winch line.

The lead jeep looked to be just coming up on the bank when I felt the snap. We immediately veered sideways with the rear of the jeep almost pointing downstream. Only my front wheels had any traction and suddenly we were swamped, causing us to roll onto our side. As Janeen fell on top of me, we were submerged in the swirling current. I pulled at Janeen while I pushed and kicked with my legs at the jeep for I knew if it rolled on us we were finished. Bouncing off the rocky bottom I felt a sharp pain in my shoulder.

We surfaced in waist-deep water on the downstream side the jeep, which had flipped onto its roll bar. Miraculously, my daypack was bobbing next to me, as it was caught up on the jeep's side-view mirror. The rest of our gear was either pinioned under the jeep or already well on its way downstream. I hooked one arm through my daypack straps and the other around Janeen.

"We can't stay here. The jeep will likely roll again. Are you okay?" I said, between coughs.

"Of course I'm okay; you know I'm a fish in water. Oh shit! Guess who dropped by for tea?" she said.

His toothless grin was chilling, but not as chilling as the water, so as the Indio reached a long sapling out to us I hesitated only slightly. With the current raging around us I realized this was our only salvation.

I yelled to Janeen, "Grab my waist and don't let go!"

With an arm through my daypack strap, I lunged for the sapling. I gripped it momentarily with one hand, but it was slipping away. With the bitter taste of panic in my throat, I stabbed out with my other hand. Janeen's weight and the powerful current had me teetering and then completely off balance, but my grasp was now firm. Janeen must have had a hell of a time getting any air, for she had no footing and was more often under water than above. Her hold around my waist was slipping and she clutched my belt. The jeep was no longer shielding us and the force of the water was pulling us away from the shore. My belt snapped and Janeen grabbed at anything—unfortunately, anything included my crotch. A powerful eddy swirled us under and a mouthful of water abbreviated my howl. Instantly my lungs were burning. I lost my hold on the sapling and panic had its icy claws tightly around my throat.

I thrashed my legs wildly and found some footing. I was able to break surface, coughing and gasping for air. Janeen, thank God, had lost her death grip on my crotch and now had a firm hold on my lower leg. My free foot found a flat-sided boulder. I pushed off of it toward shore, with all the strength of desperation. Clawing for anything stable, I was rewarded with a strong wrist. With Janeen still clinging to my leg, we were dragged up the cobbled bank to safety.

I lay there like a beached Leviathan, sputtering and spouting for air. As she had been instructed, Janeen had never let go of my person and now someone was dragging her up next to me. Regaining some air in my lungs, I tried to babble a thank you, but was kicked in the side for my effort. The force of the boot rolled me over, rendering me semi-conscious and again gasping for air. I barely felt the punch to the side of my head before soothing darkness embraced me.

"Hey, rich boy, you hear me?"

My vision was clouded and everything was surreal. Waves of pain flashed red and white in my head. I could not blink away the horrible apparition. It was that ghastly toothless grin—so close—and the smell—like wafts of stale urine as he spoke in my face.

The question made no sense. I just wanted to drift back into oblivion, so I ignored it. My head flopped sideways as a stinging slap galvanized my senses. I tried to swing my arms and realized that they were pinned. Slowly reality came into focus. Juan and Jesus were each kneeling on a forearm. *Smiley* was astride me, sitting on my belly.

Trying to blink away the sharp pain, I blurted, "What the FUCK do you want?"

Smiley just smiled his crooked grin. I made a weak effort to knee him in the back. Another hard slap left me tasting fresh blood in my mouth.

"Okay, you hold the cards, *Smiley*. What the fuck DO you want?"

"That's right, pretty boy, I be the dealer-man. My comrades here seem to think you might have found something of value and it is our fondest wish to know if this is so."

Trying to think things through, despite my stunned state, I figured our guards may have tipped him off about my nightly studies. But what could that mean to them? I had noticed that someone had been through my tent, but had assumed it was just Raul, the cook, cleaning up. I always kept the manuscript in my daypack so I had not given it any further thought.

"I don't know what the hell you're talking about, we're just doing our research," I whined, purposely trying to sound intimidated.

"You lie, you stinking, British bastard," *Smiley* screamed. He slugged me in the ear setting off an explosion of chimes and symbols in my head. "Get them up. Let's see if they enjoy the comforts of our little camp."

From my semi-conscious, kaleidoscope world I felt them flip me over and yank my unlatched belt off. They lashed my hands behind my back with it. When they pulled me upright, the action wrenched my tender left shoulder and I groaned loudly. The bastards found this funny and laughed with gusto. I pretended to be completely dazed, still having enough wits to realize our only chance of escape would come if they dropped their guard.

In front of me, two of them dragged a staggering Janeen by the arms while Jesus and Juan had hold of me. My spoken Spanish is poor, but my understanding of it is fair. I was able to follow the odd phrase of the dialect they were speaking. The only thing of interest that I understood was that they were by themselves—an advance party.

Suddenly, Janeen, who must have been dazed or unconscious until now, came to life. She started struggling against her captors and spat out a steady stream of invective that could make ears bleed. "You motherfucks! You inbred sons of diseased Llamas! Let me GO, or I'll cut your goddamn balls off and feed them to… " A vicious slug to her jaw abruptly stifled her tirade.

I could taste the fury in my throat, like bile. It took great control to maintain my outward stupor and not somehow leap to her aid. Suppressing my emotions, I stumbled along as if still woozy. I was slowly regaining my wits and by hindering their progress it allowed me to appraise our assailants and the situation.

The fourth Indio was short and paunchy. He was oddly attired like some kind of Rastafarian rapper. His multi-colored dreadlocks hung haphazardly from a balding pate. He wore ragged black coveralls and a rifle was slung over his back. The other one dragging Janeen was old Scarface, a.k.a. Smiley. He had on a shoulder harness containing what looked like a large caliber handgun and he seemed to be the leader of this motley crew.

We couldn't have gone more than a few hundred yards up the jungle path before coming to a small clearing. They pushed me into the middle of it. I fell like a rag doll next to a fire pit. Covertly assessing through squinted eyes, I took in the two crude lean-tos that served as their camp. Rough alpaca blankets hung on either side of each hut with the front covering flipped up over the foliage-covered back. It was pretty Spartan and looked quickly thrown together. Two old dirt-bikes with crates mounted on the back stood next to them.

"Huaman, what are we going to do with them now? We could maybe get a good ransom," Jesus said in Spanish.

Scarface made no reply and Juan said, "Like I've said before, this is very dangerous and we don't even have the support of our other comrades. We should just let them go before it's too late."

"It's too late, fool," replied Huaman. "We're going to find out if they actually discovered any treasure. And, maybe we'll have some fun doing it."

At this the short pudgy one giggled, "Heh, heh, yah muchacho, I like to fuck them both."

This made my skin crawl. I racked my mind for ways we might be able to negotiate our way out of this.

Huaman was rifling through my daypack and soon came upon the container holding the manuscript. He looked at it with raised eyebrows and turned it over in his hands. My breathing stopped as he pried it open with his fingers. He scowled and seemed disappointed to find only papers inside. Passing it to Juan, he snapped, "What the hell is this?"

Looking at the script, Juan said, "Looks like some kind of French scribbling—not local."

I was surprised that Juan could recognize French, but though quiet, he did seem more educated than our other workers. Buying time and trying to deflect their interest, I offered, "It's my father's diary and the gold artifacts in our backpacks would be washed half-way down the river by now."

Speaking English, Huaman said, "So, the dozy one has his tongue back. What kind of bullshit are you handing us?"

"It's not bullshit. There were four, gold Sun-God medallions-of-the-seasons. They are very unusual," I said, and rolled onto my side, with hands strapped behind me.

His eyebrows raised and his brow furrowed, as he turned this blather over in his mind. He rose from his crouch and slowly ambled around me. Kneeling behind me he leaned in to my ear, "So tell me more, amigo."

"They, they were palm-sized and had a symbol that looked like the letter R with a U shape on each side underneath the R." I remembered seeing this symbol somewhere at the dig-site and chanced that it would tweak his interest. I didn't see it coming. A kick to the kidneys set me rigid in pain and I doubled over into a fetal position, gasping.

"You fool," he hissed. "I know there were no letters or writing in such times. Juan, Jesus, you two *wasos* get back down to the river. I want that other jeep secured before it's washed away. Our compatriots will be pleased with those acquisitions for the new territory. Then search the banks for their packsacks. There had better be gold medallions or this lying trash will be very, very sorry."

"We will do our best, Huaman. Don't do anything crazy. These two are innocents to our struggle," said Juan.

"There are no innocents Juan, you *hayra*. The white interlopers have been raping our land for centuries and now it's our time to *kajchana y runa sipiy*".

"Heh, heh, yah, Huaman's the boss-man. Get going," I heard the short, chunky one mutter.

My breathing was returning to normal, and some of the puzzle was falling into place for me. I had no idea how the guards infiltrated our expedition, but old Huaman and his pudgy gnome were probably an advance foray of the *Shining Path* moving into a new area. Recognizing words from an old Inca dialect of Quechua, I remembered that Huaman means Falcon. The tattoo on his left breast was actually a stylized falcon entwined with the *Shining Path* symbol. I felt a chill creep up my spine, as I realized that *kajchana y runa sipiy* means rape and slaughter.

"Go ahead and search him, Chono," said Huaman.

That's rich, I thought, as a Peruvian hairless dog, which has been around since before the Incas, is called a Chono.

Chono tied my feet together and then rolled me from my side onto my back. Huaman sat on a stump in front of his lean-to and was rolling what looked like a cigarette or joint. He had one foot on Janeen's neck. She groaned occasionally and seemed to be coming around.

Chono searched me thoroughly—much too thoroughly. He sat his ample ass down on my thighs, and after checking the pockets of my shirt, ripped it open wide with two hands. He slowly ran his paws down me from neck to navel. Breathing heavily with a wheeze through his open mouth a rancid odor settled over me—it was something between fouled cuy fat and rotting fish. Pulling down on my pants, he got hold of my under shorts and gave a sudden, wicked pull upward that ripped them apart.

His laugh was loud, but it was more of a squeaky cackle than a laugh, "A wedgey, a wedgey." Chono cackled and shook so hard his bulk almost fell off me.

From Huaman's direction I could smell the sweet pungent odor of pot, like smoldering wet foliage. This could get really ugly I thought, as Chono's hands began to grope me. I gritted my teeth.

"Ooee, muchacho, red hair everywhere."

He stopped to check my pockets, finding only some minor currency and my Swiss knife. He got up to flip me over onto my belly, and resuming his seat on my thighs, yanked my khakis down past my butt.

"I have heard the sneaky ones will put valuables up their anus. Do you think I should check that out, Huaman?"

"Aye, lad, I think that would be a most prudent course of action," Huaman said, mimicking my Scottish brogue.

My sphincter contracted as his finger prodded at me. He continued trying to enter me, and his finger was becoming more insistent. "Fuck you," I said. What have I got to lose? I let it all go. Whatever I had, he got.

"You motherfuckin' pig," Chono howled.

Huaman, consumed by a tremendous belly laugh, fell off his perch. There was a sudden searing pain in my head and blackness rolled over me like a fog.

I had no idea how much time had passed before I started to regain consciousness. I did not want to come around, as the pain in my head and ribs was too intense to deal with. Janeen's cries were the impetus that forced me to try. I opened my eyes to a red blur. It wasn't my imagination; my face was covered in blood. Blinking through the blood and pain, it took me a few moments to focus. I saw Janeen bent prostrate over the stump in front of the lean-to. Huaman was behind her, ripping down her khakis and panties. "Oh si, senorita, what a beautiful, big ass," he said, as he slapped and squeezed her bared buttocks.

I could hear Chono chortling. He was out of my sightline, under the lean-to, holding her arms. I was now seeing more red than just blood. Rage can be empowering. I frantically worked at loosening my belted wrists, ignoring the raw chafe of leather. Janeen had broken the hasp in the water and whoever bound me must not have noticed it. I could feel the buckle of my belt beginning to slip. I worked my numb hands and the wraps were slowly loosening, millimeter by agonizing millimeter.

"Mia juicy diablo you are going to like this. Which *simi* do you think first, Chono?"

"Save the backdoor for me Huaman. I bet she's a virgin there," Chono said, with an excited giggle.

Huaman dropped his cutoffs, exposing a thick, uncircumcised erection. "Yes, Chono I think I am too much man for that hole. I'll let you loosen it up for me later."

He was stroking himself, ogling his quarry through a stoned haze, oblivious to everything around him. Janeen's angry wailing had simmered to a terrified whimper and racking sobs. Finally, I was free from my bonds. I rubbed circulation back into my wrists and arms, grimacing at the pain. Fighting off the dull ache and fog in my head, I slowly got to my knees and surveyed the situation. Huaman had removed his gun and harness leaving it on the ground beside him. I could see Chono's rifle propped up against the lean-to. I figured Chono probably had his pants around his knees, so any other weapons might not be easily accessible. Rising to my feet, I pulled my pants up, scarcely breathing. Cat-like, I circled Huaman, careful to keep out of his peripheral vision. He was kneeling across the back of Janeen's calves, positioning himself.

"This is going to be so sweet, senorita. I have such a lovely treat for you," he was saying as he began to prod at Janeen.

Yes, I thought, this IS going to be sweet, and I have a treat for you, asshole. Everything I had went into the swing of my leg. All the power my six foot, two hundred pound frame could muster. Having kicked as a rugby fly half, I found my accuracy had not diminished over the years. I was still good at kicking balls.

My boot caught him squarely and the force of it lifted him off the ground, pitching him forward. He slid right over top of Janeen into Chono, who had been holding Janeen's arms. Chono fell backward with his pants around his knees and his stiff little willey flopping against his belly. Huaman's eyes rolled back into their sockets. He curled into a fetal position cradling his groin and the only sound he made was a deep gurgling groan. He was done.

I leapt over Janeen, coming down hard on Chono's belly and chest with my knees. The air whistled from his body like a deflating balloon. I grabbed his neck with my left hand and, using my right fist like a hammer, pounded on his face. He tried to claw at me, but his body soon went limp.

"Jack, Jack enough, Jack."

I don't know how many times I hit Chono, but I became aware that Janeen had crawled off the stump and was pulling at my shirt. Shaking from rage and effort, I finally drew back. It was a few moments before I regained control. I helped Janeen up and took her into my arms. She was shaking violently, but had stopped sobbing.

"You're in shock," I said.

After a bit I stood back and closed her ripped open shirt. Kneeling down, I gently pulled up what was left of her panties and khakis.

"I'm so cold, Jack."

While I surveyed the carnage, I took her in my arms again. Huaman had passed out from the pain and his testicles were like two grotesque purple grapefruits oozing blood as if to burst. Chono's face was no longer recognizable and I was splattered with blood. I began to shake in unison with Janeen.

With Janeen on my knees, cuddled in my arms, we sat on the stump trying to compose ourselves. "Janeen, we've got to get out of here before Juan and Jesus get back," I gently prompted her.

"Those treacherous pricks! How could've they betrayed us like that?"

"Yes, I know. The authorities can deal with them, but we have to make a move to get to the plane. Their so-called comrades could show up, or our buddies may come back in a not so friendly mood. Besides, our Camisea escape route could be in jeopardy if the Shining Path are on the move."

"The Shining Path! Jack, what the hell are you talking about?"

"We can go over my theories later, Janeen. Let's just get going. I don't know what happened to my watch, but by the sun it must be late afternoon—maybe four o'clock. I don't think our pilot would leave before dusk, especially if it's Terry. That gives us at least two hours."

"But Jack, it's got to be twenty five miles to Camisea!"

"I know, but we've got those dirt bikes." She was lamenting that she didn't know how to ride such things, when I found the key of one in the ignition. "Don't feel bad," I said, "Neither do I, except once when I rode my buddy's in high school."

"Oh great, that should qualify us for the pro circuit. What's wrong with going back for the jeep?"

"We don't know what we're up against there, and our schedule is pretty tight," I replied.

I grabbed my daypack, stuffing the manuscript and Huaman's .38 Smith-Wesson into it.

"And what's this crap about your father's diary. Nothing's making any sense to me."

"We'll talk over a beer in Lima," I said, removing the carrying crate and jumping on the keyed bike. I tested the kick-start and amazingly it sputtered and coughed to life as I revved it. Grimacing in pain, I realized I must have fractured my baby knuckle on Chono's face. "Get your sweet tush behind mine darlin, this train's rollin."

She obediently did so, gripping me in a bear hug, and we jerkily headed up a skimpy path, away from the river.

"Jesus Christ you stink—what did you do, shit yourself?" I made no reply, for little did she know. "Do you know where the hell you're going?" she said.

"Maybe—as long as we're pointed southeast like this, we should intersect the main cut-line."

It was rough going as we bounced along over roots and through overhanging branches. I figured it shouldn't be more than a kilometer before we hit the cut-line. We must have gone at least two miles though, and I was starting to doubt my logic, when the ground and bike disappeared from under us. I lost my grip on the handlebars, but Janeen didn't lose her grip on my waist, as we tumbled into the ditch together. Our bike cartwheeled into the other side of the ditch, landing sideways.

"Gawdammit and bloody hell! I forgot about that drainage

ditch. You okay, Janeen?" I asked, as I wiped mud from my butt and shook the tepid wetness from my arms.

"Yah—funny how men figure they're better drivers," she replied. Janeen was starting to feel better.

I jumped across the trickle of water to check the stalled bike. Pulling it off its side and up on to the cut-line, I noticed the tail pipe was mangled. I gave it a kick and it dropped off completely. It stunk of petrol and checking the tank I noticed a dent and hair-line crack in the side of it.

"Oh great! It landed on a fuckin rock. I hope the hell all the gas didn't… " I was interrupted by Janeen's scream as she scrambled up out of the ditch.

"I fucking HATE snakes," she screeched, as she dug her fingers into my arm and spun me between her and the ditch.

"Shush, Janeen, I think I hear something." She started to say something trite about male ears, but then heard it herself. "Sonofabitch, that's the other dirt bike. Why the hell didn't I wreck the fuckin' thing?"

Quickly up-righting our bike I kick started it and it fired. "Thank god," Janeen said, as she jumped on. We hadn't even gone ten yards when it coughed and stalled. I tried again, and again, but it wouldn't fire.

"Bloody gas tank is probably drained. Shit, were going to have to … where the hell's my daypack?"

"I think it's in the ditch where we landed," she said.

Bolting back to the spot, I found it on the near bank. Just then the other bike burst through the foliage and skidded to a stop on the other bank, not ten feet from me. Leveling an Uzi at me, Jesus stood astride the bike. I froze with my hand on the daypack strap, crouched.

"*Buenas dias, muchacho*. Why do you wish to leave us? Do you not like our hospitality? You certainly weren't very appreciative to my comrades, you motherfuck," spitting out the last phrase with raw malevolence.

I saw some movement in the trickling water next to his bike. Always the gambler, I decided to take a long-shot.

"You know, boffo, this is turning into a really bad day. You are really beginning to piss me off. You're just a chickenshit little commie asshole, too fuckin' stupid and scared to get off that wee kiddies bike and walk over here like a man," I spat at him.

I could hear Janeen groaning something inaudible about my stupidity, as he swung out of the seat with pure venom in his eyes. Fortunately, for me, there was *another venom* and I had staked my life on it. He was struck immediately and the look of malice in his eyes turned to shock. He kicked his right leg out, but the slender coral snake was still attached. Its small rounded snout had taken too big of a bite. Panicking, he tried to shoot it with his Uzi. Perhaps he succeeded, but he also managed to shoot himself in the leg. As he spun into the bush screaming I rolled up over the bank clutching my daypack.

I found the .38, but it was unnecessary. I had done a little research on Peru's jungle dangers before I left Scotland. It was his ill fortune that this black Peruvian nasty with red and yellow rings, sub-genus *Leptomicrurus*, is one of the deadliest in the world. Its highly toxic venom can kill within minutes—or moments.

After waiting a few moments, I ventured a short way into the bush to see Jesus twitching only slightly and his eyes rolled back into their sockets. With great caution, I retrieved his Uzi and recovered his bike from the ditch. I did not care to meet the same fate as Jesus.

Double-quick, we were on his bike and had it wide open down the main cut-line. I hollered behind me at Janeen, "I'll bet our old buddy Juan is on his way down the cut-line with the jeep. Jesus took the shortcut on the bike. This old piece of shite won't be as fast, but stopping to investigate the other bike and his brother, will hopefully give us the gap we need."

I figured we had about an hour to make the last twenty plus miles, and that left little room for any further delays.

Dusk was fast approaching as we crested the hill and looked down into a broad selva basin. Camisea and salvation were clearly visible, less than two miles away. Camisea is an oil-processing center. The gas separators on the other side of it emitted an effluent haze that hung over the valley, a brown filmy shroud in the late afternoon heat. I was starting to say something to Janeen when I felt the machine between my legs start to hiccup. Janeen noticed too, enunciating her displeasure with a string of expletives.

"Goddam thing is probably out of petrol. Why should our luck change now?" I griped.

The bike soon died completely, but we were on a down hill grade and able to coast for a long way. Fortunately, the airstrip was on this side of the village and we were less than a mile away when the bike finally rolled to a stop. Jettisoning everything but my daypack, we started jogging, a desperate urgency driving us.

At last, the strip was in sight as we crested a slight rise, and happy day, I could see the Otter. The rough dirt road widened and became graveled just before the bridge. It spanned a lazy part of the long and meandering Urubamba River. Stopping briefly to let Janeen catch her breath, my heart began to race even faster, as somewhere round the bend behind us, was the unmistakable sound of a jeep bearing down on us.

"Quick, under the bridge," I said, ignoring the panic in Janeen's eyes.

We got out of sight just in time and as the jeep rumbled over the rickety old wooden structure. From our vantage we could see Juan was behind the wheel, looking anxiously ahead for us as he stopped on the far crest.

Trying to sound positive I whispered, "Come on, Janeen, it's just a short swim and besides, I need a little rinse off."

I realized we couldn't use the bridge, because at this point Juan wouldn't hesitate to cut us down. This part of the Urubamba was not swift, but it was up to my chest. I kept the daypack above my head while Janeen held onto my arm.

Keeping in the shadow of the bridge, it didn't take us long to wade across and scramble up the bank. I whispered for her to sneak around one side under the bridge while I snuck around the other. Stealthily I crept to the right side and cautiously peered around the trestle edge. I froze at a most unpleasant sight—the wrong end of an Uzi.

"You're a dead man if you move, Senor Jack. Where's your bitch?"

"Okay lass, you can come out from under there. Juan's not going to hurt us," I said, motioning with my head as if she was behind me.

"Don't bet on it hombre—what you did to my comrades… no funny stuff, my finger is itchy," he threatened.

Out of the corner of my eye I could see Janeen come noiselessly over the other side of the road with something in her hands. I moved slightly to draw his peripheral vision away from her, looking expectantly behind me. Just then the Otter fired up barely two hundred meters away and the noise helped cover her approach.

"Move out here NOW, Senorita, or I'm going to… "

It was then that Janeen's wet boots made a squishing sound and he whirled in her direction. I whip-kicked at his leg and at the same instant Janeen swung the bat-like piece of driftwood. His knee buckled inward at an unnatural angle. Janeen had succeeded in knocking the Uzi from his grasp and it fired a harmless wild burst. Juan went down hard, cursing in pain.

We could hear the Otter revving and beginning its taxi down the strip for take off.

"Run Janeen," I shouted. "Get on the strip and flag the plane down."

Like a shot she was already away. I scrambled to retrieve the Uzi and turned to Juan. "No, senor Jack, please don't kill me. I am only a soldier in our struggle."

Wheeling around, I squeezed off a few rounds, raking his jeep's tires on my side. Turning back to Juan, his eyes were like saucers and sweat was beading rapidly on his brow. With his left leg at a ridiculous angle, he wasn't going anywhere.

"You spoke up for us, so at least you have something of a conscience. But you still set us up, asshole." I grabbed my daypack and tossed the Uzi out into the river. Sprinting for the plane, I shot back at Juan, "You owe me one."

I threw my daypack in to Janeen and vaulted up into the slowly taxiing Otter. "Welcome aboard, shithead, you're late," Terry hollered from the controls.

"Where's my champagne and seatbelt spiel?" I said with a forced measure of levity.

"I gathered from Janeen there was some sense of urgency so we'll skip that today. Go fuck yourself," Terry shot back, with her usual rough edge.

As the throttle was opened, I tumbled into Janeen's lap face first, which wasn't such a bad thing.

"Not now, Jack," she said, with forced humor, and pushed me into the next seat.

"Thank God you were still here, Terry. You deserve a big fat kiss," I said, and made a move to get into the co-pilot's seat. I managed to duck Terry's elbow to the chops, but as the Otter lurched skyward I found myself back in Janeen's lap.

"Try that again with me, Mister Romeo, and you'll get more than an elbow," Terry barked.

"Promises, promises; I'm just so damned excited that you were still here." And I was excited—excited that we were alive. My emotions were jumbled and I was beyond exhaustion. I was euphoric, yet I was shattered.

Terry was every bit enticing as she was unapproachable. She was a dark-haired, Floridian beauty that better men than me have crashed and burnt over. Her rough, crusty personality was probably the main reason she wasn't flying for a major airline. She was one hell of a pilot.

"Dare I ask why you two are in such a panic and look and smell like shit through a wringer?" Terry asked.

"I'm not sure what the hell was happening—or why," replied Janeen.

"I have an idea or two, but after what we've been through I've got to give my battered body and brain a rest," I offered, not wanting to divulge everything anyway.

"Well piss on you bone-diggers then. Get your beauty sleep—it'll likely be ninety minutes into this stinkin' wind."

We were so drained we actually did sleep through most of the flight. When we arrived in Lima, Terry didn't wait for explanations, as she said she had to rush off somewhere due to our late arrival. I figured explaining to authorities could be done later, but I had to determine how best to tell Janeen the whole story. During the taxi ride we tried to formulate a basic plan and decided the first priority would be to change hotels. However, we still needed to go to our regular hotel to get the rest of our clothes stored there. It was the typical harrowing, anything-goes, taxi-ride from the airport. Roadways were sidewalks, construction zones, five lanes in three—and incessantly blaring horns were the rule rather than exception. Somehow though, it did not even faze me this evening.

"Jack Maxwell, you're keeping something from me. The Shining Path assholes okay, but why were they after *US*?" she asked in a low, shaky voice.

"Yes, there is more, but I think we'd better discuss it over a drink. We've been seriously beaten, almost raped, almost murdered, and are probably still in shock."

Silence then prevailed, while we rode in the fleabag taxi to the fleabag government-paid hotel in Saint Isadore.

Chapter Five

SCOTCH AND WATER

BOTH HANDS were pointing straight up so it must be midnight—at least, as near as I could tell with my murky vision. My watch was on the floor, four feet away, but it seemed like forty. I was in a drunken haze and relishing my bath in the ancient tub. Taking stock of my battered body, I figured if my ribs weren't cracked, they were at least badly bruised. My left shoulder was pretty sore, but after slamming back eight or ten double scotches and this glorious bath, I deemed it to be only jammed. A couple of welts on my face and two major lumps on my head completed the injury inventory.

I considered us shithouse lucky having dodged some of the world's worst cutthroats a.k.a. guerrillas. They obviously weren't stupid or uninformed either, as they had easily infiltrated our expedition and could speak at least two or three languages.

Discussing it with Janeen, we felt there must be some insiders with the government and accordingly we had changed hotels. How else could the Shining Path get guards on our little party? But, most puzzling of all for me, was Janeen's impassive reaction when I explained my discovery to her—especially considering she had almost as many doubles as me. Many a time had we tipped the jug together and she often became more opinionated and strong-willed than most males. The tirade never came, so when we left the little bar downstairs I made her leave our adjoining door unlocked. I told her it was for safety, but in light of the day's events I was more concerned about her mind-set.

Rocking my reverie, the bathroom door suddenly flew open and slammed into the wall with a hinge rattling crash. The swinging door had clipped my empty glass on the floor, sending it careening into the corner. I made a wild effort to leap out of the tub, but only succeeded in slipping and falling back in, splashing water everywhere.

With dulled perception I realized it was Janeen and sputtered, "Janeen for crissakes what the hell are... "

"You rotten sonofabitch. You bastard. You fuckin, inconsiderate, egocentric prick. You selfish piece of Llama dung." As she spat out this slurred slew of abuses she was moving slowly toward me, with her fists clenched and punching the air for emphasis.

I was stunned, sitting in the steamy, with my mouth still open in mid-sentence. There were tears streaming down her cheeks and her housecoat hung untied, partially exposing her.

"... asshole. Who the hell dja think you are? God's gift to archaeology? You're jus a fuckin' rank amateur. Not only that, you endangered people, the expedition, and the whole fuckin' project. You, you, ARGHH... "

Her scathing invective was running out of steam as she stood over me. She raised one foot into the tub and began kicking water at me in frustration. Partly for self-preservation, in case her foot caught something else, I grabbed it. She lost her balance and slipped on the wet tile, falling into the tub on top of me. In her rage she began to beat me on the chest and shoulders. With difficulty, I managed to get my arms around her in an effort to control her. She was racked with uncontrolled sobs and gradually went limp in my arms.

How stupid I am, I thought. Never mind my unprofessional secrecy; I should have had greater empathy for Janeen's fragile state after a traumatizing day like we had. Her sang-froid attitude over drinks should have clued me in straight off. I relaxed my grip to a loving cuddle and she seemed to settle down to simple sobs. I don't know how long we stayed like that, but the water was getting noticeably cool.

"Come on, sunshine, things will be better in the morning. You must know my intentions were sincere, though perhaps imprudent. I initially thought the text was bogus anyway. I'm sorry and I admit I was wrong. Please forgive me, lass. What else can I say?" She seemed more relaxed now, but was starting to shiver. "I guess the dumb-male-excuse doesn't work, *EH*?" and I got a small chuckle for my poor attempt at Canadian vernacular.

Her demeanor slowly seemed to change and she spoke in a subdued tone, "Jack, you just don't seem to understand the gravity of your actions sometimes." After a pause she added, "And by the way, thank you for your bravery and composure. I have to admit, without your decisive action … it was an ugly situation."

She raised her face and kissed me warmly, signifying at least a truce, if not full forgiveness. The kiss lingered, tender, as neither one of us seemed to want to break it. She started to say something, but I used the opportunity to gently probe her mouth with my tongue. She shivered again, but it was of the delicious sort, not from any chill or trauma.

Breaking it off and cuddling her in my arms, I said, "The water's cold, lass, and you need to be warm. You're probably still in shock. Why don't we warm up in bed?"

"Yah, you're probably right, but what's with this hard-on? You are amazing Jack. I'd forgotten, you're the instant erection man."

"I'm crushed, lass, how could you possibly forget."

Struggling out of the tub I helped Janeen out of her sopping housecoat. As we toweled each other off, she said, "You know I didn't mean all of those things I said. It must have been aftershock venting."

"Aye, you only meant some of them," I teased.

In response, she reached down and gave my penis an almost painful squeeze. Seizing the playful moment, I gave her puckered nipples a hearty tweak in return. Wavelets of electric pleasure arced between us.

"You know, Jack, we shouldn't start this again. Between us, I mean. I'm not even sure how I would react after today's experience."

"Sunshine, it's whatever works for you. You know how my feelings have always been—that's never changed."

She hesitated and I agonized on her hesitation. Looking up at me those Ceylonese sapphire eyes drank me in—probing, touching, searching my soul. "I have to know, Jack. Take me to your bed," she said in a whisper.

Summoning the strength fueled by passion, I scooped her into my arms and complied with her request.

The rest of the night was as incredible as the day had been, except in a very positive way. We needn't have feared about her response and I made sure it was slow and tender.

It had been fourteen years since we last had sex together. We had kept in close touch and I had worked with her once several years ago on a Mayan project. It was there that she had introduced me to my ex-wife. She even came to our wedding. As it turned, out my very rich American lass was even more spoilt than me. It had happened too quickly and we were like oil and water. Fortunately for us in today's society, these things can be dissolved as quickly as they are consecrated. Sharyl was actually paying *me* some alimony, as she and particularly her deep-pockets daddy were just happy to be rid of me. When Janeen called me on this current project, knowing I had time on my hands, I made her promise not to introduce me to any new females.

Lima's street noises and the mid-morning sunlight had been assailing my deep slumber for a while when I opened my eyes to a marvelous sight. The previous day and night came back to me in a bittersweet rush. The sweet part lay next to me on her stomach with the blanket mostly off. One large but shapely buttock presented itself in glorious creamy fullness. I could not help but reach over and knead its warm softness.

What a fool I've been all these years, I thought. Why couldn't I see that Janeen was everything I could possibly want in a woman? In the beginning I was young and foolish and then with Sharyl I was just foolish. It was Janeen who had broken it off, but I can't blame her for that.

She began to stir and my ministrations seemed to arouse her, so I let my fingers wander down the cleavage of her buttocks. She was moaning dreamily and beginning to move most sensually, when suddenly her eyes popped open.

"Holy shit! Jack! My God, did yesterday really happen?"

"Which part?"

"All of it for christsakes."

"Well, part one unfortunately yes, and part two fortunately yes. It would seem that part two is still on your mind," I answered as I continued my digital manipulation.

"Ummm … how could it not be? That was incredibly explosive, and it seemed to last all night. I knew we used to be good together, but THAT was off the Richter scale. I guess I didn't need to worry about the earlier events, eh."

"Aye, maybe there's something to that theory about severe trauma and sexual interaction. Also, I'd like to believe we still have some of that old chemistry and familiarity. It seems to strip away the inhibitions that afflict first-time lovers. We made each other's body sing like birds in the morning."

"Jack, you're not going all romantic on me are you? That much scotch would have made any hot-blooded Canuck horny."

"Aye, and may I say, you are one hell of a Canuck."

"Yah, and how many Canucks have you known? Ohh Gawd, what you're doing feels sooo good, but you'd better stop."

"Stop! Why would you want me to do that?"

"I don't WANT you to, but it must be mid-morning and we've got to report to the authorities."

"Janeen, darling, that might be dangerous. If they've got insiders that could even be suicidal. We probably should have finished off the buggers for our own safety, but I'm not that cold-blooded, even if I had thought of it."

"So what do you suggest, Einstein? We can't just pretend it never happened. And, what about the others at base camp?"

"They are either conspirators or they're dead. We have to think about *numero uno* first. My theory is that they were poking around to see if we came up with anything of value that they could ransom for their cause. What I found, they could know nothing about, but I distracted them with that gold medallion bullshit. In retrospect that might prove to be a bad move, but what else could I have done? While you were still sleeping I thought about going to one of our embassies, but an explanation might motivate some in-depth questions or even a search. I simply don't want to risk turning over the manuscript before we've had an opportunity to properly examine it."

Janeen sat up and said with obvious excitement, "Jack, I HAVE to see this so-called manuscript."

Slightly annoyed at her change of posture, but once again marveling at her full breasts, nipples jutting proudly, I countered, "Yes, yes of course, but we'd better get to a safer place first. Since my erection doesn't seem to be having the desired effect, I'm going to clean up and get some things packed straight away."

"And here I thought that mountain under the blanket was just your knee drawn up," she smiled coquettishly.

In fresh clothes, with light packs, we took a side door out of the hotel. Janeen suggested we try and contact Terry Krieg, our crusty pilot, as she frequently went in and out of the country and knew the turf better than us. Janeen had said something else that puzzled me, but in our rush to get going I let it slip by. In the taxi, however, I revisited her comment.

"What did you mean about Terry having unusual contacts as well as unusual habits?"

"Oh, uh, partly it's girl-talk and partly it's this girl's gut feeling." She let that hang without offering anything further.

"You still haven't told me anything," I said, between mouthfuls of a shared loaf sandwich and juice we had purchased from a street vendor.

Pensively, she said, "Well, I don't know how much I should tell you, or even how much you would want to know."

"Oh come on, Janeen, you're driving me crazy. We've got a lot at stake here."

"Okay, okay, you asked for it and it goes no further—agreed?"

"Aye, of course."

What Janeen related to me defied the order of my cosmos and challenged my male ego. She had no reason to relate anything other than what she truly knew or could surmise, and sometimes women are just inexplicably more intuitive than men. The *rind of realism* is especially tough for men to penetrate. At least that's what my mother used to say.

Terry Krieg's brash bravado and ample attitude were no act. Besides being gay, she was also an agent for good old Uncle Sam. Janeen knew Terry was gay, because the pilot had hit on her in Mexico five years ago. Janeen blushed as she admitted almost going to bed with Terry.

What really caused my kilt to tighten was that Terry and Sharyl had been lovers. This was one of the reasons Sharyl wound up in my arms, as she was rebounding from her fling with the *Goddess of Lesbo,* Terry. Sharyl had been more than welcome in my arms, with her radiant copper-hued complexion and slender model-like body.

Sharyl's father, Stephen Saxon, was a wealthy autocrat working internationally on sensitive projects for the United States government. He was a Texan whose grandfather had made his money in the rail and oil arenas. Stephen Saxon's father in turn had furthered their sizeable fortune through computers and national security contracts. By comparison, my family were paupers.

Stephen Saxon's travels had led to a marriage with a Latin beauty queen and this union produced the enigmatic, but stunning Sharyl. Fate has always played a big hand in my life and I now could see it looming even larger. My head was swimming with these revelations. I was barely recovering from yesterdays physical battering and now had to contend with this mental bruising to my male psyche.

"Oh come on, Jack, it's not the end of the world you know," said Janeen, sensing my shocked and disconsolate state of mind. "I'm not gay, if that's what you're worried about, and I don't really think Sharyl was either. She was just a spoilt brat who had to try everything at least once. When I introduced you two, I never thought it would lead to what it did. She seemed like a decent person and she was my financial ticket which opened doors to do those research projects I was chasing."

"You don't have to explain that side of it to me Janeen. I understand the workings and financial problems of your profession. That pre-Mayan Omtec paper of yours put you in the limelight and opened many doors for you. Without Sharyl and her Daddy-big-bucks you couldn't have accomplished what you did. It's just that I never even considered this, this… "

"Never mind, it's already ancient history. Let's deal with the present."

"Shite, I guess you're right. I'm already pushing it out of my mind," I said, without conviction. "We need to deal with the here and now. Terry seems to be our best bet, but what about her other connections?"

"She told me very little, and only hinted at her multifaceted career. It was Sharyl who enlightened me the most. Her father had entrusted her with enough information to try and keep her clear of Terry. However, that only excited her all the more. When her father realized she was actually involved with Terry he freaked and you just happened to be a temporary solution. Apparently when your usefulness expired, so did your marriage. I'm sorry, Jack. I care deeply for you, but that's how I see it."

"Fuck, that pretty much cuts it to the quick. I'll admit it; I'm pretty much numb. Old silver-haired Saxon never did take much of a shine to me, but Sharyl … I trusted her. What a naive fool I was. Well, like you said it's ancient history. Two things though: First we must deal with our predicament; and second I still care a great deal for you and always will. We have a history. That can never change. Let's just deal with this situation, and afterwards we'll see where we're at."

We were fortunate to find Terry at her hangar and she, maybe not surprisingly, seemed to grasp the urgency of our situation. We were purposefully vague about our predicament, but that didn't seem to bother her. Her suggestion of lying low at a safe village less than two hours flying time out of Lima seemed the best available avenue. Janeen made a brief call to her project administrator, Samuel Gasparojo. Then, entrusting ourselves to Terry, and filing a false flight plan, we were airborne. Terry said *Parachique* was a quiet fishing village on a large inlet. It was about 150 miles north of Trujillo and she could land there with floats. Glumly evaluating our bizarre situation, as we flew low over the terra-cotta desert coastline, I could not paint a positive picture. Our present was precarious, our future insecure, and the road we were following a miasmic path.

PART II

Chapter One

Vaucouluers

Vaucouluers, valley of colors—a verdant and sanguine place of beauty; fertile red soil, fringed by foliage of green—piquant and harmonious to the eye. Such is my enduring and cherished image of Vaucouluers.

It was a cool, clear spring day and I was in the sixteenth year of my humble life. Robert de Baudricourt's royal castle sat ascendant and brooding on the valley wall, like a gargantuan gargoyle overseeing its domain from a western perch. This was our now visible destination as we traversed beyond Burley-le-Petit.

Friar Francois and I had trekked since before sunrise to reach Vaucouluers. As a Franciscan order we were obligated to a life of poverty and service. However, we still had to sustain our monastery and ourselves. We were under the patronage of a larger Franciscan cloister at Neufchateau, but our main benefactors were Jeanne de Joinville and her husband Henri D'Ogevillers, overseers of Bourlemont and Domremy. As well, we were obliged to pledge our sectarian support to Vaucouluers and Robert de Baudricourt, who was the Dauphin's defender in this region. I had surmised from overhearing a hushed conversation between Friars Albert, Clement and Francois that we were discreetly carrying a message about impending peril for Vaucouluers and the royal Castelan, Robert de Baudricourt. It was discovered by Henri D'Ogevillers that Antoine de Vergy, Burgundian governor of Champagne, subsidized by the English regent Duke of Bedford, was planning a summer campaign to capture Vaucouluers. It was thus that a simple friar and novice covertly carried a message of earthly salvation.

Traveling on our monastery's two donkeys we were slowly overtaking two other travelers. I was excited to discover they were my friend Jeanne and her older cousin Durand Laxard. I knew Durand in passing from church events. He was easy to remember, as his hair was even a brighter red than mine. We were uncommon in this regard, especially for this region.

"Allo, and bonjour, my friends," I hailed. Francois in his stoic manner merely nodded.

"Ahh, my rouge compatriot, it is good to see you and your friar friend. What brings you up north this fine day?" Durand replied.

Jeanne smiled radiantly in recognition of me. I grinned back eagerly and started to say, "We are on… " but was interrupted by Francois.

"We are doing God's work of course. We will meet with the priest of Vaucouluers and invite him to our summer rites festival."

I realized that Francois was concerned about my loose lips but he needn't have worried. "What purpose brings my friends this way on such a fine day," I said not allowing my exuberance to be suppressed.

Durand looked at Jeanne, leaving her to reply. "I am also on God's mission, but unfortunately I have words in this regard only for Robert de Baudricourt's ears; meaning no disrespect to Friar Francois of course."

With a puzzled look on his face, Francois replied, "No disrespect is taken, young maiden, but we must hurry on to our destination."

Disappointed at such an abrupt chance meeting, I followed Francois as he prodded his ass to hurry past our fellow travelers.

"Perhaps we will meet while at Vaucouluers," I suggested hopefully.

"Yes, that would be good, as we have not met since Easter and I would like to talk to you, Alex," replied Jeanne.

I smiled at that, as my affinity and respect for Jeanne had been a constant since the incident at the fairy tree.

"Aurevoir and God speed," waved Durand.

Approaching the town of Vaucouluers there was still considerable bustle during the mid-afternoon Saturday social circle. It was a time for plebeian interaction, business and family gatherings. This writer remembers such vibrancy of life fondly, as the two years of monastic life offered little other excitement for a young person. There were wares and food being sold or bartered at the Saturday market, and there was much mingling and the noise of children.

We threaded our way through the milling people in the streets, toward the south gate of the castle. Sometimes it was necessary to duck under enormous tavern and shop signs hanging from iron rods that projected into the narrow streets. To my astonishment, I was almost unmounted by a giant tooth hanging outside a tooth-pullers shop. There were muleteers leading their ware-laden beasts and human beasts of burden bent under loads of charcoal and wood. Our donkeys were jostled and sometimes diverted from a direct course, but I did not mind. I had seen many busy centers and castles with Marie Robine and I had hungered for such human interaction since entering the monastery. Oh, the memory of those sights and smells leave a melancholy ache in my heart. Open hearths cooking such tantalizing victuals as pig knuckles in blood and fat, lemon with liver and tongue, and fresh bread to be dipped in the steaming verjuice. My mouth watered and my belly growled. Some people were eating on their doorsteps while visiting with strollers. Children were dodging in between adults and donkeys such as ours. The burning wood of ash and oak permeated the air with heavy acrid smoke, stinging the nostrils if too deeply inhaled. Confusing all these scents were, of course, the malodorous smell of human habitation, waste and excrement.

Friar Francois was his usual impatient and imperious self. He used his donkey switch to swat at riotous children who dared intersect his path. He admonished me for my lack of forbearance as we approached the south gate. I paid him no heed, but still exhibited the proper subservience outside of my feelings. Too soon for me did we reach the south gate, as I found the tumult of human activity more uplifting than my religious studies. Dismounting our asses, we left them at the royal stable and climbed the last steep steps to the inner fortress. I was fascinated by a jester juggling three balls at once, when all of a sudden he pulled a fourth from his pocket. Friar Francois grumpily pushed me up the stairs, jostling the juggler in the process. He dropped two of his balls, and cursing, had to chase them down the stairs. Three or four pesky street urchins were immediately in hot pursuit as well, trying to outrace him for the prizes.

Francois called after him, "Foul blasphemer."

His lips were a thin smirking smile and I realized he thought himself superior because he had undone the juggler's concentration. I said nothing, but thought his actions mean-spirited and ungodly. He was as callous as his immediate superior, Father Clement. When I first came to the monastery, Friar Francois seemed pious and godly, but his nature had become more and more like Father Clement.

After a long climb to the entrance of the fortress a pair of soldiers challenged us. They wore chain mail with typical conical helmets. The helmet came down over their noses with slots left for the eyes and was strapped on under the chin. These, of course, made individuals difficult to recognize.

"By the good St. Christopher could this be that rouge-top pollywog Alex del Aries?" The very large guard who spoke with the booming voice seemed very familiar to me.

"Ahah, what a miraculous surprise," I blurted with dawning recognition. "How wonderful to see the champion of the Christian world. Cedric, you old Saracen slayer."

Cedric Power, brave soldier and true follower of the Templar warrior faith. Few people would know what I knew. This Goliath-like warrior had slain hundreds of enemies of the true faith. He could wield the large broadsword in his massive hand like a carving knife. I used to sit on his knee after he and my father had returned from their second crusade to the Holy Land. I mostly remember his knee being my horse and that resonant belly laugh rolling up out of his barrel chest as he parried my imaginary sword thrusts. It wasn't long before they had me riding real horses with proficiency at a very young age. Joyfully, I threw my arms around his sizeable girth and was in turn warmly crushed by his powerful arms.

"Where have you been Cedric, my friend? It must be seven summers since you returned from the Holy Land."

"Yes, I was in Armagnac and Dijon mostly, after spending a summer and winter at thc Aquae Tarbellica in Dax. My wounds were grave and it took a considerable time to heal in the hot springs. But look at you, almost a friar, hah."

Our reunion was interrupted by the laconic Francois, "Come, come Alex, we must get along. We have important duties to attend to."

"Of course, of course Friar, I'm sure our trivial discussions can wait. Please proceed on with your important duties," Cedric retorted with jovial sarcasm. "I shall be off guard duty at sunset Alex. Meet me in front of the barracks when your important duties are completed."

"I look forward to that time, old friend Cedric. Until then," I replied and the other guard stepped aside for us to pass.

As we walked away Francois whispered, "Alex, I don't know why you would want to associate with such rabble." I said nothing, but a seed of realization was gestating in my mind as to the definition of rabble and who that might in reality be.

I stood two or three paces behind Francois with my hands folded and head bowed, as a proper attendant novice should. The audience room was enormous by my standards, as I had never been to such places, even when traveling with Marie Robine. She was always received privately at such lordly estates while I remained in the stables.

The ceiling was arched in the typical Romanesque Ogival style. Five or six men could have been stacked on each other's shoulders before reaching even the cross beams, and another two or three required to touch the ceiling. Our modest church at Coussey was perhaps half of this significant height. As the discussions progressed I stole glances at the impressive surroundings. In the light cast by the high vertical sidewall slits, I saw colorful tapestries on the walls with resonant reds and bright browns, probably stained with boar's blood and clay. There were also shades of blue and purple portraying noble deeds with white silk tassels adorning their base. There were ornate, uncushioned chairs along the walls of this large chamber, yet no one but the Lord and Master were inclined to sit, nor were others so invited.

Robert de Baudricourt lounged in his cushioned chair upon a dais at the end of the room, flanked by two advisors. The ambient light was beginning to wane as afternoon slipped on its nighttime cloak. Servants now moved about to light the candles in their massive wrought iron holders. As the candles were being lit the discussions paused.

With the servants gone, Francois continued, "Yes, good captain, it is true. Our informants have it on the best authority that Antoine de Vergy will indeed march soon against our region. The governor of Champagne is fully supported by that foul English regent, the Duke of Bedford."

Baudricourt was an imposing man. He was tall, broad of shoulder and handsome with long fair locks. He was particularly noted for his fiery temper. He had a fierce reputation on the battlefield, but it was also said, that was usually when the odds were much in his favor. As a favorite of the Dauphin, Charles VII, he could certainly wield significant power over those under him.

"Who are these informants that you speak of?" Baudricourt boomed. "I simply cannot hide myself and my peasants behind these castle walls at every rumor. It is spring and the fields must be tended to if we are to eat and profit this year. I have been building up my forces, but I am certainly not prepared to sally forth on some vainglorious expedition." Emphasizing his displeasure, Robert de Baudricourt slammed his fist on the arm of his chair and glowered down at Francois. "And what of your lord Henri D'Ogevillers at Bourlemont? Tell me of his intentions my faithful Friar." Not surprisingly, Friar Francois fidgeted and his answer came haltingly, "Your, your point is well taken my lord and, and I am but a messenger. Un, unfortunately, Henri D'Ogevillers and his wife are not currently residing at Bourlemont, so we have only such information from them through our church envoys. The information suggests that de Vergy could march in June or even earlier with additional Burgundian assistance. This is all I was told and I pray it can be of benefit to you."

"I suppose I will have to send my own scouts to determine the extent of this *'threat'*. Tell your Henri D'Ogevillers and his wench I will send two men to Burgundy and two men to Champagne. If he hasn't already done the same, with reliable men, then it would be wise for him to do so with expedience. If that is all you have to tell me then remove your sorry-self, as I have other matters to attend to."

Baudricourt's directive was spat out with finality and precluded any further discussion. I fancied I could hear Francois' knees knocking, as he mumbled his gratitude and God's blessing. We both then bowed and backed out of the chamber with heads down.

"Oh dear Mother Mary, that man makes me uneasy. He is such a brute. My water is going to overflow. I must find a chamber pot or, oh dear… " and Francois scurried awkwardly down the hall in search of relief, leaving me in his wake. I was much amused to see the usually unflappable friar so disconcerted. Unsure of what to do, I simply waited for him next to a narrow, daylight alcove.

Hearing heavy footsteps approaching, I ducked into the alcove. I was mildly surprised to see Jeanne and Durand pass, flanked by two guards. They turned and entered Baudricourts' audience chamber. Now that I had reactively secreted myself, I felt compelled by some mischievous devil to creep closer and furtively listen to my friends' audience.

Quickly, without aforethought, I crept back into the small, open anteroom. I no sooner slipped into a tiny dark alcove next to the audience-chamber doors then the guards re-emerged. I held my breath as they closed the tall, heavy doors and returned to their post outside the anteroom. With my heart in my mouth, I crept close to the doors. The latch had not been set, leaving the doors not quite shut. I could see little through the slight opening, but could clearly hear voices. Positioning myself in the archway's shadow, I listened with curiosity to an unusual audience. It has been said that a curious cat sniffing around a butcher's chopping block could wind up on a meat hook. However, being young and foolish, that thought never entered my head.

"What do you mean you already know me, girl? To the best of my recollection, we have never met," Baudricourt was saying.

"I know you, sire, from the voices that speak to me," Jeanne replied, and there was a snickering from his advisors that my ears did not miss.

"Never mind that," Baudricourt continued. "What is it you want of me that is so important?"

"I have come to you on behalf of my Lord to send the Dauphin this message. He should hold from making war on his enemies until mid-Lent, for the Lord will send him help at such time. This kingdom is not the property of the Dauphin, but rather my Lord's. However, the Lord wishes the Dauphin to be crowned as King of our land and I will lead him to his consecration." There was another short snickering, but then came a protracted silence. I was surprised to hear Jeanne speak publicly in this manner, for not only was it an outrageous statement, it bordered on blasphemy.

"This Lord of yours, who might that be?" Baudricourt broke the silence.

"The King of Heaven," she replied, and more strained silence followed.

"Take this pretender back to her father and have him box her ears before I do," finally came Baudricourt's terse reply.

Before moving away from the door into the nearby alcove I heard a confident Jeanne retort, "Let us return, Durand. Obviously

God's will is not ready for fulfillment."

As Jeanne and Durand swept past me, I knew I had to take a chance. Boldly, I slid into step behind them. Passing the guards they commanded us, "You know the way out and don't dally."

Walking away, I heard one guard remark, "I thought the novice left earlier?"

The other replied, unconcerned, "Humph, apparently not."

Jeanne and Durand looked over their shoulders at me with astonishment. I pulled my hood on while giving my head a tacit shake and they seemed to understand.

Exiting the main castle, but still within the fortress we felt it safe enough to talk and all three of us were bubbling with questions. It was a pleasant and enlightening conversation. Durand was a kind, but simple farmer and it was all rather confusing to him. His wife had recently given birth to another child and he was anxious to return home. He adored and believed in young Jeanne and her visions, which is why he agreed to arrange for the audience.

"Jeanne, my friend, you showed such audacity, especially for a young maiden. Baudricourt could have had you thrown in the dungeon or worse," said I.

"God is my master and I only do his bidding. I will be returning to Domremy soon, as Durand's wife is doing much better now. Maybe you could come to our summer rites festival again. It was so much fun last year. We must be going though, as it is almost dark and the roads are not very safe these days. God be with you, Alex."

"And with you, my friends."

At that moment, an annoyed Friar Francois rushed up to me. "Alex del Aries, I have been searching everywhere for you."

"I'm so sorry, Brother Francois, I got lost when you had to run off on your mission of mercy."

"Don't be insolent, you little whelp. You're still a lowly novice and it seems to me you could remain that way a lot longer too, with your attitude."

"Yes, of course, you are correct Friar Francois. Please accept my humble apology, as I was only making jest."

Somewhat mollified, he said, "I will be taking supper with Father Angello and then evening mass."

"Might I meet my father's friend while you take your supper, good Friar?" I asked.

After a deliberate hesitation he replied, "Very well, but be at evening mass, and remember, we will be returning to Coussey right after the Sunday dawn mass."

With a bounce in my step I made my way to the soldiers' barracks. Sure enough, Cedric was there and we greeted each other warmly.

"Have you taken supper yet, my fine pollywog?" he asked, using the childhood sobriquet he had bestowed upon me.

"No, Cedric, and my belly is reminding me."

"Well then, tonight you shall eat with men," he said, with a booming laugh and a slap on my back.

It was an exhilarating experience for me to sit with those soldiers—those warriors. Francois had not allowed me food since breakfast, because he was fasting during the light of day. They teased me that perhaps I should be joining the Dauphin's army, instead of God's army, the way I was making short work of the victuals set before me. Afterward, Cedric walked with me to evening mass, and without prodding, explained to me the nature of my father's relationship with Marie Robine and my enigmatic mother.

Chapter Two

MAGDALENA

How do I put this part to scroll? Perhaps I can heal a little, if the pain is displayed in script—perhaps not. My greatest sorrow is never having truly known my mother and the ironic tragedy by which that came to be. A tragedy that need never have been—should never have been.

My mother was a whore. She copulated with men for money or food. She did what women are shunned for doing, but my father loved her regardless. How he came to meet her was likely how most soldiers come to meet such women. She was extraordinarily beautiful, even more so than her sister, Marie Robine. Her hair was more reddish than Marie's and her physical appearance, voluptuous. She was three summers younger than Marie and possessed strangely compelling dark gray eyes. Upon hearing that, I knew she was my mother, as I do indeed have her eyes.

Women do not have many options beyond wifery and child bearing. Of course they could marry the church and enter a convent. To the other extreme they could do as my mother, and prostitute their body.

As for Marie, she was unfortunate on one hand and fortunate on the other. As was common, she had been married very young by arrangement. Her husband was nearly twice her age and an ogre of a man. He was a lower-level merchant in Avignon with high aspirations and minimal ambition. Within one church year Marie had born him twin boys, and my mother Magdalena, at just thirteen summers, went to live with them and assist. Cedric surmised from Marie that her husband felt he was entitled to two wives and took liberties with the budding flower Magdalena.

Marie's *good* fortune was that she had a gift. This gift allowed her to see things in the future that others could not. Many women with no other means attempted to prophesize, but few were honest and even fewer possessed Marie's skill of divination. By the time she was twenty summers she could no longer stand to live with her abusive husband and his glutinous affair with wine. Desperate to find a better life, she ran away from him with her children and Magdalena under her wing. Marie was wise and resourceful, but in the reality of these desperate times she had no hope of feeding and sheltering her children. Sadly she left them with her husband's family, who were successful merchants and could provide for them. With her *gift* she was soon able to impress important people and gained the ear of many courts. Magdalena, however, achieved repute as a beautiful young courtesan, at least that is until even the debauched, canaille Parisian nobles tired of her.

Cedric and my father came to cross paths with the sisters while serving as mercenaries in the service of Charles VI, Gaul's infamous mad King. They had been planning their quest to the Holy Land and, even though secretly steadfast Templars, they were not above some nighttime inn prowling. Paris has always been a diverse city with anything for any taste. Price was sometimes an issue, but availability was not. Cedric told me of the *Porte Barlette* district where bawdiness and moral laxity prevailed. With the long wars and plagues afflicting society, life and morals had become cheap commodities. It was at one of these inns, after setiers of beer, where my father was smitten by a beautiful serving wench.

Miguel del Aries de Setubal was not a large man, but Cedric said he had the strength of many. He was quicker than a cat and Cedric knew of no mortals, including himself, who could match him on the battlefield. His handsome dark features and long wavy brown hair were only slightly detracted from by his battle scars and a prominent Roman nose.

As Cedric related to me, a large *Goddam* (as the English were known) was taking rude liberties with this winsome wench who had caught Miguel's eye. His fiery Portuguese temper erupted and he was over the tables and upon the brute without second thought. The fight was quick, but messy. Cedric collared the other two smaller Englishmen with a massive arm around each neck, while Miguel picked the large Englishman off the earthen floor. It was a blood-splattering, head-butt to the face and a hard knee to the groin that made short work of the Goddam.

The Innkeeper was most upset and berated Magdalena for being the cause of another fight and more damage. He derided her as a whore and ordered her out. He then pushed her in the face with an open hand, knocking her over a stool. Calling her what she was was one thing, but when he raised his hand to her—well, as Cedric laughingly put it, "He had to hire *two* wenches to replace her, for when Miguel was finished with him, it would be a long time before he could use that arm again."

Outside the inn, there seemed to be no consoling Magdalena. Distraught and with tears flowing, she hurled foul names at my father. He was finally able to calm Magdalena by promising her a fine meal and to pay amply for her services. Cedric said he escorted them to the prestigious *Hotel Saint-Pol,* where upon he took his leave.

With a chuckle, Cedric said, "Your father may have paid the first time, but he had a reputation for being a passionate and powerful lover. I can also vouch that he was exceptionally well equipped and left many women in a swoon."

Yes, I mused privately, I am my father's son. For approaching maturity, I had recently noticed significant physical growth in that regard.

Those were the tempestuous circumstances under which they met and their love was no less torrid and passionate. Marie, of course, then came into the mix and Cedric admitted he was smitten by her. It was a love unrequited, for although Marie was a great admirer of Cedric's, she still considered herself married to the lout in Avignon. Also, her *prescient gift* had become an all-consuming enterprise.

I was born ten lunar months after Miguel and Magdalena met. When they realized Magdalena was with child they immediately became man and wife. It was a joyful union attended only by immediate friends. The marriage was, as Cedric attested, laden with love.

It was almost two years before my father and Cedric went to the Holy Land. They left in the winter on a Genoese ship out of Marseilles. They had joined a troop of French crusaders off to support Genoese and Hospitaler forces near Constantinople. The *Great Schism* within the church had finally been more or less resolved. With the internal church strife ebbing, there was now more vigor and finances directed toward crusading against the hated Islam infidels. Unfortunately, after my father's advance troop had already left, problems emerged with the Hussite followers in Bohemia. These recalcitrants of the true faith were a problem that precluded crusade efforts.

Oh, the twists and turns of tragedy and fate. The following year, Marie and Magdalena received word that my father's ship had foundered in a storm and disappeared near Malta. Magdalena was distraught, crazed, consumed by grief. Her true love was gone, never to return upon this earth. Marie tried to console her, but tragedy seems to breed tragedy. My mother, in her anguish, reverted to some old bad habits. After Marie rescued Magdalena from an Orleans brothel she felt compelled to move us back down to Avignon. A morose Magdalena then expressed a wish to see the sea that had taken her lover. Magdalena cared about very little now, so this seemed to Marie a possible salve to soothe her sister's sorrow.

Marseilles was a thriving seaport not far from Avignon. Marie hoped to prophesize for rich nobles and succor her grieving sister's need to be near the sea, so on we went, to Marseilles.

I was perhaps three summers of age, so I have very faint recollection other than the words related to me by Cedric. There was a magnificent lookout point just south of Marseilles at Croisette. It was a short donkey ride and my mother would insist on going there almost every Sunday. One could see for leagues and Magdalena would sit pining away the afternoon, looking out to sea. She would even laugh some of these summer days when I was learning to run, before I had fully mastered walking. Along with a little wine, bread, onions and cheese her spirits seemed to lift on these day trips.

At the end of one such day, Marie was packing up the donkeys as Magdalena stood near the cliff edge with arms extended in a cross-like manner. This was a favorite abstraction of hers. She liked to say she was drinking up the wind that carried Miguel's love from heaven. It was always the last thing she did before returning to Marseilles. On that fateful day, the sun was sinking like a ship into a western seascape lined with flat, gray clouds. At first, Marie thought the gusting winds were at foul play, for she thought she heard Magdalena speaking with someone. All she understood was Miguel's name, and as she turned to look, Magdalena was not there. Fear knotted her belly, as she looked about in all directions. Marie rushed to the cliff's edge and a seaward gust of wind almost dealt her a deadly blow. Teetering at the edge, she dropped to her hands and knees to peer over. Marie stared in disbelief at a twisted, doll-like figure sprawled amongst the jagged rocks and raging surf far below.

In despair, Marie left Magdalena's body to her lover's ocean. There would be little left to bury that surf, crabs and seagulls did not make short work of before the morrow.

There were tears streaming down my face as we stood before the Vaucouluers church. The big man's eyes were also brimming, as the behemoth exterior belied his soft heart. Evening mass was about to start, but I had no desire to enter.

"I think, young Alex, I might not attend mass this evening as my heart is heavy with remembrance. I apologize for relating these sad things to you, but you are approaching manhood and it will be important for you to understand your past." My look must have been puzzled, as well as sad, for he continued, "Do not worry about such things now. I will find you again soon, God willing. I have an early morning meeting with my superiors and I suspect there is a mission in store for me."

"But what of my father, Cedric?" I protested.

"These things will come to light soon enough. You must deal presently with the sorrows I have related to you. You are safe at Coussey, for Marie's intuition and forethought were wise."

He put his massive arms around me and hugged the breath out of me. We simultaneously offered, "Go with God," and he disappeared into the night.

Chapter Three

Coussey

Decidedly unhappy was I at the monastery, coping with the drudgery of monastic life. My mind flooded with confusing thoughts of my heritage and familial tragedy, but through the summer I remained concentrated on my studies.

One distressing diversion in July was the rampaging Antoine de Vergy and his English/Burgundian forces. They had stormed through the countryside from Champagne, to lay waste undefended towns like Domremy. The inhabitants of Domremy fled to Neufchateau and the protection of its fortified walls. The prize which de Vergy sought though was Vaucouluers. We at Coussey were fearful, lest our Armagnac sympathies became known, for marauding mercenaries did not always spare monasteries. We prayed earnestly for our and Vaucouluer's salvation, and apparently our prayer's were answered. After a brief siege, an uneasy truce was restored and de Vergy returned to Champagne. This fruitless campaign had only served to further decimate the land and the peasant's meager lot. Yes, I thought, tragedy and drudgery seem to be the peasant's plight through this endless strife.

Staggering slightly, I tried to keep the half-full buckets of urine clear of my body. My spirits rose to see this glorious autumn morning with a low, pale gray mist rising off the Meuse River. The leaves were turning luxurious colors and I thought to myself, this is truly to God's greater glory and I must comment on these revelations to

Friar Ferdinand. He was very sensitive to such things and would appreciate my observances on God's seasonal creations. Pausing briefly, I observed that even the dewdrops on the leaves seemed to radiate like the jeweled Holy Mary icon adorning our cathedral. Much as a rainbow, the golden jaune and orange blended into the brilliant sanguine and vert to caress my visual senses.

"Alex del Aries, you lazy little urchin, I can see you wasting God's time." I was startled from my observations by Friar Clement's bellowing. He seemed in a fouler mood than usual this morning. I scampered the short distance to the Meuse into which I dumped the buckets of foul urine. It was my third and last dumping this morning, a job detested by my fellow novice, Antoine, and myself. Hurrying back up to our enclave, I saw Friar Clement standing behind the low monastery wall, arms crossed and glowering at me.

"Why is it Antoine has finished his chores and is ready for victuals, yet you still dally over things of no concern?"

Bowing my head in a supplicant manner, I pleaded, "But, but, I was just appreciating God's beauty of nature and,"

"You are nothing but a lazy liar. There will be no breaking of the fast for you. Get to your kitchen duties now, and I will deal with you later. You will come to my study room just before compline prayers."

His hawk-like nose sniffed as if disgusted. He turned on his heal and with head high strode off in his usual imperious manner, gray robes flowing. I shivered, thinking of what might be in store for me.

I was especially diligent in my chores for the rest of the day, not wanting any further grievances to reach Friar Clement's ears. I did not trust Antoine, who was a favorite of Friar Clement's. I felt from Antoine's fawning demeanor around Clement that something was amiss. He had not seemed such a timid sort when he first arrived.

There were twelve Friars in this Franciscan monastery. Father Albert was by far the eldest and the spiritual head of the enclave.

However, Friar Clement seemed to easily manipulate him and everyone else deferred to Clement on most matters. Friar Ferdinand was in charge of gardening and I took every opportunity to be with him. He was a very gentle man who was attuned with nature. Being somewhat obese, which was unusual for our order, he appreciated the running around that I could do for him. It also kept me clear of Friar Clement.

When I had first arrived at the monastery three summers previous, I was the only novice. Friar Clement was my initial surrogate and religious instructor. His religious teaching was very zealous, and fortunately for me, I could retain everything he taught. This sometimes exacerbated him greatly. He looked for excuses to beat me, or deride me, but was frustrated by my perfection. His vexation and malicious feelings seemed to ooze from his being like sweat.

Only once while under his tutelage was Friar Clement able to fault me. I do not remember for what reason. This was the summer before my experience with Jeanne under the Fairy tree. At thirteen summers, I had no understanding of monastic punishments, but was in dire fear of my tutor. I was small for my age and he forced me down across his knees. He tossed my robe and apron over my head. Using a short willow switch he lashed my buttocks with ten severe blows, counting them aloud as he recited the Ten Commandments. Tears fell from my eyes, but I was resolved to take my beating without crying out. He seemed to be breathing with some difficulty. I moved to get up, but he grabbed the back of my neck and pushed me back down.

"You were not told to move, you miserable waif."

He reached between my legs and cupped my testicles as if weighing them. Then he reached further and I flinched as he squeezed my half-hard penis.

"This is the devil's work, Alex. Why has it grown?" he demanded.

"I'm sorry Friar Clement, I, I do not know. I do not understand."

"Never mind," he said gruffly.

I must admit, I did feel oddly pleasurable sensations when he squeezed my penis, though my buttocks stung terribly. He abruptly stood, depositing me on the cold, masonry floor.

"Get up, you lazy novice," he said with disdain. "Get thyself across the bench for the rest of God's benediction."

Not understanding, I nevertheless complied and prostrated myself across his study bench. He moved behind me and I was then puzzled to hear a rustling of his robes. A loud rapping on the study door broke the heavy air like a thunderclap. Instinctively jerking my head, around I was stunned at what I saw. It was very brief, but as he closed his robe I noticed a black patch and protruding from it a heavily skinned, gnarled appendage. The thought of a friar's penis had never crossed my young mind, but I knew there was something terribly unusual about Friar Clement and his deformed appendage.

The door swung open and Friar Ferdinand bustled in. "Pardon my intrusion Friar Clement, but the new novice is in the courtyard and I thought… "

"And THAT is your problem Ferdinand. Besides eating too much, you think too much, and God's work does not require thought. It only requires devotion and worship. More devotion and proper worship should be foremost in your addled thoughts. Very well, send him to me, and never again disturb me when I am invoking benediction."

"Pardon, good Friar, pardon," Ferdinand mumbled as he closed the door behind him.

"As for you, urchin novice, be gone and get hence to do penitence. You will recite the Franciscan dogma one hundred times before the Virgin icon and there will be no evening refection for you. GO!"

Quickly was I gone, thinking myself fortunate at Friar Ferdinand's timely arrival. I shuddered, as I thought of Friar Clement's ugly, perverse appendage. Yet, what is perverse?

That demeaning experience was now two years past and it still clouded my thoughts. Sometimes the memory of it could cause my neck to ache and flush red. Was it anger? Was it shame? Was it fear? I know not.

After Antoine's arrival, however, my life became more bearable. Father Clement found this novice more to his liking and left my education to others. I like to think I was too smart for old Clement. Antoine was a summer older than I and had little or no instruction behind him. He was very dark and smooth of complexion. Antoine probably had one or two Moorish ancestors diluting his French Christian blood. He was a good pious person and I often felt sorry for him, but I knew I could not have existed under Friar Clement's tutelage.

It was left to Friar Ferdinand and Friar Jacques to see over my instruction. Friar Jacques ran the kitchen and was assistant procurator to Friar Clement, as he had a wonderful gift for numbers. I am thankful that he greatly expanded my knowledge of numbers and edible foods. He was nervous and slight of frame, but possessed a pot-kettle-like belly, which advanced his robe like a pregnant woman. Jacques was humorless and, I felt, a certain confidant of Friar Clement. Naturally, I tried to spend more time with the jovial, but bashful Friar Ferdinand. From him I learned much about the seasons and God's marvelous ways of growing things.

As the afternoon progressed, I became more and more distraught with the prospect of going to Friar Clement's study room. I knew I had done nothing to be ashamed of in God's eyes, but Friar Clement, I now believed, was far removed from God. Finding Friar Ferdinand in the grape vineyard I rushed to seek his council.

"Esteemed Friar Ferdinand," I lauded him. "I seek your advice and help."

"Of course Alex, my favorite novice, I would be a happy friar to assist you in any godly pursuit."

Feeling immediately relieved at these comforting words I said, "I'm not sure how to explain, but I have been remonstrated by Friar Clement for something you have taught me to appreciate." His face darkened somewhat, and it was especially noticeable on his full lipped, bulbous-nosed, face.

"Go on", he said, tentatively.

"Well, as you have taught me to appreciate God's nature, it delayed me ever so slightly while dispensing this morning's excrements. Friar Clement disapproved and demanded my presence in his study room just before compline prayers, for what I fear will be punishment."

Receiving only a blank look from Friar Ferdinand, I rushed on, "I am very much afraid he has less than Christian wishes in mind and… "

"Stop! You need say no more Alex. I understand your predicament and you need not fear under God's protective wing. I am your surrogate and you may trust in me. Friar Clement knows what is best and I will always be there to speak for you."

I worked feverishly in appreciation of Friar Ferdinand's support. We pruned and nurtured many vines that afternoon. I was feeling confident and relieved as I left the cathedral after the evening vesper prayers.

"Why do you smile at me, you annoying little whelp?"

Feeling my relaxed state beginning to evaporate in the flames of doubt, I stammered, "M, M, Most eminent friar, I mean no disrespect. Father Ferdinand has taught me to appreciate nature and will testify to my holy thoughts and expedience of duties."

"Father Ferdinand!" he exclaimed, suppressing a laugh.

"Yes, yes, a faithful servant of God and… "

"A faithful servant of the Coussey monastery and thereby a faithful servant to me also, foolish novice," Clement interrupted, as he rose from his chair. My knees began to shake and threatened to desert me in different directions. With deliberate dalliance, he came around his scribing desk.

"I want you to do something for me, my little haughty novice. Your supercilious attitude affronts our One True God and you must submit to his recompense."

As those words hung in the air, I tried to imagine a blusterous but potentate Ferdinand bursting through the door. Instead, Friar Clement revealed a long willow whip.

I was sixteen Epiphanies now, and two summers had passed since my last punishment at Friar Clement's hands. Though still small for my age, I was a man now, yet any will or resolve to resist seemed to run away as water through my hands. He prodded me and nodded for me to prostrate myself over his bench. I was quaking with fear and humiliation, but was powerless to do anything against God's will. He tied my wrists to the long end of the bench in front of me and then blessed me with a benediction. There was a glazed look to his eyes and perspiration beaded in the sparse whiskers on his upper lip. He reached down my back and slowly pulled my robe over the top of my body. Walking behind me, he roughly pulled aside my undergarment leaving my nether region exposed over the edge of the bench.

The sound of the willow swishing through the air seemed more fearful than the pain could possibly be, as he tested its potency. Not so. It took my breath away at the first strike. Between each painful blow he deliberately swished the willow through the air, such that I could not tell whether a blow was imminent. He seemed to cackle and grunt, delighting at my cringes. The anticipation caused by his cruel feints of the willow was an excruciating torment and intensified the pain of a delivered blow. When the willow did strike across my buttocks or legs it seared like a hot iron. Determined not to whimper or cry out like a child, I clamped my jaw tight. I could sense my intransigent, stoical response was frustrating Clement, and my resolve strengthened—perhaps I even smiled. The blows then came down with even greater force and it felt as if they were splitting my flesh. Suddenly, in mid-swing, he stopped.

"Oh ho, sacrebleu, what is this thing. This is not the same child's thing I last saw. This is the devil's instrument incarnate."

I could feel the willow prodding at my penis, exposed under the bench edge. I was embarrassed that it had grown to its full stature —like that day at the Fairy tree.

I was filled with shame, and try as I might to will it away, it only seemed to harden further. Friar Clement chuckled, and as he rarely found anything mirthful, the tone caused my throat to constrict. I grimaced and ground my teeth as I felt his hand grip and stroke me roughly.

"This is a man's instrument, on a boy. You are a disgusting devil to possess such a thing."

He released me and backed away. I breathed a sigh of relief thinking it was over, but then I heard his robes rustling. I had heard that sound once before. I shuddered, and my heart filled with dread.

"You must be taught to be more expedient in your duties, and this, this thing… "

I tried to raise my head and speak, but as he knelt behind me he pushed my head down, growling, "Silence, and be still urchin, for you are about to receive God's punishment."

I heard him spit and then felt something slippery prodding me between my buttocks. My belly was churning and I struggled not to vomit, for such would surely incur even greater wrath. Unthinkably, I could feel his *gnarled* penis trying to force its way into my nether hole. He did not seem large, but it was nonetheless painful as he thrust his hips forward. He grasped my hips and dug in with his bony fingers, in an effort to penetrate the small aperture. Clement spoke haltingly between gasps, "For your infidelity to God … you must take this punishment … in the name of the Father … and the Son … and the… "

I heard a dull thud and Clement suddenly pitched forward on top of me. His head hit the back of my neck and his face came to rest on my shoulder. Clement's breath rushed out and then stopped. His weight was crushing, but I dared not move, unsure of what he was about. I felt his penis shrivel and it slipped from between my buttocks. It was then I heard the scraping of sandaled feet. I remained frozen in place, for my mind was filled with fear and confusion.

Two sandaled feet appeared in my vision. Blood began dripping down the side of my neck onto the floor. Splat, splat. Why am I bleeding? Could this be Friar Clement's blood? My bonds were being untied. Oh, sweet Mother Mary, blessed salvation.

"Father Ferdinand, oh bless you, bless you, bless you," I sobbed, and the tears began to fall like rain. I reached out with my freed hand around a thick leg and clutched his robe. But what was this? This robe was white, not gray! Shrugging Friar Clement's offensive body off of me, I looked up at Antoine.

Chapter Four

Revelation

Janeen sat across from me curled up in the big wicker chair. The wind was picking up and in the distance we could hear the waves pounding the rocky shore.

"A wee storm seems to be brewing out there," I commented.

"Oh, I hadn't even noticed, but I think you're right, sweetie. My mind is on overload. I just can't seem to comprehend how this manuscript, or diary, could come to be where we found it. I keep thinking this Alex fellow must have come with the conquistadors, but the beginning of the text seems to refute that. The Portuguese and Spaniards were absolute blood enemies. I suppose the mud-clay used to hide it could have been more recent, but the type of scroll material seems authentic to the Middle Ages, and the Chimu were certainly not writers." Janeen paused for a deep breath, tugging at her ear.

"The kicker though, is that the Inca advances mostly destroyed this Chimu structure, as they decimated and integrated the Chimus in the mid-fourteen hundreds. That structure existed from early to late-Chimu time and the Incas razed the late-Chimu version. You were working on the lower early-Chimu level. If you found it near the top stone masonry as you say, it may well have been left there in a corner of the floor circa late-Chimu. I don't understand how it could possibly get there any later, as this area hasn't been uncovered since it was razed in the latter half of the fifteenth century. You saw what we had to uncover. For christsakes the Spaniards hadn't even arrived yet." Janeen was basically thinking out loud and it seemed like a good spot for me to interject.

"Well, my dear scholar, this head is somewhat bursting also—from too much excessive thought. We accomplished a lot today. I say we knock off for the evening and reward ourselves with a glass of wine."

As I retrieved some Chilean red from the adjoining kitchen she continued, "As you mentioned, it was well packaged in that copper container, leading me to believe it was purposefully left for posterity. Or perhaps the author had planned on returning. But why in an apparently remote area such as this?"

Returning with two filled goblets, I countered lightly, "He probably left his memoirs for future, potential biographers such as us."

"Hey, there could be more truth to that than jest, Jack."

Lost in our own thoughts, we looked out the slatted window in silence, as the sunset's last few strands of yellow and orange were devoured by darkness.

Five days ago Terry had used her amphibious float plane to deposit us at a village on the nearby Cascaja River where it flows into the Pacific. It was arranged by one of Terry's contacts for us to rent a spartan, but adequate adobe. There was no running water, but we had a rainwater cistern connected to one tap in the kitchen and a gravity fed shower out the back. The two rooms consisted of a one-bed bedroom and a kitchen next to a sitting area. Air conditioning was provided by the sea breezes. The ocean was a hundred meters away, embraced by a craggy shoreline. We even had a bit of a view. Had our situation not been so grave, we might have enjoyed this little retreat. The local fishing village was a twenty-minute walk. At least we could get the basic foodstuffs—dry goods, fresh fish, and most importantly, wine. The local wine and beer was quaffable and, to our delight, there was also some decent Chilean Merlot available.

I was making commentary on the fine wine and speculating that, "Terry's *associates* must come here regularly, as the locals don't even seem to bat an eye. In fact," I said, "they're almost friendly. I would bet my... "

Suddenly Janeen bolted out of her chair as if lit on fire and gushed, "Jesus, Jack, Jack, Jack how could we be so stupid? Of course, of course, of goddamned course. Robert de Baudricourt and Jeanne. Did you ever study French history and the Hundred Years War?"

Startled by her outburst, I simply nodded. After a giddy giggle and a gulp of wine, she plowed on, as I knew she would.

"This is crazy, but it fits perfectly, goddamn it. Our little sweetheart, Jeanne, is Joan of Arc! It was Robert de Baudicourt of Vaucouluers who allowed her famous trek to see the Dauphin King. I must have been brain dead not to see that right away. It's just so bizarre though. How could such a text be here in Peru?" She was building steam like a locomotive, as she raced on in revelation. "And what about the mix of text—mostly French and Latin. This Alex del Aries, if he was the author, was some sort of scholar. It could have been planted at a later date, but no, damn it—I can't see that either. Wow, what a story these scripts are telling."

"Assuming of course they're true," I interjected.

This seemed to deflate her slightly and she began to pace.

"Jack, you were the one trying to convince me, and mister know-it-all is now doubting himself?"

"I still believe in their authenticity. My gut tells me that. It's just human nature to have doubts about something as unusual and incredibly significant as this."

"It's potentiall*y* significant, Jack. We will have to do a lot more work on what we've already deciphered to be sure of our interpretation. We can only do that back in civilization with the proper references."

I rose to refill our goblets saying, "Don't you agree with our interpretation? I thought it was relatively straight forward."

"Yes, but we're still not sure of certain words or phrases. Some could potentially change an entire passage—like that part about the Fairy tree. It seems to me from my studies, I read somewhere about a Fairy tree and the maiden Joan. This old database between my ears finally seems to be kicking in. Hell, that was almost twenty years ago in Medieval History 101."

There was a quiet interlude as we reflected, and the Fairy tree episode seemed to play on my mind.

"God, what a way to have a vision," I said.

"What's that look in your eye Jack? Jaaack?"

"It's the look of lechery, lass, and I think it's time for a vision of our own."

Draining my wine, I rolled the goblet across the floor and made a roguish lunge for Janeen. Giggling like a little girl she moved quickly to avoid my playful charge. She called me a pervert between giggles, as I chased her around the table and into the boudoir.

While stirring my coffee soup, as Janeen called it, my nostrils drank in the wonderful aromatic fragrance of fresh coffee. I could hear Janeen's squealing and cursing as she partook of a cold, early morning shower. With the coffee done, I played my mately roll and straightened our sleeping bags on the rudimentary board and ceiba cotton mattress. I had already shaken out the bags and mattress to keep the critters down to a minimum. This I did twice a day. We weren't in jungle and the climate was desert-like, but it was still critter country. She came in with a towel around her head and drying herself briskly with another.

"Ahh, Janeen, tis a crime. Why should you be the only one in the world with such magnificent breasts?" I remarked, in admiration.

"Jack, don't you ever get tired of them?"

"Never. I only regret the years I was separated from them."

"Hah, you knew where they were most of the time. You only had to call, you scoundrel."

"It seems to me, darlin, you turfed my sorry butt."

"I was confused and you didn't seem ready for serious commitment, Jack," she said softly and gave me a warm, but wet embrace.

"I didn't think I could have both you and my career."

"Shite, you were probably right then, but that was then and this is now."

"I appreciate that, but let's still take one step at a time. Who knows where this insane road we're on might lead us."

"Tis true, it might lead straight to hell."

She spied the table with our notes pushed aside and brightened. "Oh yum, what have we here? My favorite feast—fresh fruit, palta, peanut butter, maize bread and goat cheese."

"I'd hate to see your diet if you were actually pregnant."

"Never mind that kind of talk. Let's eat and get to work. I'm excited about the manuscript and there's a lot of work ahead of us."

"Harumph, all work and no play makes Jack craaazy."

"Hah, pretty lame—Jack Nicholson has nothing to worry about from you, babe."

We were mulling over an interpretation of an odd phrase used by *Alex*, when we heard someone hailing us from down the pathway.

"Hallooo, Janeen and Jack, are you home?"

It was Terry, and looking out the window, I saw the Barber accompanied her.

"Terry, oh I'm so glad to see you," Janeen said as she ran to greet her with a hug.

Observing their close embrace through suspicious eyes, I felt somewhat piqued. Stifling that jealous thought, I went over and self-consciously threw an arm around Terry.

"I thought I'd better pop in on you, as it's been almost a week and I figured you might be getting nervous. You don't have to worry about your security, but I have some news I'm sure you'd be interested in."

Sitting around the old wooden table I questioned Terry by discreet eye contact about discussing issues of security in front of the Barber.

"Oh, don't worry about the Barber, Jack, he's actually one of our local operatives and will take good care of you."

Her open response caught me slightly off-guard. I turned and smiled at him. He responded with a gummy grin that revealed decayed teeth. He certainly didn't fit the mental mould I had of an operative. The Barber was paunchy, short, nervous, sweaty, and ill dressed—even for a local. What little hair he had left went in several different directions. His eyes were small and wide-set, leaving the perception that you were being observed from two different angles. Even more unusual, was a pointed nose, underscored by a thin lip, which appeared to be slightly cleft.

"Amazing," I muttered to myself and could not help but ask, "Why do they call you the Barber, Amigo?"

With a deadpan look, he replied, "It is my profession, Senor. I like to shave people."

His cryptic reply left me slightly uneasy and I did not pursue the matter.

"There's good news and there's bad news, so I'll start with the bad news," Terry began. "Your camp near Camisea was wiped out, presumably by the *Shining Path*. Government soldiers went in by chopper three days ago when they couldn't raise anyone on the two-way. There had recently been a rumor of Shining path activity in the area. They found five bodies and the camp was stripped clean. They reported no sign of you two, the two guards, or the jeeps. The embassies have been notified and our friends at the Historical Agency for Research and Development are frantic over your fate. Strangely, it hasn't made the news—I think it's being suppressed."

"By who?" I asked.

"According to my sources there may be a cell with strong government ties," she replied.

"What do you mean cell? That doesn't tell us anything," I pressed with an irritated tone.

Terry looked hard at me and replied with an annoyed tone, "Cell, cancerous cell, like a tumor, like the one sometimes found between a man's ears. I dispense information that I feel you need to know. Past that, I either don't know, or it's best for everyone that it doesn't reach your *Scotch* ears."

After everything we had been through, I felt we had a right to ask questions and not be insulted by some male-wannabe pilot. It was one thing to insult my intelligence, as I only had to consider the source, but to call me Scotch, was an insouciant insult to any prideful Scot. My psyche must have been on a short tether, as I lost it. Goblets went flying, as I pounded the table with my fist.

"You witless, sorry bitch—I mean butch. Who the fuck do you… "

The left fist I had pounded the table with was now, with forefinger extended, pointing inches from her face. Before I could continue my tirade, that very finger was clasped in a steely grip and bent backward painfully. At the same instant a razor-sharp stiletto appeared where my jaw meets my neck. With lightening speed the Barber had my finger and hand bent back in a police-like grip. His other arm was around my neck and the stiletto under my jaw liberated a fine trickle of blood that I could feel running down my neck. I didn't struggle. It seemed the prudent thing to do.

Janeen was screaming for him to let me go and Terry said calmly,"It's alright, Barber, you can let him go. He's just full of hot air. Besides, I don't think I'd have any trouble handling him anyway."

The tension was thick as we returned to our seats. Janeen broke the icy impasse as she rose, "We're all a little stressed here, Terry. I think we could use a cup of coffee."

"Excellent idea, senorita. This old Barber could use a little caffeine to relax," he said dispassionately, and the stiletto disappeared into an invisible sheath inside his shirt.

"That is one of the reasons we call Michelob, *the Barber*. Besides, he doesn't like beer. Allow me to apologize, Jacko. I guess I didn't realize what a sensitive guy you are."

"Well, Terryo, if that's a sincere apology, I accept. But somehow I doubt it, so go fuck yourself, which I am sure you are quite capable of."

"Touché," Terry said, with a cold smile and cursing eyes.

As the coffee brewed, Janeen brought a damp towel and dabbed the superficial cut on my neck.

"Oh yah, another bit of nasty news, which may be unrelated," Terry resumed. "The day after the choppers found your camp, Samuel Gasparojo, the curator for H.A.R.D., was found murdered outside his penthouse." Terry's eyes were fixed on me, but it was Janeen who attracted my attention. Her face was inches from mine, as she checked my neck. She froze, and her breath stopped momentarily. She began to shake slightly, but her reactions would have been imperceptible to the others. After Terry let this news hang in the air for a bit, she continued. "My sources tell me he wasn't just murdered by some bungling burglars, he was tortured first, before being tossed from the twenty-first floor. Authorities are calling it a suicide. Now, I'm just wondering to myself, what might you two know about this, Jacko?"

"Fuck you, you're pissing into the wind," I shot back.

The air had become a little thick again, and a more composed Janeen turned and said, with forced understatement, "So Terry, I think we're ready for the good news now."

"First of all, they're busy searching between the dig-site and Camisea. No one is aware that you got out, as I *accidentally* never filed a flight plan that day. Supposedly the only one who knew you were coming out for sure, was myself and maybe, I'm thinking, our dearly departed Doctor Gasparojo from H.A.R.D. There's been no response from my sources, who usually have the insider poop on the Shining Path. Except for some silly rumor about four gold medallions-of-the-seasons, which has no apparent connection—or does it?" Terry asked, after a pause.

I couldn't quite suppress a smile—which Terry caught. With one raised eyebrow, She said, "You know, dick-head, if you're hiding some kind of discovery from me you don't have a prayer. Essentially, you would lose any support from the Peruvian authorities at H.A.R.D. and my connections as well. Your embassies would wash their hands of you in a heartbeat. You would be just as well off to join the Shining Path. Trying to get out of the country could prove impossible, and where the hell could you go anyway. Never mind trying to find a fence for your contraband."

"Jesus Christ, Terry, give us a fucking break. Who the hell do you think you're talking to?" Janeen flared up. "You're impugning our integrity and if you don't know me well enough by now you, you... "

Rising with her fists clenched, Janeen's chair bounced onto its back. Out of the corner of my eye, I saw the Barber making a move toward Janeen. I didn't hesitate. Coming out of my chair with a backhand feint, I spun and whip-kicked the Barber's legs out from under him. He landed hard on the back of his head, knocking him senseless. He was mine now. I pinioned him with knees on his arms and a forearm constricting his throat—that's when day became night.

As the painful fuzz began to clear, I realized my head was pleasantly cradled against Janeen's breasts. I focused on Terry, arrogantly standing with hands on hips and one foot on her chair.

As if in a tunnel, I heard her say, "Well stud, I guess you're a slow learner. It seems you're still not aware of our three rules. Rule number one, don't fuck with us and for rules two and three, refer to rule number one, or I may have to use *boot* force again."

Her wry humor did not escape me, but I was too dazed to reply. Janeen was sobbing quietly and the Barber was sitting in a chair rubbing the back of his head, glowering at me.

"You can be such a bitch, Terry. Jack only bullshitted the rebels to divert them from killing us. There are no gold medallions, only the confusing old text we told you about. It may be of some value, if it's authentic. By the way, did you bring the reference text I asked for?"

Terry nodded and reached inside her pack. "I had a hell of a time tracking it down and liberating it from the university. I think in recompense you need to enlighten me about the rest of what happened before I picked you up at Camisea."

After a moment, Janeen slowly related our harrowing experience. It was obvious that it was traumatic for her to recall the sequence of events. As she recounted the near-rape by Huaman and Chono, Terry's eyes narrowed perceptibly. At the end of Janeen's discourse, Terry seemed to look at me with a reserved respect, if not acceptance.

A short time later we all walked down to the village and Terry's plane on the river. "Sorry about our altercations Jack, but we all seem to be on a short fuse," Terry said, in a tone somewhere between terse and conciliatory.

Upon leaving us, Terry gave Janeen a hug and I could not help but sense an unusually strong rapport between them. In light of Janeen's previous revelations to me, it was a concept that I did not care to wrestle with.

Chapter Five

Escape

TEARS OF fear and remorse mixed with the rain running down my face. I stumbled blindly on my way through the monastery's orchard toward the Bois Chenu forest and the general direction of Vaucouluers. The rain beat upon me with a punishing ferocity. It seemed fitting that God's sky would open and castigate me for my transgressions. Tripping over an unseen vine root, I landed in a large puddle between the rows. Pounding my fists into the soggy earth I cried out to God for deliverance and in the same breath reproached him for deserting me.

I know not how long I railed in this manner, but gradually I became aware of something happening within me. I was as a frayed rope unraveling—unraveling until I was no longer a rope—until I was no longer myself. It was a strange and terrifying transformation over which I had no control. I was simply an observer. It was as if the devil within reared his frightful head and spat back in the face of fear. This feeling welled up from the very pith of my being. It gushed and erupted in a torrent more stentorian than even the torrential storm about me. Like a creature possessed, I howled and screamed at an unseen moon. I ground my teeth and leapt to my feet, shaking off the cold and damp.

My next recollection was of plowing through dense, wet foliage, well away from the main path of the Bois Chenu forest. Exhausted I curled up under a densely limbed tree and shook until oblivion overtook me.

Awakening to the morning sun breaking through the clouds, I shivered uncontrollably in my sodden robe. I did not want to waken to my circumstances, but the physical cold and mental torment would permit no further sleep. I awkwardly arose and found a beam of deliciously warming sunlight in a nearby clearing. Shucking off the robe and hanging it on a branch I jumped around and rubbed myself roughly to warm my joints. I longed for the hot kitchen hearth of the monastery. No, on second thought, that would put me too close to the fires of hell. I knew not what my afterlife might have in store for me, but I certainly did not care to find out just yet.

It had been a shock to find the devout and aloof Antoine as my savior. He explained that Father Clement had been having his way with him since shortly after his arrival at the monastery two summers ago. As I thought about it, it made perfectly perverted sense to me now. Yet what exactly defines perversion? It was shortly before Antoine's arrival that Clement had almost had his way with me. The devil within Clement had apparently (to my good fortune) preferred the prettier, cherubic Antoine and his fullness of flesh. I shivered at the thought of almost becoming Clement's regular little harlot. Poor Antoine, he suffered in ignorance until this summer.

As Antoine and I had fretted over the terrible deed and what to do, he explained that his protective angel, Saint Michael, had appeared to him during the summer-rites festival to tell him he need no longer heed Friar Clement. This confirmed his grave doubts, but his refusals then infuriated Clement. He had endured several severe beatings lately, but had not been deterred from his resolve. Frustrated, Clement had obviously re-focused on me. Antoine could see what was happening and his piety and conscience would not let the same fate he had endured befall me. Knowing Clement's secret entrance to his study room, he had let himself in while Clement was beating me. He was ashamed to admit that when he saw Clement using the same pretexts and perversions to violate me, he lost any Christian control. Clement would now impart no more sins or humiliations on mortal man. Antoine had not meant to kill him, but the silver candleholder drove the beast and soul from Clement's body. I mollified a distraught Antoine and told him it must have been the avenging hand of Saint Michael that had delivered the deathblow. He was but an instrument.

We cried and we prayed. We prayed more fervently than ever before in our lives. In shame and desperation, we even prayed that Clement might return to us. After a time, when Clement's lifeless body remained simply that, and Saint Michael did not appear to succor and sustain us, we had to choose a path. Antoine wanted to go to Friar Albert, but I strongly rejected that course as Friar Francois and Friar John, both Clement's supporters, held too much sway and our fate would be sealed. We would probably be burnt at the stake as witches, or sent to the rack to extract our true confession. Antoine seemed unconvinced that we could possibly be tried as heretics. I explained to him he might pray for the stake, rather than suffer *draughts-of-the-rack*.

Cedric's comrades at the barracks had regaled me with stories of torture by which they could elicit any sort of confession they wished. After an interminable period of being slowly stretched on the rack, thirst becomes as paramount as the blinding, wrenching pain. A long strip of gauze with embedded metal or glass is soaked with moisture. Put to victims' lips they desperately swallow, as it is fed to them with deliberate dalliance. The tormenters would then pull it out, slowly, leaving the victim to choke on their own blood. After Antoine heard this story, he was left quivering in fear and open to any solution. He had risked his life and saved me from a probable ignominious end. I knew I must choose an honorable way, even though Antoine could have been convinced of any course. He was, I realized, if not a simpleton, at best a simple person to be used by the monastery's hierarchy. With sudden clarity I could see I was at a crossroads. My fate could be the same, or my Templar blood could be my strength and impetus for liberation.

Non novis, Domine, non nobis, sed Nomine, Tuo da gloriam. The words of the Templar dictum rose unbidden from my past. Somehow I found them comforting and they gave me hope.

Antoine would remain innocently at the monastery. I would be gone, implying my culpability. No more would be said. I would deal with my fate.

The morning was warming up nicely, thanks to the bright October sun. Early October was not usually this gentle, but perhaps God had spent his wrath in last night's storm. I retrieved a slightly soggy crust of bread and gobbet of cheese from my leather pouch. While escaping through the kitchen last night, I had liberated some bread and cheese from the larder. My main concern was now one of simple survival.

From my vantage point I could see the cart path down near the Meuse River and there was usually some traffic of ox-carts and occasional horsemen. As I considered my next course of action, I thought it strange there was no one on the road below. I almost expected to see a royal guard in hot pursuit of the murderous novice.

Perhaps I should get to Vaucouluers and find Cedric. He would know what to do. Getting there was the problem. Certainly it would not take long for news of such a heinous crime to spread. I might be expected to run to Neufchateau, the closest large center, or Francois might remember my chance meeting with Cedric and direct the search to Vaucouluers. If the latter were to happen I was likely doomed. I had no idea where Marie Robine might be, if even alive in these troubled times. I was certainly in a quandary, but knew I must decide quickly on a course and act quickly.

Concluding that Cedric was my only chance, I leapt to my feet with renewed determination. Next to the clearing was a noisy little rivulet so I shed my garments to wash and sated my thirst. Relieving myself beside a large oak tree I found my organ to be somewhat afflicted by that swelling problem, but had no time to reflect on that now. Rounding the tree to retrieve my robe and under-apron, I was shocked to be met with squeals and commotion. Three young females had just emerged from the other side of the small clearing and I was caught in the open. Should I hasten back into the bush or race to my robe but a few paces away? Well, I resolved, what has a novice on the run to lose anyway. Defiantly, I strode to my robe with my member a-bobbing. Too late, I abashedly realized one of the girls was Jeanne. She turned away immediately, but Hauviette and Mengette looked on brazenly. I thought I heard Mengette whisper to Hauviette, "I have seen my father's mule, but I did not know boys could grow such things." Hauviette's response was a nervous titter.

"Are you maidens in the habit of sneaking up on people while they bathe?" I boldly countered, while donning my robe.

This seemed to disconcert them, but Jeanne shortly answered, "Alex del Aries de Coussey, have you quite finished covering your insolent self?"

Shame afflicted me with a rush of red to my face and I stammered, "Yes, I, I apologize for causing you maidens any discomfort and meant no disrespect."

"None taken," Hauviette replied in an odd, husky tone.

Jeanne turned and seeing me clothed, fixed her intimidating glare upon her two friends. Clearly, they looked up to Jeanne, as they immediately became like timorous mice under her scrutiny.

Breaking the cool impasse, I asked, "What brings you young maidens into the Bois Chenu this fine day?"

Jeanne replied almost cheerily, "Alex, do you not realize this is St. Remy's day? All the people are domiciled this day for rent collection and election of officials. My father will likely be reinstated as mayor for Domremy and Bourlemont. It is a holiday, of course."

Feigning nonchalance, I replied, "Oh yes, yes. I had forgotten as I left early this morning to forage nuts and berries for the monastery." They looked at me a little quizzically, but I rushed on, "I have not had much luck, but where are you off to?"

"We were accompanying Jeanne part way to Bourlemont castle, as she must fetch the stock inventory for her father," Mengette proclaimed.

"Yes, but we must soon be returning to help put on the midday feast. Maybe you could be so kind to escort Jeanne, as it is almost on your way back to the Coussey monastery," suggested Hauviette.

The thought of going anywhere near the monastery made me quake, but then Jeanne smiled and said, "Yes, that would please me, as long as you can keep your robe on." At this the other two girls burst into gales of laughter. And so it was that I chose my path. After a little inconsequential conversation, I left with Jeanne to test my fate at Bourlemont castle.

Along our route to Bourlemont, Jeanne talked mostly of religious concerns affecting our diocese, the Dauphin, and the Armagnacs. Looking upon her more closely I figuratively painted a vignette in my mind of this girl who so infatuated me.

She had a melodic voice. It was as sweet as purity itself, with a pleasant resonance, never downcast or faltering. Her face was perfectly proportioned with a strong, dimpled chin. She had a dark, but clear complexion, and passionate, dark brown eyes. Though not large, those dark pools had a haunting beauty that held my attention whenever she spoke. Her nose was slightly up-turned and slender. It was underlined by heart-shaped red lips, which never seemed to be without that demure, confident smile. Except for two marred lower teeth, darkened by a horse's hoof as a child, she had fine, straight white teeth. Her medium-length, dark auburn hair shone such that she seemed to wear a halo in the sunlight. Below the birthmark behind her ear, that matched my own, she possessed a strong neck and square shoulders. Her erect noble stance with shoulders back, had the unintentional effect of making her small breasts stand out pertly. Jeanne's hips were boyish, yet sufficiently proportioned to give her a strong frame and balance. She would make a fine rider. From a distance she seemed unremarkable, but once within her aura she was as dazzling as a freshly fallen snowflake—one of a kind; my one and only true love.

Together on future travels I was also to discover other wonderful things about her physical and mental character. This heart pines in bittersweet remembrance. Foul or fair, I admit, I will always know this unquenched fire in my loins, until I have no more breath to draw.

Nearing the castle, I knew I had to make a decision. Though chatting amiably with Jeanne all along the way I fully realized the desperate danger I might be in by accompanying her to this place. Stopping at the edge of the forest where it opens onto the Bourlemont hill, I decided to lay bare the burden of my horrific tale. Of course, I left out the most perverse details, but she seemed to grasp well my tone of desperation. When I was done she looked long and deep into my eyes before replying.

"I believe you, Alex." It was the first time she had ever called me simply by my Christian name. "You are likely in grave danger, but today is St. Remy's day and officials probably have other priorities. Perhaps you are best not to run to places they may be looking for you. The local diocese appears to be Armagnac supporters, but I am sure they would blow with the wind. I have been to the bishop's seat in Toul and found that there are many conspirators against the Dauphin within the clergy."

I was surprised by Jeanne's apparent knowledge of ecclesiastical and royal politics. She could see my quizzical look and continued, "I must get to the Dauphin. My visions have instructed me so. This is why I had Durand also take me to Toul, but again non-believers thwarted me. The time may be soon at hand and perhaps you are a supporter sent by God to assist me in my mission. Or maybe even an angel," she jested, and laughed to alleviate my tension.

It worked and I replied excitedly, "This poor orphan would be proud to assist you in your noble cause. When I was younger and with Marie Robine, she related to me a vision, which had at first disturbed her. While at the Dauphin's father's court perhaps twenty years past, the King had asked her of Gaul's future. The vision she had invoked was of a woman in pieces of armor and bearing many bloodied weapons. This upset her, because she felt it might be herself wearing the armor. Later she was enlightened by another vision that told of thc kingdom being betrayed by a woman and restored by a young maid. Is it possible that *you* are this young maid, Jeanne?" At this Jeanne laughed demurely, but it was a nervous laugh.

"Well my friend perhaps I am and perhaps I am not, but I do find it interesting fodder to ponder."

She said she knew well the caretakers of Bourlemont castle, and they were much indebted to the D'Arc family. There was a stable where I could find refuge until it was time for her journey. She knew not when she might go to the Dauphin, but my educated background of reading, writing and languages might prove of great use to her. For one so young she was a wise and caring soul, so without hesitation I decided to put my life in her hands.

Jeanne introduced me to Pierre and Nathalie Marlet. They were a young, hard-working couple who maintained the Bourlemont castle and grounds in the master's absence. Jacques D'Arc, her father, had indentured them for this purpose. They showed much deference to Jeanne, I'm sure because of her father, but also because that is just the way Jeanne seemed to affect people.

Jeanne explained my plight but offered fewer details than I had related to her. Immediately they went in search of some clothing to replace my telltale robe. Once I was attired in Pierre's ragged work clothes Jeanne and her devout friends gave me a tour of the castle and its immediate surroundings. It was somewhat run-down from disuse, but I was nevertheless awestruck. Up close it was more impressive than from down the hill at Coussey. Its six towers were puissant in structure, but, lacking thicker stonework, not defensively formidable. Perhaps that is why the masters were not living here at this tumultuous time.

The stable was a solid wooden building that looked no less comfortable than my old austere monastic quarters. Little did I know this was to be my home for the next three full moons.

Chapter Six

BOURLEMONT MIRACLE

THROUGH THE course of my time at Bourlemont, Pierre and Nathalie Marlet became my very good friends. He had been the fourth son and Nathalie had been the third daughter of their respective families. As such, their futures in our plebeian society held no promise. Their lot in life was no better than my own, but as young people are wont to do, they had fallen in love. To make matters worse, Nathalie had become pregnant before they were married and was cast out by her family. Her father was dogmatically devout and unforgiving.

It had been a cruel experience for both of them—so much so, that a distraught, castigated Nathalie lost much of her beautiful long hair. Shortly thereafter she also lost her baby prematurely. Nathalie confided in me that death was at her front gate, but she escaped out the back on the wings of Pierre's love.

She had been seven full moons pregnant and staying in a stable of Pierre's uncle. She could have gone to a convent, but that would have meant leaving Pierre and her baby would have been a bastard. The stable aspect of their story reminded me of Jesus and the manger, but unfortunately the result of her time there was not nearly as blessed or happy as in Bethlehem.

A compassionate priest had married them shortly after, but the miscarriage had left them disconsolate and forsaken by their own families. They left their home at Fierbois, a desperate pair of castaways in a desperate land. Their wanderings took them to Domremy where they were befriended by Jeanne's parents.

Nathalie Marlet, nee Romee, was a second cousin of Jeanne's mother, Isabelle D'Arc. Showing great kindness, Jacques D'Arc indentured them to caretake the lands around Bourlemont castle. This allowed them a cottage and to survive by living off the land, but not much more. In the five years since they were wed they had been hoping for a child, but it seemed God had struck them barren for their earlier transgressions.

I record this mostly because of the Nativity season I spent with this loving couple. Joyously, Nathalie had discovered late that summer she was finally pregnant again. She felt she should come to term about two full moons after the Nativity. My being there these many weeks served good purpose for them. I could help Pierre with the heavier tasks rather than Nathalie. Heedful of my possible peril, they disguised me in Nathalie's clothing when I was out working the castle's meager fields. Twas not much different than my novice's habit, I remarked, to their laughter.

Scant news had reached us as to my previous predicament. Interlopers or travelers generally did not bother us on Bourlement hill for it was off the main route. Shortly after my arrival, Pierre and Nathalie had heard of a murdered friar and a delinquent novice when they were at a church service. It was said that the novice was not to be found in Neufchateau or Vaucouluers and was suspected of having fled to Paris. After that, there was no more word. Hah, and there I was, right under their noses at Bourlemont—or should I say over their noses.

That fateful day of Nativity was cold enough to make water as glass. There was a light snow falling and a bitter wind blew. Returning from the Mass of Christ service in Domremy had been an arduous trek for the pregnant Nathalie and she seemed in a sickly state. Because of the foul weather, I made sure the hearth in their little cottage had a fine fire blazing. I wanted to surprise them with my gift. Having learned something of basket weaving at the monastery, I had collected the finest reeds and wove an infant's bassinet. Though it was not detailed craftsmanship, I was proud of my handiwork. It cheered Nathalie greatly when I presented it to them on their return.

The ebullient mood was fleeting though, as Nathalie then began to grimace with what seemed regular pains. I knew little of birthing, but could sense what Nathalie and Pierre cared not to think of. She soon became deeply distraught, not so much from the birthing cramps, or even the lack of any feminine support, but from past tragic memory.

"Pierre, oh Pierre, this should not be happening now. I know I am not yet to term. I, oh, ahhh, oh—it is happening all over AGAIN! No, no, please dearest Christ, not on YOUR day of birth, it is much too soooon. Have we not paid penance? Have we, oh, oh, aieee… " and she began to weep in despair.

Pierre and I tried our best to comfort her, but she seemed only to worsen. Finally, in desperation, I took Nathalie by the shoulders and shook her gently, but firmly. Looking into her eyes to hold her attention, I commanded, "Nathalie, look at me, listen to me. YOU must help us. We have no experience in these matters. If you can guide us, God will do the rest."

I was not confident in what I said, but at least it seemed to calm her—and also Pierre. He had been trying to cuddle and soothe Nathalie, but there was a lost, frightened look in his eyes. Nathalie had been attended by a mid-wife on her last premature delivery and Pierre had not been present. Here I was six years younger than they but, perhaps since I had not experienced their last terrible ordeal, I felt more under control and confident. In hindsight, it was but false-bravado. And false-bravado can be the sword of success, or the sword of Damocles.

I continued talking, hoping discourse could get them thinking clearly. "You've been waiting six years since your last birthing Nathalie. You *MUST* remember what is to be done and if you simply tell us, we will do your bidding. It will be a fine child. It will just get an early start on life is all. I feel that is what happened to me, for I was always small for my age. But, look now, I am beginning to catch up." She grimaced again, but did not cry out in anguish this time. "Just think, six years ago you were my age and... "

"Shut up now, dear Alex, and add some wood to the fire, for I fear to be chilled," Nathalie interrupted me with a sudden calm to her voice. "Pierre, get those clean blankets and, ohhh, ahh. The pains are getting closer together. Help me onto the bed, Pierre."

Pierre said nothing, but he now moved with purpose. I busied myself stoking the fire. There was no thought of modesty as Nathalie shucked off her garment and Pierre helped her remove her wet under apron. Disrobed, he wrapped her in blankets upon the bed leaving her lower region partly exposed.

"Alex, bring me a sturdy twig in case I need something to bite on."

This didn't make any sense to me, but I did as instructed.

With conviction, Nathalie then said, "Sit above me and hold my hands, Alex, and take care I don't break yours. I am about to deliver a baby. Pierre, father of our child, you will receive God's gift... " and again Nathalie was wracked by pain—and indeed, as she had forewarned, she very nearly crushed the life from my hands. "Look closely now Pierre, can you see the child's head?" she gasped.

It was all happening quickly now and I was witnessing the miracle of miracles. I was shocked at what came out of that tiny aperture. Not that the baby was large, for it appeared quite tiny, but it would seem getting a pamplemousse through a keyhole would be as easy. Never before had I seen a birthing, not even of livestock at the monastery.

After considerable effort, on Nathalie's part, a little bald head fully emerged. I felt Nathalie strain and I heard the twig crunch between her teeth like dry leaves underfoot. She then gave forth a deep guttural groan through clenched teeth and the babe slipped from its womb into Pierre's trembling hands. Behind it came some other bloodied matter like the casing of *saucisse,* and I trembled with alarm that it might be Nathalie's stomach falling out. Feeling my dismay, Nathalie assured both Pierre and me that she was doing fine, and everything was as it should be. Newborn babies are not beautiful, but birth is beautiful—indelibly beautiful.

Panting heavily with much sweat upon her brow Nathalie was not quite finished. "Pierre… is… is the cord attached?"

"Yes, my love, there is a cord," Pierre said, shakily.

"Cut the cord near the child's belly leaving enough to knot it and then do so. Then clean its mouth and gently shake our child upside down. I think that is what to do. Make sure the afterbirth is out also."

All these matters of birthing were dizzying my head and I must have fainted.

I next recall lying on the straw-stuffed palliasse next to a proud mother with a crying baby girl in her arms. Nathalie was trying to suckle the babe and seeing my eyes open, said with a beaming smile, "Joyeux Noel, Alex, what a wonderful gift on the very day of Christ's birth."

It was upon my birth date of Epiphany that the message came from Jeanne. I was chopping wood and had to scurry out of sight as the soldier rode up to the castle. Though I was dressed in feminine attire, I did not wish to chance my discovery. Pierre was taking his mid-day meal and came out of their cottage to greet the stranger. The soldier hailed Pierre cheerfully, who in turn bade him welcome and asked, as was the custom, if he might sup with them. The invitation was accepted and, after tethering the horse, they disappeared into the hut. I was in a state of anxiety not knowing whether to run or remain, for strangers, let alone soldiers, rarely had occasion to stop at Bourlemont. Not long after, however, Pierre emerged and called out for me. Hesitantly, I came forward.

"Be not afraid, Alex. Come in and meet a friend of Jeanne D'Arc's."

I admit I was still much fearful and chary to enter, but I put my trust in Pierre. The soldier was laughing and cooing as he played with baby Isabelle in his arms. Seeing this, I was much relieved and began to relax. He said his name was Jean de Nouillonpont, but his friends knew him as Jean de Metz. He had come from Vaucouluers and he had a message from Jeanne D'Arc. Dumbfounded, I could only nod, wide-eyed and breathless.

"She wishes you God's blessing on your common day of birth. The time is near at hand for her mission and she bids you come with me to her side."

I realized my mouth was agape and made myself close it, lest my heart escape.

I was not long in readying myself, for I had but the clothes on my back and a second ragged set of Pierre's, re-sewn by Nathalie. I remained in female attire, as all agreed it would be a prudent measure. There were hugs and tears as we said our farewells, and especially, kisses for little Isabelle. De Metz proffered his arm and I hopped up behind him on his tall chestnut steed, with a heavy heart. I looked back and waved at my friends, somehow knowing we would never cross paths again. Nathalie looked away, her eyes brimming as mine.

So there I went on my seventeenth birthday. Only Jeanne could have known of my identical birth date, so I felt safe to accompany this stranger. It was comforting to know others, such as soldiers, believed in her mission. Jeanne thought it best for me to stay close by at Burley-le-Petit with the Laxarts, de Metz explained. I would be safe there. As we rode, de Metz told me of his first meeting with Jeanne.

He had chanced to meet her through mutual friends, Henri and Catherine Royer. She seemed to have fired the interest and approval of the townspeople, de Metz related. On her second visit to Vaucouluers she professed to any who would listen of her need to see the Dauphin and have him crowned according to her visions. Orleans had been besieged since December and it had also become her mission to raise the siege. Upon hearing of Orleans's plight, she came back to Vaucouluers to once again beseech Baudricourt. She was again rudely rebuffed, but this time did not return to Domremy. She stayed instead with the Laxarts or her other family friends, the Royers in Vaucouluers. It was felt public opinion was actually beginning to sway Baudricourt. So much so that he had sent a message to the Dauphin in Chinon. In fact, when I asked of my old friend Cedric, de Metz thought it was likely Cedric who took the message to Chinon. De Metz told me he had been much intrigued by Jeanne and one day he queried her intentions, as she waited in vain to see Baudricourt.

"I am a staunch believer in the Armagnac cause, Alex. The Dauphin is the rightful heir and the Anglais are but opportunistic interlopers. And those treacherous Burgundians," de Metz paused to spit on the ground, "can kiss the Goddams' backsides all the way back to England. Fearful was I that the Dauphin was only a fainéant—a puppet Merovingian incarnate from Clovis, ruled by others beneath him. I was prepared to give up, but then… " And he paused, as if reflecting on his own tenet. "But then I was much moved by this seemingly simple farm girl possessed of such tenacity. One day I had observed her at the collegiate church of Notre-Dame next to the west gate, which was my post. She came there almost every day, and this particular day I had observed her weeping pitiably, prostrated at the statue of Our Lady of the Vaults. As she was leaving, I asked, 'what are you doing HERE? Must the Dauphin King be driven out of his kingdom and must we all become ENGLISH?' This set her off on a long dissertation covering all manner of royal political intrigues, which impressed me greatly. She also said, 'There is no help but through me! And yet I would much prefer spinning at my mother's side, because it is not my condition. But I must go and do it, because it is my Lord's will'. I asked who her Lord was and she answered, 'God'. I am not an overly religious man, nor am I unreligious, but I was moved. The English have beaten us down for almost one hundred years—so why not this girl, with the halo about her head?

Then and there, I promised the Maid, pledging my word to her by touching her hand, that with God as my leader, I would bring her to the King. I asked her when she would leave and she said, 'Better today than tomorrow, better tomorrow than later.'"

De Metz had asked me little on our ride to Burley-le-Petit. I was grateful not to have to answer questions and simply absorb news of my friend, Jeanne. He informed me he might soon escort Jeanne to the castle at Nancy where Charles II, Duke of Lorraine, had granted her counsel. Perhaps she could solicit his aide in her mission if Baudricourt would not acquiesce. Blessed darkness enveloped us with its safety before we arrived at Burley-le-Petit, and it was a happy reunion with the Laxart's.

Chapter Seven

THE JOURNEY

ALMOST ANOTHER full cycle of the moon passed before Baudricourt finally granted Jeanne her wish to leave for Chinon. During this period, we learned much of soldiering and warfare from some well-wishing compatriots of Cedric's. I helped Jeanne accomplish some simple things, such as signing her name, improving her riding skills, and how to dress as a man. How peculiar it seemed that I dressed as a woman and she now as a man.

Jeanne showed her giddy, girlish side when she first dressed in gray doublets and breeches. She purposely wanted to counter my predicament. She thought it great jest and laughed with glee at how we looked. It soon became her mode accoutrements, and even part of her selfhood. For me, my female guise was prudent and passing. For Jeanne though it was treading on dangerous ground, as the Church's dictum was clear. Women were not to wear men's clothing. Such guise was considered the Devil's work, and in extreme cases was punishable by stoning, or even burning at the stake. The only exception was if the woman felt her virginity was threatened, and such a thing might be difficult to prove.

Jeanne's forbearance was considerable, but Baudricourt's intransigence was equally considerable. There were rumors that he had sent a messenger to the Dauphin asking for his decree on the matter. Supportive people would surround Jeanne on the street asking of deliverance from the Anglais, and she had lately begun to chafe at these questions. To allay her frustrations, she decided to accept an invitation from Charles II of Lorraine to visit him in Nancy. She made the journey with de Metz to try and rally support from that province. Unfortunately, Charles was only interested in having his health and love life presaged. She returned to Vaucouluers in disgust.

Not long thereafter, our time came. It was the first Sunday in Lent during the month of February, after the arrival of a royal messenger. Baudricourt finally relented, with the Dauphin's countenance. He presented Jeanne with a gelded black steed and a finely burnished sword. Within a day, Jeanne's little troop was prepared to depart, and as they mounted at the west gate, Baudricourt charged them (rather tersely I thought), "Go, go, let come what may."

I had climbed into the tower guarding the west gate. From this height of almost two lance lengths, I could survey the exodus. There were many people there to see them off including the Royers, the Laxarts and others who had been so generous to both of us. There were seven of them in the party including Jeanne. Jean de Metz and his squire, Bertrand de Poulengy, Richard the Archer, Julien and Jean de Honnecourt comprised the company. The royal messenger, Colet de Vienne, who had arrived from Chinon with the Dauphin's approval for Jeanne, decided not to return with them. Apparently, discretion was the greater part of valor for him, and he would wait for a larger, armed force before returning.

Jeanne, hardly appearing the quiet girl I knew, was a *foudroyant* sight. She was dressed in black doublet and hose breeches, brown high boots with long spurs, and a black cloak flowing behind. Her head was unhooded with hair cut short round, and her face shone white in the torchlight like a beacon. Mounted high with her black charge snorting steam in the cool night air, she rode through the west gate. Jeanne looked up and caught sight of me. She smiled, and with a twinkling in her eye mouthed the words, 'We go with God. See you soon, my friend.' And then, above the cheering of the well-wishers, sang out to the melody of a traditional children's song of worship:

"Chinon on the blue Vienne,
four hundred miles away.
For God and France and Liberty,
we go forward on this day."

Jeanne had bequeathed to me the horse purchased for her by Laxart and Jacques Alain. I would rendezvous with them that night to take the place of the squire. Apparently, the squire had no taste for warring after all, and was happy to be released of his bond. At last, I could doff my female habiliment and begin the adventure of my life.

As prearranged, I found the group just south of Alainville. The young squire seemed much relieved to be released from his duties. To my amazement, he announced he had decided to become a Franciscan friar, dedicating his life to God. I shook his hand and strongly suggested he ride south to Avignon and avoid Neufchateau or Coussey.

As we hoped to reach Saint-Urbain before resting, Jeanne suggested he might stay with us awhile. There was a Benedictine abbey there at which he might be accepted and the Abbot was related to Baudricourt's wife. The poor frightened wretch was blubbering with gratitude at this suggestion, and we all agreed it would be a good solution for him.

Where once had been fertile fields, the countryside was ravaged or overgrown. This heinous never-ending war was eating Gaul from within and without. If it wasn't merciless armies, it was unconscionable marauding mercenaries raping our land and people. These were the blackest of times and we were as ravaged as by the plague. I was glad that most of our journeying was at night whereby we need not witness these depressing sights. It seemed to worsen each year, a fact I heard my compatriots discuss at length. The province of Lorraine was certainly not healthy, but some other areas were completely devastated. I prayed to God that our savior Jeanne would accomplish her mission and a semblance of order be finally returned to our land. More than once she was asked if she would actually do what she proposed. Jeanne would reply, "Do not fear. I am commissioned by God to do so. Even four or five years ago my brothers in paradise and my Lord, that is God, told me I must go to war to deliver the kingdom of France." Her faith was resolute, her mission irrefutable and we had no doubt that she bore us upon the winds of destiny.

Our first night of travel was long and arduous. The Ornain River was so swollen with heavy winter rains that we followed it south, avoiding Gondrecourt, past the confluence of the Maradite and Ognon streams. There we forded the two streams separately with greater ease. It was daybreak by the time we reached Saint-Urbain, wet and exhausted.

We were dry and refreshed when we left at dusk on the next eve, leaving the timorous squire under the abbey's aegis. That was to be our last stop of comfort for several days. Many times we were alarmed by nightriders in the distance. Each time Jeanne said simply, "Have faith my friends." And indeed, it came to pass that every menacing looking group failed to take notice of us, no matter how exposed our position. Fate must have been our ally and God our beacon, for we passed through dangerous Burgundian territory and forded many swollen rivers. We could not keep to the main routes and we slept damp and cold with no fire to comfort us. Victuals were scant, but we flourished with the food of faith. Jeanne complained not, but rather encouraged and sustained us through example. Like us she slept fully clothed, on cold ground with but the horse's blanket for warmth. We passed deserted villages and occasionally were fortunate to sleep in barns with a straw bed. With weapons at hand, we ensured Jeanne was protected as she slept with Poulengy, De Metz, and myself all lying close to her. A posted guard was *de rigueur* at all times.

About halfway through our journey, Jeanne insisted she must attend mass. Jean de Metz felt it was folly, but Jeanne would not be swayed. Disguising ourselves as best we could and claiming to be merchants, we attended mass at the pro-Burgundian town of

Yonne (or Auxerre as some called it). This audacious act was further proof of Jeanne's invincibility and uplifted the spirits of our little troop. It was a voyage of destiny and yet for me, as I know now, it was only the preamble.

We crossed the wide and swift Loire on an unguarded bridge near Gien, and once on the other side we were in somewhat safer Armagnac territory. After another eight nights and days of hard travel we reached Fierbois and were but a half days ride to Chinon when Jeanne decided she must attend the chapel of Saint Catherine's. Exhausted, we were only too happy for what turned out as a three-day rest there. Jeanne seemed to find an affinity with this chapel and I remembered Fierbois was where Nathalie and Pierre Marlet had lost their first child. I related the story to Jeanne and it brought tears to her eyes. Immediately, she went to the chapel to pray for them and their new child.

Saint Catherine's was a historic chapel, renowned as a sanctuary for knights returning from battles and crusades to the Holy Land. The interior walls were adorned with many swords left behind by crippled crusaders. Nathalie had spoken of witnessing one such knight, in apparent great despair, lamenting near the altar. About to turn around and leave him with his misery, Nathalie stopped when she noticed him oddly scratching at the earth near the north wall of the nave. He dug at the hard ground, heedless of his bleeding fingers. It was then Nathalie said she noticed he was missing his right hand, yet that did not deter him from using the stump to also tear at the earth. She thought this a strange and harsh means of self-chastisement. After he had carved a bloodied hole that was a few inches deep and shaped like a trough, he placed his sword in it. In tearful anguish he buried the blade and worked on the earth until it was flat once again. Nathalie said she took it as a sign and quietly left the chapel, thinking her anxiety must be trifling next to his great sorrow. C'est la vie—when you think your woes are blackest, someone else shows you how much worse it could be.

When we continued on to Chinon, three days later, the rains had abated and the sun shone brightly upon us, as if anointing our noble quest. Chinon castle was a towering edifice. Its gray, crenellated battlements rose as if to touch the gates of heaven from atop the right bank escarpment of the Vienne. We climbed a steep, winding road to the castle's east gate and entered across the moat that protected its northerly flank. Our arrival was expected and there was a large crowd of curious onlookers waiting. We entered with great expectations to a warm, but reserved welcome.

I was riding behind Jeanne when the pleasant scene was suddenly befouled. There was a lull in the clamor and a loud churlish voice exclaimed, "Hah, is that the maid? If I had her for one night, she would no longer be a maid." A small, but discernable chorus of coarse laughter followed this.

Immediately, the hackles on the back of my neck rose, and I turned with de Metz to the side from where the rude voice had emanated. It was one of the gate guards, a rather large and ugly brute. I instinctively swung my mount in his direction to defend our maid's honor, but De Metz grabbed my horse's reins. "Not now, Alex, not now," he hissed.

Not wavering in her course or pace, Jeanne ignored the insult. We followed her lead and continued on. Looking back over my shoulder though, I glared at him, engaging his fierce eyes with unreserved rancor. His response was but a mocking laugh.

As I dismounted at the stables, I was grabbed from behind and lifted off the ground by one I thought had the strength of two men. Struggling against my foe, I could hardly breathe, let alone free myself. I was tossed into a straw pile and a familiar, resonant laugh burst forth.

"Cedric, Cedric you champion of right and old Saracen slayer!" Jumping to my feet, we embraced with gusto.

"I said I would find you, Alex, but tis you who found me. By the good Saint Christopher, you look hale and hearty and have grown a good handspan these many months."

"Oh, I cannot say what a blessed coincidence this is. How is it that you are here Cedric?"

"Well, you know I would only be where the action is, my fine young colt. But what of you?"

"Have you not heard of the maid, the Maid of France? I am her squire and she is here for the salvation of the Dauphin and France."

"Well, yes, yes of course but, how did you… "

"Here, my friend let me introduce you to our savior, Jeanne D'Arc," I interjected.

Gazing upon her, he was suddenly transfixed. Cedric later confided to me that he had paid little attention to the rumor of a maiden savior, as all sorts of rumors were rife in this time. His reaction was therefore all the more astonishing. Filled with reverence, he dropped to one knee in supplication, unable even to utter a greeting.

Jeanne's eyes widened, as if in recognition, and she said, "I know of you, Cedric. You will be my champion of Orleans." Nothing further was said. Cedric then rose and backed away in apparent awe-struck silence.

We were then shown to our temporary quarters arranged by the Dauphin's stable squire, Gobert Thibault. When de Metz and Poulengy explained to Gobert how we had ridden across much of Burgundy without hindrance, he shook his head in disbelief. It did not take long for word to spread of our seemingly incredible feat.

Once at our meager quarters behind the stables, Cedric took us to his friend, the kitchen-master of the garrison. As the others sat down to victuals, I pulled Cedric aside and explained there was something I must do immediately. Willingly he agreed, on the condition I enlighten him as to my situation and purpose. Leaving out some personal details, which might embarrass us both, I brought him up to date on my sojourn as we made our way back to the east gate.

"There was a guard at the east gate who gravely insulted Jeanne's decency. This cannot go unanswered, as I believe it could jeopardize her entire mission."

"Yes, I did see something of that from a distance, but what do you propose my favorite pollywog? Er, maybe I best not call you that anymore, my feisty young colt." He laughed and playfully thumped me on my back causing me to stagger forward.

"I don't know yet, but I must confront him and extract his apology."

At this Cedric's smile disappeared and he said with great levity, "I think I know this Armagnac scoundrel and he is a seasoned, ill-tempered warrior, not to be trifled with. Perhaps I should just toss him into the moat for you." And his smile returned.

"No, no Cedric! If I am to become a man in the maid's service I must face such rabble. Besides, there is nothing to fear, for we are under God's wing. Did we not brave worse to arrive from Vaucouluers?"

The squeamish feeling in my entrails was not entirely in accord with such bravado, but having spoken thus to Cedric, there was no turning back. He looked at me strangely and said nothing more as we approached the gate.

"Sire! SIRE!" I challenged, stridently.

They were in the process of changing the gate guard, and four burly soldiers turned to the source of disruption.

"You on the right, what is your name, that I may address you?"

He had an incredulous look on his face and seemed speechless, looking back and forth between Cedric and myself. With a furrowed brow he finally said, "What business is it of yours, whelp, and what has this overfed northern mercenary to do with anything?"

Sensing that Cedric was moving hand to sword, I put my arm in front of him. To quell my shaking hands I then braced them on my hips and moved toward the beast slowly, not sure what next to do, yet trying to exude a sense of purpose.

"He has nothing to do with this, and I asked of you a simple question, if indeed your simple mind can remember your own name. You have blasphemed the maid and there must be retribution," I said, surprised at my own belligerence.

His face, ruddy and reddened under a scruffy beard, was turning purplish. He growled, "Why you little piece of canard shit… "

He started to slowly circle me in a menacing manner as I drew closer. The other three guards, wearing sinister smiles, were gradually positioning themselves to my rear when Cedric spoke.

Drawing his broadsword he said, "Lest any of ye three have ideas of interfering, ponder this wee thought."

There were two dogs growling at a small mangy dog within a long pace of Cedric. Before a breath could be drawn and with his feet barely seeming to move, Cedric's right arm flashed out in a backhanded manner. Wielded as if weightless, the heavy sword severed the mangy dog so neatly and quickly in two that blood only spewed after the two portions landed an arm span apart. In an instant the other two bigger dogs were upon the spastic, spurting remains, tearing at and devouring its flesh in a frenzy.

"Do not doubt it, lads. I would cut you into dog meat and feed your offal to the cats."

One of the younger guards was audibly gulping back bile, as was I. They moved a good distance away, but my adversary continued to stalk me, pressing me onto the drawbridge. He seemed uncowed by Cedric's action and said, "So you wish to know my name, you little dog fart. Very well, since it will be one of the last things you may hear. I am Aout La Tremoille and… "

For some reason, perhaps anxiety, or perhaps fear, this made me break into almost hysterical laughter. Aout was completely nonplussed, left standing with his mouth half open. Trying to control myself and not knowing why I would think such a thing, I said, "Aout you are very late. It is already Fevrier and this is not your month at all."

In a confused rage he lashed out at me, but I ducked, backing against the drawbridge chain. Though his movements were slowed by his heavy armor, I was no match for his strength. He swung again, and again I ducked, but this time he anticipated and tried to knee me in the head. He only partially succeeded as his leather plated knee glanced off the side of my head. I wound up in a crouch with my head between his legs. Awkwardly, he bent over to collar me, in what would have been a death grip, but I grabbed him round the back of his knees, buckling them. Drawing upon every reserve of strength I possessed, I uncoiled upward and back. Even without armor he must have been a heavy man, but God and fear made my young legs Herculean. Panicking he let go of me and clutched for the drawbridge chain. He was unsuccessful.

It must have been three or four lance lengths to the moat and, bawling in anger, he hit the water on his back with a resonant WHOP. If not immediately dead, he was soon drowned, as his heavy armor dragged him to the bottom. We all stared in stunned disbelief at the ever widening circle of ripples and the dissipating frothy bubbles at their center. Not a word was spoken. A small crowd of curious peasants had come upon the scene and they too were silent. After I had regained my composure and breath, I said aloud, "Bear witness all—that Jeanne the Maid is here for the salvation of France and our Dauphin. She is NOT to be reviled, as she is on GOD's mission."

Upon still shaking knees I strode off, with a half-smiling Cedric in my wake and a burgeoning legend for Jeanne in the making.

Chapter Eight

THE MEETING

THERE WAS much favorable talk of Jeanne in Chinon, but the Dauphin, Charles VII, seemed to be deliberately delaying her requested audience with him. After waiting three long days and being subjected to a wearisome, captious inquisition by Charles' council, she was told to appear in the main hall at sunset.

Led by the Dauphin's seneschal, de Metz and I escorted Jeanne to the meeting. Ascending the exterior stone staircase of the recently constructed tower, we were favored by a panoramic view of the sunset. There were resplendent shades of orange capped by a gray haze, as the sun dipped itself into the waters of the Vienne running west from Chinon. That, I reassured myself, was a portentous sign of great things to come.

We were admitted from the foyer and I was at once daunted by the great hall and the throng of people therein. Especially imposing, was the grand fireplace situated at the gable-ended far wall. Several men could have stood within it. It was meant to impress those entering and for simple folk like ourselves it certainly succeeded.

It was said Charles had it built to please his wife. I suspect he needed to, as it was known in privileged circles that he was much infatuated with his current mistress, Anne. Fortunately, these improprieties were unknown to Jeanne. She had wasted no breath before admonishing Charles II, of the province Lorraine, on her aforementioned futile trip to Nancy.

As related to me, what happened there was thus: Charles of

Lorraine had granted Jeanne the audience because he was in ill health and heard she was something of a clairvoyant, perhaps possessing curative powers. When he queried her in this regard she enlightened him as only Jeanne could, for his improprieties were commonly known.

'Sir, you may never recover unless you redeem yourself by living again with your good wife, Marguerite de Baviere. You should forsake your mistress Alison May. I am no magician. My purpose here is other than what you seek.'

Such unabashed, moral honesty certainly ruined any chance of support, but it should be noted Charles of Lorraine returned to the bosom of his wife shortly thereafter and indeed did recover. As I said, it was likely fortuitous for Jeanne's success that she was unaware of the Dauphin's libertine tendencies.

The main hall was brimming with courtiers, aides, advisors, family members and anyone of significance in Charles' court. Some were bizarrely costumed, as mid-lent being a drab time of year, it was customarily a time of revelry among the privileged.

Mostly it was the men who were costumed. Color was the popular theme with an array of striped and checkered vestments and pantalettes, often worn inside out. I found this particularly amusing, for lower class prostitutes were made to wear checkered or inside-out raiments. Besides a variety of odd, floppy caps, the one common piece of attire was *poulaines*—long pointed shoes, often tied up to the calves. The clergy detested these shoes, decrying them as a display of devil-like vanity.

Fashionable tall conical hats with decorative silk appendages crowned many women. As was the fashion, bulbous wrapped protrusions of hair adorned either side of their heads. They wore rich flowing dresses and carried hand-held masks for disguise.

Looking at de Metz, I could tell he, like myself, felt somewhat uncomfortable in these circumstances. Jeanne on the other hand was completely oblivious to the fete-like milieu. The throng became hushed and separated before her advance, much like the sea must have parted before Moses. Jeanne approached a group of obvious hierarchy gathered around the fireplace, and we followed closely on her heals. The group stared at us fixedly, and one of them then spoke out loudly over the low muffled din.

"What have we here? Tis the Maid of Lorraine come to rescue the Dauphin. Please come forward and greet me, my loyal subject and savior."

De Metz then covertly whispered into her ear from behind, "They must be making jest Jeanne, for that cannot be Charles. Oh, ho, look to the right of the fireplace—the uncostumed, dour looking one with the conspicuous nose. That is the Dauphin I would wager, for I have seen his likeness and that nose ... well, perhaps that is why his mother renounced his legitimacy."

At this irreverent and rude comment Jeanne gave de Metz a look that could have frozen the Vienne. Not privy to de Metz's whisperings over their own susurrations, the courtiers anxiously awaited Jeanne's reaction to the imposter. After visually redressing de Metz, she turned away from him and strode with purpose and confidence directly to the imposter. He was costumed in the flowing robes of a Sarasen chieftain and stared at her smugly while tugging at a small red beard upon his chin.

"You, sir, are not the reason I am here." With that she turned abruptly right and moved to address the one indicated by de Metz.

Kneeling in supplication she said, "Gentle Dauphin, I have come to your aide as instructed by my Lord, God. If you would grant me private audience I would enlighten you as to my legitimacy."

The din of muffled noise had completely abated. Jeanne spoke softly to the Dauphin, but her words were audible in all corners of the hall. A tense and breathless silence followed as everyone awaited the Dauphin's response. The corners of his thin lips curled up in what could have been a smile or a smirk and he spoke simply, "Very well then." And he moved off to an empty corner of the hall, indicating Jeanne to follow.

Deferential chatter and movement resumed while the maid and Dauphin conferred. I was sworn to secrecy as to what Jeanne later confided in me. However, that was my *old world* and I'm sure such an oath could not apply to this private journal. As related to me, the conversation was thus:

'My kind and gentle Dauphin, soon to be king, my mission is your deliverance. Do you not know it has been prophesized that France would be lost by a woman and raised up again by a virgin from the marshes of Lorraine? Your very mother was that woman, but her councilors and her treacherous Burgundian allies betrayed her. The Treaty of Troyes is a blasphemous scroll, deserving of no respect or legitimacy.

My mother was a dedicated subject to the House of Anjou and occasional aide to your mother Isabelle. She confided to my mother that none of her offspring were actually legitimate, for your supposed father Charles VI's mental malady, also rendered him incapable.

Indeed, she even told my mother of Odette de Champdivers, who bore a striking resemblance to the Queen. This horse-dealer's daughter was sent to Charles' presence when he required the need of feminine comfort. Such profane dealings make my heart sad, but the Queen could not deal with his ravings when the darkness overtook him. Even the aged and venerable physician Guillaume de Harsigny could not completely cure him.

Your true father was actually Louis of Orleans, so said my mother. Yes, that may shock you, but it is true, for my mother had attended your birthing, bearing garlands of flowers. It was then that your mother, in a state of malaise, whispered to her these truths I have related.

It was perhaps a fortnight later that Louis was set upon and foully murdered by the henchmen of that Burgundian, John the Fearless. So you see, when you had a hand in the execution of John the Fearless, it was divine providence—for it was he who had murdered your true father. Indeed, Louis would have been a legitimate heir to the throne."

Charles' eyes were wide with wonder at such brash and astounding statements coming from a mere country girl. The possibilities must have intrigued him, for it was said that he harbored great guilt over John the Fearless' murder.

After a pensive pause, he replied, "I know not the truth of everything you speak, but if what you say is so, whether I am bastard or king matters not, for divine providence must surely be my ally and perhaps you its instrument. But I do not understand how your mother, a commoner, could be a confidant of my mother, whether she toiled for the House of Anjou or not."

Jeanne's reply was the coup de grace. "I had hoped not to divulge this, but I believe my mother would understand the necessity. My dearest Dauphin, it is for your ears only that we are of the same maternal bloodline. I see the shock and disbelief in your eyes, my gentle Dauphin, but indeed it is true. My mother's parents were originally from Bavaria, the same as your mother. Our mothers are cousins. This was not to be known, as your mother was—how shall I say—an enterprising and opportunistic courtier. She would not want to be associated with the untitled side of her family. My mother was born later than yours and was named Isabelle in her honor, as our maternal grand-meres were close and loving sisters. In Bavaria, my mother's maiden name is Romel—in France, it is Romee. So there is the truth of the matter, for these cousins were confidantes.

It is up to you, beloved Dauphin—to be France's savior. If the decision of legitimacy is left to the courts and such things came to light, the English would have further fodder to substantiate their claims. This is your divine providence, my Dauphin. My visions have told me so, and through them, God has sent me to aide you. We must act immediately and aggressively, or France is lost."

The Dauphin was in a state of consternation at such revelations. With narrowed, suspicious eyes he finally said, "If you are speaking truth, my cousin, what is it you hope to gain?"

"To but serve God and my King. Once you are anointed from Clovis' bowl in Reims, you will be our divine King and my mission shall be accomplished."

After a lengthy period of thought the Dauphin decreed to her, "Very well, my intrepid one, I will want to have your faith and character examined by my priests and council. I would not want my divinity compromised by those who would consort with the Devil. Should you be deemed as you say, I would have you lead my providential army." Charles' eyes then wandered dreamily and he stroked his chin as he mused aloud, "This denouement does indeed uplift my spirits if what you say of Louis is true. Evil was the only thing of which John was fearless. I hated the large-headed, unkempt, graceless runt for having consorted with my mother, yet felt grievous guilt for my actions. But, if Louis was my father ... and John his murderer ... yes, yes, it MUST be divine providence."

It was obvious he was greatly pleased with their conversation. He abruptly returned to his courtiers and was no longer dour, but rather cheerful and buoyant of spirit with apparent tears of joy glistening in his eyes. Jeanne, for her part, was in a state of bemused ebullience at the sudden and positive vertiginous spin of events in her favor. That very day, though late, Jeanne was taken by the Dauphin's mother-in-law, Yolande d'Aragon, and examined as to her chastity. With the powerful matriarch's tentative approval, destiny now shone brightly upon our mission.

Chapter Nine

Jerusalem to Fierbois

Delay upon delay—interviews, interrogations, explanations and examinations. Our little entourage had been walking among the clouds after Jeanne's initial meeting with the Dauphin. But now, frustration weighed heavily upon Jeanne. She wore it grumpily, like a sodden cloak after a rainstorm.

Jeanne, de Metz, and myself as their squire, were moved to the Coudray tower. Jeanne was accommodated in the upper room, while de Metz and I slept below, near the entrance of the keep. Our quarters were now more comfortable, but they left me with some grave misgivings. There were unusual carvings and scratchings in the wall near the entrance of the tower that invoked in me a sense of foreboding familiarity. So eerie was this feeling that I could not even bring myself to discuss it with de Metz or Jeanne.

Some of the symbols were lines within boxes that intersected each other randomly. Others were strange crosses with arms curved to the right. There was an apparent haloed Madonna with child. Another was a quartered moon with an ominous eye. And, most striking of all was an inverted teardrop radiating rays like that of the sun. The markings must have been there a considerable time as they were partially defaced, or at least so they appeared. Whoever was responsible for these had taken great care and considerable time to etch them so permanently and perfectly in the stone. Consciously, I tried to ignore their presence, but when the firelight danced across them, they seemed to come to life—magical, beckoning.

We were all greatly relieved when Jeanne was finally summoned for another interview. This time she was to travel to Poitiers to be examined by the Archbishop of Reims. Blessedly, I would have a respite from slumbering under the scrutiny of the markings.

It so happened that my good friend Cedric commanded our escort, so I had ample opportunity to converse with him. Finding it necessary to appease my curiosity I tentatively asked him about the cryptic markings.

"Ahh, yes my bold young squire. I was wondering when you might bring that up. It is not at all surprising you could feel the spirits within the Coudray keep. Among others, your great grandpere, Jacques de Molay, was imprisoned within those wretched walls."

Seeing my astonishment, he said it was time for me to learn further of my Templar heritage. Cedric reminded me of my great grandpere's illustrious life and his demise at the hands of King Phillip's henchmen. He told me of the Templars who were imprisoned for years, with the grim choice of either recanting their faith or being burnt at the stake. Somehow our faith still survived, though hidden from those who would persecute us. Cedric began his tale with a startling possibility.

> "To the best of my knowledge, Alex, your father may still be alive. After all the terrible things we saw and did in the Holy Land he returned a different man. He no longer possessed that indomitable fire which made him seem invincible.
>
> What those foul savages did to us in that stink-hole Saracen prison … he could have easily succumbed to despair and allow himself to die. It was, I now know, the thought of his beloved, Magdalena, which kept him spir-

ited. Unknown to him as we rotted in that hole was that the shining light, for which he pined, had already…

We were being held for ransom, chained in the dungeon of a small fort outside of Jerusalem. They had caught us by surprise several leagues south of there and we were overwhelmed. Though their numbers were superior, twas not that to which we succumbed.

Twas the heat of summer's mid-day when they attacked and we, in our iron cocoons, were almost burned up in the hellish heat of battle. They, in their cuircasses of quilted cloth and with small swift horses, were eventually able to prevail. Our force had been moving a recently captured, high-ranking Mullah to a secure place, when they turned the tables on us.

Your father was our captain and he had a considerable reputation with the Saracens. They knew he was much valued by our French commander. It was an opportunity for them to demand a sizeable ransom for him. After disarming the survivors of our guard they slaughtered them like cattle. It took five or six of them to tie me down when I realized what butchery they were about. They had a great laugh, saying they would ransom me by weight. This was the first time we had ever been captured in all our fighting years together. Your father did not take to it kindly and was as a saddle burr to his gaolers.

After several days, the very Mullah we had captured came to our fetid cell. He demanded information on military plans and the fettle of our lads. He said there would be no more food until we complied with his questions. Miguel glowered at him and snarled without forethought, 'You dung-eating infidel. We treated you honorably and fed you what we ate. You even dare to call this offal slop food?' With that he spat on the Mullah's feet and threw the bowl of gruel at him, splattering it over his already matted beard.

Needless to say, Alex, the two guards and the Mullah were enraged. All three attacked Miguel, beating him senseless. Suddenly the Mullah cried for them to hold. Though my knowledge of *Farsi* is not good, I understood the incensed Mullah ordering the guards to hold him on the floor. In Miguel's weakened stupor they were easily able to do as instructed. The Mullah took one of the guard's scimitars and stood over your father. I was wild with rage and strained against my chains, but they only reached a long arm's length from the wall. Your father's chains were long enough that they could pinion him on the floor with arms extended. The Mullah seemed to consider the scimitar for a moment and then threw it carelessly into the corner, just out of my reach. Bending down, he withdrew your father's *stolen* sword from its scabbard hanging on the kneeling guard's side.

Breathing heavily and shaking with fury the Mullah spat out with venom, 'I am the nephew of the great *Bajazet*, known to all the faithful as *Ilderim*, or Thunderbolt in your infidel tongue. This insult shall not go unpunished. To the greater glory of Allah it is fitting your own weapon shall take the hand that has defiled our people—YAHH, AEIII!'

I strained to reach the cast aside scimitar with my foot, but it was too late. The sword flashed in the dim torchlight and clanged sharply as it cut through flesh and bone before encountering the upraised stone. Miguel immediately regained his consciousness and an ungodly caterwaul arose from within him, threatening to pierce our ears. With incredible Herculean strength Miguel cast off the guard. Falling backward, the infidel cracked his turbaned head hard against the wall. Meanwhile, I managed to hook the scimitar with a toe and drag it to where I could grasp it. As the Mullah and other guard attempted to restrain Miguel, he instinctively swung at them with his now free stump of an arm. The blood spurting from his terrible wound temporarily blinded the guard as Miguel struck him in the face with the stump. The fury of Miguel's crazed reaction stunned the Mullah and the spurting appendage caught him in the face also. In the melee the Mullah had dropped the sword. Gagging in revulsion, he turned and staggered to the door.

I now had hold of the scimitar—just in time to lash out at the Mullah's legs. I caught him on the back of his leg and he collapsed with a howl, headfirst into the open cell door. I could hear the gaoler charging down the hall to see what all the tumult was about. He came through the low doorway with his scimitar protectively crossed in front of him. His attention was immediately drawn to Miguel choking the conscious guard with his uninjured arm. That was all the opportunity I needed. From my position outside his line of sight, I lashed out with all possible strength. It was not a glancing blow like the Mullah's, but a clean strike, severing his scrawny leg just below the knee.

The keys were about the gaoler's waist, so I dragged the convulsing infidel closer by his remaining leg and dispatched him to his afterlife. It was surprising good fortune that the second key I tried unchained me. I rushed to your father's side, finding him now insensate and sprawled over the now very dead guard. He was fast losing his rouge strength and earthly life. After tying off his right arm with the guard's belt, I ran to the passageway and plucked one of the torches off the wall. I stretched his forearm flesh down as much as possible and cauterized his wrist. The stench of his burning flesh made my innards heave. I have been in many blood-lust battles, but when it is your best friend and you can barely stand on a slippery floor awash with blood …

As I was relieving the foul bile from my gullet the other guard and Mullah were both regaining their senses. The dazed guard was rising, but he slipped in the blood to his hands and knees. He looked up to the hiss of my scimitar and the next thing he may or may not have heard was the thud of his head hitting the stone floor. With mouth and eyes open wide, it bounced and skittered to a stop against the wall. I then prepared to do the same for the Mullah. He was crawling on his belly into the corner and babbling gibberish. He knew his life dinna mean a thing to me, but what he babbled made me stop and think whilst I gripped his scrawny throat. He said that if only I would spare him he could save us. Miguel, at that moment, began to groan and seemed to be rejoining us from his swoon. As the Saints will attest, he was white as a virgin's habit at the altar.

'Hold Cedric! You must use him … Tis your only chance … Use him as your shield,' he gasped.

'What do you mean by YOUR, Miguel. Two of us leave here or two of us die here,' I vowed. I may have been squeezing the Mullah's throat just a mite too tight, for he started choking and turning color. His troublesome squirming was interrupting our discussion.

'Nay Cedric, do not finish him … I agree we'll both go … even though … I will be but half a man for Magdalena … the sons of CAMEL WHORES!'

'Not to worry, old friend, we'll get out of this stink hole and nay will you be half a man. Even a half a man makes three of these like. So let us not dally, my brother.'

I inspected the Mullah's leg and though there was a lot of blood, he was only missing a sizeable piece of fat off his flabby thigh. He moaned pitiably, as I roughly bound his wound with a part of his robe. It was his loose flapping robe, which had saved him initially from a severed leg and it was perhaps to our good fortune also. Miguel tried to rise, but once again fell into a faint.

The Mullah protested at having to carry your father, but a gentle slice of his ear with Miguel's wonderfully balanced sword seemed to convince him. It seemed a long trek up the dank, sloped passageway to the jail entrance and the Mullah soon began gasping for air under his burden. Peeking out the jail door, I could hear the wailing of evening prayers commencing. I said a silent prayer of thanks for this diversion, as all I could see was one guard at the stable and one guard at the gate. I found a length of rope and used it to tie Miguel to the Mullah. Miguel was now conscious and I told him I wanted the Mullah to call the stable guard over. But we were in luck, as the guard was already heading our way, unbidden. I whispered to Miguel, 'Here is a dagger my friend, keep it at the Mullah's throat. Can you stay conscious?'

'I will see that I do, even if I have to prick myself with this child's sword.'

Just as I positioned myself out of sight beside the door, the stable guard entered. It must have been a shocking sight to see the Mullah, his ear dripping blood, his leg soaked with it, and your father lashed to his back holding a dagger at his throat. Miguel saluted Saracen-style with his grotesque stump and bade him welcome. The guard froze with his mouth agape and in that manner he almost met his maker.

'Nay Cedric, spare him, for I feel he would be more than willing to saddle us two of his finest and fastest Arabians.' An amazing man, your father, for he must have been in a terrible state of feverish pain, yet his wit and foresight would not abandon him.

Disarming the stable guard, I peeked through the small barred window and saw that there were now two guards at the south gate. Luckily, the timbered gate had been left open. They were kneeling on their mats droning incoherent chants toward their Mecca. With blades at our captives' throats we hugged the cobbled walls and made it to the stable posthaste. And praises be to God, we found several speedy Arabians already saddled. Apparently a Saracen patrol was prepared to depart after prayers.

At knifepoint I had the guard tie the Mullah onto a saddled horse. I chose the largest of the small steeds for myself and attached a tether to the Mullah's mount. Miguel said if he could not ride on his own, we had no chance. He was right of course and, though in great pain, he rode bravely. The guard was spared on the condition he tells their force that the Mullah would die if there were any attempt at pursuit. If they did not try to pursue us, we gave our oath to release him unharmed once we were safe.

We burst from the stable, and herding all the other horses ahead of us, galloped through the south gate. Those wee brown, gate guards got a rousing wake up from their prayers. Twas a sight—didn't even know what hit them, as they tumbled all curled up under those pounding hooves.

Aye, that ride to freedom into a glorious sunset was more sport than any bloodlust rout I've been in. We were even wise enough to tether two spare Arabians, as we had a long ride and they would not be accustomed to such large lads as us. I had borrowed the stable guard's skin of water and his skin of wine. For Miguel, the wine was a godsend.

By morning, I felt we were far enough removed to rest and I was about to release the Mullah as promised. That goat-fucker must have secreted a dagger from the stable guard. I was turning to untether his horse when Miguel cried out. I moved enough that he narrowly missed my heart and vitals, but he ripped my back open from armpit to waist, nicking a few ribs. Achh, he dinna ken any better—that such a wound with such a toy could only irritate this Scot warhorse. AND, by the good Saint Christopher, he tried to stick me again. Well, that was it. I was so annoyed that I took his little toy away and broke his wee goat-fucking neck. Tis a shame, Alex lad, some people just never learn.

Aye, I make jest and you laugh Alex, but BLOODY-HELL, I had to come back to France because of that. We recuperated for a time at the crusader's roadhouse in Malta. Twas a bonny, avant-garde infirmary that. It even had iron hitching rings next to our beds for our horses. Now that's progress. I mean, what is more important to a crusader than his horse, I ask you?

Your father's arm healed surprisingly well, but he was returning with much trepidation because of it. My plaguey scratch was more troublesome—the nuisance was want to fester and make me fevered.

Ohh, twas a terrible, terrible thing when we finally found you and Marie Robine. Some people weep copiously—some weep without tears—some rant and berate—some are even self-injurious. Portuguese are a most demonstrable people and thus your father bore all of these afflictions. He wept for days until he was empty—and then he moaned—ohh, how he moaned. Ich dinna ken if you could call it a moan, but it was the somber sound of sadness. Sometimes I would have to retrieve him from running through the nightscape wailing and moaning as a madman. We even had to move out of the village near Avignon, away from you and Marie. It was then that he pulled most of the hair from his head in raging fits. And then… then he drank. He almost never spoke—he answered only rarely when spoken to. When he drank copious wine he occasionally spoke, but rarely did he make sense. He tried several times to go to *Croisette* where his love had perished, but I would forestall him from doing so, for fear of dire consequences. Eventually, the wine seemed to dull his grief, but there remained only the sodden husk of what was Miguel.

Months passed. My wound was still slowly festering and it was beginning to eat me from within. A local barber in Dijon had said I must take the curative waters of Aquae Tarbellica in Dax. Because of Miguel's condition, I agonized over the decision to go. It was then that a strange, but miraculous thing occurred.

Miguel awoke one morning in his usual sad state and shuffled off to procure more cheap wine. He did not return by late afternoon and I was becoming vexed with worry. I was sitting upon our stone fence burnishing my sword when this monk approached our dwelling with his arm about Miguel. There were tears streaming from Miguel's eyes into his unkempt beard, and I feared he might have regressed even further. But to my great surprise and delight, he smiled and began to speak coherently.

He explained that he had heard this hermit monk of the order of Saint Austin, lecturing to a gathering in the square of Saint Peter. His scripture reading was that of Maria Magdalena and her salvation. It struck him like a cannon ball to the heart and he realized he had prostituted his life to the Devil.

How he ever came to such conclusions was beyond my simple mind, but his bewitchment of grief appeared to be miraculously exorcised. It was like a leaden weight was lifted off this Scot's heart. To see Miguel smile, as he hadn't for many new moons, made my spirits soar.

We sat down to our humble victuals with the hermit, known as *Jean Pasquerel*. He was on his way to Tours, where he would reside at the Saint Austin convent. Jean had noticed Miguel wander in to his gathering with a pitcher of wine in hand, seemingly captivated by his scripture reading. Next he knew, Miguel was weeping passionately at his feet. Knowing this to be a troubled soul, he gave him benediction after the reading and his change in mien became noticeably uplifted. Miguel informed us that the scripture reading was a parable of his and Magdalena's salvation. Jean told us of other miraculous encounters he had achieved, but none so dramatic. It was a wonderful evening we three spent, for once again I had my friend.

It was not long after that we left for Dax by way of Fierbois. Your father, encouraged of course by Jean Pasquerel, had made up his mind to join the hermits of Saint Augustine in his native Portugal. He decided he could no longer be a soldier, because of his new relationship with God and his physical incapacity. He wished me to travel with him to Fierbois, so that we might visit St. Catherine's chapel. For generations it has been a revered sanctuary for daunted and downcast crusaders or even distressed commoners. My heart was heavy, knowing I was losing my comrade at arms. Yet I was joyous to see that he had found his peace. On our journey to Fierbois he had some moments of bitter remorse, but it was obvious he was a new man. I had never seen him so devout. Though we were Templars, we had never observed the rites zealously. It was with great sorrow that we embraced warmly and followed our own paths from Fierbois. He to his hermitage and me along the only path I know.

We were a half-day ride yet to Poitiers. We had made camp in a densely forested area that provided meager protection against the spring rains. By the time Cedric had finished his discourse all the others were abed. Twas a fitful sleep I had that night. So many images and new thoughts from what Cedric related assailed my head like buzzing flies. I had many more questions, but they would have to wait. It took a long while before sleep became my ally, and it wasn't only Cedric's tale or the cold ground. There was something else tickling my memory from his story, and I could not quite unravel what it was that piqued my thoughts.

Chapter Ten

Poitiers and Tours

Poitiers proved a very vexing tribulation for Jeanne. There were further delays and certain indignities to which she was subjected. A forum of clergy and commissioners, presided over by the Archbishop of Reims, addressed her.

The last interview was farcical. I was appropriately positioned behind Jeanne, and could tell she was losing patience when she beseeched, "In the name of GOD the soldiers will fight, and God WILL deliver them."

There was a somnolent cleric who intoned in a thick provincial accent, "And what dialect is that you speak with?"

"A better one than you, sir," she replied, boldly.

Then came another innocuous inquiry, "Do you believe in the true God?"

Having been asked this many times before, she responded tersely, and I thought, recklessly, "Better than you do."

The Archbishop then interjected, "We need proof, or a sign that God really sent you."

To which she replied impetuously, "In the name of GOD, I did not come here to give signs, but take me to Orleans and I will show you the sign for which I was sent."

At that, the Archbishop privately conferred at length with his clerics while Jeanne chafed and waited. Finally, came his smug dictate, "Very well, Jeanne *La Pucelle*, you must present yourself to the rector's study at noon on the morrow. There we will examine you for your chasteness. As all know, those who are witches and consort with the devil could not be virginal. If you are unblemished, it is our decision to rule in your favor." With that they all rose as one and departed the chamber. I was aghast and appalled that they would actually subject Jeanne to such scrutiny. Jeanne's eyes were brimming but she complained not, for she had a purpose and an end. Destiny would not be deterred by the small of mind.

That night was another fitful one, as I remembered back to the Fairy tree. Could such an incident damage her virginity? I understood a little more of such matters now. But my mind and body were still celibate, for opportunities to learn and experience had not been presented to me. My perverse experiences with Father Clement I did not feel were relevant.

I needn't have fretted, for Jeanne passed their inspection without ado. After that, things began to move along rather more quickly. When the clergy legitimizes you, it is a wonder how many gates open.

It was more than a fortnight before we returned to Chinon and then we left the very next day for Tours. This was where Jeanne was fitted for her armor by the Dauphin's finest armorer. While there, she studied different modes of combat, tactics and weaponry. As her squire I was at her side most of the time.

Certainly, implements of war such as we examined and parried with, must have been conceived by a mephitic mind: Long cudgels with spikes and hammer ends, usually with fur grips; Razor-like sickles on poles; Poles with deadly sharp barbed iron points; Various types of grappling hooks on long poles to bring down riders; Dual axe and hook instruments; Yet, the most odious option was a U-shaped contrivance on the end of a pole to slide past a man's neck with tensioned iron barbs not allowing the neck to escape unless torn asunder, and a needle sharp point at the bottom of the U to penetrate the throat even if armored. Assorted daggers and broadswords complimented all of this.

My mind was filled with macabre thoughts after that first day and we hadn't even yet visited the gunnery and cannon foundry, where lay man's most recent method of mass destruction. As I laid myself down that night, I shuddered at the thought of what carnage such weapons could inflict. War no longer held the same allure and I had not yet fought my first battle.

It was then, with great revelation, that I bolted up in bed and scratched my tickled memory. 'Dear God, the soldier at the chapel of Saint Catherine—the sorrowful man described by Nathalie. It could only have been my father!'

The next morning I was bubbling with excitement from my nocturnal revelation. Jeanne was the first I was able to tell as we broke the fast together. She smiled happily for me, as I also related that my father might possibly be alive back in Portugal. She even suggested that this was perhaps a significant sign for me and that his sword may serve me as successfully as it had him. I had not thought of that possibility, but it now intrigued me. I was left to think on this as Jeanne left for prayers after her usual meager breakfast.

What a learned day that was in the ways of waging war. Monstrous iron tubes, called cannons, could incredibly propel large stones or iron balls high and far, causing havoc and destruction. I had heard of such things, but had not envisioned the magnitude of their destructive power. The biggest problem was their inaccuracy. They were unlike the light portable *culverins*, which as I discovered, could at least have some measure of accuracy and even penetrate light armor.

I decided such weaponry was more my kind of war tool; twas not for me this slashing and hacking. It made me shudder to envision a foe's face glowing with bravado and bloodlust in the heat of battle. Yet, perhaps that face was only shadowing the terror within his true heart. My own face, I knew, would mirror such terror, for the suffocating dread of being mutilated would seep from my body as a stench. It would reek of horror and putrefaction like that of the living dead in hell. Such moribund thoughts pervaded my mind in the same manner, as had the lectures on Satan's hell, so fervently expounded by Friar Clement. For me the battlefield became the slaughterfield when I thought of fighting with such severing implements from hell. Yes, I decided, gunnery would become my forte.

While awaiting Jeanne's suit of armor, I took full advantage of the opportunity to learn the art of gunnery. Jeanne, of course, was the prime recipient of this instruction, but by paying rapt attention I garnered much of this new military science.

The master of the foundry and gunnery expert was Louis de Monteclair. Much did I learn from this gruff, short man. Though I was growing rapidly this past year, I was still only of average height and Louis was almost a head shorter. It therefore made perfect sense to me that Louis became a warrior who could kill and maim from a distance. Though short in height, he was broad and possessed heavily calloused, powerful hands. No, sharpened steel was not to his advantage, but as a bombardier and forger there were none better. He taught me the intricacies of powder, shot, flint, maintenance and loading. The latter was of great advantage, as many gunners have maimed or killed themselves rather than the enemy during an ill-executed loading of their gun.

I was desirous to learn more of shooting these instruments, but Jeanne had other designs. Specifically, she wanted to visit one Hamish Power. Hamish, I discovered, was a half-brother to Cedric and a retired mercenary. He had since become a craftsman in the design and weaving of standards, and when we three arrived, was working on Jeanne's personal standard. Hamish was a smaller and older version of Cedric and they greeted each other with great bear hugs. After introductions, Jeanne asked me of my opinion on her standard. I replied honestly to the standard's august essence, simplicity and visual purity. It portrayed Jesus flanked by two angels, richly embroidered with shades of gold thread upon radiantly white pure silk. She later had another standard crafted for her company, but this one seemed to embody the quintessence of Jeanne's cause and virtue.

When Jeanne excused herself to attend mass, I had the opportunity to taste a draught of beer with Hamish and Cedric. I felt rather guilty at not attending mass with Jeanne, but that feeling was soon lost in the glow of my second pint.

Cedric and Hamish exchanged some raucous tales that I listened to with youthful veneration. When I was on my fourth pint, and they likely on their sixth, the conversation turned to bawdy women they had known. Such things were mostly foreign to my ears, and whether from beer or not, I could feel my face flushing rouge. This did not escape the sharp eyes of Hamish who said,"Hold Cedric. What have we here? Our young friend seems to be discomfited by our little tete-a-tete."

His comment seemed to make the heat in my neck and face more inflamed.

"HO, HO, by the good Saint Christopher! Alex, my lad, I had almost forgotten your tender years. Though you are seventeen summers, I believe you have lived a sheltered life. Aye, Hamish, the good young Alex has spent the past few years in a monastery."

"Achh, Ich dinna ken, Cedric. I've heard stories about some monasteries that would seem to fall short of piety. What say lad? Have you ever dipped your quill in a ladies ink pot?" Hamish bantered.

"I … I have never had such, such an opportunity," I stammered, abashedly. To my chagrin this elicited fits of deep-bellied laughter from them.

Cedric tugged at his beard and with a roguish smile said, "I think perhaps when we return to Chinon the morrow after next we should do something for this young warrior. It would not be fitting for him to risk his life on the battlefield without having tasted certain fruits of life. Dinna you agree, Hamish, my brother?"

"Aye, Cedric. Twould really be a cursed shame if it were otherwise."

There were more guffaws and laughter, liberally mixed with ribald suggestions. I knew it was unlikely to come to pass, as my fealty and chasteness belonged to my heroine of the *Fairy tree*. The beer flowed freely and sometime later, my senses took their leave. I am not sure how I got back to our lodgings, but I suspect it was upon Cedric's sturdy shoulder.

Chapter Eleven

LOST INNOCENCE LOST

As Cedric predicted, Jeanne's armor and standard were ready the next evening and we were on our way back to Chinon the following morn. Such was a good thing that our departure was not immediate, for I was feeling rather sickly the first day after my encounter with Hamish's beer.

When we arrived in Chinon this time, it was with considerably more pomp and adulation than had previously been the case. Attired in her elaborate armor and brandishing her resplendent standard upon a prancing white steed, Jeanne was an impressive figure. The suit of armor was immaculate in its highly polished state, manifesting a silvery white aura about her person. Oh, such a sight she was that the remembrance of it brings dampness to these old eyes.

As her squire, I was responsible for the donning of her accoutrements. Such was a learning process for both Jeanne and myself, and it was not without a measure of mirth at the initial tribulations. Firstly, over her usual tunic and leggings went a padded leather tunic. Next, went the fitted hauberk of chain mail from neck to knee, and I must have seemed the jester in my efforts to get the snug accoutrement into place. There must assuredly be an adroitness acquired over time at accomplishing such awkward feats I fretted, silently. Not the least impeding was Jeanne's merry laughter at our predicament of not being able to get her second arm in place. It was only after achieving this feat that the armorer returned, and with much merriment, informed us the hauberk must go *under* the leather tunic. With his help we corrected things and added the gleaming breastplate with its many clasps. Also added, were gauntlets of linked plates to protect the hands and a white plumed helmet with hinged visor weighing over half a stone. Impressive though she looked, comfort could not have been possible.

The city was abuzz with anticipation, and many others were now arriving to join the fray. Two of Jeanne's brothers had arrived and were being treated much above their plebeian status. The Duke Jean d'Alencon immediately requested an audience with Jeanne and offered his services to teach her in the matters of combat and tilting. Things were indeed beginning to happen and the city was alive with activity.

I was not much impressed with Jeanne's brothers, Pierre and Jean. I sensed an air of opportunism from them that was decidedly the opposite of Jeanne's altruism and sanctity of purpose. D'Alencon however, was a much different hogshead of herring. He was young, handsome, dark, tall and cut a fine figure of flamboyant nobility. Even Jeanne seemed to be somewhat taken by his élan and knightly manners. This had become an age of militaristic anarchy and fear. Chivalry and morality had become mere words. Like childhood aspirations they were spoken of, but rarely practiced. It had become a callous and wicked world. Perhaps d'Alencon was the fresh breeze above this reeking caldron of enmity—perhaps not.

My attitude was ambivalent. On one hand he seemed a nobleman worth looking up to. On the other I detested his fine ways and manners. This was mostly, I must confess, because I was jealous. He spent far too much time with my heroine. As her first squire, I was privy to all the subtle nuances of their interaction. There was one such instance on a misty morn as Jeanne practiced on the quintaine. She misjudged and it swung wickedly, knocking her from her steed such that she landed hard upon her derriere. Rushing to her aid I reached her an instant after d'Alencon. He helped Jeanne to sit and raised her helmet visor. Taking her gently by the hand he asked if she was injured. Though blushing crimson she smiled warmly, and looking at their joined hands made no effort to disengage. "I am perfectly fine, save for a sore hip and bruised amour-propre, my gentle Duke."

The next day d'Alencon presented Jeanne with a fine, white war-horse, charitably citing the other mount as the culprit for her fall. The powerful *destrier* steed would surely be the envy of any knight.

Try as I might I could not cleanse my mind of choleric, jealous thoughts toward the married d'Alencon. It was usually deemed acceptable behavior of nobles to pursue extra-marital romance. Most marriages were arranged for political expedience, and love was not a consideration. But this was JEANNE, and his winsome ways were odious and profane to me. Anger would sometimes rise in naked resentment from within my breast—palpable, like regurgitated indigestive in one's throat—choking off any other thoughts. I was in such a mood that fateful night when Cedric and Hamish confronted me after evening victuals.

Hamish had come to Chinon to deliver an inspiring standard for Jeanne's newly formed company. It was a glorious Annunciation scene, sure to galvanize its followers. I had forgotten about their threat to deflower me prior to battle and soon discovered refusal was not an option. Truthfully, I offered little resistance, for my mind was in a rebellious and depressed state. To my mild embarrassment, they had also brought along a small entourage of fellow libertines. They explained these would be some of the men I would live and die with, so this was an opportune time for our first foray together. The three others were Etienne de Vignolles (known as La Hire), Allain Bussier (known as Buzzy) and Gilles de Rais.

I knew La Hire was a sometimes fighting mate of Cedric's. He was a brigand for hire who led his own brigade and had a reputation for efficient ruthlessness. Of de Rais I knew little, except that he came from wealth and was a friend of La Hire's. It was common custom for the privileged to have clean-shaven faces, but de Rais indulged himself with a small red beard upon his chin. He seemed especially enamored of it, as he had the habit of constantly tugging at it. I subsequently noticed that he even died it blue on occasion. So there we went five well-seasoned, fierce firebrands and a virgin, to do battle in the brothels of Chinon.

As we toured the steep cobbled streets of Chinon outside the castle, I found comfort in our number. With all the preparations for a major battle, various miscreants and rabble naturally surfaced from Lucifer's den. Enforcers of the peace were either preoccupied with battle arrangements or simply ignored most transgressions during such times. As I was to discover later, our little group was as chilling and barbarous as any—especially one Gilles de Rais. He seemed to hold some measure of sway over our motley group. It was only later I discovered that he was a close confidant of Georges La Tremoilles, who in turn was a close advisor of the Dauphin.

Cedric and La Hire were like the two Pillars of Hercules with Cedric only slightly larger the La Hire. La Hire was an ostentatious man, with a flair for garish dress. He was rough-hewn, but certainly more likable than de Rais. His scarlet cloak had many tiny bells sewn upon it and he claimed each bell was for a foe that had dared to cross his path and not survived to see another sunrise. These bells, he said, served as a dissonant warning to others. Buzzy was more like Hamish—shorter and paunchier in stature, but with a wit and joie de vivre which entertained others and us as we tried to pay homage to every inn in Chinon.

La Hire was explaining to me that he used to pound cobblestones into roadways and now pounded men instead. Coarsely laughing at himself after an enormous belch, he showed me his massive hands, one of which swallowed both of mine. La Hire, he explained, was the iron-shod pounding tool used to drive cobblestones into place. How fitting, I thought, for him to be called *the mallet*. Without warning a boisterous bellow erupted from Cedric, as he slammed his empty mug upon the rough planked table.

"Tis time lads, tis time. Tis time for young Alex to enter manhood."

"Aye, tis time indeed," echoed Hamish.

"From proper experience, I know just the place. Though not cheap, I highly recommend the *Fleur de Lys.* It is but a spear shot away," offered Buzzy.

"Very well, lads, let us be off then," ordered Cedric.

With great laughter and many lewd remarks I was prodded and pulled along, while offering only token resistance. I had exercised some caution on my volume of beer so as not to lose my wits as I had in Tours. I had perhaps four pints through the evening, but the others had quaffed two or three times that amount. We were a roistering, swaggering, staggering lot, cuffing anyone who dared obstruct our path. Particularly crude was de Rais, as he tried to fondle a young passing couple who likewise seemed to be in such a sottish state. La Hire dragged him away, admonishing that he must wait, because we had other business to attend to.

There was a simple, small wooden sign hanging over the door with three white flowers upon it. I expected the inside to be much like the other inns we had attended that evening, but was pleasantly surprised. The floor was planked and swept clean. It stunk only slightly of beer. There was another most pleasant scent, which reminded me of springtime fragrances in the Bois Chenu forest—melilot and pine perhaps. There was something about the scent and surroundings that was distinctly feminine. Perhaps, I thought, I have spent too much time with my smelly, incorrigible companions. This was obviously a finer establishment and all, except for de Rais, complimented Buzzy on his choice. De Rais complained that he had been here before and had not been happy with the service. Given his churlish nature that was not surprising, I mused to myself. There were only two other patrons and they looked like proper gentlemen, sitting in the corner sipping their beer, with mellow smiles upon their faces.

As we were sitting ourselves at a planked table, a door behind the bar swung open and out flounced one of the largest ladies I have ever encountered. She approached, or rather flowed toward us, in her filmy yet proper gown. Opening her arms expansively, she gushed with an excited shrill, "Buzzy, Buzzy my puppy, Buzzy my pony. Where have you been, you scoundrel?"

She enveloped him as he laughed uproariously and tried to lift her. She was a pleasant woman to look at, but exceedingly large in every way, especially the breasts.

"Have you brought all these friends for a visit, mon amour?"

"We are here on a special mission, Celeste, ma cheriee. But first, we are very thirsty tonight."

Buzzy explained my delicate condition, much to my embarrassment, as she poured a round of ale. Finishing her task at hand she conversed in a genial and flirtatious manner with all. Celeste then came round the bar and proceeded to *inspect* me.

"My, he's a handsome one. Looks healthy too." She moved within breathing distance of me and her scent was not the least unpleasant. In fact, her proximity was causing me to perspire and her floral redolence excited me. "You know, Buzzy, I might be tempted to initiate this one myself. He seems delectable, as long as the hardware works." My throat was parched as the dust blowing through a withered vineyard. Reaching for my mug, I shakily brought it toward my suddenly scorched lips. It was then she grabbed my crotch and playfully, but firmly, squeezed my member. My throat constricted, permitting no ale to pass. Jerking the tankard from my mouth, ale ran down my chin. From my chin, the cold wetness of the beer slopped directly onto my crotch. I had been half hard, but now my penis shot up like the freed arm of a catapult. Her eyes grew wide and her mouth gaped, but she emitted only a slightly startled, "Ohh!"

After a moment, she smiled broadly and broke into a throaty laugh, eliciting laughter from my curious companions as well. "Gentlemen, this is no boy. As much as I would love to bed this young horse, I will forego that pleasure and send him up to the lovely young Isabeau, if he promises me his rapture for another visit." She smiled wickedly, giving my member another squeeze before finally relinquishing it. And it was well that she did, as I was embarrassingly close to releasing my tension.

"Pray tell my winsome wench, who is this lovely Isabeau of which you speak?" Cedric said with a decided slur to his words.

"Ahh, my good sir and much-muscled, mountainous specimen of a man, allow me the pleasure of etching her portraiture upon your minds," Celeste answered with surprising eloquence.

"By all means," chimed in Hamish, slapping the table with impaired emphasis and almost falling off his stool.

"She is a breath of fresh air after a spring shower. Her demeanor warms you, like the sun breaking through the morning mist. She is not yet twenty years, but has the wit and grace of one much older."

"Such as you perhaps?" de Rais cut in with unadorned sarcasm.

She turned to him and there seemed to be a spark of recognition. Her puzzled gaze turned to a cold glare. Looking back at me, her beneficent smile returned, and she continued.

"Her body is only now reaching perfect maturity, yet it still retains the resilience and sauciness of youth. In a short time with me as her instructress, she has learned the tricks of our trade almost to perfection. Soon she will rival me as the virtuoso of this fine establishment."

There was a snort from de Rais and he opened his mouth to speak, but a sudden jingling of bells foretold an elbow by La Hire.

"Sacre bleu, my girthsome cheriee," Buzzy chortled, "You are the one with words to make a man's appendage permanently hard. Take me to your boudoir and I will make amends for my absence, if you promise not to strip my purse bare."

"Dear Buzzy, for being so tardy it is unlikely you will leave here with any purse at all, but you will be grinning from ear to ear."

This brought on raucous laughter from everyone, including the mellow gentlemen in the corner.

"And what of your other whores? I want a young one and she needn't be experienced," de Rais broke in, fouling the levity of the moment. We all looked at him askance.

"My other ladies are busy for the night, I'm so sorry to say, sire," Celeste replied with gossamer-thin veiled contempt.

Cedric suddenly burst forth with a rollicking drinking song, thumping his empty mug on the table. Everyone happily joined in to alleviate the tension and Celeste called out for more ale. A very old man hobbled out from behind the bar and our mugs were soon replenished. After negotiating briefly with Buzzy and Cedric, Celeste then rose. Smiling almost demurely, she motioned for me to follow her up to the loft. She winked at Buzzy and said, "I'll be back for you. I want to ride that pony I've been missing."

Looking at Buzzy, I couldn't imagine his grin getting any bigger that it already was.

Oh the poignancy of my first experience, sweetly piquant, indelibly etched in my mind. There were three loft rooms that I could see, as I waited nervously in the hall for Celeste to come back out of the far room. I was not at all sure of what to expect, but I was met with a most pleasurable vision as they emerged.

She was slender, and though not a classical beauty, seemed to have an inner allure that overflowed its sumptuous vessel. Her aura radiated like warmth from a hearth. Her demure smile struck me as being like the sun just before it crests the eastern horizon on a clear morn. Celeste could see I was happily agog so she quickly introduced us and left with a maternal smile upon her face. Or, could that have been a contented business lady's smile? It matters not, for whether this girl was a virgin or a whore, I was smitten.

Her hair was luxuriously long and a light, reddish brown. Her complexion was most fair with a hint of freckles. The eyes were glistening emeralds of a greenish blue hue, and she possessed a full-lipped, rather broad mouth. Unfortunately, her nose was crooked like a dog's hind leg. For me however, it only seemed to enhance the character of her beauty.

Isabeau later explained that the spiteful matron of her orphanage had first broken her nose with a ladle, and more recently a dissatisfied client bent on sodomy rearranged it. She laughed with dark humor and said that she now would allow no man ANY measure of DISsatisfaction. She perhaps had had a wretched life, but still seemed to possess a rare indomitable spirit. And it shone through—shone through any disfigurement—shone through any adversity. As I later discovered she could outshine the sun when showered with a little love. She reminded me very much of my other *sunshine*, but I digress from my bawdy tale.

Without a word she gave me a sly, but seductive smile that would captivate even crusty old Lucifer's icy heart. Those eyes—those eyes were as stars—dancing with delight in the anticipation of pleasure. Taking me by my fidgeting hand she led me into her den of pleasures.

Her boudoir was a simple, windowless affair. The bare-timbered, sloped ceiling was so low that I had to duck under the main beam. There was a waist-high bed set against the far wall. The white blankets were drawn back from a clean-sheeted, wool stuffed mattress. And again, there was that alluring melilot clover fragrance that I had noticed earlier.

She pushed me down upon the bed, and stepped back to disrobe in a most seductive manner. "As you know, sire, my name is Isabeau, but my friends call me Izzy. I hope you like what you see, because it is for you to enjoy. Think of me as your toy and I will think of you as mine. Do you remember the anticipation of a new toy as a child, however simple? Well I am that new toy. What do you think of it? Would you like to play?"

She had untied the chenille about her waist and slipping the emerald gown past her shoulders let it fall to the floor. I could simply say that she wore nothing underneath, but that would be a disservice. There was enough candlelight in the room to behold the creamiest white unblemished skin. No fluffy, effulgent white summer cloud could boast alabaster perfection such as she. Her shoulders were delicate, but not bony. She instinctively drew them back and thrust her breasts forward—offering them. Her breasts were as two large pears upon a tree. They were capped by two swollen, pink rosebuds reaching skyward. Following my eyes, she placed her small hands under and around them, squeezing as she did so. This engorged the nipples, causing them to stand out like ripe dates. Moving toward me she presented them to my face and I obediently drew one into my mouth. She had such a fresh scent about her that my head swam with euphoric delirium. When I bit down lightly she flinched, yet pulled my head suffocatingly closer and whispered, "Be gentle, my prince. They are for sucking, not for eating. Oohh, yes, that's it. Let me help you out of this hindering apparel."

Gently pushing me onto my back, she straddled me and began to untie my blouse. I rested my hands upon her flared hips, kneading their firmness and the soft fleshy protuberance of her buttocks. Gazing downward, I beheld a gillyflower-like blossom of red orange down, growing profusely at the juncture of her thighs. What a marvelous coincidence, I thought. Dispensing my blouse, she bent forward to kiss me upon the lips. Ohh, what word can better describe rapture? Her lips were tender and sweet, sweet and wet as warm honey, almost sticky, with just a hint of mint. And her tongue, her tongue did things that robbed me of any breath in my body. Presently, she moved down to my chest and I gasped for air. While kissing about my navel she deftly undid the ties of my breeches and slowly pulled them downward. Part way down she giggled with delight. "Oho, we are twins, we are twins … Oh my—*OHHH!*"

I was acutely embarrassed. Desperately wishing not to be an *outre rara avis* in the eyes of this erotic angel, I attempted to cover myself.

"No, no my prince. Do not be ashamed. Celeste told me you were prodigious, but… " and she gently pulled my hands away, "Ahh, we will do our best and I am sure neither one of us will be disappointed. We will just have to go a little slow, that is all." She smiled that seductive smile and bade me to lay back. Those eyes, those eyes were as stars in the night, dancing with delight, in anticipation of.

Dispensing with my breeches, she knelt between my legs and took my burgeoning self between her two petite hands. Drawing my minimal foreskin slowly back she looked at it with what seemed great curiosity and veneration. For my part it was good to be lying down, for I was dizzy and weak with passion. Slowly, she stroked me and began to kiss the underside up to the crown—and then it happened. Beyond my control, a euphoric sensation rose rapidly from my loins with intumescing urgency. My hips involuntarily jerked upward and Izzy exclaimed, "Oh damn, damn, damn."

It did not deter her, however, for as my seed shot into the air she stroked me faster. I could not help but cry out in ecstasy. Then as the rapturous convulsions began to subside she did an astonishing thing. She put the head of my shaft in her mouth and began to suckle it. This renewed the convulsions and ecstasy to an excruciating degree until I was drained and cried out for mercy.

It took a while for my senses to return and when they did she had hardly moved. Her head laid upon my belly, with my partly withered appendage still in her grasp.

"I, I am sorry Izzy. It just came and I could do nothing for it."

"Do not worry, Alex, my young prince. I should have realized this being your first time that such a thing might happen. Oho, what have we here? Is our young soldier coming to attention again? Why, yes, just as I suspected. He is far from finished."

She was fondling me and I was rapidly rising to her ministrations. But first I had queries for her that begged to be asked.

"Izzy you must tell me why you placed my, my member in your mouth as I was… "

"Spewing your seed, my dear, is what I call it. The greater enhancement of your pleasure was my goal, especially since it was most premature. It is a method many men enjoy."

"It was incredible. But what of you? Do women spew when they do that? Do we not have to couple to procreate? And would a man suckle a woman's quim?"

"Yes, yes my curious one, people must copulate to procreate

and that is how women *spew*, as you say, though in a different manner than men. I do not think men would suckle a female's quim, but I am only twenty years into my young life so perhaps I know not everything."

I asked her if I might make a closer inspection of her quim, and with mild hesitation she acceded. I found it a most strangely exciting little creature. It had a musky yet provocative odor, and its nearness was causing me a heightened state of arousal. On an instinctive whim I did what she had done by kissing and then suckling at the lips. At first she flinched and drew back slightly, but as I persisted she relaxed and even presented her quim to my face at a more advantageous angle. She murmured breathlessly, "Ohh, sire, you do that wonderfully. No man has ever done that for me. Ahh, yes, do that with your tongue if, if you please. Oh yes, there, yes. Oh, ohh, Celeste could do no better."

I raised my head in surprise. "What was that you said Izzy? What was that about Celeste?"

"Oh, never mind that, my prince. It was, well, it was when I came to work for Celeste a year past. She told me it was part of my training and demonstrated how she liked it done. Not to worry, cherie, it is even more exciting when you do it."

I was confused, but decided this was not the time to dwell on confusing things and returned to the pleasurable matters at hand. No sooner had I returned to my experimentations that I noticed a bounteous secretion emanating from her quim. Her murmurings were becoming more urgent and I wondered if I was causing her pain. When I looked up into her eyes, they seemed glazed and in a dream-like state.

"I think I am ready for you my prince. Perhaps another time we could experiment further, but now is the time for you to, how do they say, dip your quill in the inkpot?" Pulling me up and on to my back she swung around and straddled my thighs. "Please be gentle at first and allow me to ease you in, dear Alex."

I was not sure of what to do, so I was quite content for Izzy to lead. Upon her knees she grasped my tumescent appendage at the base and positioned it at her quim. Slowly, slowly it seemed to disappear within her and it was with great difficulty that I was able to keep myself from thrusting or moving. Both of us emitted many groans and moans throughout the process. As she moved up and down rhythmically I once again could feel that indescribable urgency beginning to churn within my loins. This time, however, it was not so sudden and with incredible pleasure and satisfaction I felt both controlled and controlling. Izzy leaned forward and as we kissed deeply we both erupted in cataclysmic rapture.

"Oh my dear, dear prince, I don't understand. This never happens. I am here for the pleasure of men, not for the pleasure of Izzy," she lamented after we had regained a measure of composure.

"Izzy, what do you mean? If I were to die now, I would die a happy and fulfilled man."

"Thank you, kind sir. And thank you for your tenderness and caring. I have not had such an experience for a long while. I am proud to be your first and I hope you think well enough of me to visit your adoring Izzy again."

"No doubts could shadow my thoughts of you Izzy. You were all that I could hope for and more."

Bounding down the steep stairs I doubt that I touched but two. With a warrior's whoop I announced my coming to the faithful followers. La Hire, de Rais, and the now three gentlemen stood and applauded with great hurrahs. Hamish was snoring upon a bench and Cedric was slumped over on a table, glutted to insensibility. Celeste emerged from the back room and joined in the applause.

"A round for the house on Alex del Aries. A man among men," I announced loudly, with my chest puffed out and my head among the clouds. There was more applause and great guffaws, not the least appreciated and encouraged by Celeste. She even made sure the dormant ones were served to fatten her purse, but I was in such a state of bliss that I cared not.

After quaffing the celebratory ale in short order, La Hire and de Rais were chafing to return to their barracks. Looking upon poor Cedric, I wondered who might have the strength to assist our hibernating bear.

"Not to worry about our slumbering stallions. They are safe here and I will rouse them out at the break of dawn. Buzzy sleeps with a smile upon his face, but I may have more to say about that to the lazy lout," Celeste cackled suggestively.

The other three gentlemen bid adieu and were on their way. "Well, I must return to my lodging also, for my good mistress Jeanne will need me for quintain practice in the morn," I proclaimed.

"Yes, if you would be so kind as to send these besotted beauties homeward at the cock's crow we will be obliged," La Hire agreed.

With that we took our leave and staggered back up the steep cobbled streets to the castle. It seemed peculiar to me that de Rais was now in a much-mollified mood. Perhaps it was the copious ale consumed that becalmed his ill-tempered nature—or perhaps, more the likely, darkness was his cloak of comfort. I did not dwell long on such matters, for my thoughts were more of being pleased with my newly discovered worldly ways.

"Hold Alex, hold. What is thy rush? I must stop and relieve myself of all this ale. Sacrebleu, what a foul pity and waste of fine ale so laboriously acquired." La Hire chuckled at his own humor and we stopped at an alleyway to relieve ourselves.

"Oh ho, what are those queer noises coming from this alley?" whispered de Rais as we performed our task. Listening more closely I could indeed discern some grunting sounds, but could see naught in the dark recess. Perhaps it is animals mucking about in the garbage, I surmised. Finishing my business, I looked beside me to see de Rais obscenely stroking his member. La Hire meanwhile, seemed to have no end to his ale storage and punctuated his discharge with rude farts. My mood was suddenly weary of these two inveterate churls.

"Well, my good gentlemen, the evening has much exhausted

me. I care not whether those noises be man or beast for I must make haste to my barracks. A squire's day starts afore a knight's, you know."

Whilst they peered into the dark alley I hastened off, leaving them to their curiosity. Indeed, I was back at the Coudray tower and blissfully asleep upon my palliasse long before them.

The next morn, as I broke my fast at the barracks, Cedric and Buzzy entered wearing dour looks upon their ruddy faces. "Ho, ho gentlemen. You look like you have just waged a mighty war ... and lost." I slapped my knee and laughed, as did the other soldiers around the long table.

Cedric sat beside me and after a time said, "You know, Alex, I would wish for my demeanor to be the after effects of ale, but I'm sorry to say it is not." I looked at him in silence and he finally continued, haltingly, "On our way back to the barracks we came across a gruesome discovery. Tis a shame. It started out as a bright, fair morn. That young couple we crossed paths with last night near the Fleur de Lys. We noticed an arm sticking out of a dark alleyway and I thought it a drunk, but Buzzy went to investigate and called me back. ACHH, MERCIFUL MOTHER MARY, I wished he hadn't. The young lad had his breeches about his ankles. Perhaps he was caught in an awkward situation with his lady friend. He was stabbed in the back of his neck up into the skull—fairly bloodless—instant death. But the young lady. Ich dinna ken. Ich dinna ken."

I had never seen this battle hardened warrior in such a vexed state before. He pushed his bowl away, rose and left without saying more. I looked across the table at a quiet Buzzy, his brow deeply furrowed and a far-a-away look in his eyes.

"Twas awful, Alex. Even Cedric... " and Buzzy's eyes seemed to wander without seeing.

"What was it Buzzy? What could have happened?"

His eyes narrowed and he spat out with startling vehemence,

"I knew the young wench. She was a friend of my daughter's. She was face down across the end of a barrel with her garments thrown up. And her head … her innocent young face… " Buzzy choked back angry sobs and I knew I did not wish to hear more, but sat transfixed, as did the other soldiers about us. "They cut off her beautiful head and sat it upon the barrel beside her." Buzzy spoke these last words with a whispering, vacant tone and then paused. The silence was like the silence of death, for there were twenty men present and you could not hear a drawn breath.

Finally he continued, "The kids were probably having their fun and caught unawares. Her buttocks were horribly slashed. Dear God, WHY? They were innocents. What are we coming to with this damnable warring and anarchy defiling our land? People are sinking to such baseness. No, not people, *ANIMALS*."

His invective was laced with increasing bitterness. I could stand to hear no more, so I bade him stop and left for my duties.

I walked to the stables on shaky legs to ready Jeanne's steed for tilting. This was a shocking, senseless act, even for these troubled times. A dark thought enshrouded my inner soul, like a black plague. Could it be? Could de Rais and La Hire be capable as such butchery? If so, then was I not responsible as well in God's eyes? Perhaps I could have somehow prevented the tragedy. Had my selfish, lustful thoughts and euphoric state of mind cost the young lovers their lives? Certainly I had been aware of de Rais' foul mood. And what was La Hire capable of? No, I temporized, how could I have known? What could I have done? My suspicions were compelling.

I have done many things in my life not to be proud of though they cause me no great distress. Yet, for this, I cannot help but feel the barbed pangs of culpability.

Chapter Twelve

THE SWORD

THE NEXT two days were very unsettling for me, as I grappled with my inner-self over what I should, or could do, concerning my dire suspicions. It was a blessed distraction to be on an errand with Jeanne to get her saddle adjusted.

Foolish though it might be for me to love Jeanne, worse yet was my inability to dislodge Izzy from my thoughts. We happened to be near the Fleur de Lys and while waiting for the repairs I found myself strolling toward that very establishment. Passing by, I longingly looked up to the loft area of the building's stone and rough-timbered façade. It was windowless, but my eyes nevertheless imagined her sitting there primly, waiting for me and me alone. I was too embarrassed to stop. Winding my way through the throng of mid-day traffic, I glanced back one more time and collided with a lady, spilling the load of bread sticks from her arms. Immediately bending over to assist, we knocked heads sharply, and fateful Saints in heaven be praised, it was Izzy.

We embraced with unabashed delight and she began to chatter away excitedly. About what I know not, for my head was amongst the clouds. Her beauty was enhanced in the light of day. I was smitten all over again.

Helping her into the Fleur de Lys with her booty, I had no sooner deposited the loaves upon the bar then out came the gregarious proprietress. She enveloped me as if I were a long lost lover, swallowing me in her bulk and breasts to drink in her flowery scent. Though a woman of great girth, she moved with agility and dignity. I could see why this paramour would enamor Buzzy. After some small talk I begged of their leave to return to my duties.

"Alex, you devil. You come here on a whim only to tease these hungry ladies. I am still waiting for a sample of that sizeable rapture you promised." Celeste brazenly reached down and squeezed me. Awkwardly, and with reluctance, I had to pull away. "My apologies, dear ladies—with the battle fast approaching there is much to prepare. It is my fondest wish that I could stay, but duty unfortunately is an onerous priority."

The disappointment on Celeste's face was unconcealed and I suspect more for business reasons than that of unrequited rapture. To my delight, Izzy insisted on walking at least part of the way with me.

We spoke of inconsequential things and about the coming battle. I told her of the mistress I served and could detect a subtle coolness, though I explained of Jeanne's chastity and mission. Of herself, she would only say that she was an orphan, and that Celeste was the only mother she has known. When I asked her how she turned out so pleasant and even-tempered she giggled girlishly. "You sir, do not know Izzy as Izzy can sometimes be. I can be devilish and petulant at times. Women sometimes choose their moments to best advantage. We must be wily to outwit you irascible men."

I laughed at this and she smiled coquettishly. "I fear you are more worldly-wise than I, sweet Izzy, and you have me at a disadvantage. I wish I were wealthy and could afford you everyday. But alas, I have but a few deniers in my purse. Oh, damn! Here we are at my destination already."

As we stopped, there was a moment of awkward silence and then a blossoming smile broke across her face.

"Well, my fair prince, I find you much to my liking, so fear not the lack of gold. Tomorrow is my own day. I enjoy walking along the Vienne, especially since spring is in the air and if you would be so inclined… "

"Oh yes, yes, that would be wonderful," I stammered.

"Very well then—I will meet you at the bridge when the sun is high, cherie."

With that she put her arms around my neck and gave me a lingering, exotic kiss that made my head float among the clouds. With an impish grin, she winked at me, and was gone amongst the throng.

I was still in a daze as I entered the saddlery works. To my shock, Jeanne was just inside the entrance with an uncharacteristic black look upon her face. Her eyes were fierce and squinting, piercing me like arrows.

"Where have you been Alex, you laggard? Do you call yourself a squire, making me wait like this?"

"No, maid Jeanne. I mean yes … I mean… "

"And WHO was that you were so lewdly embracing in public?"

I had initially felt the color draining from my face and now I could feel a rouge wave surging from neck to forehead. Completely taken aback, my mouth was agape. How could I possibly lie to Jeanne?

"Well, speak up, Alex. She dressed and acted like a harlot. Could this be so?"

I was mortified. Bare and exposed like a wretched rat, debased, vitiated. I felt my eyes burning and I blinked away searing tears. "I … Please forgive me, Jeanne. I just … Please forgive me."

My voice was faltering and trailing away to a whisper. She shook her head in a sorrowful manner and spoke to me for the last time on this day.

"Let us be gone then."

So perplexed and distraught was I that the evening victuals were of no succor to my churning belly. I decided to return to the bosom of the church to seek guidance. I had not frequented masses of late and felt ashamed more for that than any wrongdoing of the flesh. Having tasted the potent elixir of love, I could not understand why God would bestow this facility upon us if it were such a base sin. I begged of God's forgiveness and that Jeanne may not disown this humble squire. In a final act of despairing piety I prostrated myself at the altar, quietly weeping and beating my palms upon the stone floor. When I rose to leave, it occurred to me, my father had subjected himself to similar penance and that too was in relation to the love of a woman. It was then I sensed, without seeing, that I was not alone in the chapel. As I left, I saw Jeanne in the wings. She overtly ignored my gaze and went forward to the altar where she knelt for her evening rumination.

As a beaten dog, I dragged my heels back to my lodging. I looked upon the Templar frescoes, seeking some sort of sign or direction from my ancestors. How might I placate my beloved Jeanne? But what of Izzy? She was, it seemed, an innocent, victimized by our brutal society. Was it wrong what she did to survive by her wiles? I sighed loudly, tasting the bile of sardonic fatalism. For yes, even my mother was a prostitute. Should I have loved Magdalena less, had I known her now? I think not.

Extinguishing the candle and laying upon my palliasse, I was trying to ignore the cacophonous snoring of de Metz when a possible avenue of reprieve occurred to me. So perfect was the inspiration that I bolted straight up in bed. Like the sun erupting in immediate brilliance from behind blackened clouds, a denouement presented itself. I could retrieve my father's sword and present it to Jeanne. I had no desire to fight with such cutting instruments myself. It would be richly symbolic for her—a significant gift from me to prove my adoration and absolute allegiance. With renewed hope, I vowed to arise early and polish my plan. I allowed a new measure of confidence to seduce my wearied head and joined de Metz in harmonious repose.

Rising before the sun on a cool crisp spring day, I was stoking our fire when I was blessed with further inspirations. I fervently wished to keep my rendezvous with Izzy, yet did not want to further alienate Jeanne. I now realized, as much as I loved Jeanne, her God was the love of her life. And if ever that should change, there was d'Alencon. I was but her lowly squire. Together we had come far in a short time, but it was she who was the darling of destiny. I would have to find my own destiny and be content to help my true love succeed in hers. Perhaps our destinies would one day coalesce, but I was having grave doubts of that. As a young man, I now realized, I needed more than spiritual love and that would be the best I could hope for from Jeanne. I wanted to further explore the person of Izzy. It seemed my appendage had its own agenda and moral scruples were not its concern.

My inspirations were thus: Firstly, I must convince Jeanne to let me leave this day to retrieve my father's sword from Fierbois. Secondly, I would let it be known that Jeanne had clairvoyantly foretold of a providential sword to be found at Saint Catherine's chapel. God willing that I find it there, the sword could be the icon to represent her legitimacy and a portentous sign of imminent righteous victory. Thirdly, the timing would allow me to keep my rendezvous with Izzy.

Perhaps, dear Izzy, men can be wily as well, I reflected. I had some misgivings about the subterfuge involved, but the expedience of my plan made it the pre-eminent solution. The sun was cresting the eastern horizon, replacing the cold grays with warm yellows as I rushed to where I knew Jeanne would be. Though the morning was cool, I was warm with apprehension, as I waited discreetly for her in the chapel's vestibule. When she finally emerged, her temperament was one of exuberance. It was to my great relief that she greeted me cordially and warmly.

"And a merry morn to you, Alex, on this dazzling spring day with which God has blessed us. You are back again so soon for solace and forgiveness in God's house?"

"Uhh, yes, yes Jeanne and a merry morn to you. Pray tell, might we be working with the quintain again today?"

"Perhaps only briefly—I have an interview with the Dauphin's military leaders to discuss how arrangements are progressing and the deportment date."

"That is marvelous, La Pucelle. We will finally move forward in achieving God's will," I said, avoiding any discussion of yesterday's fiasco. "I, uh, I had a wonderful thought and I am sure it would be worth mentioning at your interview today." Her eyebrows rose with interest as I unveiled my plan in the most positive light. To my surprise and pleasure she was immediately receptive and, as I espoused the benefits, became enthusiastic.

"Yes, Alex, you are wise. Such an oracle would serve God's cause. I must meet with the advisors at midday. You should leave then and take my chestnut, palfrey mount, who has an apparent aversion to the quintain."

I could hardly believe such auspicious fortune. Certainly the reverie with my Templar ancestors last night must have cast a positive light upon my fate. That, or God had blessed me for last evening's penance. As I went about my day with a decided spring in my step, I thanked both God and my ancestors. My world was well. I was back in my adored maid's good graces and could serve her cause auspiciously. Oh, and yes, my unconscionable appendage was pleased as well.

As I think back now I realize, though I loved Jeanne, I was already giving up on that dream. Izzy was there to embrace and she intoxicated me with passion. She taught me things most men have yet to dream of. That afternoon on the Vienne will always have a special place in my memory.

I pulled her up on my palfrey, across my lap. She kissed me long and tender, wet and warm. We rode down the river's edge and her long red tresses were streaming past my face, tickling my ear.

"Go faster, go faster my prince," she exclaimed, above the rushing wind and splashing hooves. She laughed and laughed, as on we charged in dangerous delight. We shed our garments and swam as carefree children on that warm spring day. The Vienne was still icy cold, but even that could not cool our fiery ardor.

It was late afternoon before I actually left for Fierbois. I rode hard and was exhausted when finally arriving late that night. After sleeping in the stable with my horse, I met Cedric, Buzzy and one of the Dauphin's personal clerics, as prearranged. There were some inquisitive looks from Cedric and Buzzy as we met outside Saint Catherine's chapel. My bedraggled look and separate arrival had tweaked their interest, but I pressed on with matters at hand.

"The Maid said it would be here," I said, pointing at my feet. Close behind us came the local Abbe having been forewarned of our proposed excavations. Now that there were credible witnesses I prayed God the sword was indeed here. We tilled down two handspans over the area, and to my horror, found nothing. I was holding my head in a woeful manner as the others looked at me skeptically.

After a short period of silence the Abbe offered in a timorous, squeaky voice, "Well, if the location of the chancel is significant, it was moved from over there, perhaps four or five epiphanies past."

Unable to restrain my sudden joy at this revelation, I grabbed the startled elfin Abbe and kissed him upon his bald pate. After but a half handspan of tilling we unearthed the providential icon. It was dirty and rust encrusted, but as we cleaned it the rust fell away to reveal a beautifully crafted weapon. There were five holy crosses carved upon its length (a Templar vestige I was to learn) and an ornate hilt of braided serpents. Everyone was suitably astounded and behind me I could hear a surprised Cedric murmur for my ear only, "I have seen this weapon—this would-be icon."

Upon my return to Chinon, everyone was suitably impressed with the astounding discovery of the providential sword as foretold by Jeanne. In the eyes of most this affirmed her destiny beyond doubt. As I explained to Cedric, sometimes even providence is in need of *Zeus' aegis.*

Chapter Thirteen

On To Orleans

Over the following fortnight before we left for Blois and Orleans, Izzy and I spent every possible moment together. Much to Celeste's annoyance, Izzy complained of sickness, that we might steal away together. Lovesick, Celeste would snort. Suppressing pangs of guilt, I likewise found pretexts to slip away from my duties almost everyday. When the time came for our company's departure it was with great melancholy on my part. I was excited about the looming clash of forces, but somehow realized I was passing from a very special interlude in my life.

Izzy and I had no illusions as to our future. She had no proclivity toward marriage and nor did I. She wished to finish her indenture to Celeste and somehow start her own pre-eminent house of pleasures. Because of her past experiences she wanted no part of being reliant upon anyone but herself. I realized her ambition would be a most difficult feat, but I had no doubt this sprightly, assiduous nymph would succeed. Already she had triumphed over much adversity in her life. I loved her in many ways, but knew it was not our time.

With pomp and ceremony we rode out of Chinon upon equally anxious prancing steeds. There was a large throng of well-wishers along the route. It so happened we passed by the Fleur de Lys and I was thrilled to see Izzy and Celeste among those gathered there.

I was riding between Buzzy and de Rais with Jeanne and de Metz leading our entourage just in front of us. To my chagrin de Rais had been appointed as one of Jeanne's captains and his close presence was unavoidable. Boldly, Buzzy briefly held up the procession, and Celeste fairly pulled him from his mount as he leaned over to embrace her. After accosting his lips with a long sloppy sounding kiss she loosened a long piece of gossamer from the tresses of her hair and wrapped it about his neck. At this, there was much laughter from the gathered throng and an agile Izzy, following example, leapt up to join me on my mount. Playfully, she rode with me a ways to the great delight of the onlookers.

"My brave soldier, God speed you safely on your noble quest. Come back and see me someday, as I will be a rich and famous courtesan. I will miss you terribly." These things she said with a mixture of laughter and solemnity. As she was about to disembark she noticed de Rais smirking at my side and her countenance blackened. "Watch out for this one, cheriee, for he is the evil devil who rearranged my nose." And with a last delicious kiss she slipped away.

I swung my gaze from her fading figure and there was murder in my heart as I glared at the vile de Rais. My doubts were receding that he was the bestial rapist loose in Chinon, for more than one instance of unexplained butchery had occurred recently.

But something most strange then happened. I could sense something else, something intangible, and I could feel a mortal chill course through me. I looked up ahead and with a start, realized it was Jeanne. She was half turned around in her saddle and those dark eyes were boring into me. When she locked on to my eyes, I felt as though struck. There was no question that she was filled with rage, perhaps even jealous rage. Once again, like a black wave, a profound sense of shame swept over me.

It was an interesting, but uneventful trip to Blois. Our military procession gradually became a cortege. At each village there were a few more curious and adventuresome, who having heard of the savior maid, appended themselves to our force. By the time we reached Blois it was a rather ragtag looking column, but its numbers were nonetheless heartening. Our immediate group had swollen appreciably before even leaving Chinon. There was another squire, appointed by the Dauphin, one Jean d'Aulon from Barrois. He seemed immediately devoted to Jeanne. But I thought him somewhat timid and knew he could not possess the sort of insight into Jeanne as did this birth-mate.

There were two pages and two heralds, as well as a personal chaplain from Tours appointed to Jeanne. Because of my busy personal schedule, I had not even met this cleric until we reached Blois. Upon hearing of him, I was most intrigued that his name happened to be Jean Pasquerel—the very name of the priest who had cured and converted my father. At first opportunity I approached him privately and expressed my curiosity. With a beatific smile he readily acknowledged that it was indeed he who knew and had blessed my father.

"Yes, my son, Alex, it was my most joyous conversion and healing. I have experienced many blessed events, but Miguel's exorcising was of particular satisfaction for me when he took up the cloth."

"Do you know Father, if he is still alive and where he might be? Cedric said only that he was returning to Portugal."

"Yes, that is true. In fact I had a letter from him perhaps two epiphanies past. And how fares that gentle giant, Cedric?"

"Oh, did you not know? Cedric rides with us. I believe he was near the rear with our spare horses and is currently quartering them. But what news of my father pray tell" I prodded, impatiently.

"Oh yes, hmmm, I believe that was his second letter." He thought aloud, almost absent-mindedly. "He knew I was lector at the convent of Tours and could communicate through church channels. He was at the Saint Augustine heritage a good while, but left there to become a chaplain and confessor for Enrique of Portugal. Ahh, I see by your mystified look ... a, yes, Enrique is the third son of King Joao.

This prince seems to enjoy building sailing ships and spends most of his time at Sagres near the port of Lagos. That is from where your father last wrote me. Prince Enrique also has the title Protector of the Order of Christ in Portugal. I gather Miguel might have been somehow associated with that troublesome brotherhood, but thankfully, it has died out in most parts of our Christian World." Pausing reflectively, he continued, "Anyway, I hope he stays away from those devilish ships. They just might sail off the earth into the abyss."He laughed awkwardly at this, but I could tell he did not doubt the reality of his jest.

"This is most interesting news, kind Father. Someday I would like to once again see my father for I was but an infant. Firstly though, we must follow the Maid and drive the blasphemous English goddams from our land."

"Yes I hope, nay, I most fervently hope, those who should constantly take the Lord's name in vain would suffer retribution. This horrible, never-ending conflict has protracted the Great Schism and pitted brother against brother. I pray God the maid is our salvation. Oh dear, I sometimes do ramble on. You will have to excuse me my son, my duties await. May God bless you and protect you."

"Thank you Father, you have been most enlightening." I was excited about finally reaching some resolution regarding my father's fate, and comforted by this, I felt more at peace within. I was now content to deal with the present, and let the winds of destiny decide my future.

The countryside from Blois to Orleans was mostly flat, with a good portion of it cleared for tilling and seeding. Much of it was now overgrown, for terror and anarchy stalked our land as the locusts had Canaan. There would likely be no crops again this year. We were cautious in our advance, sending several small parties of scouts ahead. Although in Armagnac territory, we did not want to risk being intercepted by any sizeable marauding enemy bands, as a good part of our force was still making preparations in Blois.

Orleans had been under siege for seven months. Count Dunois, the bastard brother of the Duke of Orleans, had been staunchly defending the city. The Duke, having been previously captured, was being held for ransom in the Tower of London. As they were attacking his city and he was unable to defend it, the contemptible English were breeching commonly accepted rules of civility in warfare. Jeanne in particular felt this opened the gate to allow the use of certain tactics previously shunned. She confided in me that she would press for quick forays to keep the enemy off balance. There would be no more 'wait until the honorable foe is prepared'. Honor was no longer respected and upheld as in times past. Perhaps a change in attitude and tactics was in order. It was brash of a novice like Jeanne to even think such thoughts and it caused heated disagreement among the staid military hierarchy. She even outrageously predicted it could save lives.

Inexperience was both Jeanne's foible and puissance. More than once it placed her in, and retrieved her from, the doorway of disaster. For her, fear was fictional, or at most an irrelevant emotion. God was truth and she was his representative of righteousness. Thus did she believe, and thus did she exude. It seems incredible that this girl could excite and unite such a force of myopic military might and miscreants. The irascible La Hire—the despicable de Rais'—the seasoned Powers—the irrepressible Bussiers. It was true. I was there. I saw it. I lived it. There was no doubt. She was salvation, spiritually and desperately, for this oft-beaten rabble. She was the wave, and we rode upon her crest. I have seen much in life, but nothing more miraculous than this simple farm girl with visions—visions personified by rapture.

Cresting the escarpment on the south side of the Loire River, my eyes drank in a panoramic view of Orleans and its milieu. I could easily discern that Orleans was a formidable fortress. It was bracketed, at various distances, by several small enemy fortifications. The landscape was slightly undulating and covered by a mix of wild growth, badly pocked by warring activities. No fields had been tended, and with the growth of spring, it left one with an impression of an unkempt, colorful beard. The wide Loire ran high and brown with the rich sediments and melt-waters of springtime. Ahead of us to the east could be seen the Tourelles fortress and its twin towers protecting the bridge to the south entrance of Orleans. There was a small deserted monastery in front of the Tourelles. The south side of the bridge had been breached—dismantled by the Orleans defenders to prevent access by the Anglais.

It was decided to make contact with the defenders of Orleans first. The eastern entrance, the Burgundy Gate, was still accessible on the Loire's north bank. This was the sustaining lifeline for the city's inhabitants, but the noose was slowly and inexorably closing. The problem was that we were approaching from the south side of the Loire. We widely skirted the monastery and Tourelles. The English had captured the Tourelles fortress and it was now their stronghold, choking off the usual southern access. The English may have controlled that crucial point, but it did not allow them access to Orleans.

We met an Orleans group of defenders who, led by Dunois, had earlier crossed the Loire in expectation of our arrival. Jeanne was in a choleric mood as she had hoped to disrupt the Anglais and fight our way to Orleans. It was probably through the influence of La Tremoilles and de Rais that we found ourselves sneaking in the backdoor. This was customary French military caution, avoiding direct engagement or ungentlemanly surprise.

As I think back, and from subsequent events, I believe La Tremoilles was unquestionably serving his own interests. The rotund waddler enjoyed his position of privilege as Charles' advisor and would use any means to protect it. Others had already left this earthly world who had been at odds with him and he was not about to let this vexatious virgin erode his influence. What amazed me most was that his brother, Lord of Jonvelle, was chamberlain in the Dijon court of the hated Burgundian duke, Phillip the Good. Incredibly, such ambivalence of loyalties seemed to escape the Dauphin. Unaware of these political manipulations, a spunky and determined Jeanne came face to face with Dunois—Dunois, the courageous protector of Orleans, he who least expected or deserved the brunt of her wrath.

"Are you the *Bastard of Orleans*?" Jeanne inquired sharply.

"Yes, I am, and happy that you are here," replied Dunois.

"Was it you who suggested I should come on the south side of the river instead of going directly at Talbot and the Anglais?" she pressed.

"Yes, my Maid. And others, cleverer than I, gave this advice, thinking it would better serve the safety of our enterprise."

It was obvious Jeanne was not mollified, but uncharacteristically she held her tongue.

The weather had turned foul and all were bemoaning the impossibility of ferrying across the Loire this day. Jeanne was unfazed and commanded that, as the foul conditions would imminently change, we prepare to cross. The local delegation looked upon her askance, but shortly before sunset, indeed did the winds diminish and a small party of us crossed unscathed. Initially, I was amazed that the English did not challenge us. Perhaps being a sizeable force of several hundred may have been enough to cow them and cause hesitation. As Dunois explained to us, the English had the Tourelles well defended, but their main forces were west and north of Orleans. They had erected several small bastions in those directions from which they harassed and attacked Orleans. Being well fortified with walls higher than two lance lengths, had so far been the Orleans inhabitants' savior. Our timely support would hopefully sway the balance, for should the English cut off the Burgundy Gate, a dire situation would soon become an impossible situation. Yes, the potage of siege and conquest was slowly coming to a boil, but Jeanne was a spice they had not contemplated.

Jeanne was irritably impatient and allowed us little time for irresolute thought. Barely had we banked on the Loire's north shore then she was mounted and away. Dunois' pleadings for a prudent pace fell upon deaf ears as we scrambled to catch up and maintain her pace.

Approaching the Burgundy Gate, darkness was rapidly descending and the sentries' trumpets heralded us. Jeanne called for her standard so that we may enter with proper dignity and eclat. We were exhilarated, for when we passed into the city there was an anxious, elated multitude clamoring to greet their savior. Many torches lit the way and people pushed forward to touch the Maid. Amazingly, for a city under siege, we were showered with medlar, quince and spring gillyflowers. The street was narrow and so filled that a careless torch set Jeanne's standard ablaze. With a brief gallop into an open square Jeanne waved the standard about, extinguishing the flame. This brought a tumultuous cheer and heightened celebrations from those beleaguered and superstitious residents. Such was our welcome and such was the faith generated by rumors preceding us. Jacques Boucher, Mayor of Orleans, received our delegation. We were led to his residence near the city center and sequestered there for the interim.

The next few days my Maid was constantly in council with the local powers and leading captains. Jeanne had previously sent a message from Chinon to the Duke of Burgundy, which went unanswered. The envoy did not return. From Orleans she sent a message to the English commander, Lord Talbot, and again there was no courtesy of a reply. After a second request to Lord Talbot that he withdraw and avoid bloodshed his reply was thus, "Tell this little French cow-girl to return to her goddam farm where she belongs, or I will see her burnt."

Obviously, not one easily rejected, Jeanne rode out on the sabotaged bridge to within haling distance of the Tourelles bastion and demanded they surrender in the name of God. Their reply was a diatribe of insults hurled from behind the walls. I was braced to attack the foul-mouthed *goddams*, especially after they defamed our escort as a bunch of faithless pimps. Jeanne could not comprehend such a coarse response and tears welled up in her eyes. I suspect her sensitive feelings stemmed more from the realization of unavoidable bloodshed than from a smitten amour-propre.

Having discovered that the English captain, John Fastolf, was on the way with reinforcements, de Rais hastened to Blois to speed the marshalling of the rest of our forces and to procure additional supplies. Our group was left in a frustrating and precarious position, but at least I was able to put the delay to profitable use.

Jean de Monteclair was reputedly the premier master gunner of his time. Like Jeanne, he was a Lorrainer, so through her I was able to make his acquaintance and study further the wonders of gunnery. While we were in Chinon, Cedric and Buzzy had taught me many of the intricacies of swordplay, but as afore-mentioned, I was desirous to learn the avant-garde art of gunnery in warfare.

De Monteclair was a very precise person. To operate such weapons of destruction, precision was the difference between life and death. As I discovered, to discharge one of these gargantuan iron tubes could as easily end your life as that of your foes. The technique by which it was primed for ignition meant life or death—especially for the gunner. The ingredients of the magical pounce, if not correct, could result in disaster, success, or nothing. If the weapon was not properly aimed the whole exercise would be either futile or disastrous. It was a trial and error procedure, and hopefully, error did not result in catastrophe. According to de Monteclair this was the future of warfare and he was as animatedly excited about such weaponry as any Frenchman expounding on a passion could be.

Jean was much like his brother Louis, who I had met in Tours. He was almost as short, but even broader and possessed of a barrel chest and powerful arms. Perhaps experimenting with cannons in the foundry gave him such strength, for he could move these weighty tubes around with relative ease. He was not as gruff as his brother and readily took me under his wing when I showed an interest in his forte. A memorable character was he and a true craftsman of cannon.

Grinding, grinding, grinding, finer and finer—it was a laborious task with the mortar and pestle, but Jean insisted I first practice with the ingredients, so that I could appreciate the intricacies of the magical pounce. Jean dispensed the secrets of the death-dealing powder to me reverently, as if he were passing on the Holy Scriptures. I felt much privileged to receive his tutelage. The fact I had spent so much time with Louis did not much impress Jean, for they were adversarial siblings. But being with the Maid from Lorraine, and recommended by an old fighting mate La Hire, I soon became a favorite student and assistant to master gunner Monteclair.

Charcoal, saltpeter and a substance called sulfur were the necromantic ingredients used to deliver death to the enemy's door. The ingredients had to be ground to flour fine consistency, and mixed in exacting proportions. We would use a tincture over four parts saltpeter to a pinch under three parts each of charcoal and sulfur. The proportions were critical, and because of the nature of the ingredients, they had a tendency to settle out and even escape their containers in a cloud of dust if moved about. Many a bombardier and soldier were injured when flame found this floating peril. Another problem was that discharge would leave behind a black residue inside of the cannon. Sometimes after only a couple of firings the cannon would become useless unless arduously scrubbed out.

I was with Jean for only half a fortnight before the real fighting commenced. I learned much over this short period, including about Jean's love affair with ale. I suppose his hazardous profession led him to such indulgence, but he was amazingly resilient from the enervating effects of ale. The same cannot be said for me, for one night he coerced me along on one of his bouts of immoderation. Sorrowful was I the next day, as I forced myself from my palliasse in the workshop. My discomfort became greatly intensified, for I could tell by the foul smell that I must have earlier rid my innards of their sour bile into the waste bucket. But then worse, far worse, I had mistakenly relieved the beer in my belly into the larger bucket of finely ground precious pounce. Oh, woe—woe was I that Jean should see his valued alchemy befouled by this lowly squire. I stirred it up to hopefully dissipate the moisture, but only succeeded in causing it to ball in corn-sized kernels. And then, to my great disconcert, I could hear someone shuffling down the stairs—and I knew that heavy shuffle. I wedged my contretemps under the workbench—barely in time.

"Ho, ho, bonjour my sorry looking young squire, it smells fairly foul in here. Did something disagree with you last night?" This was followed by Jean's dissonant laughter, causing my head yet further anguish.

"Jean, you are a better man than I, for all that ale did not care for my gizzard. Please forgive my weakened state. I am not used to such partakings."

"No worry, Alex. Your constitution will improve with practice," and he laughed heartily once more. "Forgive my laughter, but I am in a fine mood this morning. I think we should fire off a few rounds at those stinking Anglais Goddams. We need to break in my new iron tube. It will never rupture, as I have fortified it with iron banding and it is sorely craving some action. I will take the pounce and you can bring the ignition tools."

My heart almost stopped, for I feared he would look for the bucket that I had fouled. Fortunately, there was another large bucket of pounce and as he hefted that onto his shoulder, I hastened to follow.

Considering that Orleans was under siege, the morning streets were surprisingly busy. My throbbing head did not appreciate of the chaotic din. A passing crier sounded his familiar refrain above the cacophony, "Calling you to bathe, Messire, and steam yourself without delay. Our water's hot and that's no lie."

The luxury of bathing would have been most welcome, especially since public baths were not always available to those under siege. However, his strident urgings only accentuated my head's discomfort.

We climbed up to the highest point of the castle's walls overlooking the south bridge and the Tourelles fortress. Jean had placed his newly reinforced iron tube at the precipice and aimed it toward our foes across the Loire. Jean, obviously feeling far more cheery than I, set about his task with fervor, and a soft intonation of a war chant escaped his lips. Not only was the entire tube constructed of cast-iron, it was braced upon its length by many iron hoops. I was much amused as Jean excitedly showed me the name engraved on the cannon's side. Proud gunners would give a fanciful soubriquet to their preferred weapon of destruction, as they might a favorite child or animal. *The KYNG'S ANOINTER* was boldly embossed along its length.

"This will be a test for you, Alex. I have shown you previously how to load and fire. Now we will do it for real. Speed and accuracy are the goal. I will be your assistant bombardier," Jean said with a broad smile across his ruddy, rouge face.

Nervously, but quickly, I set about my task. Knowing an error in loading or lighting could be the death of us, I found it hard to maintain my sang-froid. First we rolled back the monstrous Anointer on its wooden, spokeless wheels. I then carefully remixed the pounce, as it had a tendency for the ingredients to settle out. Next I filled the barrel, tamping the mixture down until the tube was about one quarter full. Our projectile was a heavy stone, chipped into an almost perfectly round shape. As cast iron balls were much more expensive and difficult to produce stones were more frequently used. I tamped the stone in place and then reached for the quadrant. This sighting instrument was crude, but far better than trying to aim with an unaided eye. I inserted the long end of the quadrant into the repositioned barrel and noted the inclination from the dangling plumb bob.

"I think this is a good angle, Jean. What do you think?"

He shrugged and said, "Perhaps yes, perhaps no. It depends on your pounce mix, the amount, the tamping, the stone weight and the patron Saint of bombardiers. Are you happy with your witches brew, bombardier?"

Looking it over again and gazing at La Tourelles through the dreary morning haze, I reached for the red-hot wire heating in the brazier. This was a tricky process, for I now had to plunge the wire down the vent on top of the cannon's rear to ignite the pounce. I prayed to the patron Saint of bombardiers that my methods were correct. With great histrionics, Jean grabbed his head and ran for cover, sending two on-looking soldiers into fits of laughter. Sweating profusely and filled with anxiety, I plunged the wire into its vent and dove for cover. Looking up, I saw fizzling smoke shooting from the vent and was crestfallen that the cannon had not emitted a might roar. But that was only for a moment, because the monstrous tube suddenly bucked violently and reared back into the wall behind it with a thunderous discharge. Scrambling to the parapet we were disappointed to see our projectile fall well short of its mark.

"DAMN the pounce!" Jean cursed. "No fault of yours Alex. I would have loaded and aimed exactly as you. We will need more pounce and slightly more angle."

Rapidly I reloaded the Anointer, filling it almost half full of pounce and raised the angle slightly with the quadrant. Once again we were short, but at least hit the base of the fortress wall. Now we had the enemy's attention and we could hear them laughing and haranguing us with insults. Jean seemed most pleased by this, as he and the soldiers shouted insults back at the foe while I once again reloaded. Unfortunately, that was about all the damage we could do for the pounce seemed only strong enough to do minimal damage to the fortification's walls. We tried raising the angle, but could not quite reach the inner sanctuary of our tormentors. After three or four firings the cannon bore became fouled with the black grit.

Dejectedly, Jean left me to clean the bore and returned to his shop. As I scrubbed out the Anointer I remembered something Louis de Monteclair had shown me in Tours. He was experimenting with a different lighting method using hemp soaked in saltpeter. When lit, the hemp would burn so intensely that sparks flew. He said this could be much safer, because the bombardier did not have to stand next to the cannon, inserting the hot wire. He could insert the hemp, light it, and head for cover. I had briefly mentioned this to Jean, but since he and his brother were virtually antagonistic competitors, he was not interested in listening. Such stubbornness made no sense to me and I resolved to experiment with the method myself.

Returning to the workshop, I was unable to find Jean. I took the opportunity to soak some hemp in saltpeter and laid it out to dry near the hearth. Later that afternoon when I returned from polishing Jeanne's armor, the hemp was dry. Cutting it into appropriate lengths, I tested one. It burnt wonderfully. Knowing it was unlikely Jean would consent to testing his brother's idea, I decided to be bold and risk it myself. My only problem, I realized with chagrin, was that I had no pounce. All that was at my disposal was the fouled pounce I had hid under the bench next to the hearth. Pulling it out I tried to stir it up so it would be more of a powder, but it still wanted to bead like kernels of corn. I did not fully understand the alchemy of it, but decided due to darkness falling soon I would have to use it such as it was. It would take too long to regrind, and tomorrow the battle was likely to start in earnest.

Stealthily, I returned with my cargo of hemp and pounce to *The Kyng's Anointer*. It was the dinner hour and the guards were taking their victuals, not paying any attention to this passing squire. Using all of the pounce I loaded and tamped the Anointer half full. Carefully I fed the hemp into the vent having had to peel off some strands to allow for easy insertion. I left a handspan free from the vent to allow me plenty of time to back away after lighting it. With great effort I was able to roll the heavy iron tube on its wooden carriage back into the battlement's crenellation. Looking out at the Tourelles I noticed two figures at a parapet pointing in our direction and thought they would be as good a target as any. I knew with this probably spoilt pounce, there was no way I could reach them, so I didn't even bother to adjust the low angle. Breathlessly, I lit the hemp and moved a few paces away. It burnt beautifully, but slowly. The sparks disappeared into the vent, and then to my dismay, emitted only a hissing smoke. Dejectedly, I approached the *Anointer*. That was when everything became a brilliant orange. I had a brief sensation of floating in a suffocating sea of pain, and then fell into blackness.

I must be in a cave. It was very dark, but there was a light, very far off. My love Jeanne was calling me and I wished to reply, but attempting to do so caused me great pain. I tried to recede into the comforting darkness of the cave, but Jeanne would not let me and was persistently calling me back. Her voice was echoing, far away, unreal.

"Alex, Alex, please speak to me. Please wake up. Do not die on me yet, dear one."

Hearing those endearing words I tried to fight through the pernicious pain and the abyss of blackness. I felt my eyes were open yet everything seemed a reddish blur.

"Oh yes, Alex, yes. You are here. Praise be to God. Can you speak, dear one?"

I tried to reply, but it was only a croaking, as my throat was lacking any moisture. Someone put a cup of watered wine to my lips. I greedily slurped at it. That was a mistake, as the swallowing caused a resurgence of painful explosions in my head. Someone was groaning aloud—twas I. Fighting through the swirling malaise in my head, I focused on the beautiful face of the angel before me.

"Jeanne, Jeanne, where am I? What has happened?" I rasped, hardly recognizing my own voice.

"You are upon your palliasse. It seems you did something very foolish yesterday."

"Yesterday?" I asked with shock.

"Yes. It has been more than a day since you blew up Jean's *Anointer*. We thought you might never return from your delirium. The barber examined you and was disturbed that you bled from every orifice of your head. Your arm is bound on your left side for he had to rearrange it at the shoulder."

Just mentioning this seemed to bring all my pains individually to the fore. The ache in my head was excruciating, but suddenly my arm spoke to me with volumes of torment. My shoulder, my ribs, my face, all voiced their choleric complaint.

"Oh, oh Jeanne, why does my face hurt so?"

"It has been burnt from the blast on the right side, but the barber said it should heal. He said if you awoke today you would likely survive your folly."

"Folly indeed! My beautiful *Anointer* is no longer beautiful, but at least it left its mark on those Goddams, HAH!" Jean's resonant voice boomed from somewhere behind Jeanne.

"What? What is that Jean? Did I harm *The Kyng's Anointer*? Please tell me no," I lamented as I saw Jean's face swim into my narrowed vision.

"Should you not be in the state you are I would lash you to a pulp," Jean blustered, and then in a more temperate tone said, "I do not know in what manner you loaded and fired the *Anointer*, but it ruptured at the vent where I thought impossible. What is most amazing though is that it also did some consequential damage to the Anglais. Looking at the firing angle it must have been a pounce more powerful than any before, not to mention a magical stone with eyes. Our spies tell us the fortress commander, Glasdale, was showing the Anglais leader, the Earl of Salisbury, *his city for the taking*. Hah, what a jester. I cannot stay angry with you Alex, for you *anointed* Salisbury and blew his bloody head off." Jean's laughter became exuberant and it pained my head sorely, but a smile was upon my lips nonetheless.

The next morning my thoughts were much morose, not simply from my bodily pains, but more that I could not assist the Maid in her sortie against Saint Loup. Jean's wife, Annie, was a kind lady, and happy to help me through my recovery, especially she said since I was now a heroic bombardier. At first I was not sure recovery was the best option, but gradually the pains in my head and body subsided. My arm seemed not to be broken, but my left shoulder was in great pain. My left index finger was certainly broken and someone had bound with a twig. Annie applied a wonderfully soothing salve to my face's right side, which she said would minimize scarring. The rest of my pains were more temporary and Annie said good fortune was on my side, as she had seen far worse inflicted on compatriots of Jean's. I realized that had I lit that devil's brew with the hot wire, instead of the saltpeter fuse, I would certainly be at the Gates of Saint Peter.

Hostilities had resumed with vigor. Jeanne, Annie said, had been blessed with another vision yesterday. Immediately after, she rose from her palliasse and rode out to assist a small force engaging the Anglais at Saint Loup. Saint Loup was an abandoned cathedral a half league east of the Burgundy Gate. The Anglais were in the process of fortifying it so as to choke off Orlean's last line of supply. Dunois rode out with a small force and a fierce fight ensued. The fight was not going well for Dunois, when Jeanne, brandishing her white standard high, led her group of irregulars into the fray and stemmed the tide. However, the Anglais leader Talbot, seeing this, was able to deploy forces drawn from the other fortifications to attack Jeanne from the rear.

Providentially, de Rais had just returned from Blois and, realizing the peril, hastily mustered La Hire and his seasoned group of mercenaries. Charging out from the Burgundy Gate the mercenaries tipped the balance back to our favor, striking the attackers at their rear and overwhelming them. This uncoordinated and ill-conceived foray actually resulted in a dramatic and inspiring victory for us. Most importantly, we had re-secured our lifeline and served notice that we could be victorious in a significant battle. This was a feat we had not accomplished for a long time. Jeanne's folly had actually magnified her mystique, that certain nimbus which surrounded her, and instilled our forces with an unfamiliar sense of invincibility.

It was three days before I could rise from my pallaisse. During that first day I had been unconscious and the following two were spent in great pain. Annie informed me that the war council was not in favor of any other foolish forays. Ignoring them, Jeanne had just ridden out at the head of an enthusiastic, though mostly inexperienced throng of several hundred.

Dragging my battered body back to the parapet where I had nearly died, I was able to view the engagement as it unfolded. Once again showing a foolhardy brashness she surprised the Anglais. She attacked Les Augustine, a fortified monastery standing outside the Tourelles fortress. Disaster was once again avoided as de Rais, La Hire and d'Alencon rode with their troops to her support. The Anglais, seeing the arriving reinforcements, conservatively retreated to the safety of La Tourelles and Jeanne immediately laid siege to this bastion. Darkness was now falling and I could no longer sit back and watch. I must somehow assist the Maid. It was my duty. Nay, it was my mission—it was my crusade.

Jeanne returned that night to Orleans and I was at the gate to greet her. The fact that I was up and about so soon, cheered her greatly.

"Alex, my friend and confidant, what a marvelous day you have made this. First our success at Augustine, and now to see you in better health."

"Yes, I watched from the south parapet. It was a glorious sight to see you send those Goddams into their hole," I answered joyously.

"Things are turning in our favor, Alex. We will soon have the Anglais running to Normandy." She dismounted and I took the reins of her white steed. "Follow me, my favorite squire, as it is time to finally set this war council on course."

Fortunately, her horse was an agreeable beast, for with my left arm strapped down to a tender body my strength was greatly diminished. After pausing to instruct a stable boy, who was in awe to gaze upon the Maid at such close proximity, I turned to find myself alone. Far down the cobbled street

I saw Jeanne striding along purposefully. Hurrying as best I could, I caught up with her just before she reached Jacques Boucher's residence. Jeanne had been residing here and this was where the war council held most of the meetings. Jean de Monteclair had let slip to me that many decisions were apparently made in her absence. I had a feeling she was about to change that.

The council was already underway. Looking upon Jeanne's face as we entered, I observed a now decidedly black countenance. After a short awkward silence, discussion began between de Gaucourt and Dunois as to retreating and fortifying Saint Loup to our advantage. There was little talk of advancing to secure Les Tourelles. From my inconspicuous position in the background, like a fly upon the wall, I watched Jeanne step forward and loudly interrupt the proceedings with barely bridled disdain.

"You have been in your council and I in mine, and believe me, the council of the Lord will be carried out and will prevail. AND YOUR COUNCIL SHALL PERISH."

A stunned silence descended over the small room, hanging as palpably as the morning mist upon the Meuse. De Rais was the one who at last responded, cutting through the tense mist with typical acerbity.

"Well, it appears our fearless femme du jour has once again been instructed from above… " He paused, but his attempted wit bore no fruit of laughter, for everyone cringed under Jeanne's black glare. In a surprisingly acquiescent tone he then continued, "I for one am in accordance. After all, she is our leader and follow we must, at the Dauphin's dictate. Today's success could be parlayed into a great gain if we seize the initiative. The peasants and even my own soldiers would follow her through Hell's portals, if she promised salvation on the other side." After a brief pause, a smirk creased his face and he concluded. "By all means, let her lead us, to salvation."

As cynical as his statement began, I was amazed as it unfolded.

He was obviously a pragmatic man and I knew sincerity would not be in any dictum he embraced. As everybody grudgingly approved his recommendation, I resolved to be wary of his actions on the morrow.

Chapter Fourteen

The Tourelles

Under the mantle of darkness many supplies and armaments were ferried across the Loire. At this time of year the river normally ran high and fast, but perhaps due to Jeanne's guardian Saints, it was noticeably less treacherous. I had been up long before dawn readying my heroine's armor and saddling her *destrier* in the torch-lit darkness. Though my shoulder was in a poor state, I unstrapped my arm from my body so that I might ride alongside Jeanne.

As we left through the Burgundy Gate, the Bailiff, likely on the council's orders, attempted to turn her away. There was a sizable throng of militia, independent mercenaries and assorted adoring rabble at our back. In the cold spring predawn, our breaths were visible like campfire smoke, but it was the excitement that warmed us more than any campfire could. Jeanne confronted the Bailiff and proclaimed for all to hear, "God's will shall not be denied. In fact I may be injured today, but we will prevail. Stand aside." Paying no further heed to the Bailiff, she rode forward and he had no choice but to step out of her path.

The bombardier's assistants had ferried and carted five cannon from Orleans through the night. Jean and the other bombardiers were now positioning them and unloading the kegs of pounce, as morning broke.

It was going to be a fine spring day for the bloodletting to come. As if to portend that, the eastern sky was bright rouge-pink in the manner of blood purling in a shallow, torpid pool of water. The movement of so many people, beasts and loaded carts made the air thick with dust. The fine powder of the pounce was also evident, from the heavy acrid, oppressive odor, like fouled eggs. There were no morning fires nearby as we entered the Saint Augustine monastery grounds. This was not so much for safety from our tormentors, but the danger inherent to movement of the fine pounce. Inopportune sparks while moving pounce could have deadly consequences. Other combatants kept a goodly distance from the eccentric death-dealers handling this weaponry.

Already, I could smell the stale sweat of soldiers mixing with the odorous offerings from our beasts of burden and the pounce. There were also the scents of freshly oiled and burnished steel, leather, linseed, and that tainted taste of fear that left my senses afloat on a pungent sea. It must have been evident to anyone observing me that this was my first battle. Agog, I beheld a bristling form of organized confusion. Adding to the growing cacophony, I could hear the *Goddams* in the distance shouting taunts and insults. An occasional puff of smoke could be seen, as they fired culverins in our direction to harass us. The monastery was fenced, providing minimal protection from the Tourelles fortification overlooking us. From the fencing it was but a long spear throw to the foot of the high masonry protecting the Tourelles. The fortification was on built-up ground leading to the ruined bridge. Within its walls rose the Tourelles, well defended and menacing.

The cannon were being moved forward slowly, behind large wooden shields. These shields were posts lashed together and attached to horizontal pinions, which in turn were mounted on large wheels. The pinions allowed them to swivel up for firing and down for protection while reloading or moving. Long scaling ladders were constructed and brought as far as the monastery fence. I espied Cedric and La Hire supervising the activity of constructing and deploying siege implements and asked Jeanne for permission to join them for the nonce. Busy conferring with Dunois, and having squire Jean d'Alulon present to assist her, she readily acceded.

I had not seen these two titans the last few days, except when Cedric came to congratulate me on blowing the English leader's head asunder. Salutations were necessarily brief and La Hire immediately put me to work constructing scaling ladders. I was disappointed at being given only this menial task, but realized I was not capable of much more. Jean de Monteclair came over to wish me well and asked if I was strong enough to help him man his cannon. I was eagerly agreeing when he reached out and squeezed my left shoulder. The sudden intense pain caused my body to convulse and my knees to give way. Only his quick move to support me prevented an embarrassing collapse.

As I gasped and blinked away the stars of pain, I heard Jean lament,"AHH, just as I suspected. You will be of no use to me, young Alex. Tis a shame though, as you have more potential than any of my other assistants. You will be of more use here doing what you can. I hope good fortune and marksmanship blesses me this day, as it did you."

Offering no argument and smiling weakly, I bade him, "Go with God, Jean de Monteclair."

I toiled on the ladders a short while, until my shoulder could do no more. It was then that a raucous, rolling clamor arose from front to back, as the signal was given for the bombardment to start. Not far from me, at a breach in the monastery's fence, I could see de Montclair's protective shield swing up as he applied the hot wire to the ignition vent. The thunderous blast dwarfed the din of noise about me and shook the ground beneath. There was a brief, breathless silence, and then a goodly portion of the guardhouse roof atop the battlements erupted into splinters. What an uplifting first shot. A tremendous cheer rose up and three more iron tubes belched their brimstone and fire. The *Goddams* at the battlements scurried from sight as one of these shots blasted away part of their battlements. Most impressive, I marveled, as two significant hits of four was an auspicious beginning. Under cover of this initial barrage, the fifth cannon was moved closer to the Tourelles. From its forward position the cannon could do even greater damage to the fortification. It was not long before de Monteclair's practiced gunners were loaded and firing again.

Looking around for my Maid I saw her pressing to the front as everybody was now massing for a charge at the bastion. La Hire was not far in front of me and I could hear him inciting his mercenaries. He turned his face skyward then, and in a loud, lusty voice invoked, "God, I pray you that YOU will do for La Hire what you would wish La Hire to do for YOU, if La Hire were God and YOU were La Hire."

After a few more barrages the hue and cry from our anxious soldiers rose to a deafening crescendo. Through all the confusion I had lost track of my mount. Desperate, I climbed up a broken section of the monastery's wide, stone wall to try and sight my charge. The chestnut gelding was nowhere to be seen amongst the teaming, surging sea of combatants and beasts. Then, at the head of our main force, I saw Dunois motion forward with his raised sword and let out a fearsome war-cry. At this signal, the trumpeters blared in chorus and our heroes surged forward in a fury. I was tingling with excitement from the resounding trumpets and tumult. Though not cold, I felt a shiver rush through me. My body hairs stood out and my skin became bumpy like that of a plucked goose.

And there she was—standing out as a shining icon in her armor upon her white steed, carried forward on a sea of frenzied followers. With my father's burnished sword held high and reflecting in the sunlight she exhorted them onward. Through a deadly hail of arrows, culverine and cannon shot did they forge. It was as a torrential rainstorm, but this downpour dealt death instead of sustenance. Most were on foot, occasionally stumbling over fallen comrades. Soon they reached the walls with ladders at the fore. Miraculously, the projectiles seemed to fall everywhere but upon Jeanne. In her mystical presence, with salvation almost assured, there was no fear to slow our onslaught. Her white and gold standard, silvery white armor and white steed presented a beacon all could see and follow.

I was about to rush to her side on foot when I noticed de Rais. Well back of Jeanne, he casually and cautiously moved laterally with his shield up protectively. Bedecked in ostentatious blue armor upon a leather-girded, immense, black destrier he was an imposing, if not participating figure.

Frustrated though I was at being both horseless and injured of shoulder, I temporized that a bird cannot fly with but one wing. Perhaps, I thought hopefully, I could provide assistance by simply observing. Grandiose thinking perhaps, but I had few other options.

We were attacking on all three faces of Les Tourelles. A part of the Loire was diverted in front of the twin towers that were accessed by a drawbridge. The powerfully walled compound sitting in front of the Tourelles was entered on the eastside over another drawbridge. The battle raged on and on. Like insects, our leading infantry bravely scampered up ladders with shields held before them for protection and swords at the ready. Our archers and crossbowmen harried the defenders who were trying to push off the scalers. There were boulders, hot oil or ash, caltrops, swords, and maces to greet our scalers. It seemed more of them were pushed and beaten to their demise from this lofty height than made it over the rampart. And those who did were attacked as by ravaging locusts and then cast to their death. Our iron tubes were doing their infamous work, however, and our total effort was causing significant attrition to their forces. Grotesquely, it seemed the scalers had a nearer summit to reach as the dead piled up beneath them. I could see blood running upon the ground among the twisted limbs, and in places even the ramparts ran rouge.

The pall of death and malaise of confusion seemed to gradually slow and disrupt our concerted effort. Looking up at the sun I realized it was at its apex and the battle had been raging for half the day. I noticed that supplies were now being delivered by fishing boats and barges near the East Gate. These operations were mostly unharried by the preoccupied Goddams. Perhaps I could be of use in such operations. I was about to climb down from my perch when my eyes beheld the unthinkable.

Clearly, I saw Jeanne shot. My fists were clenched tightly down by my sides as I screamed my protest aloud to God. Every fiber and sinew of my being was taut like the string of a winched arbalest. My horrified shriek was like a fragment of leaf in the wind, against the tumultuous backdrop of battle. Leaping down from the wall and ignoring the jarring to my shoulder, I raced to be by her side.

She was actually trying to climb a scaling ladder when the arrow caught her in the neck. I had seen her slump back into the arms of a following soldier with the arrow protruding. This could not be happening. She was on God's mission. Blindly in panic did I run, but only seemed to get hopelessly mired in a human mass surging in the opposite direction. I was finally getting near the place where I had seen her shot, when I stumbled and fell. I landed on something wet and soft. Choked and blinded with dust I tried to wipe my face, but only seemed to make it worse. Dearest God, my hands were covered in blood and I was lying upon a disemboweled corpse. I swallowed hard, trying to control an impulse to vomit. Looking up, I glimpsed something coming at me and instinctively rolled away. There was a loud thud next to me and the sound of splintering wood. It was a scaling ladder with a soldier still clinging to its top. Obviously, it had been pushed over backwards and had almost landed on top of me. I was starting to crawl away, still in search of the Maid, but something familiar made me stop. The soldier on the ladder had a filmy strip of gossamer attached to the back of his helmet. As he lay groaning upon his side I rolled him onto his back. It was Buzzy.

I saw a large dent in the side of his helmet, as I untied the strap and removed it. His eyes were open, but wonting to roll back into their cradles. A trickle of blood ran down from a large lump on the side of his head. He had probably been dealt a blow from a mace or heavy cudgel. If that hadn't already finished him, I was sure the fall must. His eyelids flickered, then closed, and then opened wide. When he recognized me he tried to speak, but could not seem to form the words. Not knowing what to do and realizing he was unlikely to survive, I simply stroked his brow. Tears were beginning to run down my bloody and begrimed face and I could do nothing to make them stop. There was much commotion and danger about us, as our forces were pulling back, but it mattered not to me. Again his eyes focused on me, and a smile formed on his deathly pale face.

"I, I guess Celeste's good luck tress possessed insufficient luck. I must have needed two," he said, through clenched teeth. I realized I was holding part of the tress tightly in my hands. Attempting to sound hopeful, I said, "Perhaps you are right, but this turn of events is only temporary. I will get you to safety and we will mount another attack."

His eyes became glazed and he spoke faintly, "I think not, my friend. I am a soldier and I have fought the good fight for God. My time is nigh and Jeanne has shown me the way. Yes, yes I believe I can even see a lighted path awaiting."

His body's breath seemed to escape his lips, as a soul might leave. His eyes rolled back—open, not seeing.

I was numb. None of this should be happening. My mouth was open and salty tears flowed in through the corners. *Whoosh, thud, whoosh, thud, whoosh, thud.* In rapid succession arrows flew past one ear and then the other to penetrate the earth deeply in front of me. The third hit my lower right leg and drove into the earth through my loose pantaloons. I was kneeling beside Buzzy with my back to the ramparts so I rolled to my left. It was immediate fear which jolted me into action more than the searing pain. Pulling hard to free my pinioned leg, I ripped my pantaloons and realized I had only been grazed. *Whoosh, thud.* Another narrow miss. Someone had a mark on me. Fear made the pain inconsequential and I sprang to my feet with legs churning. I could see but a few stragglers fleeing the battlefield and realized my great peril as a remaining target.

I darted over and around the dead and dying bodies of beasts and men. With little breath left in my body I reached the safety of the fenced monastery. Dazed and gasping, I simply huddled under the fence's protection. After a time, I realized there were others in a similar state as myself nearby. Most, however, were far more bloodied than I. A barber and priest were moving about attending the most seriously injured. As my senses and breathing returned, I checked my leg to find but a minor wound.

'Jeanne!' It was like a hammer between my eyes as my head cleared. Leaping to my feet I ran off, not knowing where I was going. Running from one beaten and bedraggled group to another, I desperately sought my Maid. No one knew where she was, only that she had been gravely injured. In my state, I know not how long I ran about in search.

I finally found her in a meadow behind the monastery, with de Rais, de Metz, de Gaucourt and squire Jean D'Aulon. She was conscious and being attended to by a barber and Jean Pasqueral. I prostrated myself at her feet and wept.

"Rise, Squire Alex. Why do you weep? This is but a minor setback. We shall prevail yet this day." Her courage was to marvel at and I could see the grave looks on the faces of the others present. She continued, "Beneficent barber, how see you the arrowhead? It must protrude from the blade of my shoulder does it not?"

"Yes Maid. It does, only just. I would be loath to pull it straight through, for though it appears not to have pierced any vitals, damage could still be done to your inner self."

"Well then," she said, "you must break off the head and we shall pull it back out."

"Oh, dear Maid! I don't know if you could withstand such pain. I… "

"Enough of such talk. I cannot be seen in this manner. Must I do it myself? Soldiers must endure these things and I am a soldier in the army of God. Do not talk to me of pain, for I am on God's mission and this is of no consequence. Break off the arrowhead."

Immediately did the barber comply and rightfully so, for doing it before further thought or discussion, surely minimized the distress. Using a fine saw from his bag, he etched and broke the arrowhead off with a practiced motion. Then, as all present agonized how best to now extract it, Jeanne simply gripped the shaft where it entered her neck and withdrew it. The arrow came free with a wet sucking hiss, followed by a goodly spurt of blood. Quickly, the barber staunched the wound with a hot iron. The sickly sweet smell of burning blood and flesh brought to me the vision of plucking and gutting chickens. Jeanne's already white face became a gray pallor, yet there was not a whimper. Her eyelids fluttered and then closed causing my breath to cease.

"She will be fine. The pain has caused her to swoon. I fear though the battle is perhaps over for her," the barber mollified us.

"Tis perhaps over for all of us," added Gaucourt.

"Best to not let the Maid hear such talk," said d'Alencon.

Thoughtfully stroking his wispy little red-brown beard de Rais said, "I don't know. Perhaps we could prop her up on her mount and send her out. Her very presence, in whatever state, would incite and invigorate our rabble and worry the Anglais."

All of us looked askance at de Rais who quickly added with a smirk and palms turned upward with feigned innocence, "Just a frivolous thought."

Dunois then arrived with a group of captains and a lengthy, heated discussion ensued as to our next course of action. Yesterday had seen numerous Anglais dispatched to their maker at Saint Augustine. However, their number was still comparable to our present forces and they were safely rooted within the ramparts of the Tourelles.

"Gentlemen." All turned, surprised by that unmistakable melodic though now strained voice. With the barber's assistance, Jeanne struggled to sit. In the bated quiet she looked from face to face through slightly glazed eyes. "I have been counseled that salvation awaits for all. Victory is at hand. We will yet this day return to Orleans triumphant and we shall enter through the South Gate." Again she glanced from face to face. Her eyes were now clearer and confidence exuded from her steady gaze. "I will rest until just before dusk and then I will lead us to victory. Watch when the tip of my standard touches upon the ramparts. Go now and renew our attack. Let the bombardiers do their damage, so that we may prevail. Let the people of Orleans know to prepare our way across the bridge. Go with God", and closing her eyes she laid back down.

There was a consuming silence, such that a leaf could have been heard striking the ground. Dunois was the first to speak, "Jean de Metz, since victory is imminent, return to Orleans and have Jacques Boucher organize an expeditious restoration of the bridge. Thereby we can harry them from behind as well. You may take a squire with you. And make haste."

De Rais was the next to respond as he ordered La Hire and another captain to go make preparations for the next surge. He inquired of the whereabouts of Jean de Monteclair and then was off to renew bombardments. The sudden flurry of activity uplifted everyone. De Metz bade me follow and we were on our way back to Orleans.

The townspeople and soldiers, left to defend Orleans, eagerly went to work acquiring and expropriating construction materials. Dusk was almost upon us, as we feverishly labored to repair the damaged bridge support-arch.

"De Metz, my friend, what if the Goddams turn on us and

charge across the repaired bridge. Could we stop them?" I asked.

"Perhaps not initially, but with our troops on their tail it would be a fruitless venture for them."

"But couldn't they do murderous damage to us in the meanwhile?" I persisted.

"I cannot foretell that, but their fate would be sealed regardless."

He ignored my, "But, but," to concentrate on his labors. I too labored diligently on the bridge with wooden guttering, spare ladders, planks and anything else that was useful to facilitate repairs. My fear of disaster did not much lessen, for if the Goddams were to attack Orleans with their other forces from any direction, the consequences would be grave. Those were thoughts I'm sure none of us cared to consider. It was only the buoyant comradeship of all present and the Maid's promise of salvation that made catastrophe seem inconceivable to most.

Four men had poled over a barge from the south bank to deposit more materials, and looking upon it gave me an idea. I stumbled and slid my way down the steep dirt mound of the arch to help unload the barge. I met three young men and they explained the older one was their father El Capitan. Even his sons addressed him as El Capitan. Perhaps a jest, I thought, since barging was his *métier*. Sturdy men they all were, which was an obvious advantage for poling this river.

The father, I immediately discerned from his rough-hewn regalery, was a short-tempered brute with a decided hatred for the Anglais. When I explained my idea he gave a frown such that I thought he might crack my skull with his poling oar and spit on my grave. To my great relief he broke into a thunderous laugh. Unfortunately, he then slapped me on my left shoulder. This sent me gasping to one knee, and the broad smile left his hoary face. Though older and not quite as large, the well-muscled brute reminded me of Cedric. I had told him I was the Maid's special envoy, which I thought was a half-truth that shouldn't much affect my time in purgatory.

Before I recovered from his playful blow and realized what was about, we had pushed off and were returning with the aid of a tether rope to the south bank. This had not been in my plans, but I decided it might be for the best after all.

Our docking spot was not very distant from the Tourelles east gate and I could see the fighting there was reaching a frenzied pitch. I helped load the barge and offered some instructions on how best to achieve our goal.

I found it difficult to divert my eyes from the hostilities as we worked. Our scalers must have breached the ramparts and severed the drawbridge ropes. The portcullis was probably damaged when the Goddam's overpowered the Tourelles, for it was only halfway down. There was a slight knoll close by and I could not resist moving a few steps up it to view the raging battle upon the drawbridge.

The *Anglais* were being driven back through the narrow gateway, but there our advance was suddenly halted. This stoppage was entirely due to one gargantuan *Goddam*. Goliath himself could not have been more fearsome. He had a broad-bladed axe in one hand and a broadsword in the other. A normal man would need two hands to wield either. Yet swinging these heavy weapons like carving blades he parried and dispatched men to their maker as if they were pesky children.

There was a brief cessation in fighting as our side drew back to gather itself. It was then, in the relative quiet that a dreadful, baying arose, such as Satan's beasts would jealously accede *dignari*. It seemed to be emanating from the center of our horde. And then I saw him. He was a massive figure. He stood a full head taller than any of our other Armagnac combatants. As this warrior pressed through to the front, I realized the brutish war-cry was born from this behemoth—a behemoth no less fearsome than as described by Job in God's bible. Our soldiers parted and he came face to face with the Anglais Goliath. Recognition made my eyes grow wide, for I realized our behemoth was Cedric.

The two giants paused, visually taking the measure of each

other while exchanging scowls and taunts. Huge though Cedric was, the Anglais was still a head taller, but Goliath knew from our soldiers' deference that this was no ordinary mortal he faced. From my vantage I could even see the sweat dripping from their faces. Their visored, conical, metal helmets became hot as Hades in the pitch of battle. Suddenly, Cedric cast his shield aside in an amazing show of bravado and disdain. Slightly crouched, he moved slowly in a semi-circle about the enemy. The *Anglais* stood firm, glaring. As Cedric neared the wall at the side of the entrance, he let out a ferocious roar and attacked the Goddam. The Anglais moved to parry, but was surprised, as the amazingly nimble Cedric spun on his heel leaving the Anglais to flail after his feint. There was a half cheer, half laugh from our soldiers and an angry growl from the Anglais defenders. The embarrassed giant squinted his eyes and took a step toward Cedric. I surmised that this was perhaps what Cedric wished. If he could draw him out of the gateway arch his chances would improve. Cedric feinted again with a savage, yet mocking, high-pitched cry. This time the Anglais flinched only slightly and then laughed as if amused, though no smile crossed his face.

"What do you send to do battle with the Great Gregor? Is this some kind of over-stuffed jester, who prefers feinting to fighting?"

The Anglais' taunt brought about an apprehensive silence from the throng and a loud gasp escaped Cedric's lips. Most odd, I thought, for nothing I could imagine would cause such a reaction from a seasoned combatant such as Cedric. It was a ploy, as suddenly Cedric charged again and the Anglais set himself for the onslaught. But it was yet another clever feint. The Anglais giant threw his head back to laugh—but no, it was only the feint of a feint, for Cedric's sword became a blur and the Anglais was barely able to deflect the worst of the blow with his broad axe. It glanced off his helmet leaving a crease that would have finished a lesser man. Cedric's foray did not cease, but he wisely shifted to a sideways attack, not letting the giant retreat into the constricting, protective archway. It was all Gregor could do to fend off his rapid, powerful blows.

Having seen what Cedric could do with one hand on a broadsword, two hands seemed almost an unfair advantage. Big Gregor was stunned and staggering, his broadsword driven from his grasp. He was near to being forced off the drawbridge when ill fortune cast an evil eye upon Cedric. One of our own dead soldiers aided the Goddam, as Cedric stumbled over the corpse. This brief reprieve allowed the Anglais to regain his balance and counterattack. He now fully realized the worth of his battle-wizened foe and counterattacked with all that he possessed. A high arcing swipe with his axe forced Cedric back. Cedric replied with a thrust while Gregor was off-balance, but it glanced off the side of his breastplate. Battle-axe and broadsword flashed relentlessly and the violent clanging of iron rang out like church bells. Unfortunately for Cedric, Gregor was now able to maneuver himself back into the semi-protective archway.

It was a momentous clash of Titans. The battle raged on and on. Each side of supporters roared at every thrust, swing and parry. It seemed all were mesmerized by this incredible struggle. Even the busy bargers stopped to watch. They wailed with every setback and whooped with every success. Everyone knew what was at stake, for these gargantuan foes were fighting for all of their lives. Nay, more than that, they were fighting for the future of France and salvation itself.

We observers marveled at the strength and endurance required for such a prolonged, intense effort. The blows were becoming slower, the defending parries weaker. Glancing strikes were mostly absorbed by armor, but there was a profuse amount of blood mixed with the sweat on their arms. It was then that the Goddam made his mistake. Swinging haphazardly through weariness, he completely missed the agile Cedric and stumbled forward on to his knees, embedding his axe in the drawbridge planking. Cedric's sword flashed toward the back of his neck for the kill, but in the same instant my champion slipped in a pool of blood. His unopposed blow glanced off the top of Gregor's helmet pitching the Goddam onto his side while Cedric landed, almost humorously, on his backside. There was no laughter—only a collective gasp of anxiety from a thousand throats. Gregor freed his axe and while Cedric rolled onto his knees, the Goddam rose upon one knee and swung wildly with both hands gripping the shaft.

My eyes could not accept what they saw. Time stood still in a frame of abject horror. One fortunate swing of the broad axe had cleaved Cedric such that he seemed two. The wild, but mighty blow, caught my hero where the neck meets the shoulder and is least protected by armor. His shoulder and chest were hewed to the heart. Blood gushed forth in a torrent, suffusing both combatants. His eyes wide, Cedric teetered, and then fell forward. The axe slipped from its gory cleavage and his face hit the planking with a splattering thump.

Gregor stumbled to his feet and raised his axe high letting out a mighty victory bellow. The rest of the Goddams followed in kind, but as I was screaming my grief a strange thing happened. Gregor's face erupted as a ripe melon dropped upon cobblestones. As everyone watched in disbelief he fell backwards with arms and legs splayed. What was left of his face seeped through his helmet onto the planking beside Cedric. A short distance behind the front of our forces I noticed some dissipating smoke. It was Jean de Monteclair upon a cart and he was now calmly reloading his culverin. A culverin is a most inaccurate hand-held cannon, so he had just made an incredible shot.

Commonly, the losers of a one on one confrontation are demoralized and run for their sorry lives. This however, was a stunning reversal. After an initial stupefied silence, an angry rolling roar cascaded through our ranks and they surged forward with a renewed and vicious vigor. So suddenly did the events turn again in our favor that the Goddams abandoned the drawbridge and ran for refuge inside the towers. Our forces poured through and a haphazard battle ensued within the fortress leading to the bridge.

I could not draw my eyes away from these scenes, especially the vanquished giants, who now lay pitiable in a massive pool of blood. My heart wept in great anguish for Cedric, and my vigor ran out of me like wine from a fallen chalice. The world was spinning about me, when I faintly heard someone yelling my name. El Capitan had hold of me, shaking me from my torpor.

"What're you standing here for, squire? Get your blubbering arse to the barge, we're almost loaded." He grabbed me by the scruff of the neck and pushed me toward the bridge.

With great difficulty, I forced myself to put the horror out of my mind and to think of what I was about. The barge was piled high with dry branches and firewood. There were three barrels of pitch on board and I noticed there was still two more remaining on shore. "Let us take the other pitch as well, my friend, for more is better than less."

Grumpily, the hoary old barger complied and we pushed off back to the bridge arch.

With the help of a rope dropped to me by de Metz, I had been able to clamber back up the steep arch mound and onto the bridge. Slowly, but steadily, the Goddams were being driven back through the tall portals leading on to the bridge. From this vantage all was now visible.

Glasdale, the Anglais leader, was recognizable—and not only by his standard bearer. There were always two of our soldiers trying to best him, but he fought as a man possessed. Truly, he was not their leader unjustly, for he could not, would not, be bested. As one of his front soldiers fell, he would take on yet one more adversary, inspiring his troops with his great courage.

Finally finishing the patched over bridge with our makeshift materials, our town-force, though mostly poorly armed, charged across to attack the Anglais' rear. This bravado did not last long, for as each Goddam turned to fight he could dispatch two of our poorly armored, untrained, villein fighters. A few wore surplice armor, but this could not long stand up to the Anglais' blows. Our few armored, regular soldiers on the bridge fought bravely, but as our foes became more desperate in seeking a possible avenue of escape they turned on us and fought their way on to the temporary crossing.

I haled at the bargers to strike a spark to the huge stack of wood and pitch, but they had already done so. Grabbing a pitchfork from a fallen farmer, I joined the fray, desperately trying to staunch the Goddams' retreat. Their rear guard, though small, was proving difficult to keep at bay. The growing flames and thick smoke began adding to the Anglais' confusion, as they fought desperately on both fronts.

One of our town soldiers was getting the worst of the swordplay with a hulking Goddam. Without aforethought I charged with my pitchfork. I caught the foe under his arm, but his armor deflected my striking fork upward. It pierced his underarm deeply and the force drove him back onto the temporary bridge. He collapsed, rolling into the legs of his comrades. It was at this moment, the provisional bridge works seemed to shudder and flames shot through, licking at the panicking Goddams. It was as if the trapdoor of hell suddenly opened—for they all disappeared into the flames of eternity. Through the thick, choking, black smoke I could see our forces driving the remaining Anglais into this abyss of hell. Some were roasted on the barge pyre below, but most simply drowned as their heavy armor quickly dragged them under in the fast rushing Loire. Last to go was Glasdale. Never yielding to the end, he was finally driven into the Loire after his compatriots.

I witnessed Glasdale land upon another wretch, flail about in the rapid waters, and then abruptly sink into oblivion—an ignominious end to a valiant foe. Tears welled up in my eyes. I did not understand what this tearful malaise was that gripped me with such suddenness, but the melancholy enveloped me like a suffocating blanket. Perhaps it was God's hand, humbling me to the sanctity of life. Why must man always come to this to resolve his issues? How many other souls, good or bad, perished in this bitter conflict? How many Buzzys, how many Cedrics, how many Glasdales? How many God, how many? Silently I lamented with my eyes searching heavenward for an answer, but none came. There was raucous cheering all about me, but I could find no solace in my heart.

I was told afterward that Jeanne's reaction was as tearful as mine. Perhaps our mutual day of birth made us mates of the soul in some ways. As the celebration and din grew about me, I fell to my knees and unleashed what bile was in my gullet. The bloodlust and carnage had assuredly addled my mind. Of the rest of the evening I can remember nothing.

As Jeanne had predicted she did indeed enter Orleans that night across the south bridge from the Tourelles. I was later told that our euphoric warriors had labored with great zeal to remake the provisional bridge span. My next recollection was of marching out the next day from the north gate to confront the remaining bulk of Anglais forces. I knew naught of what occurred the previous victorious evening. It was like waking from a dreamless sleep to find myself once again on the battlefield of the dead. I was not terrified—I was simply numb. This was not the glorious, God-given victory I had imagined. For me, yesterday's victory held no romance or repletion, only revulsion and emptiness. Such was the pervasive feeling which imbued me.

Looking about me with first realization, I found myself astride my gelded, chestnut palfrey and on Jeanne's right hand side. Slowly we were marching with a multitude of fierce and determined-looking warriors abreast us. Behind us I saw a much greater multitude of warriors, their eyes all seeming to blaze with a passionate and malicious intent. In the distance I could see the Anglais aligned and obviously determined to do battle unto death. There did not seem to be any fear for me, only a ubiquitous feeling of remorse and resignation. I did not understand these feelings. I was simply a player it seemed, in a jester's deck of corrupt cards.

In my stupefied state, there was suddenly a light of retrospection, though reassuring it was not. In my travels with Marie Robine, a scholar had instructed me in the writings of Honore Bonet. His studies determined that war is of no great marvel, for these battles first originated in heaven between Lucifer and God. And such shall it ever be until earth becomes Paradise. To my perpetual shock he determined that sodomy was the ultimate sin over war. Oh, how is it possible, I wailed within, that life can be so irreconcilably convoluted?

Jeanne had given strict instruction not to attack unless provoked, for today was the Sabbath. Time was frozen. It stood still, like a raptor observing a snake. Our cortege had come to a halt, perhaps one hundred paces from the Anglais forces. On the gently rolling plain we stood—endlessly we stood. The sky was clouded gray as was my mind, and our mounts pawed the ground with their hooves, snorting in anticipation. After a while they simply stood—confused by our inaction. It seemed a force of wills. This was the moment of providence and neither side flinched.

Even the customary shouted insults were not exchanged. Jeanne, de Rais, La Hire, de Gaucourt, Dunois stood side by side, glaring, yet not advancing. I imagined I could smell the Anglais—they stunk. Perhaps it was I, for there was no wind. The sun eventually emerged from its lair of clouds. Its position indicated it had made one quarter of its daily pursuit, and the impasse continued. My back ached, my legs quivered, my neck cried in silent complaint. As I felt the bile welling up in my gullet for an innumerable time, something inexplicable happened. They simply left.

In an orderly fashion the enemy turned toward Melun and, led by Talbot and his standard bearer, they marched off.

Chapter Fifteen

THE *YAKUZA* FACTOR

"WOW, THIS journal just seems to get more and more believable," Janeen said, between mouthfuls of grilled mud-shark. I had rigged up an open-fire barbecue outside not far from the short cliff and craggy shoreline. Our grill was a discarded refrigerator rack balanced with stones over the fire pit. The principle fuel was coconut husks. They made even better cooking coals than charcoal. As Janeen was a better interpreter and historian, cooking mostly fell to me and we shared clean up. It had been two weeks since Terry's visit and work on the journal had been progressing well. We were averaging at least eight pages per day of this voluminous historical account.

The day after Terry's visit Janeen had told me that Samuel Gasparojo had indeed known of our escape and predicament. It was he she had rung from the Lima auxiliary airport. Whoever got to him could have only learned that we were somewhere north of Lima, if indeed, that was what they were after. With some difficulty, I was finally able to convince her that she was in no way responsible for Doctor Gasparojo's death.

We were startled this afternoon by the Barber. Suddenly he was just standing in our doorway with a crooked, gummy grin on his round face. Now that we knew the capabilities of this incongruous, overgrown gnome he seemed very sinister indeed. He had come to inform us that Terry would likely be paying a visit tomorrow. He also stated that as he had been taking very good care of us, perhaps we might consider giving something for his impoverished family and circle of trusted helpers. It was a thinly veiled threat that I was about to take serious objection with, but Janeen wisely intervened. She strung him along with a line that once our safety was assured and we could leave there would be something in it for his most-deserving family. Though he was not entirely mollified by this, it seemed enough to fend him off for the present.

Janeen was prattling on about the journal over dinner and I tuned back into her commentary. "I figure it must be a type of colloquial participle," she said. "That's when I finally achieved clarity with regard to his verbal inflections. We should be able to make even better progress now—eh?"

"Aye, darlin, that we will," I agreed, not wanting to sound inattentive, though my thoughts were more on the Barber. "But we need to discuss tomorrow's social engagement with our protectors," I prompted while crunching on some type of tasty tuber root. "I dinna think we should mention the parchment text yet, for I see no advantage there. And, if it's soon safe enough to leave this lovely little hide-a-way, what would our plan of action be?"

After pondering for a few moments Janeen replied, "Well, we're gonna have to come clean sooner or later, but you're probably right that now is not to any advantage. I would like to return to Machu Mochita and rework the level of the excavation that you found the bundle at—meticulously. We need to finish the translation first, though. We're about half way, so to extrapolate and if we don't hit any major snags, it might take another two or three weeks of concentrated effort. I'm sure it's not a perfect translation, but it's good enough under the circumstances, and the linguistic purists will have their day to massage the details."

I was more than a little stunned at her suggestion of returning to the dig. "Dear Gawd lass! You would go back to that, that Macho Mocha killing ground we narrowly escaped?" I replied with a thicker than normal brogue, as sometimes occurs when I am perplexed.

My question was met with convulsive mirth. "Ma-ma-macho mo-mocha… " It seemed she could not catch her breath, and her staccato laughter rose to compete with the cacophony of seagulls and surf below.

"Achh, Janeen, give me a break. You know I have trouble with these peculiar names."

Catching her breath, she took a sip of wine and continued. "Jack, you must know I don't relish going back there, but if this script is authentic, as it seems, I'm sure as hell not letting any details of such a wild find escape me."

We finished our supper in silence while observing a remarkable Peruvian sunset. There were shades of orange and red that I never knew existed. It was like a subtle rainbow that seemed as one flowing, rippling color. As Sol dipped his toe into a passive Pacific the descent suddenly seemed to accelerate. Though a normal phenomenon, with the horizon as a close reference point, it nonetheless never ceases to fascinate me. We were mesmerized by the gradually expanding darkness. The seascape seemed to swallow the sun and its rainbow-like halo whole—greedily, like a wolf of the night.

"Breathtaking," Janeen exhaled, as the final tendrils of day disappeared.

"Aye, sadly gone ... though nighttime-town is but daytime turned upside-down."

"That's poetic, Jack. Is that another side of you I don't know?"

"Of course, my beauty. There's a wee bit of Robby Burns in every true Scot. You should also know my passionate side by now, and especially, that breathtaking sunsets make me exceeeedingly horny." With a wicked grin on my face, I rose at a profile that she might notice my bulging trousers in the blossoming moonlight. As the full moon bloomed so did her smile, for it had been a couple of days of all work and no play. I cleared the rickety old wooden table with a roguish sweep of one arm. In rapture did we survive the moon's intensity—the table, however, did not.

"Maxi my love, we should have settled some things last night, but I'm glad we didn't, you stud Scot you," Janeen murmured in my ear between soft, moist kisses. Her breath was sensuously warm and spiced with a darting tongue as she moved on to my neck. As I was so deliciously drawn from slumber, early morning sunlight, our alarm clock, was seeping through the trees behind our adobe.

"Aye, we have some unfinished business to discuss, but the business we finished last night was of even greater urgency my sweet. Tis bonny to hear you call me Maxi again—you haven't called me that since university."

"I haven't felt this way since university. That poor table—we'll have to eat off the floor now. Umm, it was like the very moonlight was stroking me Maxi. Shit, what time is it? We should be getting an early start."

She bounced out of bed with her usual go-get-em morning energy. I watched the full twin orbs of her backside shimmy and shake provocatively as she padded into the other room.

"OHH! My God! Terry! Jesus Christ!"

Janeen came flying back into the bedroom with her marvelous breasts bouncing discordantly. As she jumped into her dungarees and shirt, I sat up in a fit of pique, having guessed the situation.

"Damn, I prance outside for a whiz and Terry's sitting there," explained Janeen.

"Nothing, I'm sure she hasn't seen before," I said with dripping sarcasm. Janeen flashed a pained look at me and I wished I could have pulled the foot out of my mouth, but I couldn't even find the knee. A stony expression was on her face as she tossed her head and left the room without another glance. Stupid fucker—stupid, goddamed asshole—I berated myself silently while dressing. When will I ever learn? Jamming my hands in my fatigue pockets I sauntered outside. Though I may have looked brooding, I mostly felt ashamed of my reaction. Janeen was asking Terry if she wanted some coffee. I thought our pilot looked a bit rough in the early light.

"I'd love some, Janeen, and it looks like sleeping beauty-boy could use a happy cup too."

With an exaggerated smile I replied facetiously, "Top o' the mornin to you, Terry, lass. So nice to see you bright and early. Excuse me while I take a piss." Rudeness often comes easy to me, especially when dealing with people I find annoying. As Janeen saw to the coffee I merely stood on the edge of the stone pad and let'er rip.

"Nice touch, stud," said Terry, and she moved inside.

Shite, I thought, I'm really getting this day off to a bonny start.

Splashing some cold rain barrel water on my face proved a bit of a tonic for me. Returning inside, I found Terry explaining why she was here early. Apparently, she had flown in late last night in the dark and snoozed in the canvas chair outside. There was definitely something odd about Terry. It was her eyes. They seemed vacant, dark, sunken.

"You landed on the inlet in the dark?" I asked, somewhat surprised.

"Yeah, sometimes you gotta do what you gotta do. It was cloudless, a full moon, high tide, and no wind—piece of cake." She said this matter-of-factly, but Janeen and I looked at each other, appalled. Janeen's father had been a bush pilot and we had taken a couple of flying lessons together years ago at her insistence. We knew just enough to be dangerous in a pilot's seat. One thing we could take to the bank though was that such a stunt was definitively dangerous. Terry continued, "Unfortunately, I had few options. Two *Yakuza* thugs broke into my apartment." "What, what are you saying Terry? What happened? And what the hell are *Yakuza*?" Janeen asked, anxiously.

"It seems to me I heard about the *Yakuza* when I was in Japan. Aren't they elite Japanese Mafia types?" I asked.

"Go to the head of the class, Jack," said Terry, sipping her hot coffee noisily. "Maybe they weren't planning to kill me at first, but knowing how they operate, it was probably inevitable—especially after they found my mini-satellite and weapons. It also occurred to me that these are probably the same scum-suckers that did the Gasparojo toss."

"So what the hell happened?" Janeen said, impatiently.

"By the way, Jack, Janeen is the only non-agency person in this country who knows my background. So if you develop a case of lucid lips I'll have to kill you—dead—just like those Ninja Turtles." There was no humor in Terry's voice and no smile on her face.

"I wouldn't doubt that, Terry," I said, forcing a hard edge into my tone that belied the chill floating up my spine. "But your story sounds bogus. What the hell would Japanese Mafia be doing in Peru? And why would they waste poor old Samuel Gasparojo? They're not normally politically motivated."

"That's my point, Jack. And that's what brought me here a day early. Besides, my cover's probably blown now. One of the Yakuza's specialties is fencing rare art and artifacts. There is a significant Japanese presence in Peru, and the Yakuza are not averse to dealing with revolutionaries like the Shining Path if it furthers their own ends. I've seen them operate and they're one of the most ruthless subversive elements I've ever encountered. These facts lead me back to the four gold medallions. Not so surprisingly perhaps, they were inquiring of those very items," Terry said, and locked her eyes on me.

"Ach, for chrissakes. This is unbefuckinglievable! I already explained that was a wee fib to buy us time. Bloody-hell, what'd they do?" I asked, in frustration.

The improving morning light was revealing a couple of ugly welts on the left side of Terry's face. Looking closer now I noticed swollen lips and what looked like burns on the part of her neck not covered by her collar. Janeen rose and reaching over to Terry pulled the hair back from the left side of her head. There was a bloodied gauze bandage on her right ear. Janeen gasped and her eyes welled up with tears. It was then I noticed the shirt under her flight jacket was matted with blood near her waist.

"Don't worry, Jenny, they only took the earlobe … nothing serious." It was the first time I had ever heard Janeen called Jenny and had to stifle a jealous reflex.

"Terry, Terry what happened?" Janeen said, as she made Terry stand to remove her jacket. Terry seemed to be sinking into a tired stupor and made no reply or resistance. "Come on, let's lay you down and get you cleaned up. My God, look at the blood … ohh, Terry."

After getting Janeen some fresh water and medicinal salve I went outside and tried to make some sense of this ugly twist. The coffee had suddenly turned bitter in my mouth. It seemed this Occidental express was hurtling downhill through a dark tunnel with a flashing red light in the distance.

It was mid-morning before Janeen joined me outside.

"It wasn't pretty, Jack," Janeen explained. "She'll be okay, but… " and she cleared her throat before continuing. "I bathed and dressed Terry's cuts and burns as best I could with what we had available. The cuts were all shallow and limited to her abdomen and upper thighs. They may not be individually painful, but they were done with something razor sharp and the cumulative effect must be excruciating and psychologically devastating. The burns on her nipples, chest and neck are also shallow though they must be painful. Scarring will hopefully be minimal if we can make her rest and allow them to heal evenly."

"Did she say what exactly happened?" I asked.

"No, she said very little. She seemed spent, drained emotionally and physically. Perhaps she was beyond the pain … perhaps that's how she deals with it."

I didn't know about Janeen, but I had become very chilled and qualmish. I moved into the sunlight and sucked in the fresh air. It seemed like the gruesome cauldron of events that Janeen and I had been tossed into just kept on fermenting. Perhaps these damnable scripts were cursed.

Cold steel on my lips … just a dream. NO, not a dream. Reality and raw fear ignited me into a trained response, but my limbs were unresponsive, restrained. The cold steel forced its way into my mouth, cutting lips, scraping teeth, gagging me. Hot, garlic-laced breath abused my nostrils and a dark face eclipsed my world in the dim.

"You are chewing on a silenced Beretta little lady. Silence is a requirement unless you prefer a nine millimeter slug down your throat."

Someone else must be on my legs as the gunman had positioned his knees on my arms. Fuck! How could this happen? Was it the sleeping pill I took for the suffocating heat after the air-conditioning went down? How could I be so careless? The rage that flashed within me was monumental and directed mostly at myself. I felt a handcuff clamp around my wrist and the weight on my legs shifted off. The gunman grabbed a handful of my hair and dismounted me. I was dragged through the gloom into my living room. When the light flashed on I was painfully reminded of my nakedness, but they seemed not to take notice. The second one yanked my arms behind me and handcuffed them around the brass pole in the archway. Finally the gunman released my hair and removed the Beretta from my mouth. At almost the same instant he kicked my legs out from under me. I slid down the pole and plopped hard on my ass. They were efficient and professional I immediately realized.

"Now, little lady, we will have a chat, but first, Ono!" Somehow I knew what was coming, but that did not lessen the searing shock of pain as the truncheon stung the left side of my face like a bullwhip.

"So ... I need to know, I really do need to know, the whereabouts of four gold medallions," the gunman said with casual malice. His English was almost perfect. Better than mine probably, but it still had a faint oriental inflection and the slanted eyes beneath the thin balaclava left no mistake. The second one came into view and he was dressed identically in night-stalker black. He lit two cigarettes and passed one to the gunman.

The second one ogled me for a moment and then said, "No fuzz on this peach, heh, heh. Nice little tits ... too nice."

"I know of no medallions and you need to get some clothes

for me immediately. Please, don't even think to take advantage of me—you won't get away with it," I whimpered, trying to sound credible and buying time to think.

The gunman replaced the Beretta in its shoulder holster and reached behind his back with the other hand. He produced a small kukri knife, curved and razor sharp. Cigarette drooping from the corner of his mouth the ogler moved back behind me and grabbed a hunk of my hair cracking my head against the pole. The gunman sat on my legs and then there was a glint of steal. My consciousness gapped.

Now they were both before me with the gunman dangling my dripping earlobe in front of me.

"Earrings will only cost you half as much now," chuckled Ono the ogler.

It was like an old, silent, horror movie. I tried to scream, but there was no sound. What I was seeing was a jerky and grainy picture show. Parts of scenes seemed to be clipped out and odd childhood memories spliced in. There I was on the backyard swing—my mother pushing me—my step-father and brother watching intently—my dress billowing up … and now, I'm exposed again. They're burning me again with a cigarette. I must have screamed—a burn per scream they said. I don't even feel the Kukri cuts, but I'm bleeding, very slowly I'm bleeding. How many cuts now? How many questions that I can't answer?

Early dawn is filtering through the curtains and my horror movie is coming into focus again. They must have got bored with me. The gunman is ransacking my bedroom. Now the other one is pissing on me. He thinks I'm a fucking urinal—FUCKING PIG! Oddly, it occurred to me that you can piss on your wounds to help cleanse them in a pinch—urine is initially sterile. "Thank you, asshole … better make sure I'm dead," I mumbled.

"Ono, come in here. The bitch has a mini-satellite and … EIYEE, looks like a sniper's case," the gunman called out.

As weak as I am this is my only chance. They think I'm half dead. Old injuries can be useful sometimes. It's painful, but I can pop out my left shoulder and have learned many contortions as an advanced yogini. Gritting my teeth, I popped out the shoulder and contorted one leg at a time through my arms to get turned around with my wrists crossed. I popped my shoulder back in with less pain than I had endured the past hours. Standing on the sofa I soundlessly slipped the cuffs over the brass pole just above the dropped tile ceiling—the decorative pole was only bolted at the floor.

This measure of freedom fired my senses. I could feel that familiar tingle of alertness return as I surveyed the situation. The balcony door was slightly ajar. They must have got in through the balcony—probably from the roof. It's an old stone and concrete structure—almost soundproof, but not quite impenetrable. I got to my spare weapon—a beautiful piece—a Swiss Sphinx, nine millimeter, ambidextrous magazine release, with slide latch and ten rounds—perfect for a southpaw like me. It was hidden above the coat rack—precautions pay dividends. I could still hear the pricks jabbering. Sliding along the wall I got to the bedroom doorway and the jabber suddenly stopped. In the reflection of the hall mirror I could only see one of them. His back was to me. He was on his knees inspecting my satellite. Surmising the other one was in the closet or bathroom, I moved into the doorway. I can hit a keyhole at fifty feet—this was only fifteen. The top of his head erupted and he pitched forward. In that instant as my Sphinx recoiled, the door slammed into my shoulder knocking me into the doorframe. The blow knocked me down and jarred the gun from my grip. The other one must have been behind the door sifting through my dresser. From the corner of my eye I saw the black figure lunge at me and the flash of his kukri. I'm sure he didn't expect my speed or agility. My kick caught his extended elbow and it made an audible pop. He yelped and went down as the kukri clattered off the wall. Immediately, he rolled to retrieve his knife. I rolled with him and caught him flush in the temple with a whip-kick as he reach for it. There was the mushy cracking sound of heal breaking cheekbone and I knew he was done. I was on my hands and knees in a stupor and the stunted horror picture seemed to be enshrouding my mind again. I needed to get to my feet now, but those grainy blacks and whites were making me dizzy. I found the wall and pulled myself up the door frame. I looked in the hall mirror and tried to assess what they had done to me.

"Fucking *Yakuza*!" I spat. Had to be *Yakuza*, I reasoned, as my head cleared once more. My mother was Italian. I needed to dispense a little Mafia justice. I found the handcuff key in the dead one's pants and cuffed the live one as they had cuffed me. I tied the plastic bag over his head. There was no mess and there was no noise. I sat cross-legged on the floor and watched with passive interest as he twitched and then violently gasped, sucking the plastic into his mouth. It fascinated me that the image of his face reminded me of Munch's, *The Scream*. Then I cut their balls off with his kukri knife and stuffed them in their mouths. Their bodies were completely tattooed—a *Yakuza* trademark.

I called Jiminez, my reliable *provider*, who never asks any questions. He found an old steamer trunk for me. It was a perfect fit. As I was paying a smiling Jiminez three times his usual fee I asked him the only question needed to be asked, "Jiminez, amigo, do you know where the Japanese embassy is?"

Cold steel on my lips ... just a dream. NO, not a dream. I tried to scream as the old, horror picture show began another rerun.

"Terry, Terry my darling wake up, you're nightmaring again," Janeen soothed, as she wrapped her arms around a struggling Terry. Terry's struggling gradually subsided and she settled into a steady shiver. It was getting dark out and Janeen began to tenderly redress Terry's wounds.

Apart from the bandaging and loose clothing Terry almost looked and sounded her normal self the next morning. She was keen to go back to Lima and sort out the crazy sequence of calamities. She finally relented to rest a few days, but only after Janeen graphically elucidated on Terry's potentially permanent disfigurement if her wounds were not properly cared for. Not only that, she would assuredly be on someone's hit list, I added.

Terry said she had not offered any explanation of her night arrival to a surprised Barber and had left him to pull her amphibious Otter up on shore and camouflage it. The Barber, she noted, would have black market access to get the proper healing salves and painkillers. We mutually concluded that as far as we knew, this was still a safe-house and it would be best to remain here. This worked well for our translation goals also, but it would necessitate confiding in Terry about the scripts.

I was growing an unfamiliar affinity and respect for this spunky agent. Or was it just charity? There was one odd thought though that tugged at my perverse psyche. Might have Terry arrived in time to observe our prolonged bout of robust lovemaking last night? Thinking about it seemed to give me a vicarious thrill.

Chapter Sixteen

Champion of Jargeau

RIOTOUS CELEBRATION took place on that eighth day of May after the Anglais raised their siege. There was a great victory march through the streets and Jeanne was proclaimed savior of Orleans.

The exploits of many heroes were recognized and I was especially pleased at my own laurels. For my good fortune in causing Lord Salisbury's demise and showing forethought by torching the bridge, the mayor, Jacques Boucher, presented me with one hundred livres. I was shocked, but the adulation and recognition was even more remarkable for this humble novice-cum-squire.

My senses were dazed by sudden glory, but my heart was heavy with loss. Buzzy, the incorrigible, who had died in my arms—and all the colorful, wonderful characters that I knew but briefly. Especially though, I was heartsick by the loss of the stalwart, mountainous man who had been my family—the indomitable Cedric. Twas only a twist of fate, an unfortunate slip upon enemy blood, which decided the depth of his cup. This was the hardest for me. All else was now irrelevant. Cedric, oh Cedric, what shall be your epitaph?

To assuage my grief I spent much time in Jean de Monteclair's workshop and foundry. It seemed any ardor for war and bloodlust that I may have possessed must surely now be forever sated. Work seemed a salve to sooth my conscience. Concentrating more on the alchemy of metallurgy than the destructiveness of pounce, I was able to learn much from Jean. At his insistence, I had explained with blushing humility how the pounce I used in *The Kyng's Anointer* may have become so potent. After initial disbelief, his reaction progressed to guffaws and then to unbridled belly laughter. I could not help but join him in mirth at my impetuous *faux pas*.

After my confession, he found it even more sensible to spend time at his favorite inn. Fulfilling the necessary task of enhancing the pounce, he justified. I was easily persuaded to accompany him and found some solace for my sadness in Orleans brew. Most of May was spent in this manner, either at the foundry or within the sottish confines of the Lapin Noir tavern.

Jeanne seemed to be in constant prayer or military meetings with Dunois, d'Alencon, La Hire and de Rais. She had given me free rein. I was happy for that, but it also afforded me the opportunity to misspend my time and new found riches. More than once did I find myself in a sotted state and staggering to the sweet smelling loft above the Lapin Noir.

Though sweet it was these pleasures could not compare to those of my peerless Izzy. The winsome wenches were most persuasive, and initially, had little difficulty coaxing my purse's and breeches' drawstrings loose. With difficulty, I was eventually able to keep secure my drawstrings. Jean encouraged my lascivious side, but was resolutely celibate himself. He did, however, quaff prodigious amounts of ale under the pretext of furthering his pounce experiments.

After a month of work and occasional debauchery I was happy to hear that we would be leaving Orleans to advance on Jargeau. We would begin our drive to Reims, and there, the rightful coronation of Charles VII would take place as foretold by Jeanne. He would be properly anointed from Clovis' bowl like his royal predecessors.

Like leaves from a shaken tree in autumn did our foes fall: Jargeau, Melun, Beaugency and Patay all fell in less then a fortnight. As I was by Jeanne's side throughout these battles, I could see the adulation in our soldier's eyes without exception. Her "*Beau duc*", d'Alencon, as she occasionally liked to call him, was also constantly at her side. This was a burr on my backside. I could only endure his flirtatious manners with the Maid and his indifference toward me. It brought bile to my throat when I heard Jeanne vow to his wife that she would return him safely. He had not fought at Orleans because of an unpaid ransom debt. The code of chivalry required he pay this remaining debt before taking part in any fighting. His capture was four years previous at Vernevil and I learned that the balance was conveniently paid off after the Orleans battle. An opportunistic knight to be sure.

Jargeau was a crucial victory and further imbued us with a sense of *savoir-faire* as a fighting force. After Orleans and Jargeau nothing could sway our soldiers' belief in Jeanne's invincibility.

The Anglais led by the Earl of Suffolk, William de la Pole, defended Jargeau staunchly. Initially the wide moat at Jargeau held us at bay, but we attained our goal with a concerted attack on the eleventh day of June. I tried to set my bloodletting bias aside and to fight bravely by Jeanne's side.

Our soldiers had been subjected to boiling oil, hot ashes, caltrops and blasphemous taunts from the defenders upon the walls. But what incited our troops the greatest was when Jeanne was dealt a deflected blow upon her helmet by a caltrop. All those who saw, held their breath as one. As I helped her back up she was dazed, but cried out for all to hear, "UP FRIENDS, UP—THE ANGLAIS ARE OURS."

When we had finally breached the walls, the carnage began in earnest. I could see the bloodlust in the eyes of our soldiers—that fearsome, crazed, unblinking intensity. I sensed with surety that plunder and defilement were soon to be the product of such rage. Jeanne, perhaps not realizing what would ensue, exhorted us on across the now lowered drawbridge.

"Go Alex, go. Go in the name of our Lord and the Dauphin. The town will be ours. Help secure it. God will protect us."

Heeding my Maid's bidding I raised my sword and charged

across the drawbridge on my chestnut gelding. Most of our warriors had already preceded me and there were small skirmishes being fought everywhere. The inhabitants fought for their lives, but unless one was a knight of significant rank, they were dispatched without mercy. Vanquished knights of rank were hobbled and chained together, kept alive only out of the prospect of potential ransom.

Seized by the moment, I chased two Anglais foot soldiers down an alleyway. As I thundered down upon them one veered right, into another alley. Ignoring him, I charged after the other. It happened so fast that I hardly realized what was about. The soldier who had veered right slashed out with his broadsword as I passed. It caught my gelding's foreleg just below his leather-protected chest. It severed the animal's leg and it collapsed with a shrieking neigh. I was pitched forward and landed hard on the cobblestones, skidding for several paces. Gushing blood from his leg my mount was kicking wildly in panic, unable to rise. In the narrow alleyway the flailing beast prevented its assailant from immediately attacking me so the Goddam took flight in the opposite direction.

The other Anglais, however, had turned and was now bearing down on me with sword held high. Though dazed, I was able to roll enough that his blow glanced off my helmet and the leather armor protecting my arm. Instantly he was upon me again. Cornered, and having lost my sword in the fall, there was no hope against this wild-eyed Anglais.

I could already hear the jingling bells of heaven beckoning me as his sword flashed. But then, there was another lightning glint of steel. In mid-arc there was an ear-piercing clang and the Anglais' sword flew from his grasp. Off-balance, the Anglais stumbled to his knees. Stupefied, he only had time to look up as the broadsword came down again, cleaving his open mouth and neck through to the shoulder. His partly decapitated head lolled to the side and its stump spouted a torrent of blood as he fell dead on top of me. This is a most grotesque and terrifying dream, I thought, as I looked up to see La Hire, my savior. There was pure bloodlust in his eyes, but incredibly he was missing his waist armor and apron. Most absurd of all was the fact that his protuberant member was exposed and waggling obscenely.

I felt something underneath me move accompanied by a shrieking squeal. Realizing I was lying in a pile of garbage I pushed the dead soldier off me and tried to sit up in the stinking mess. A large rat scurried from where I had lain.

"Hah, you are a most troublesome squire, Alex. Tis a fortunate thing I was here to save you from your folly. Sacrebleu, must I deal with your beast as well?"

With two hands he plunged his sword through my gelding's heart, ending the beast's misery. I tried to rise, but slipped in the growing pool of blood about me.

Somewhere I could hear amongst the general tumult an anguished female wailing. Looking up from my hands and knees I saw what was obviously a young maiden, bolt from a nearby doorway. She was stark naked with long dark disheveled tresses flowing down to her small buttocks. She glanced at us with such a look of wide-eyed terror that it chilled my already quaking soul. Turning to run in the other direction she tripped over a pile of refuse in the alley. As she struggled to regain her footing in the muck, one of La Hire's henchmen, Regnault Dailly, emerged from the same doorway. Before she could take a second step Dailly caught her by those lovely long tresses and viciously yanked her backward. With a slapping thud she landed upon her backside and Regnault proceeded to drag her back into the dwelling. Pitiably, she screamed and struggled, to no avail.

"Ha, ha, almost got away on you Regnault. I will be right there to finish what I started." La Hire turned to me and smiled a wicked smile. "Come, Alex, off your knees. I believe this one is a virgin and I was just about to draw her first blood when you so rudely interrupted me. I'll even let you have second go, ahead of Regnault and Gerard. Besides, those barbarians usually prefer a young willing mouth anyway." His deep-bellied laugh made my stomach churn.

As he disappeared back into the dwelling the sickly sweet smell of blood and the insanity of the moment caused me to release all that was in my gullet. I heaved until I had nothing left. Though it was not cold, I was shivering. I rose on wobbly legs, and using a rag from the garbage pile, wiped off what I could of the blood afflicting my person. My beautiful chestnut gelding's eyes were staring blankly at me. I could not bear this, so I stumbled over to him and closed them. I found my sword, and dragging it behind me, moved hesitantly toward the doorway. With great trepidation I forced myself to look in. The crying, the moaning, the groaning and grunting, foretold the horror I did not wish to see. Yet, I could not stop myself.

They had her pinioned face down across a table. La Hire was rutting on her from behind and there was blood trickling down her white thighs. Gerard and Regnault were doing something I could not see on the other side where her head and hair hung over the table edge. In the far corner I could see an old woman lying awkwardly, with her legs askew like a discarded wishbone. A young boy had been cast carelessly across her like a rag doll. Gaping wounds in their throats told of their demise.

My initial despair and horror was transforming into a black rage. BEASTS—and they were my comrades! How could God let this happen? Were we not fighting the *good* fight? My eyes were wet without, but my heart howled in stormy anguish within. What was I to do? Should I charge in and hack these beasts to bits? La Hire had just saved my life! The other two I barely knew, but surely they deserved to die a horrific death for this atrocity. My head was spinning and felt unattached to my body. Black thoughts and powerful emotions were smothering me. I could not breathe.

My next recollection is that of running through the main square toward the fortified inner tower. It was the enemy's last line of defense and our forces were attempting to breach it. Wailing and shrieking I rushed into the fray, slashing and hacking at any enemy whom dared present himself in my path. There were no thoughts in my head. No moral, no immoral; no right, no wrong; no thought of living nor of dying; no devil and, and no God! Blindly, I fought as a man possessed. I fought without mercy against a panicked and retreating foe.

Was it bloodlust? I do not believe so. Was it for God and King? I do not believe so. Was it hate? I do not truly know. I was crazed—not like the idiots who beg in the market, but like a distempered animal. Perhaps it was the devil in me. Or perhaps, it was the man in me, and man is the true beast.

There was then another darkened period of which I remember nothing. I pray God I was not possessed by such bestiality, as were some of my comrades. I next remember rushing up a narrow, circular stairwell to the tower's lookout room. I know not why I was doing so, except perhaps, providence. I arrived at the summit to see an Anglais knight impaling an Armagnac knight beneath the chin. The force of the sword thrust drove him deeper through the crenellation where he had been apparently cornered. The Armagnac fell backwards over the parapet edge. In his death throes he desperately grasped at anything, finding only the broadsword in his neck with his right hand. With his other hand the armor-clad glove clawed at the parapet and I can still hear that grating of metal on stone. Unable to scream with the sword in his throat, he slipped backward over the edge. I would rather have heard his screams than to have seen those bulging, silent eyes.

With a warrior's roar of anger, I charged the Anglais with sword high. My inexperienced effort to cleave him in two flailed at empty space, as he dove and rolled out of harm's way. In his effort to escape my charge he had relinquished his broadsword to the Armagnac's deathly embrace. I swung to attack again and he sprang to his feet, drawing his short-sword. I hesitated and we slowly began to circle each other, assessing each other's measure before the mettle. He moved like a young man, but I could see by his lined face he was a man of substantial years. There was a fire in his eyes that made me hesitate. He had a rich, ornate suit of armor, though he had lost his helmet. Even though I had the superior weapon, I sensed this was a very dangerous and seasoned warrior. My presence of mind was returning to me, but my arms were weary and my body cried enough.

"Why, you're not even a knight, you young whelp. I think I'll just take that sword away from you and carve out your gizzard for dinner," he said, with menacing calm and in perfect French. He feinted forward, brandishing his short-sword and I backed away with a defensive swipe. Suddenly my broadsword seemed very heavy. My throat had been parched, but now its dryness was inflamed to constriction by my hot, rasping breath. I could not swallow. He laughed, probably smelling my escalating fear, as only weathered warriors can. He actually began to stalk me, despite my superior weapon. In a disdainful manner he held his short-sword nonchalantly at his side. There was a smile upon his face, but his eyes were narrowed and concentrating on my every flinching, appraising every weakness. Moments before, I had been crazed with anguished bloodlust, but suddenly weariness and fear pervaded my being. I had become as a fly in a spider's web, staring into the face of death, its arms reaching out to receive me. His eyes were mesmerizing me.

Without my realizing, he had closed our distance to where my outstretched broadsword was within arm's length of his chest. He moved so rapidly that I could not react. His short-sword slapped aside my broadsword and as one movement thrust forward inside my defenses. Backing away at the same time, I stumbled and fell in my panic.

Oh the fortune of fools! Off-balance, his short-sword grazed off the top of my helmet and he landed on top of me. He wrapped his arms about me and we rolled over several times, losing our weapons in the process. His strength for an aged warrior was extraordinary. Though not a large man, his grip was crushing the life out me. My armor was fortified leather, but his was of the finest metal. With my arms pinioned he had me at a severe disadvantage. He wrapped his legs about me, securing a firm grip around my thighs. I was weakening rapidly. An instant of reprieve was granted me, as his arm shot out to retrieve his short-sword.

Chivalry was no longer a consideration for me and perhaps he underestimated that possibility. Gasping for air, I rammed my hand up under his apron and found his sweaty sack. I squeezed his chestnuts with all my strength and he howled in agony while he groped for his short-sword. His grip on me now only half as fierce, I was able to drive my helmeted head into his face. I caught him on the bridge of his nose with great force. It was an unexpected blow. Blood gushed immediately and we rolled over and over. His vision impaired, he swung wildly, trying to slash at my head with the short-sword. Barely was I able to divert the blade and it clanged off the masonry floor. He must have been in excruciating pain, for I am sure my unceasing grip was near to neutering him. His agonized caterwaul threatened to pierce my head from ear to ear and one of his legs shot straight out, allowing me to flip him off. He began to shake and could stand it no longer. Dropping his weapon he clawed weakly at my offensive hand. Seizing the opportunity, I released him and scrambled for the short-sword. It was unnecessary, however, for he was no longer conscious.

I crawled to the closest wall and leaned against it, for I do not think I could have sat up otherwise. Looking upon him in my groggy state, I noted that he was a handsome old, gray-haired knave, even if he was a Goddam. I did not think I had killed him, but perhaps he would not father any more Goddams, and that was probably a good thing. Wiping his blood from my face, I struggled to my feet. If he regained his senses I'd best be prepared.

By the sound of the turmoil below us, the conflagration was still brewing. With a pang of regret, I briefly considered the terrible things that had happened this day, and that my culpability was lamentable. This was not something I cared to address, so I pushed it from my thoughts. Looking upon his festooned helmet in the far corner, it was obvious he was a knight of some stature. He began to groan pitiably and curled up in a protective manner. I did not want to test fate a second time so I rolled him onto his back. I placed my foot upon his plated chest and my sword at his neck.

His eyes opened, but at first they were glassy and unseeing. As comprehension dawned, his bloodied eyes grew wide with defiance and fury. What manner of man was this, I thought, to react thusly? I was his vanquisher and held his life in my hands. I was not sure if it was from pain or anger, but I could hear his teeth grinding as his jaw moved perceptibly. It was apparent that the battle was moving up the stairwell, for the tumult was growing ever closer. He seemed to realize this and spoke with difficulty.

"So, squire, or have you yet achieved that lofty distinction?" he said, with disdain.

I was speechless at such haughty disregard of circumstance. I stammered briefly without emitting anything of consequence and he smiled, almost tauntingly.

"Kill me … yes, kill me. Tis easy … you hold the power. Pierce my neck through. Tis easy … do not be a coward. DO IT."

His neck muscles stood out, and his eyes were crazed, bulging. He pushed upward causing my blade to prick and draw blood from his neck. I was finally able to respond, "Sir, you have fought bravely. I know not who you may be, but no more blood need flow. The battle is done. I am the Maid's squire and she would bid you live. If we believe in the same God, then let this be finished!"

There was a pause and his demeanor gradually changed.

"You do not fight civilized like a true knight, but I believe you speak truth. So believe me when I say, I am Lord Suffolk, Champion of King Henry and Protector of Jargeau. I could never surrender to a lowly squire. Should you wish me to live then permit me the grace of knighting you that I may surrender with honor to a fellow knight."

I was nonplussed—astounded. Of such, I had not even dreamt. Perhaps he was jesting. I was not sure I even desired such an honor. Deserving, I could not be. Fatuous though the situation may be, I could not help but believe the dauntless knight.

"Sir, perhaps we could wait for a French knight to arrive and then… "

"Don't be ridiculous, boy. That would be meaningless. Though you have defeated me in such a manner, you are victor nonetheless. Finish me, or... "

When my frenzied comrades charged through the lookout entrance they were met with an astonishing sight. Tapping this kneeling squire upon either shoulder with my own broadsword, a bent and debilitated Lord Suffolk was heard to say, "Rise, Sir Alex, Champion of Jargeau."

Chapter Seventeen

Izzy, Dear Izzy

The burgundians and Anglais were on the run, retreating to safer enclaves. Townspeople were switching their allegiance, as does the whim of the wind. Charles emerged from his protective burrow, and like a *hero,* joined the cresting wave as it rolled toward Reims. It was happening exactly as the Maid had predicted. In early July we entered Yonne. The town capitulated willingly and it seemed a different world from our last clandestine visit four months past.

The Earl of Suffolk had preserved his dignity and bequeathed me a dubious knighthood. This allowed me many privileges, but I declined most, so as to remain at my Maid's side. The Dauphin, upon hearing of my adventures, was seized by a fit of great mirth, I was told. As we rested at Yonne I was summoned to an audience with Charles. Sorely was I vexed at what might evolve when I was ushered into his presence. Fortune once again smiled upon me, as I was presented with a fine new steed and another 100 livres. The much-amused Charles congratulated me on my exploits and was far from his normal dour self. He was particularly pleased at the prospect of a sizeable ransom being paid for the Earl of Suffolk. I was walking among the clouds and felt as a parvenu, for I was now a man of means. No, I was a knight of means.

Life is a strange calamity of extended events. There always seems to be a balance when things progress too well, or too poorly. Sometimes fortune might seemingly follow you without ebb, but be assured that misfortune will always be lurking in the shadows.

Other times, it is misfortune that is the only apparent mistress in your life while fortune is witlessly biding its time elsewhere. Such seems to have been the turns of my life.

It was a joyous shock the day after my audience with Charles, when an ebullient Izzy accosted me. I was just emerging from my temporary quarters."Ma cherie, ma cherie. It is you … yes, yes… " she exclaimed while embracing me in her intoxicating arms. Overcoming my initial surprise, I responded with kisses and embraced her with passion. Lifting her off her feet in my arms I spun us about like a child's top. There were tears in her eyes as she held my face in her precious hands, slowing my dizzying pirouette. "I have found you. Praise be to Saint Christopher for keeping you safe."

"This is wonderful, Izzy, but how is it that you are here my precious vision?" finally finding my voice. Her radiant smile darkened slightly and there was a long pause before she replied.

"Take me aside, my princely knight. I have already heard of your prowess in battle, but let us find a space without so many inquisitive eyes, dear one." Looking about me, I realized for the first time that we were making something of a spectacle. Passersby had slowed and most smiled indulgently at our joyous reunion.

Arm in arm, we walked down to the river's edge. Jeanne was in a meeting with the Dauphin this morn so my responsibilities were minimal and there was no need for me to rush off anywhere. We were able to find a quiet, shaded piece of riverside a little way upstream. I ceased our chatter with a passionate kiss and caressed her covered bosom. It seemed those creamy mounds were tantalizingly larger than I had remembered and I endeavored to release them from their confines. Though far from unresponsive, she gently resisted my efforts and bade me wait, as she must talk of certain matters first. Puzzled, I laid back with a broad smile. "Regale me then my beautiful, buxom maiden, for I listen with rapt attention." Then, with mock sternness, I said, "But take care not to waste a knight's time with any badinage."

"Fear not brave knight," she replied with a pouting smile, "for I have news for you that you may find of great interest. Oh, my goodness … our peccable friend is also displaying his rapt attention." My shameless member was straining at its confines, creating a bulge in my apron.

Her mien changed slightly and she continued with a more serious, hesitant tone. "Alex, I, ah, I have missed three menses. This is the first time for me. I have never missed my menses before." She hesitated and then rushed on. "I had been with none other than yourself during that period of time. Celeste has become most annoyed with me. Now that I am sure of it, I felt that you would be the kind of man who would want to know."

Her big blue-green eyes were brimming. She reached out and began to twirl my dark red locks in her fingers. I moved my lips, but no sound was escaping them. It took a short while to sink in that she was actually carrying my child. The thought seemed so outre to my young mind that I knew not what to say. Her eyes were beginning to overflow.

"Oh, Alex, I am so sorry. I always douche, but with you I did not, for whatever reason," she said with tremulous voice. To allay her angst I took her into my arms and stroked her light red, rampageous hair.

"Dearest Izzy, fear not. Why are your eyes wet? Should this not be a joyous thing? For me it is startling news to be sure, but it would seem to be God's will. I would be honored to have you bear my child."

"Honored? Alex, Oh Alex—but, but I am just a… " and her shaky voice dwindled to a murmur, "I am but a whore."

"Izzy, my mother was a whore. There shall be no obloquy spoken against her or you," I said with conviction. "There need not be further discussion on this, for you will be a fine mother and I will be a proud father." Not sure if I said these things through kindness, love, or perceived duty, I said them nonetheless.

There was a profound smile on Izzy's full lips. I kissed them long and tenderly. We made rapturous love on the riverbank. Mounting her frontally, I took great care not to penetrate too deeply, fearing injury to her or the unborn. As we reached ultimate bliss in unison, she grabbed my buttocks, digging her nails in deeply, and pulled me into her fully. Waves of euphoria swept over us like the warmest waters of a gentle sea.

After a time, I was vaguely aware of strange noises some distance off. Annoyingly, the noise continued and I realized it was some kind of clapping and clamor. Reluctantly, I disengaged myself and Izzy complained, "Whatever the hell is that din?"

Izzy sat up closing her splayed legs, and emitted a startled scream. Turning, I looked in the direction of her dismay and was disgusted at what I saw. De Rais and three others were jeering at us and laughing. Regnault actually had his member exposed. He was pointing at it and motioning us to come over. The rushing water had masked their untimely approach. They must have been on reconnaissance and stumbled upon our little show.

"Come, Izzy, let us get back. Do not pay any mind to those barbarians. They are cow-dung."

With taunts of "Encore! Encore! Save some for us, famous Knight of Jargeau" following us, we hurried off. It was not long before the smiles returned to our faces however, for there were grander things to think of. With full, happy hearts and a passionate parting embrace, we agreed to meet in the main square that evening.

"Do you think we would ever marry, Alex?" I was much taken aback by Izzy's question, but perhaps I should not have been. I was only seventeen years, seventeen epiphanies, young, but obviously not too young. After a reflective pause, and seeing Izzy unable to hide the concern so upon her face, I responded.

"I have thought on these matters only this day, Izzy, my sweet, and I will be honest. Simply put, yes. You are a very special woman and any man of merit would be proud to have you as his wife. I care not of your past experiences, only that you are what you are. We all take paths on this journey of life, judged in our own hearts to be the proper path for that situation. It is not for us to sit in judgment of others. It is for God, and God alone, to determine the worth of one's life. I have seen, in my short life, many contradictions of right and wrong. So this I say to you, Izzy. You are a precious jewel, and it would be a cruel God, or a vile man, that might spurn you."

A relieved Izzy embraced me and her eyes, which had a moment before been brimming with tears, now sparkled and danced with joy.

It seemed we were on a floating barge of contentment, while we lolled amongst the noisy throng of evening strollers. I could see peace and serenity upon Izzy's face as she gazed up at the heavens. She was marveling aloud at the vault of heaven, which was alight with countless stars. But I was gazing at her. I can still see her profile—her delicately square jawbone, her blue-green-almost-emerald eyes, her sculpted erratic nose, and that fine red hair with a mind of its own. Yet, there was more to her. It was, I believe, the serenity of her nature. Surely, Achilles could have had no finer Helen. It was then my realization of love became fulfilled. If the Maid was my first, perhaps Izzy would be my last.

Izzy was not given to much consumption of wine, but I insisted we celebrate the day by stopping at an old woman's stall to purchase some very tasty *hippocras*. Common people rarely got to taste this pleasurable, spiced wine, as it was usually only afforded by nobles. It soon accented Izzy's giddy mood in a most delightful manner.

Giggling like frolicsome children, we next stopped at a vendor who was displaying shawls of exquisitely fine silk. These filmy articles were popular for women to wear about their necks at night and sometimes they attached them to their hair or pointed headpieces. It was only in recent years that traders had discovered and began bringing silk back from the far eastern lands. It was said that worms spun the silk, but I was not so gullible as to believe that. Still, they were an exotic treat for any woman and I decided this would be a perfect gift to present Izzy in celebration of our reunion. There were wonderfully vibrant new colors of yellow and orange that captivated our eyes. The vendor showed me a tiny purplish sprig from which these salient colors were rendered.

"Oh, Alex, these are truly incredible colors and the material is like a baby's skin, but this rogue would have you pay four livres. Why, it would take me half a fortnight to make, er, save… " She paused, awkwardly, then continued. "It is too much for you to afford, my love." Amused at her needless anxiety, I laughed aloud. It fortified my belief that she had indeed fallen in love with me and was not aware of my newfound bounty.

"Do not fret, my love, for you are the treasure and this bauble but a suitable adornment." I then turned to the vendor and the bartering began in earnest. "Ah, yes, this bright yellow-orange one would be most suitable," I said, "but I could not in all conscience pay more than one livre." The aged vendor's eyes flew skyward, as if he were struck. He moaned—he groaned—he wrung his hands.

"Oh sire, honorable young sire, how could you do such a thing to this honest old merchant? This is the world's finest silk, from beyond the land of the great Kahns. It is dyed with the priceless pigment, saffron. Made with exquisite care such that it will never run, nor fade. Surely your beautiful maiden is worth more than one livre—as surely as I know this precious shawl is worth at least three livres."

Barely suppressing a chuckle, I played the game and replied, "Yes, my gilded-tongued friend, you are right. My beautiful maiden is worth much more than that. Yet, honesty and reality dictates my purse strings. I would perhaps loosen two livres from my purse, but that would be my final offer and only that much in veneration of your age and wisdom."

He shook his head and a sorrowful look creased his brow. "Alas, I could not possibly. Such fine material I am sure will fetch me four livres in Paris. Just feel this amazing texture."

With an exaggerated shrug I smiled and took Izzy by the arm, turning to leave. We had taken but two steps, and I could already sense resigned disappointment in my lover's stride, when there came a voice from behind us. "Hold, sire. I cannot bear to see this lovely maiden without my resplendent material complementing her magnificent red tresses. Such a match is heaven-made. Two livres it shall be."

With an excited giggle, Izzy spun around and rushed back. She scooped up the precious material and caressed her cheek with it. "Oh, Alex, you spoil me so. No one has ever before bought me anything of value. Only Celeste has ever provided me with anything other than crumbs." Her glorious green blue eyes looked up at me adoringly, and my heart swelled with happiness.

The evening smells of braziers cooking various delights set our mouths to watering and we went in search of grilled pig's knuckles with bread and verjuice. As we were about to make this purchase from a food vendor, I chanced to see the Maid entering the square with de Rais at her side.

I stood frozen, instantly stunned by the possible implications and consequences if we four were to meet. There were many people in the square. Perhaps we would not be noticed. The possibility of such a confrontation had not occurred to me. With vivid horror, I remembered Jeanne's reaction at seeing me with Izzy previously. Immediately, I returned my purse to its waistband and seized Izzy by the arm.

"Come, my beauty, I am no longer hungry. Let us leave this vexingly busy place." Izzy was startled at my sudden change of countenance, but offered no resistance. There were four accesses to the square. Reaching two of them meant passing close by Jeanne. Another was blocked off by a dancing Gypsy troupe. Reaching the last and closest required crossing their paths, but at a distance. I chose the latter for expedience and tried to keep a low profile amidst the strollers.

Chancing a glance in their direction, I lucklessly locked eyes with de Rais. His bushy eyebrows rose in recognition and he immediately bent to whisper in the Maid's ear. Cursing my ill fortune, I pressed on, staring straight ahead. We were almost at the archway when an accursed little gamin bolted into the square and accidentally hurtled into Izzy's legs. I was affrighted at the delay, but Izzy laughed, and bent to help the little urchin to his feet.

"WHORE!"

I knew the voice, but it was the strident vehemence that was unnatural. It had cut through the din as a sharp blade through flesh. A pervasive silence fell over the area around the archway as all turned to see what was about—all except Izzy and me. Izzy released the obstructive little gamin and he scurried away. I was as Lazarus—in a state of death and stupor. Izzy glanced sideways at me questioningly, but I had nothing to offer.

We were beginning to turn about when a collective gasp rose from our audience. I heard a whoosh and Izzy pitched forward as if stuck by a broadsword—she indeed was. I tried to cry out, but my throat had tightened like old rolled parchment. There was Jeanne—her eyes enraged, seething with enmity. Her hands hung in front of her, clenching the broken haft of my father's sword. My legs were lifeless and they gave way as I fell to my knees. I crawled to where Izzy lay sprawled face down with the broken sword beside her. Incredibly, there was no blood. How could this be, my befuddled mind questioned? Izzy moaned and she rose to her hands and knees. I touched her back and she winced. The cloth on the back of her gown was split and beneath it a long red welt was appearing. I realized Jeanne must have struck her with the flat of the blade.

"Izzy, Izzy are you very hurt?"

There were tears of pain and humiliation running down her face as she turned to me. "No, I am fine. I am … I am fine, even for a whore," she said, with grim bitterness and looked directly into Jeanne's eyes.

"Be gone from our sight, vile fornicator with the brazen orange shawl. Camp followers that desecrate God's soldiers and their mission are not welcome."

There was a tense silence as Izzy looked hard upon Jeanne, then at me, and then again at Jeanne. I remained in a pitiful Lazarus-like state and could not seem to respond to what was happening. I was caught between the two most important people in my young life and I was powerless. I moved my mouth in some sort of protest, but no words would come forth.

"And you, foul Alex, get to thy stable for you are no longer my knight. You have shown that you are but a squire, impersonating a knight."

Outraged, I stood with fists clenched. Yet, I still could find no words. Looking at de Rais, I saw that typical smirk upon his face. His eyes were not upon me though, for he was concentrating on Izzy, and there was something lewdly sinister in his overt stare. Suddenly, Jeanne threw the broken haft at my feet.

"Tis your choice squire … God's mission, or damnation." Turning on her heel she stomped off with de Rais following in her wake.

Tears stung my eyes as I watched them go and I felt as if everyone was looking at me, whispering, snickering. The noisy milieu had returned, and after a few moments I broke from my morose reverie and turned to Izzy. She was gone. Frantically, I looked about and thought I saw a flash of orange, well beyond the archway. The throng of strollers had closed in about me. I called out her name—then I shrieked out her name. Retrieving my father's haft and blade, I forced my way through the clogged archway, leaving the curses of those jostled and trodden upon in my wake.

I searched well into the night, but to no avail. Like a beaten dog, I returned to the stables—as instructed.

Sorely did I sleep that night. It was hot and moist, making the stable stench most insufferable. I dreamt of terrifying things. I awoke before dawn in a drenching sweat and a scream upon my lips.

I had seen anguished floating heads of the dead and living. Their body parts were strewn about, twitching, sometimes reaching out, as if seeking their owner, or the perpetrator of their state. Charles and Jeanne and de Rais sat upon a throne seemingly as one, for the face kept changing, as if three-sided, rotating. Sometimes they laughed and sometimes they cried, but their fingers were always pointing at me. I tried to run, but was trapped in a thin, rope-like circle of orange. I was simply too weak to leap out of it and they were coming for me.

I think my own scream awoke me, for the horses were neighing and stomping in their stalls. Exhausted, I went outside where it was cooler and fresher, and lay upon my blanket under the stars. I drifted back to sleep, but this time I dreamt of wondrous things. I dreamt of the prophecy Marie Robine had foretold—of my *propitious and peregrinate destiny*. It seemed she was there before me, reminding me. I reached out to her. I ached to have her hold me, secure in her caring arms again. No, she could no longer be in this life with me, she said. It was time for me to fulfill my *own* destiny, for hers was complete. Strangely, she imparted this to me without actually speaking. I tried to question her, but she simply shook her head and faded away—a beatific smile upon her face.

As the sun's cresting rays awoke me, I arose imbued with a purpose. I decided what I dreamt must have been a vision and perhaps Marie Robine was no longer among the living, but somehow she had made my ordained path clearer. She had seemed in a most contented and serene state, such that it left me with a sense of joy for her. Of the earlier vision, I could cull only a profound sense of dread. Though I loved Jeanne, I could not believe she was the light upon my path any longer. Her path was strewn with blood. Innocents were raped and murdered. Deceit and intrigue stalked all about her, and she was blind to it. If this was God's quest for Charles, then he was a callous and unseeing God. I would go in search of my father, for he must somehow be linked with my destiny. First, I would find Izzy and give her what things of value I possessed. Perhaps I would return, but I knew it was time to go. The direction of my footprint would decide my destiny, and the winds of fate would fill my sails.

We were to leave Yonne that day and march to Troyes, with the Dauphin finally at our lead. Since I had been relegated, at Jeanne's command, back to being a simple squire, my normal duties would be to dress and saddle her white steed. I was also again responsible for her personal armor, along with fellow squire, Jean d'Aulon.

He was of lesser time in her service, so the more important duties fell to me. However, I considered my knighthood and squire duties now equally relinquished. I worried not that I was treading on dangerous ground, for who would be concerned about a deknighted squire in these times. Jean d'Aulon was capable and he would likely be cheered by my departure.

Searching the busy morning streets diligently and checking the inns, I had no luck in finding Izzy. Finally near the river at a modest inn called Fleur de Jaune the keeper acknowledged she had been there. Its name reminded me of the Fleur de Lys as I'm sure it did Izzy. I cursed myself, for I should have considered such possibilities earlier, or even yesterday.

"How long ago did she leave, sir, for it is imperative that I find her?" The bald, big-bellied innkeeper looked me up and down as he responded across the rough planked bar.

"Be you a friend of hers?"

"Why, yes, I am a good friend."

"That pleases my ears, because she went out last evening after dark and has not returned to settle her debt."

"She is not a dishonest person, sir. I am sure she will return to settle it." I said this without great conviction, as I was now becoming much worried for her.

"So you say. Past experience tells me to expect otherwise. Perhaps, as a good friend, you would be willing to settle on her behalf. Besides, I might be encouraged to tell you more of her odd departure." The dank smell of stale beer suddenly did not sit well with me, and my gizzard tightened.

My eyes searched his face for deceit, as I said, "Of course, I would be happy to clear the maiden's debt. And what of this odd departure?"

"Maiden! Hah! Pretty perhaps, even with a bar wench's nose, but a maiden traveling on her own? I think not, my young gudgeon. For two, er, three nights, yes, three nights she owed, it will be three livres."

The lying, foul-mouthed pig I chafed silently. To think of Izzy in such a manner and to overcharge—certainly he would not have permitted a second and third night without some fore-payment. Reaching for my purse, where I had discreetly tied it under my armpit, I withdrew three livres and flipped him one. He fumbled with it excitedly and almost dropped it.

"Now tell me what you know before I give up the other livres," I said, with barely veiled malice and contempt.

Peering at me through squinty eyes in the dimness of the empty inn, he grinned an almost toothless grin. "It was a soldier who came looking for her. He seemed to know her, as he asked for the redhead. But when she came down she didn't recognize him. She didn't look herself. She had come back earlier and didn't partake of any victuals. She probably had had a bad customer, heh, heh. They left and that is all I know." He held out his hand.

With outward innocence, I placed another gold livre on the near edge of the bar. As he reached for it, my right hand moved faster than his eye could follow. I had taken to carrying my sheathed short-blade strapped down with haft forward upon my hip—a practice used by the infidels for expedient attack and shown me by Cedric. He never saw it coming. I plunged the blade through the meaty part between thumb and forefinger, burying it deeply into the plank bar. He looked down in shocked disbelief and opened his mouth to scream. With my left fist I punched him in the mouth so hard that it stung my wrist. Then grabbing him by the hair on the back of his head I slammed his cheek down into the bar. My voice seemed not a part of me, as laced with menace, it hissed into his ear, "I need only ask this once old man, for you will listen carefully and answer truthfully all you know. If not, you will have another toothless grin, below your chin and you will lie no more." I paused so that he might digest his dire peril and suspected from the smell that he might have fouled himself. He was shaking violently and emitted a pathetic, whining mewl. Slowly, and with emphatic clarity I demanded, "Who was this soldier? Where did they go? What did they say?" He began blubbering incoherently. "Be still, old man. I do not understand your babble.

Is that all you have to say? It would be so sad—please, let us not part this way."

"Nooo—yes, I have something to tell you. He was a soldier under someone's orders, but he never said. She did not wish to go, but he forced her. I heard him say, his master wished to see her down by the river. I could do nothing. He … he paid me and told me to mind my own affairs. He told her it was just a game, not to worry. Ohh God, please, please don't kill me, sir. I did no wrong." He was blubbering again, and my gut was churning with great angst. Wrenching my blade free, I let him slide off the bar onto the floor in a whimpering, cowering heap and raced out the door.

Thinking back, it is surprising that I acted with such ruthless violence. As a pot of porridge upon the hearth, my simmering soul had become enflamed past the boiling point. Many terrible things had I seen and much had been inflicted upon me. The innkeeper was lucky. There would have been no equanimity for him. I was no longer the same Alex.

I have always been fleet of foot, but I'm sure I was even fleeter as I raced to the river's edge. Instinctively, I ran along the shore in the direction Izzy and I had been previously. I could see an old bargeman and a young boy running toward me in what seemed a state of distress.

"Oh God, dear God, it is awful! Get the town guard, get the barber!" the old man gasped, out of breath. The boy was pale and shaking, moving his lips soundlessly and pointing from whence they had come. I pushed past them and ran upon suddenly leaden legs. Coming upon the naked body, I staggered to a stop, my eyes not wanting to comprehend the horror.

Chapter Eighteen

Suspicion and Sensual Phenomena

I WAS INTERPRETING rapidly. My interest piqued, I could not stop myself from charging headlong down the moribund path this tragic tale was taking. I knew I was missing the odd elemental phrase, colloquialism, or connotation. Janeen was usually all over me when I got sloppy like this, but she was strangely silent. As I turned over to the next parchment, I looked up at her. There were tears welling up in her eyes and one escaped to slip down her slender nose. She had stopped typing on her laptop and was staring at me. But her mind was elsewhere.

"Janeen, what's wrong?" She didn't answer for a few moments, so I put my rule and magnifying glass down and moved to her side of the table. As I put my arm around her she spoke."Maxi, oh Maxi … this is a true tragedy. I can't help but believe in its authenticity. Whether it happened yesterday or five hundred years ago does not lessen the appalling events. Must mankind always be its own greatest affliction?"

"Don't fret so, Jenny. It may be true of mankind, but we also have a great capacity for compassion and love. I've always believed physics is akin to physiology. As for every physical action there is an opposite and equal reaction. So also, for every evil perpetrated, there is an equal, if not greater, kindness accorded."

"Certainly an encouraging credo to believe in, Maxi," she said, as she squeezed my hand. "You sometimes amaze me. You are a conundrum. Thank you for sharing those thoughts, but there's something else weighing on my mind."

"What other misgivings are rattling around in that pretty head of yours?" I asked.

"Well, as I've said before, I took one course on medieval history many years ago, so I'm no authority. However, I do remember a thing or two. One Gilles de Rais did indeed ride with Joan of Arc. I now remember why that left an impression. He was also the infamous child butcher, Bluebeard.

"Sonofabitch! That bastard! Aye, I remember him from some Shakespeare play in high school. Didn't he have a blue beard though?"

"I think that was one of Shakespeare's inventions, Jack."

"What the hell was one of Shakespeare's inventions? What bizarre tangent are you two off on now?" Terry had just returned from her morning jog and was puckishly poking fun at us. Her wounds were healing nicely with the salves. After the first week it had become increasingly difficult to keep her down.

"It's the same tangent, Terry, just a little more enlightening," responded Janeen. "This script is starting to make so much sense, it's scary."

"Well, when Jack starts talking Shakespeare with an air of familiarity it scares me," Terry jested. I ignored her tease, but logged it in my I'll-remember-that-one file. "I may know squat about history, but I do know Shakespeare was a couple hundred years after Joan of Arc," Terry added.

"Yes, of course, Terry," Janeen said, patiently, "but you didn't catch the whole conversation. What we're finding is more validation and accord between this journal and historical fact. Brain cells from our aging memories kick in when their mood suits, it seems. This Gilles de Rais, and Shakespeare's Bluebeard are one in the same. Historically, that's a known fact, so it adds major credence to these scripts. I suppose we could be being duped, but my gut tells me this isn't the case."

"Well, I'll leave you two to it," Terry said as she turned and headed out the door. "I'm going to shower and salve up. It seems I might even be normal one day if this stuff continues to work."

Not being able to resist I called after her, "Normal by whose standards might that be?"

"Jesus, Jack, that fucking shower head is down to a dribble again. I thought you fixed it?" Terry complained, as she came in with a large towel wrapped around her.

These past few days, due to our unavoidable close contact, I had seen Terry partially clothed like this before. I had been deliberately ignoring her, but today for some reason, perhaps my inactive libido, I found myself appraising her anew. Shoulder-length, wet dark hair framed a tanned and ruggedly pretty face. Her eyes were somewhat deep-set and very dark brown. Though she had a strong roman nose, it was not disproportionate. Her lips, though not full, hinted at delicious softness—or, depending on the circumstance, hard implacability. There was something sensually exciting about her, even if her mannerisms were slightly butchy. Her figure, as much as one could see, was slender and well defined with sinewy muscle. She was taller than average and carried herself with confidence. I supposed if I found her sensually attractive, bordering on beautiful, women who were so inclined might also.

"Well, I don't see a piano tied to your pretty arse," I said, in jest.

"I've never played the piano, but thank you for thinking me musical," Terry retorted, with unusual good humor.

"Well, it's almost lunch time anyway. Let's take a break, Janeen. I'll check the shower head and shower up," I suggested.

"Works for me, Jack. Gawd, my neck is stuck," Janeen said, stretching like a cat and slowly rotating her head.

"I know an oriental massage technique that'll fix that in about two minutes. I owe you at least that much for your Florence Nightingale salve ministrations, Jenny," offered Terry, as she disappeared into the bedroom. Terry slept on a cot in the main room, but used our bedroom for changing and salving.

"I'll make some sandwiches after salving Terry," Janeen said, as she headed for the bedroom.

"Righty-right, lass, I'm a starvin." Grabbing an apple on my way out the door, I got a most pleasant surprise. As Janeen briefly pulled back the curtain to enter the bedroom, Terry was removing her towel and laying it on the bed. Seeing her naked form from behind certainly got my attention. Her buttocks were smallish, perfectly formed and rock solid. She did not have large hips, but her slim waist accentuated their flare.

"Damn!" I mumbled to myself, and proceeded to the shower. Stripping down, it was visibly apparent that my two tantalizing roommates were playing on my mind. I cranked on the shower, thinking that would cool my ardor. Shit, it really was a dribble. The problem had been an accumulation of debris in the showerhead so I turned the tap off and unscrewed the showerhead to clean it out. I was surprised to find it free of debris. "Oh bloody-hell!" I cursed aloud. I would have to climb on top of the shed to check the small cistern. Eroded slate flakes from the water supply trough were probably clogging the shower feed.

It was a bit of a feat getting up there, especially naked. Sure enough that was the problem, I soon discovered. As I reached down into the narrow aperture to scoop out the grit, I raised my eyes to a view that ignited my senses like an electric shock. From this height I was looking directly down at the bedroom window about ten meters away. The curtains were open. Because the adobe was built on a higher patch of ground than the immediate surroundings, it would have been otherwise impossible for anyone to see into the bedroom.

Terry was turning over, as Janeen had apparently just finished applying salve to the back of Terry's neck and shoulders. As her breasts shook into view, I was impressed. Though not large like Janeen's, they were full and stood out from her chest as if somehow suspended. They were crowned with very dark brown, swollen nipples—the aureoles appeared shrunken, perhaps cold—or perhaps, excited.

I was transfixed, as Janeen's fingers moved delicately and quickly, dabbing salve on the barely visible, healing scars. I could see Terry physically shiver, and wondered if it was from the cool salve, or from acute sensual delight. As Janeen's finger dabbed salve around a nipple, Terry's hand came up and covered Janeen's. She closed Janeen's hand over her breast and moved it in a circular manner. Terry's eyes were closed and she smiled in obvious delight. Janeen was saying something, but I could hear nothing over the distant surf and rustling branches. Using her other hand Janeen freed herself gently from Terry's grip. I was hardly breathing and my mouth was suddenly dry. I found myself aroused and yet in a state of confusion. I should be upset with such familiarity passing between them, but the voyeuristic demon within seemed to be holding sway.

Janeen now shifted to a sitting position on the edge of the bed, while Terry moved behind her to massage her neck and shoulders. At what appeared to be Terry's insistence Janeen then, somewhat reluctantly, removed her khaki shirt. Janeen had taken to not wearing a bra during our internment and her pendulous, pearly-white breasts flowed free of any confines. The side view of these two lovely ladies held me spellbound. Janeen and I had not had any opportunity for sexual dalliance since Terry's arrival over a week ago. My libido had, until now, seemed to be coping. Terry's ministrations soon effected a countenance of cat-like contentment on Janeen's face. Terry had risen to her knees and now casually allowed one hand to slip down Janeen's front to cup and knead a breast, while still massaging her neck. A sharp intake of breath was Janeen's reaction, but she did not thwart the advance. Terry then bent to nibble at Janeen's neck and I groaned aloud—partly from the evocative carnality and partly from jealousy. My sexual soul was being tormented and I felt powerless to do anything but watch the scene as it played out.

Terry was now gently moving Janeen on to her back. This afforded me a complete frontal view of Terry, if only for a moment. What a creature! She was perfect. No better could an artist have molded the female form in clay. Most surprising and provocative, was the pubescent nature of Terry's body. Her prominent mons was clipped bare—exposed like a ripe nectarine upon a tree. This tree, however, was a sinewy marvel, hewn to perfection by disciplined training. Yet it still retained a feminine allure. Terry bent to kiss and embrace Janeen's breasts, which dipped off the side of her prone form. As her fingers fumbled with Janeen's belt something happened. It was as if Janeen awoke from a trance. Her eyes opened to an exaggerated wideness and she sat up, almost knocking Terry off the bed. An animated discussion ensued, though the exchange was gentle. I was surprised to find myself somewhat disappointed as Janeen rose and donned her shirt.

It was a bizarre, unsettling experience and my limbs were unsteady as I descended to finish my shower. I was filled with mixed emotions. Confusion, anger, arousal and frustration all parried for pre-eminence in my mind.

The unexpected voyeuristic experience was still weighing heavily upon my mind as I returned to the adobe to find my two ladies in a heated conversation. Ignoring them, for lack of a better solution to my dilemma, I sat down in only my cutoffs and began devouring lunch.

"Two very good reasons, Terry: firstly you need another week of healing, and secondly we need more time here on the scripts," Janeen said, forcefully.

"Fucksakes, Janeen, I can go out by myself. If everything is safe, I'll come back for you, and you lovebirds can continue your business under better and maybe even more romantic conditions."

The spiteful tone of Terry's voice seemed to hit Janeen hard, for her expression changed from one of determined calm to one of emotional hurt. Terry was obviously piqued at Janeen's rejection of her sexual advances. Janeen's eyes bore into Terry, as if trying to read her mind and understand the acerbic attitude.

"What the fuck are you two trying to prove?" I said between mouthfuls, unable to hold my tongue. "I saw you! I'm not sure where I stand here, but let's not let this kind of bullshit jeopardize our safety and especially this discovery. And believe me, Terry-lass, that this could be the discovery of a lifetime. You should know Janeen well enough that she wouldn't bullshit or jump to conclusions." Heedless of their shocked expressions I plowed on. "What you know of me is nil, so we won't go into that. Ich dinna think anyone else would have a clue as to what has been found. And that's a bonus for us, a big fucking bonus. You're bloody well right about one thing, Terry—we need to know what's happening in Lima. But let's not get off course. I say give it another week. Then you can slip back into Lima much healthier to scope the scene."

Terry's lips turned up wryly on the corners, realizing with an air of aplomb, that I had witnessed her attempted seduction of Janeen.

"Hum, do we have a Peeping-Tom here then? Oh, I'm sorry, I meant Peeping-Jack?" Terry quipped acidly.

"Screw you. And you didn't exactly get lucky, did you now!" I retorted quickly, before sanity could catch up to my runaway mouth. It went deathly quiet for a moment and I feigned indifference by stuffing my mouth with a sandwich. Suddenly, glasses and plates were flying in different directions, as Janeen slammed both fists down on the table with calamitous results. Vaulting from her chair, the movement jarred the table from its rickety equilibrium and spilt helter-skelter whatever remained upon it.

"YOU BASTARDS! Am I some kind of object? You can both go fuck yourselves. Yeah, that's it—because you deserve each other. I don't need this garbage!"

With tears spilling from her eyes, Janeen stormed out of the adobe. Terry and I turned to each other, and wordless, exchanged a look of mutual regret. I was no longer hungry and the food in my mouth had suddenly become tasteless. I swallowed it as a lump, not wishing to be bothered with it any longer.

"Jesus Christ, Terry, it's been over three hours! Where the hell d'ya think Janeen's got to?" I said, entering the adobe. I had been out on the point trying to read, but mostly the pages went unturned as I watched in vain for Janeen.

Looking up from her book, Terry tried to appear nonchalant, but her dark eyebrows were furrowed with concern. "Sporting of you to care so, Jack. Uhh, sorry—that wasn't called for—just a reflex. Janeen's too savvy to let anything stupid happen. Yet, it's beginning to bother me too. Maybe we should go down to the village and check around, just in case. There's nowhere else to walk to from here."

"Aye, I agree, so let's head out. I'm taking the .38 with me just in case."

With a crooked but forced smile she countered in a deep masculine tone, a la John Wayne, "Good idea, pilgrim."

"Ich dinna understand your gist lass, but a smile does wonders for your features." Her smile broadened slightly, but then vanished, and she looked away as if flustered. Strange, I thought, but was too concerned with Janeen's whereabouts to reflect on this further.

The structure and layout of the old building was very rudimentary. It was a large adobe-style, square building with a peeling whitewash inside and out. There were simple wood tables and uncomfortable, straight back, reed woven, wood-frame chairs. The bar stretched across one end. There were eight or ten tables with the tattered chairs scattered about haphazardly.

"Ferr Crissakes! Look what the damned dog drug in! Machos stud and studdette." This slurred greeting was followed by a falsetto-like laughter, which was girlish and out of character for Janeen. I was surprised to see two seedy characters sitting with Janeen—likely local fishermen, I surmised. There were no other patrons in the bar. Locking eyes with each interloper in turn, I glared at them. Taking the not too subtle hint, the two men chose to vamoose to another table.

Janeen's eyebrows raised in an exaggerated parody of shock and she slurred,"Oooo, you two look positively scary. Have you come to rescue a damsel in distress?"

Looking at Terry, I noticed that her expression was every bit as menacing as mine. Perhaps it wasn't just me who had cowed the locals. Bartenders in such backwater Peruvian bars rarely cleared tables and I could see six empty glasses at Janeen's elbow. Only when they ran out of glasses, would the bartender collect them to be dipped in tepid sink water for reuse. No doubt, these six glasses were probably on Janeen's second cycle, as her eyes were having difficulty focusing. As we sat down in the vacated chairs, I was turning over in my mind several ideas on how to deal with the predicament.

Terry bellowed at the bartender in rapid Spanish. The best I understood with my shaky Spanish was, 'Bring us some chickletes and beer in fucking clean glasses. And tell the Barber to get his ass down here, pronto!'

"What the fuck are chickletes and why the fuck do we need the barber?" I asked.

"I just want to make sure those two scruff are nothing more than that," replied Terry with a steel-hard edge to her voice. Her eyes were raking the bar and our surroundings, never leaving reconnaissance mode. Though she appeared outwardly calm, I sensed from her an air of coiled tension.Meanwhile, Janeen, trying her best to ignore us, turned away and moved to cross her right leg over her left. This exaggerated, nonchalant action resulted in her kicking the table's leg and sent two glasses to their demise on the clay-brick floor. The barman, who was wiping glasses, looked up, and flashed a disgusted scowl. But when he met Terry's glare, he turned away in silent subjugation.

"Janeen, darlin, we're both bloody sorry for what was said. You know how I feel and I'm sure Terry would agree we dinna want to hurt you. We were worryin for your whereabouts. What's the big idea startin a bonny party without us? Bloody hell, it's Saturday and we're all due for a good ripper." My attempt at levity only drew a toss of Janeen's head, as she cleared a lock of hair from her face.

"Jack's right, Jenny. No one meant to hurt you. We only let personal differences get in the way. Strange, you're the object of affection, and you're the one who gets beat up. I'm truly sorry, Jenny."

Hearing Terry's heartfelt words, I felt a grudging, but growing respect for this complicated macho female that I had not anticipated. The surly but subdued barman deposited three foaming beer bottles and three short glasses that were half full of a murky brown liquid.

"What the bloody hell is this, radiator fluid?" I blurted.

"Damn near," Terry said, and as the barman shuffled back to his roost, Terry quietly got up and followed him.

Puzzled by Terry's actions, I glanced over to see the reaction of the other two shady patrons. They had shifted to a corner table and seemed quite drunk, but were keeping a wary eye on Terry. As the barman rounded the corner of the bar Terry thumped her forearms, hands down, with a resonant wallop on the bar. He reacted with an anxious start. Leaning forward, Terry spoke to him in tones low enough that no one else could hear. He nodded and shrugged his shoulders every once in a while. Then she stretched across the bar and tugged on his shirt, bringing her face very close to his for a moment. She turned, one elbow on the bar, and glared at the other two briefly. And then, smiling, sauntered back to our table. The bartender's jaw had gone slack and his demeanor turned from tepid nervousness to overt fear.

"What the fuck are you about, Terry? Why'er you antagonizing the locals?" I asked, as Terry sat down.

"Just lookin after business and makin sure no one bothers Janeen again, Jackie-boy."

Janeen slammed back the foul looking radiator fluid and chased it with a swig of beer. Rolling my short glass between my hands, I cringed at the thought of downing it. "What the fuck are we drinking here—chickletes! Never heard of this shit."

"Not sho bad," slurred Janeen. "Smells like sweet fish. Tastes like smooth white lightning. Reminds me of Maritimer's white lightening. Good fer what ails ya I say."

"It's a local appertif," Terry explained. "I think it originated in

Chiclayo, which isn't far from here. They call it Chinquetes because it's made from rotten fruit, but it smells like fish. The locals fry a thin sardine-like fish called Chanquetes and the smell is similar to this moonshine—hence the name. If you can get past the smell, it's a really smooth but wicked brew."

"Hah, reminds me of other fishy things more to do with the female genre," I quipped.

With an uncoordinated wave of her arm, Janeen retorted, "Ahh, fuck you, Jack—you wouldn't know pussy if it slapped you in the face. An that goes fer you too, Terry." With that riposte, Janeen slumped forward onto the table, her head coming in for a soft landing on her forearm.

"Bloody hell! Not too often does drink get the better of this tough Canuck cookie," I said, in surprise.

"Probably just as well, Jack. She'll be easier to get outta here without any argument. We'll just have to borrow a wheelbarrow for the journey home."

Laughing at that image, I said, "A bonny idea. I'll toast to that," and I drained the devil's brew with a grimace. Surprisingly, it was rather decent and my grimace unfolded into pleasant revelation.

Terry was seized by a sudden fit of laughter at my reaction. "Jack, Jack, you're too much. Some of your expressions just kill me. Especially for a tough-ass, hard-drinkin Scot stud like you," Terry said, shaking her head. The fact she didn't say Scotch stud, did not go unnoticed by me. Maybe there was hope for this hard-case yet. She actually opened up a little then and we had an amicable conversation about our present predicament, past mutual encounters, and future objectives. For her to open up, even so slightly, was somehow a heady tonic for me—assuming, of course, that this was an exchange of realities and truths. I would think it uncommon for professionals, such as her, to open up at any time. Accordingly, I viewed this exchange with some reservation.

As we ordered our fourth round the young messenger finally returned. Cortez, as Terry had called the barman, informed us nervously that the Barber had left the village and would not be back until tomorrow. I knew Terry was uneasy about this, but she calmly ordered Cortez to tell the Barber to contact us pronto upon his return. Obsequiously, Cortez promised this would be done without fail. The bar was now empty and we finished our drinks mostly in silence.

We had to prop up Janeen between us, as we made our way back to the adobe in the waning light. Climbing the brief talus slope leading to our dwelling, I stumbled and fell—more due to Janeen's discordant pace and my own insobriety than the loose rock. My fall caused a chain reaction that ended with my face getting planted in Janeen's crotch and Terry's face in my crotch. The hilarity of it was magnified by our mutual stupor.

Terry interrupted our uncontrolled mirth with mock seriousness, "Jesus Christ, Jack! This rod between your legs is hard as steel!"

With that, she reached into my flap pocket and rummaged around, a mischievous glint in her eyes. In doing so, she actually brushed my penis, causing a galvanic reaction in my loins. Looking up I saw Janeen raise her head and her glassy eyes focused in surprise.

Terry pulled out the .38 and exclaimed, "Ahah! You sly pretender."

At this we rolled around in drunken delirium, unable to stop laughing for several minutes. When we finally staggered into our adobe, Janeen and I had a major case of the hiccups that gave cause to further jests from the equally inebriated Terry. It was an evening of surprises and Terry's positive change of demeanor left me mystified. I asked Janeen about this the next day, but she casually shrugged it off, replying, "That's just Terry—she has many faces … more good than bad, actually."

The Barber arrived early the next morning. Terry went outside with him and from a distance I could see his responses to her apparent grilling were rather animated. I surmised it must have been over his absence. Terry's mien was calm, but I sensed a deadly tempest brewing just below that veneer. After their initial sparring the tension seemed to dissipate and he departed on apparent peaceable terms.

"I think we're going to have to find another safe-house soon," Terry said when she came back in. "We've been here long enough and my cuts seem to be mostly healed."

"It's something to do with the Barber and security, isn't it?" Janeen asked, before I could.

"I don't know. It's just a feeling. He supposedly went to meet another agent for an intel update, but had nothing new to tell me."

"Goddam all to hell, Terry. We're making good progress on the scripts. I sure as fuck don't want to waste time running around the country at this point," Janeen complained irritably.

"We may not have a choice, Jenny. I'm going down to check out my plane. I want it ready just in case we need to bug out."

After Terry had left, I looked at Janeen and said, "We might as well trust Terry's judgment. She's supposed to be the pro. What say we get to work while we can? If we bear down there's a chance we could finish this in the next few days."

"Humph, that's the first time I think you've ever agreed with Terry," was Janeen's only reply.

Chapter Nineteen

DELIVERANCE

IZZY'S HEAD had been hewn from its torso in the same manner as the young girl in Chinon. It had been placed with deliberate purpose on a prominent rock. The beautiful red hair was carefully arranged around it and the rock pedestal was red with a mixture of blood and hair.

Finding her discarded cloak, I covered her once beautiful and now desecrated body. I wished to do something with the gruesome specter of her head, but all I could effect was to prostate my form in front of it, numb and distraught. I wept copious tears and know not how long I remained so.

There was the sound of horses' hooves and the approach of clamoring people. As the noise surrounded me I forced myself to look up. Standing about me were many townsfolk, their expressions of disgust plain. Among them, at the fore, were three mounted horsemen.

A sudden fit of revulsion and rage pierced my bowels like a smithy's red-hot forge iron. It was de Rais. Regnault and some other odious minion flanked him on their mounts. Still kneeling, I locked eyes with de Rais and he seemed to squint—no, he smirked at me. I knew then beyond doubt who the foul perpetrator of Izzy's murder was. In fact, I am sure he wanted me to know. My reaction was instant and predictable. With a guttural growl emanating from deep within my being, I drew my dagger and leapt to my feet. I charged him, my growl escalating to a base, primitive howl. Startled by my immediate reaction, he swerved his mount to thwart my attack. Not caring the consequence, I slashed out blindly, catching his destrier on the chest. My thrust was deflected by the beast's breastplate armor, but slashed its foreleg deeply as it reared back. A flying hoof caught me on the jaw, knocking me off my feet. Dazed, I struggled up and renewed my attack. The injured horse spun such that de Rais could not draw his sword, for he needed both hands to fight the reins. From the corner of my eye, I saw the flash of Regnault's sword. I raised my dagger to deflect it and did so well enough that the flat edge glanced off my shoulder. Still, the impact knocked me to the ground again. Rolling, I bounced to my feet, ready to renew my attack. An unfamiliar townsman then jumped in front of me and I thought he had come to my aid. Instead, all I saw was the blur of his staff as it crashed upon my head.

There was something terribly wrong. My arms were being extracted from their shoulders. I was drowning in a sea of red and yellow. As I fought to find the surface of this painful sea, my knees were battered upon a rocky seabed. My head was bursting, but I could not bring my hands up to comfort it. My eyes gained a measure of focus and I saw that my knees were being dragged across cobblestones. I tried to get my feet under me, but only succeeded in stumbling back to my knees. I realized I was being dragged through the streets of Yonne. My wrists were tied in front of me with a staff passed through my arms behind my back. Trussed in this manner, two sturdy townsmen each had an end of the staff and were hauling me along mercilessly. There was a din about me with sporadic shouts rising above it. They seemed to be yelling for my head, my very life.

"Hang the butcher!"

"Send him to the rack!"

"Draw and quarter the devil!"

"Let us stoke a stake for him!"

I could only see clearly through one eye, as the other felt like it was caked with blood and swollen shut. Someone jumped in front of us and I recognized the fat innkeeper from the Fleur de Jaune. One hand was swathed in a bloodied cloth and his lips were grossly swollen. This interruption of our progress allowed me to gain an unsteady footing. He suddenly revealed a butcher's cleaver in his good left hand and raised his arm to strike. I knew I must immediately make my peace with God, for surely this was death staring me in the face. His arm swept toward me and hobbled as I was, could do little to avoid it. In that instant I heard a familiar tinkling of bells and a very large arm shot in front of the innkeeper's. It seized the offensive wrist halfway toward my head, stopping its progress abruptly. The innkeeper howled with rage and was rewarded with a fist to his battered mouth. As the innkeeper crumpled to the cobblestones, I recognized my savior in the hulking form of La Hire.

"There will be no crowd justice here," La Hire loudly proclaimed. "Justice shall be meted out by the superiors to whom this soldier must answer. So clear the way!"

For a mercenary like La Hire to show a taste for justice was most unusual. I attribute his intervention as motivated by soldiering kinship only. Normally, a mob scene such as this would only be an amusing dalliance to entertain him. I thanked God for my preservation, but realizing everyone must blame me as Izzy's butcher, knew my future did not look promising.

The Yonne gaol was a filthy affair. It was a sturdy wooden structure abutting the castelan's fortress. I was cast into the dug out level, which offered no light or anything more than stale, putrid air to breathe. My tiny oubliette was but dirt walls and floor with a low timbered ceiling.

The gaol was rife with rats scurrying about in the sloped corridor that led down to my Hadean hovel. Occasionally I could hear these creatures scratching at my door. There was a buried block under the doorframe which made it impossible for them to dig their way in and also, as intended, impossible for a prisoner to dig his way out. There was a small gate over this block, latched from the outside. It was just large enough to pass hands and then feet through to be manacled or unmanacled and to allow access for the daily plate of gruel. I was obviously a demented murderer, so I was left manacled in my cell. There was a rough board on the floor for a palliasse and a pot in corner for human waste. The narrow eye-level slit in the door permitted only the faintest light and it was not possible for me to discern if that be daylight or a distant candle. Consequently, I had no concept of time, except when I received my morning gruel.

There was almost complete silence, save for the occasional faint groan of another prisoner. When I tried to rest I could feel tiny vermin upon me, or at least, so I thought. This may have driven me to dementia, but the excruciating pain in my arms and shoulders weighed more heavily upon me. Worse though yet, was the consuming grief, which seeped blackly into every crevasse of my being. Even in sleep there was no escape from the horror and my sense of failure. Surely my life was over and the horrific dreams were purgatory incarnate. The gaolers' canes interrupted my first night's sleep. Two of them were beating me without mercy—waking me from my screams. Apparently my demented shrieks were a bother to them. Battered and bloodied, I thereafter screamed silently.

It must have been my third day in that mole's hole, for I had been twice fed and my empty belly told me it must be getting close to the next *soi-disant* feeding time. I had not much stomach for eating, yet my survival instinct somehow made the prospect of dry molded bread and thin gruel almost appealing this day.

I could hear the gaoler fumbling with his keys at my cell door. But wait, he was opening the door instead of the little gate and I realized there were other voices. Voices other than the gaoler's, who often enjoyed conversing with himself. Immediately did I quake for I knew it would be the stake—my dreams had told me so. My purgatorial dreams were vivid and real. I had seen myself burn—felt the interminable sting of the flames licking at my body while Izzy looked on approvingly. Izzy's head was not quite attached in these dreams. It floated above her torso, as if on a tether. And now, now they were coming for me. So be it, I resigned in my stupor. It was my just desserts for failing Izzy.

I was blinded. The light was more intense then the mid-day summer sun. Oh dear God, they were bringing the flames *to* me. My doom was palpable and imminent. "Most honored Maid, I pray thee not to enter, for he is demented and dangerous."

The answer was sweet and clear, like that of an angel's soft breath, bringing light and warmth to darkness and cold. "God is looking down upon us this moment. There is no danger in the presence of God, excepting for those followers of Lucifer. Here lies a Christian and friend of France."

I took a chance and allowed my hopes to soar.

"Rise Alex … friend, squire, knight, so that you may greet your Maid civilly."

I had thought there could be no more water remaining in my eyes to beget tears. I was wrong. I cried and trembled uncontrollably upon hearing Jeanne's angelic voice. Perhaps she had come to take me from this purgatory and deliver me to heaven. I struggled to my knees and focused on the eerie, brilliant vision in white that stood before me.

"Remove yourself from our presence gaoler. I will summon you if needed."

The gaoler briefly protested, but daunted by her hard gaze withdrew as a vermin into the darkness. There was a passage of time where only my sobs blighted the silence. Slowly, through the tears and brilliance of the lantern, my radiant Jeanne became manifest. There was an uncharacteristic furrow upon her brow as she finally spoke.

"What have you done, Alex? What have you come to? Am I to believe the heinous things being said? That you are not only a consorter with whores, but a foul butcher as well?"

"Je, Jeanne, my angelic Maid, you must know that such a thing could not be true. She was a wonderful person and I loved her, as

I love you." I responded, trying to control my sobs. Jeanne's angry, raised voice then struck me as might a mortal blow.

"How dare you! To love her is almost a sin in itself. But to say you love us both in the same breath insults both God and me. What has become of you, Alex? You cannot be the innocent boy I lo … cared for. Innocence has been washed away by the sin in which you wallow."

I was suddenly empty. All the fear, the pain, the bitter hatred, fell away from me as putrid flesh from a corpse. I was only the skeleton—no longer hurting, but no longer feeling—merely lifeless. I now knew that truly, Jeanne had loved me as I had her. It had hovered upon her lips. She could not say it, nor could she ever. And consummated it could never be. She was wed to God. There could never be a place for me in her heart, especially now. I could not raise my head to look upon her. She seemed to be waiting for my response, but with none forthcoming, she finally said with a sigh, "Oh, Alex, poor Alex, I do not believe you are capable of what you stand accused. I have managed to forestall a judgment against you, but we are to march this day for Troyes. The best I could accommodate was to have you sent back to Orleans, for public opinion is strongly against you here. When the Dauphin, soon now to be king, returns with de Rais and La Tremoilles, you will be dealt with fairly."

And then she was gone. Oh, dear God, she was … gone.

I was numb, sullied and beaten. I could feel nothing in my limbs, or heart. My pained body moved as if in a trance and the trance in which I swirled was a crucible of sorrow. No longer did I care about life or death. I knew I was doomed, for de Rais had most effectively plotted my ruin to cloak his depravity. I felt I was suffering from some form of dementia and I was powerless against it.

A few hours after Jeanne left, I was shackled in gyves and taken from my cell. It was night as we emerged from the gaol and the air was blessedly fresh, like a recent dust settling shower. Not long was I able to savor this small joy. A two-handed blow across my back from the gaoler's staff drove the air from my body and pitched me forward to the back of an ox cart. I was roughly hefted in and then further shackled to its side. The streets were empty. Jeanne probably arranged the timing, for as I think now, the masses would not have let me leave alive in daylight. Of that I am certain, for between de Rais' people and the Fluer-de-Jaune innkeeper, my fate would have been sealed.

The cart bounced along at a good pace, delivering further abuse to my battered body. Leaving Yonne's outskirts I began to be aware of my immediate surroundings. It was a warm, clear night with a full moon. There was a young man of my age handling the reins and a horse, presumably his, tethered behind the cart. There was also an older mounted guard attired with ill-fitting soldier's garb, riding alongside the cart. This did not seem unusual, as conscripted peasants would often don accoutrements stripped from fallen foes. What tickled my mind, though, was that there was something familiar about these two.

The other odd thing was the bundle in the cart beside me. It seemed a human form wrapped and tied in a blanket, as might be a plague victim on its way to the pyre. The pyre! Sudden fear gripped me in its cold claws and I cried out, "Oh God! Why have you deserted me? Take me now! Strike me down if you must, but spare me the PYRE!"

"Be quiet, Alex. Do you want to have the townsfolk down upon you?"

It was the older, mounted one who spoke. Realizing he had addressed me by my name I turned to look upon him more closely. He was a large man, with a full grizzled beard. Recognition came slowly, as his hoary old face became that of the bargeman from Orleans. As my contorted mind absorbed this fact, he laughed aloud at my look of confusion.

"El, El Capitan!" I sputtered, not quite comprehending the situation. "How is it that ... Am I in a dream?"

After another snorting laugh he related his tale. Caught up in the flush of victory at Orleans, he and his two oldest sons had offered their services to the Dauphin and Maid. They had fought at Jargeau, Melun, Beaugency and Patay. They had cheered my success and the news of my knighthood at Jargeau. When they heard of my murderous crime in Yonne it was with total disbelief.

Fate had played its rueful game with their lives as well. His eldest son had dispatched a foot soldier at Jargeau, but the foe had managed to wound his mount. The beast in its panic tossed his son from the saddle. El Capitan watched helpless, as the son fell upon an enemy's broken lance. He was pierced gravely in the side, but it was not sufficient to kill him. Alas, potions and bleeding of the bad blood by a barber could not staunch the slow flow of life from his body. He had died two days past. Twas him tied in the blanket, going home to his mother for burial. Even in his grief, El Capitan thought of offering his services to escort me back to Orleans, so that I might have a chance at fair judgment. He confirmed all my fears that one of France's professed heroes, de Rais, had foully accused me and incited the townspeople. How dare I so cruelly butcher a fine young wench and then turn on de Rais the valiant! Such was the mood of the locals.

As the sun showed its bright face from the direction of Domremy, I thought of how much I had lived through in such a short time. Much had I seen and done, but what good had come of it. What was the purpose of all this … this pain and passion and anguish? Surely, God had not intended it so.

Only at mid-day did El Capitan finally decide it was safe to rest and break bread. "We should reach Orleans on the morrow," El Capitan proclaimed, through a mouthful of bread, cheese and wine.

"Mama would perhaps wish it not so, when she receives Duarte," Pedro said. He had spoken very little on our journey, so when I became aware of the brothers' names I asked El Capitan about them.

"Ahh, yes, you wonder at my sons' names being Portuguese. My mother, as well as my children's mother, is French, but my father was a fisherman from the county Portucale. I am proud to say that I have named my sons after the sons of King Joao of Portugal. I served under the *great man* when I was young and captained several vessels protecting his coast. My youngest son, Enrique, remains at home protecting our barges.

King Joao's third son Enrique has taken up the sea much more so than his elder siblings. Like King Joao, I have been blessed with fine sons. But the pain of losing the eldest is something I hope the great man does not have to bear." With that, he hung his head as if it suddenly became very heavy, and conversation ceased for a time.

After victuals, El Capitan rose and retrieved something from his horse's panier. When he unwrapped it my eyes grew large in surprise. It was my father's broken sword. As he presented it to me, he said, "The Maid brought this to me just before I came for you." He chuckled then and, reaching inside his travel bag, tossed me a jangling purse, which I recognized as the purse I had hidden in my barracks. "Oh yes, I almost forgot this minor thing called money. I was sorely tempted, but… " With that he rose, withdrew a key from his purse, and proceeded to unshackle me. I was bewildered, and my mouth must have been agape, for he said, "Best you close your mouth lad, lest it tempt the flies. It seems the Maid went to your barracks to check your belongings, as such things tend to quickly disappear when one is incarcerated."

Indeed this was true, I thought, for the bit of money I had with me had somehow disappeared off my person. I was still at a loss for words, so he proceeded. "Twas a strange conversation I had with the Maid. She instructed us to deliver you to Orleans, but also alluded that should you escape, you would need these personal items."

I rubbed my chafed, raw wrists and ankles as the last gyve fell away. I started to speak, but El Capitan held up his hand and continued, "She told me to let the Lord be my conscience and rectitude will result. She also said, if this event were to happen, you must leave France and seek no vengeance, for retribution is God's alone. It was then she did as Pontius Pilatus and rinsed her hands in a basin, saying that she is done with you and may God be with you always. It seemed to me there were tears upon her cheeks as she left." El Capitan looked at my face intently, perhaps searching for truth. What he saw was a silent, steady stream of tears escaping my eyes.

This seemed to puzzle him and he shook his head muttering, "Young people, young people—huh."

El Capitan was making ready to ride on, when he spoke further, "There is something else I know of you lad. You are of Templar heritage."

The look of shock that came upon my face amused him. "Do not fear, my friend, for you are in the company of Templars. The past hundred years have not been kind to our brethren and it is wise to be tight-lipped about these things. Jean de Monteclair is one of us and he knew of you from Cedric—God rest his large soul. When your peril became evident I did what any Templar would. It was fortunate I was in a position to help."

I was invited to ride upon Pedro's horse while he drove his brother's hearse. My battered body was grateful, for to be unfettered and on a mount was far more comfortable."I am indebted to you beyond words or deeds, El Capitan," I said. "But it would seem to me, you put yourself at peril by unshackling me."

"We have more than unshackled you, my friend, Alex. You are free to go. As God is my conscience I worry not of any peril in this world. I have done many foul things in my life, and my evil deeds dealt upon others would be too many to count. My time for atonement is now. Perhaps I may lessen a lengthy purgatory for having followed the Maid and abiding with her suggestions."

"I thank you, good Templar friend," I acknowledged. "Perhaps I may yet return from death's door … although it pains me sorely to think of leaving Gaul."

We rode on in silence for a while and I considered my fate. My addled head was beginning to function and slowly an idea was blossoming into a plan. "El Capitan, how would you suggest one to travel to Portugal? Particularly, one not wanting to be noticed," I asked.

"Yes, that is a prudent consideration. In fact I was thinking also of that very same notion. Firstly though, I have decided that you met your end while foolishly trying to escape and drowned in the Loire while still shackled. Unfortunately, we were unable to recover your body."

I smiled for the first time in days. "It would seem to me, esteemed friend, that you have some experience in these matters."

With a resonant belly laugh, El Capitan agreed. "Tis not alchemy, lad. When one has learned to live by one's wits, such things come naturally. We are fortunate so many are on their way to Reims and these roads are empty. Let me think on things awhile, for I feel the seed of a plan sprouting."

Between El Capitan, Pedro and me we agreed on a plan. I would ride ahead to Gien and, keeping my face from view thanks to Pedro's cloak, take the Gien ferry across the Loire. It was not likely I would be recognized, but caution is safety's angel. From there I would ride to Saint Jean Le Blanc across the Loire from Orleans. El Capitan's home was close to the ferry dock at Saint Jean Le Blanc and I would watch from a distance for their arrival via the Orleans ferry on the morrow. They would then hide me in their home and send me off the next night in monk's clothing.

El Capitan recommended I take one of his coracles down the Loire. Seeing a monk paddling down the Loire should not arouse suspicion, he insisted. I would be floating past Blois, Tours and the distant Chinon. At the town of Saint Pierre, I was to leave my boat and strike off on foot to the south and west. I could recognize Saint Pierre by a beautiful chateau towering high above it. It was the once powerful Duke de Berry's favorite chateau—a sometime employer of El Capitan's. The duke was to be avoided as untrustworthy, he warned.

El Capitan had friends in the port of La Rochelle. They were mostly pirates and other such characters, but some were Templars. With his seal of trust, and the occasional gold livre, I would be reasonably safe. The reasonably part plagued me, but what could possibly be worse than my present predicament. Whether in the company of pirates or not, I knew I must get to Portugal. My mission was now to find my father and leave this godforsaken country of my birth. I must leave behind the pain, the love, the sacrifice, the people, and … and Jeanne d'Arc.

Marie Robine's words returned to me once again. With clarity and cogency did they re-awaken me to my life's direction. As I touched the star-like mark behind my right ear, I could hear Marie's counsel, *'Alex, dear Alex, you will have a most propitious and peregrinate destiny. You are among The Destined and your Templar heritage will be the beacon to your future'.*

Chapter Twenty

Going Home

As I drifted and paddled down the Loire there was much time to reflect on what my future might hold. It took me three days to reach Saint Pierre. I stopped only for short periods to sleep or stretch and ate sparingly of my bread and cheese. I took wide courses past Blois and Tours, and of Chinon, I was too distant to worry. By the time the magnificent chateau at Saint Pierre came into view, I had resolved what my plan must be.

I prayed my father was still serving Prince Enrique, as Father Pasquerel had related to me. Surely my future must be in Portugal with my father, for it seemed forces I could not comprehend were drawing me there.

El Capitan had related more of his history to me so that I might be successful in my journey and have some understanding of Portugal. He even told me of his christened name. Few people knew of it, as he did not much care for it. Only his closest confidants and fellow Templars knew his christened name, Robert Pequeno. Knowing this, he said, would serve me well if I were in the company of Templars who knew him. It would be for me, his seal of trust.

El Capitan regaled me with exhilarating tales of the sea. He told me of the first voyage of exploration Prince Enrique had sent out, some seventeen Epiphanies past. As commander, he sailed beyond a place called Cape Nao. He had to keep a stern hand, for his men were ever fearful of sailing off the edge into the great abyss. There were stories of boiling waters that would swallow a ship and of waters so shallow that a ship might be marooned forever, far from land. That is, of course, if you could first survive the sea demons.

El Capitan was a fearless man of strong character, for he laughed at such stories as he recounted them. After that voyage, his French wife, Maurina, had inveigled him to move them to her hometown of Orleans. Their second son, Pedro, had been born in his absence, and she would have no more of his trying to sail off the edge of the world. It was with great reluctance that he left Portugal, but apparently, Maurina was of even stronger will than he. She was still a beautiful woman, I discovered. When we returned Pedro to her arms, it was a most heart-rending sight to see her terrible anguish.

Previous to sailing with Prince Enrique, El Capitan had first fought with King Joao of Avis at Tui many years past. He told me that after the Battle of Tui he was commissioned to help rid the coastline of those wicked, plundering Castilles. Prince Enrique later took up residence near Lagos at the most southwesterly promontory called Sagres and persuaded his father to give him men like El Capitan. Many expeditions have been made since El Capitan's daring voyage, but the progress of exploration was slow. It did not take much encouragement from my Templar friend to stoke my fires of adventure. I resolved to cast off my cloak of sadness and disappointment, and to be reborn. I knew, as I stepped from my coracle at Saint Pierre, that my life was once again twisting and turning in the winds of destiny.

I did not spend any time in Saint Pierre though it seemed a fine village. El Capitan warned me of Duke de Berry's transient political disposition, which was always predicated by his avaricious nature. Much like La Tremoilles, his interests swayed with pecuniary circumstance.

De Berry's father had squandered the dukedom's riches on all manner of eccentric frivolities. If it was Charlemagne's tooth, he must have it. If it was Christ's cup from the last supper, he must have it. If it was a rare animal or exotic bird, he must have it. If it was a priceless sky blue pigment, he must have it. It was said, according to El Capitan, that he ground gold and pearls together as a laxative. And all this in the midst of the calamitous black plagues and a destitute peasantry. The son, and current Duke de Berry, had inherited these obscene proclivities, as well as an insolvent dukedom. Certainly, he would be a grasping, greedy sort to avoid for a ransomable fugitive such as myself.

I purchased a rather decrepit horse in Saint Pierre, but the beast served me well. I also did not wish to look conspicuous as a humble monk. Though I was far removed from my tormentors, it was prudent to exercise caution.

Making my way on what roads and trails I could find to the south and west, I entered land that became steadily higher. I passed through a town called Argenton and crossed a fast, but shallow river known as Sevre. I was loath to ask many questions or directions so I muddled my way along slowly. To my best recollection I could not remember traversing this region, though I had traveled extensively and widely with Marie Robine. I foraged for berries and made the occasional purchase of cheese, bread and wine. This high region was slightly better off than other more ravaged areas of France. The days were warm, yet the nights required a fire or sleeping in close proximity with my beast. Parts of this land seemed almost untouched by the conflagration, and the people I talked to led a simple, but contented life. Regrettably, I took no time to savor this area, for my goal was Portugal.

Once through the highlands I started a gradual descent and passed through a very poor village known as Chantonnay. There I encountered a small river that the locals called Lay and followed its sometimes rapidly descending course. I knew I was approaching the sea by the scent of salt and seaweed in the breezes. Quite suddenly, its massive breadth and reflected brilliance at mid-day was before me. I had not seen the sea since my early youth, but as an old friend, it warmed me and bestowed upon me a sense of peace.

La Rochelle—ah, La Rochelle—it is my last memory of France and not at all unpleasant. La Rochelle has always maintained a self-sufficient, independent disposition. Its leaders guarded and affected their autonomy with zeal. The one thing, which kept me especially wary, was that this was La Tremoille's home ground. In fact, that very danger kept me constantly vigilant and thereby enhanced my safety in this notorious seaport.

Approaching La Rochelle from the northern headlands, I was kept in a constant state of awe by the vastness of the seascape. The shoreline was pleasantly pocked by small sandy coves. They beckoned invitingly, but I pressed on. In the distance I could see a large island with La Rochelle's Vieux-Port in its lee. This island I came to know as Ile de Re and learned it was a refuge for many ships engaged in illegal activities.

Arriving at a particularly sandy beach not far from La Rochelle, I chanced to meet a peddler with a heavily burdened ass in tow. He was pleased to trade some food and clothing for my horse. Such a bargain he would not have dared hope for and was consequently most informative. The old hump-shouldered peddler even knew of the particular person whom I sought—one Emanuel Machado de Portucale.

Emanuel was a lifelong friend of El Capitan's and a fellow Templar. I had been told he would be my safest contact in La Rochelle. The peddler informed me that if Emanuel were currently to be found in La Rochelle, it would likely be at the Inn Rue Thiers, not far from the Tour de la Chaine. Perhaps, I thought, my fortune had taken a turn for the good. It was late afternoon, so I decided to rest upon the warm beach and test my fate in La Rochelle on the morrow. Twas an inspiring sun that sunk into the sea that evening—surely an auspicious sign—and thus it was in peaceful comfort I slept for the first night in many.

With a decided measure of savoir-faire I rose to greet the morning light and I was not disappointed at the day's end. I found the Inn Rue Thiers and was informed by the proprietors that Emanuel was indeed in the region. He had recently arrived as the first mate on a merchant ship. However, two days past he had sailed with another crew over to Ile de Re. He was reportedly to be gone only a few days.

I had a pleasant visit with the innkeeper Georges Iribe and his wife, Jocelyne. They were a gregarious pair and told me of many local features and customs. It was a surprisingly pleasant inn and I was lucky to obtain a room. That night the cheerful rotund Jocelyn Iribe cooked a stuffed-duck, the fineness of such I had never tasted in my young life. It had been many weeks since I had tasted meat. Running rich with grease and permeated with sage and apple from her garden it was a delight to remember.

I had spent that afternoon along the main quay, gaping at ships of all shapes and sizes. Most were fishing crafts, but there were also many merchant ships and even a few war ships. The next few days afforded me the opportunity to study these vessels and I savored the experience.

After bathing in the ocean and a sound night's sleep on a soft straw palliasse, I was treated to more of Jocelyn Iribe's fine cooking. Fresh bread, creamy butter, anchovies and even fresh boiled eggs cooked in her blazing hearth.

Strolling round the horse-hoof shaped quay, I took closer note of the two edifices guarding the narrow passage into the moorage bay. On the west there was the massive Tour de la Chaine and on the east, an even more impressive Tour Saint-Nicolas. Their seaward pointing cannon would have a decided advantage over any foolish aggressor approaching by sea. Thick walls began at each tower and completely surrounded the town. They looked formidable though they were not high such as Orleans. I learned that negotiation and political alliance were the greater forte of La Rochelle. Little wonder then that La Tremoille prospered in Charles' court, for his home ground was well steeped in the artifice of successful intrigue.

Stopping to scrutinize a large warship, I observed that it had two tiers of ports on either side. Each port would project a long oar and I could envision the ship's great speed and maneuverability with a skilled crew. It was of narrow prow and beam, enabling it to cut swiftly through the water. I learned, however, that this design did not allow for either much cargo or for stability in rough seas. There were culverins mounted fore and aft, with six cannon on deck. It would surely be a wicked fighting machine at close range, where foes could be damaged and boarded. Certainly, however, it would be limited to coastline warfare, as it appeared too light to face the rough open seas.

The merchant ships were usually fitted with sails on one or two masts and appeared much more cumbersome. They were broader of beam with fewer oars, often lacking ports for them. I learned many things by observation and from any seaman who might stop to answer my lean-witted questions. Ships were always guarded from intruders and no amount of cajoling could gain me access. This was a busy port and though punishments were harsh, thieves lived and often died in the sly procurement of other's booty. Theft was high risk, but simple survival could dictate such reckless acts. The harbor and its milieu enthralled me and it was there I spent my time in anticipation of Emanuel's return.

I felt I must have been viewing an apparition. The similarities were so great that Emanuel could certainly be El Capitan's brother. Emanuel was slightly shorter and broader with eyes black as night, but otherwise he was a twin. Perhaps it was the bushy, black, grizzled beard that made the similarities so striking. I rose from my dinner chair as Georges Iribe made introductions.

"Oho! Tis a pleasure to meet a friend of my old friend, El Capitan." His reaction was loud and boisterous and he was obviously glutted with wine. As we clasped hands his grip all but crushed mine. Such a large, rough, leathery hand I had never encountered before. Many years upon the sea, spent pulling on wet stubborn ropes and oars had transformed his paws into scabrous anvils. Not much conversation occurred as Emanuel slurped and grunted his way through dinner. After devouring an enormous quantity of food he pushed his plate away and released a resounding belch while breaking wind. We were the last in the kitchen, save for Jocelyn, and I was shocked when she turned from her labors at Emanuel's deplorable actions and said, "Thank you, kind sir."

I later learned that such noisy expressions were considered a compliment in the infidel, Moorish culture. Traveled sailors sometimes picked up such habits, or at least that is their pretext. I was disappointed at meal's end, as Emanuel's head soon slumped forward and he proceeded to snore fitfully. With some difficulty, Georges was able to rouse him enough to guide him to his room. Unfortunately for me, he was led to the other bed in my room. I was subjected to such a thunderous serenade of snoring that little did I sleep that night.

I rose early the next morn and was surprised to find my sleeping mate already up and gone. Perhaps it was the quietude that had awakened me. I found Georges stoking the hearth for his wife. He informed me that Emanuel had gone down to the quay to supervise the loading of his ship, the Santa Marta, for they would be setting sail for Lisboa two days hence. My feet were flying as I rushed to the quay in the early morning light. With some difficulty I found the Santa Marta, for it was not the only ship loading at this hour.

Emanuel's ship seemed not so impressive to me, for it lacked the sleekness some others possessed. It was called a Barca, but was, at 4000 stone weight, considered a smaller sort. It had one mast amid ship mounting two large square sails. There was one smaller square sail rigged off the forecastle, and aft it had an angular sail called a lateen. Its length may have been four lance lengths and its breadth perhaps one. I found that even after it was fully loaded, it bobbed like a wine cork. Its span amid ship was bowed such as a loaded arbalest. At the time, I could not appreciate its design and purpose, but confidently assured myself that this conveyance was to be my aqueous chariot to salvation.

After briefly observing the craft and the loading procedure, I began assisting the crew. There were three large carts whose contents they were transferring to the hold. The crew seemed to pay me little notice as I helped move large bundles of wool textiles, coiled rope and chain link to the ship's gangway. Emanuel was on deck bellowing instructions to those on and off the ship. It was a little while before he noticed me, and there was then a conspicuous pause in his sonorous commands. He frowned, so I looked away and labored ever more diligently. After a while my arms were aching such as they might fall off. The morning was cool, but I was sweating profusely.

"Here, *poco mozo*! Get your sorry arse up on deck."

At first I was not aware the stentorian directive was meant for me.

"Are you deaf, as well as dumb?"

Looking up, I realized Emanuel's invective was directed at me. Flustered and anxious, I hurried up the gangway, tripping onto the deck and landing upon my chin at his feet. Those upon the deck found this a jolly joke and took time from their labor to laugh heartily. Emanuel, however, only glowered and crossing his arms sternly reproached, "What game is this you play, *mozo*? We are not in need of any fools upon this ship."

Mortified, I stammered, but nothing of consequence came forth.

"Stop this babble! Stand up and speak as a man."

I scrambled to my feet and attempted to gather my courage and dignity. "Sir, Emanuel Machado de Portocale, revered seaman and friend of El Capitan," and then I whispered only loud enough for him to hear, the name Robert Pequeno, before raising my voice again. "I am here at his direction, seeking employment and passage to Lisboa. I humbly… "

"Enough!" Emanuel roared, with an impatient wave of the hand. "Perhaps providence shines upon you this day," he said in a much lower tone. "One of my oarsmen had his hand pruned of a few fingers while fighting over a wench last night. Have you ever manned an oar before?"

I gulped, briefly, choking back a lie. "No, no sir. Only that upon the river, but I am strong and will not disappoint you."

"Harumph … apparently honest, if nothing else. Well, for my old friend, El Capitan, you shall have your chance. Though you may be the sorrier for it," he said with a sagacious smile. "Now back to work and be quick about it."

With buoyed heart and gusto did I return to my toil, eager not to disappoint.

Twas an eerie feeling rowing through the port passage at my cramped oar station. I said my silent prayers and farewells, for I knew not if I would ever return to my native soil. In fact I felt sure that fate had me in tow and my future no longer included France.

Upon reaching open water, oars were ordered raised and withdrawn. The winds were in our favor and all sails were allowed to blossom, speeding us along to our destination. Coming upon deck with the other seven oarsmen, I found it remarkable how little room there was for a crew of fourteen when assembled. I looked back at La Rochelle and its twin portal towers a last melancholic time. Then I looked ahead to the open sea, allowing the brisk breeze to caress my back, pushing me on. My moment of reverie was dashed by Emanuel's bellow that I get forward and help liberate the jib sail. I was an oarsman in name, but a deckhand as well. I was soon to learn that if I had thought a novice's lot lowly, my new station as an oarsman meant being nothing more than a beast of burden. I learned much rapidly, for if I forgot or knew not, a cuff was quick in coming from the hand of any superior lurking about.

As the winds were favorable, Captain Rodriguez decided we should make our way directly across the bay of Biscay. On the second day a calm beset us and it was to the oars we went. For almost three days did we row with only occasional respite. Two deckhands rotated through with every emptying of the small hourglass. This allowed a measure of relief, but my virgin arms and hands suffered terribly. Raw and bleeding were my hands. My arms quivered of their own accord and screamed at me in protest. Thankfully, my back was young, for it was subjected to torturous exertions. At night we were allowed a half-night's rest and then were back at our station before sunrise. Food was ample, but hardly could I move it to my mouth with such shaking and blistered hands. On the second day of rowing my senses left me and I collapsed over my oar. A bucket of cold seawater and a sound cuff by the second mate soon revived me. Affronted and ashamed, I renewed my exertions and loudly sang the refrains of the oarsman's chanty—twas the only thing that kept me going. The chant seemed to smooth the torturous regimen. My body became one dull aching mass, but the chant empowered me to lessen the pain and get from one stroke to the next. The *Celeuma Chanty*, as all called it, is forever committed to my memory. Whoever would lead the chant would sing the first half line starting with a very loud 'OH'. We would stroke at that sound and sing the refrain.

OH, God aid us;
Who are your servants.
OH, we would serve you well;
Preserve the faith, the Christian faith.
OH, thrash the pagan;
Confusion on the Saracen.
OH, throttle and kill the dogs;
Sons of debrahin.
OH, they do not believe good though it is;
They do not believe the holy faith.
OH, the holy faith of Rome;
From Rome comes pardon.
OH, Saint Peter great helmsman;
Saint Paul his companion.
OH, who rule God be with us;
And with others sailing,
OH, in this world we are so many;
Westward I say and eastward.
OH, eastward the sun rises;
Westward it glows.
OH, maiden long live love;
Young man rejoice.

On the fourth day at sea the wind returned in our favor. With great relief, the oarsmen, particularly one Alex del Aries, welcomed it. Not that my labors ended there, as scrub brushes were broken out and I toiled upon the deck. I was becoming not so enamored with this future, but vowed not to submit to despair. Captain Rodriguez drove his men hard, but they all maintained a grudging respect for him. He was a smallish man and almost as fair-haired as myself. His modest stature belied his strength and inner fortitude, which became evident to me through tales, told me by both Emanuel and his crew. There was a deep scar on the side of his face that ran from just below his left eye to his jaw line. Perhaps he wore it as a badge of courage, for he made no attempt to mask it beneath a beard. Asking Emanuel of this, he said it was from a Moorish pirate's falchion and that the Moor had fared much worse.

On the sixth day we sighted land and I was told it was the northwest headland of Galicia. Emanuel explained that Galicia lay to the north of Portugal and was loosely allied with the Castiles. It was therefore to my surprise that our captain's course took us into a gulf port of Galicia called La Coruna. We docked only for the night and unloaded six casks of wine. By the ornate well-constructed nature of the oak casks, they must have been the finest of wines. Also unloaded were several finely designed woven carpets and tapestries. No one was permitted ashore and there was some grumbling, but as we had not been long out of port complaints were few.

Twas a seasonably hot night. All crew, excepting the captain and first mate, always slept forward with minimal protection against the elements. Captain and first mate had small cabins aft. I found myself restless toward morning and arose early for my watch. Gratefully, the other young oarsman retired and I was left to gaze from the helm upon a dark, sleeping La Coruna.

It was full-mooned night and deathly quiet upon the calm waters. I heard the aft door creak and boots upon the stairs. On this placid night those sounds were like canon shots to my ears. I was surprised to see Emanuel and Rodriguez emerge from their quarters and disembark without a word. When they reached the quay, three other men with a torch appeared and exchanged greetings with Rodriguez and Emanuel. They were obviously familiar with each other and conversed at length. As they parted, I recognized one of them as being the recipient of the cargo unloaded earlier. Rodriguez and Emanuel again paid me no heed as they returned to their quarters. Rodriguez had with him a small bag which noticeably jingled, full of livres.

Much later, in a moment of candor, Emanuel explained that this kind of exchange was necessary to lessen the risks of piracy. In this manner everybody gained, even the shipping merchants, for most of their goods actually arrived. Feared seafaring men such as Eduardo de Aviz used their noble lineage to full advantage. Everyone took their ladle of potage from the pot, including Rodriguez and Emanuel. Eduardo de Aviz was the local powerbroker. He used his influence to milk this system and these were the waters he plied with his formidable fleet of warring craft. The only blessing was that he actually did lessen piracy. It was a workable, if corrupt system, said Emanuel.

The rest of the voyage to Lisboa was mostly uneventful. Several times we had to put oars to water, but only for short periods. A day out from Lisboa we experienced some very large rolling waves from the west. Being out of sight of land it had an unsettling effect on this novice seaman. The others had expected these kinds of waves on the Bay of Biscay and were surprised we should encounter them now. Several times I was very near to losing whatever was in my belly. For a time, this was great amusement for my more seasoned mates, but by god's grace I was able to survive the terrible affliction.

As land, and eventually Lisboa, came into view my disposition improved greatly. Nearing port in the wide mouth of the Rio Tejo, I was astounded by the number of craft and incredible bustle of uncountable people. Goods were stacked high everywhere on the huge quay and it seemed like a mass of confusion. Such pother put me in mind of Friar Ferdinand's beehives. As we came about to our destined anchorage, it felt as if an incubus of haze was lifting from my head. The sails were full and the sun was high in a cloudless azure sky. Leaning from the rail with the wind in my face, I drank it all in as a fine elixir. It was a passionate and powerful wave of emotion that suddenly surged through my being—overwhelming, like unbridled ardor.

I was home.

PART III.

Chapter One

THE GAUNTLET

"GODDAM YOU, all to hell! Shit, shit, SHIT. Jesus, Jack, I knew this climate would screw up the scripts. But no, I had to let you talk me into interpreting them here."

There were tears of frustration welling up in Janeen's eyes and I felt it better to let her tirade run its course. She had been ranting around for the past half hour since we discovered the last three pages were deteriorated beyond legibility or repair. Perhaps she was right. Perhaps my selfish zeal to investigate the scripts under these unsafe, unscientific conditions cost us the last valuable tidbit. We had used extreme caution in the handling and cataloguing process. And they had been carefully stored in plastic, but this was still not a research lab. At last she flopped into the wicker chair, her hair disheveled and one remaining tear trailing down a flushed cheek.

"Jenny, Jenny, it only appears three pages are unsalvageable. If we get the rest of it to a proper environment, it is still a find for the ages," I offered, solicitously.

"Oh, Jack, don't you see how unprofessional we've been in all of this. I'm sorry to dump on you. I'm just as much to blame, if not more so. I got caught up in the excitement of it also. Who knows what those last three pages may have told us. Each and every page is precious. The text seems to end completely enough, but what of that last tantalizing tidbit? Maybe it explains how the scripts came to be here in Peru."

"Aye, sad to say, but I guess we'll never know now," I said, with resignation.

I carefully returned the damaged parchments to the airtight copper receptacle, and silence prevailed, save for the constant, distant surf. Darkness began to abet the already cool evening and I moved to sit at Janeen's feet, hugging a leg over each of my shoulders. With the back of my head resting between her legs she stroked my hair in an affectionate, almost apologetic manner. There seemed no need for talk, or least of all, any need for further recriminations.

Our peaceful state was suddenly and traumatically dashed, as Terry burst through the door. "Move your slack asses. We're buggin outta here, NOW!"

Terry's tone of urgency brought us scrambling to our feet.

"What's the deal?" Janeen demanded.

"We've been cross-haired. I don't know how or by who, but we gotta scramble. I was checking my plane and caught this local lizard doing some dirty work to my engine. I had a bad feeling this morning, and thought I should make sure my bird was gassed and ready. I had told the Barber to look after it yesterday. I noticed some movement under the tarp. The little prick was messing with the gas line. He didn't hear a thing. He never will now. I knew he wasn't some Good Samaritan mechanic. He was one of those dorks from the bar the other night. His pants are full of rocks and he has a big smile under his chin—at the bottom of the inlet. You've got two and a half minutes and then I'm torching this place, so move it."

We didn't hesitate, for she had a container of gas in her hands and was starting to spray it around with deliberate gusto. Terry was clearly in her agent mode. She had calmly related her chilling news and though completely composed, her eyes subtly flitted around in a state of hyper-awareness. We stuffed our backpacks with only those things of prime importance and Terry directed us out the back way around the adobe. She then struck a match to a packet of them and tossed it inside. The effect was immediate and the adobe lit up the early night like candles on a giant ninetieth birthday cake.

"Bonny cold evening for a bonfire," I quipped, as we clutched our precious backpacks and dashed down the narrow path behind our adobe.

I had been down this path before, but had aborted my exploration at a narrow, fast running creek. Terry, taking the lead, splashed across it in knee-deep water. Obediently we followed her, barely keeping our balance with packsacks held high. Stumbling out of the water, we raced headlong down an obscure path in Terry's wake. Suddenly, Janeen stumbled over an unseen tree root and I catapulted over top of her. Janeen and I both cursed loudly. Terry, darted back to us, cursed us in turn and told us to stifle the racket. We helped Janeen up and charged on, but I soon realized there was a serious problem. She was limping badly and I could hear her sobbing with each step.

"Terry, Terry, where the fuck are you?" I called after her. "We have to stop, Janeen's hurt."

Terry re-appeared from the shadowed foliage ahead, and pushing me aside, checked Janeen's ankle.

"Jesus Christ, it's already swollen like a grapefruit," Terry lamented. We had only made about two hundred meters from the adobe and Terry's look of disgust was black as a rain cloud. She reached behind her back and retrieved a large blade from its sheath. Its girth and glinting razor-like reflection in the moonlight reminded me of a Bowie knife. My heart stopped, as she raised it and brought it down toward Janeen's ankle. One more swipe and a two-inch sapling fell next to Janeen. Like a surgeon, she stripped and split the sapling to rapidly fashion a splint. Ripping off her shirt, she tore it into strips that she used to tie Janeen's ankle snug between the two pieces of splint. Only briefly was I distracted by Terry's tantalizing, sweat-drenched, t-shirted profile in the moonlight.

"Okay, Jack, you'll help Janeen along. Try to keep up. I'll be out front on point and you'd better not lose me, because I'm not coming back for you again."

We struggled up the gentle rise, which seemed like a mountain now. I carried Janeen for a ways, but soon realized we were better off if she hopped along and used me as a crutch. My shirt clung to me like a wet rag. We were sweating so profusely from the exertion and humidity that, more than once, Janeen almost slipped from my grasp. That it was a cool evening seemed a blessing now. We crested the promontory and came into a desert-like clearing. Over our raspy, labored breathing I became aware of a distant, pervasive noise. Looking down along the coast, I could see a flashlight procession approaching the brilliant inferno of our abandoned adobe. The town by comparison was dim. I realized that people from the fishing village were trying to reach our adobe and give assistance. Obviously, this was the ruse Terry had planned on. Our little structure up in its nook was mostly visible from the village and it didn't take long for the villagers to notice our supposed plight.

"Come on you shitheads," Terry chided us, as we had paused to look down on the scene and catch our breath. Then she was gone again, following some arcane path on the other side of the clearing. Plunging into the still swaying fronds of fern and palm growth where she had been enveloped, we almost lost our balance. The ground was now sloping and its slatey surface slicked with evening dew made the sudden descent precarious. As we skidded and staggered Janeen moaned only occasionally. I knew she must be in considerable pain though, from her grimaces and taut quakes. The path was difficult to make out, especially in this dim, hazy moonlight and the occasional pocket of fog. With our state of anxiety and flagging energy, I had to concentrate intently to keep on Terry's track. Fortunately, the necessity of vigilance dictated Terry's pace. Every once in a while I could catch a gray glimpse of her, moving stealthily, but steadily down the path. We plodded on blindly for what seemed an eternity. Without warning, we broke clear of the foliage and cascaded as a waterfall of arms and legs down a slippery slope. Near the bottom was Terry and she abated our slide with her strong, wiry arms. Janeen was now shaking and sobbing almost out of control.

"Jesus Christ! Can't you hold on to Jenny any better than that?"

I almost slugged Terry in frustration, but then I saw her eyes. Those eyes were wide with alarm as she looked at Janeen. I looked down to see Janeen's other ankle, previously uninjured, and now bent at an unnatural angle.

Terry pulled back the pant leg and saw it was not compounded, but certainly fractured. She then turned around, and while squatting on Janeen's leg, abruptly straightened the ankle. The audible crunch sent a shiver up my spine. Janeen tensed tightly and opened her mouth to scream, but her eyes rolled back into their sockets and she passed out with a shudder.

"Lord blethering Jesus Christ! You fucking near killed her," I wailed.

"Better that than the alternative," Terry replied, without offering to explain what that alternative might be. "At least now, Jack, you'll be able to carry her more easily. She won't feel the pain."

I didn't know if I should hammer on Terry's practical skull or scream in frustration, but she left me no time to pursue either course.

We were now on the edge of the village and Terry was off again, skirting it by the landward side. With no alternative, I hoisted the insentient Janeen up over my shoulder and staggered after Terry. Cussing gently at Janeen, knowing she could not comprehend, I chastised her for her ten stones of dead weight.

The little village seemed almost deserted, as everyone was likely off to see the inferno. Finally, we made it to the wide, but rickety old river dock, and it was none too soon, for my physical limit was fast approaching. I had almost caught up to Terry when she slowed and then stopped. Warily, she stepped onto the dock. Crouched and wielding a small gun that appeared from under her t-shirt, she proceeded. Her right hand gripped her extended left gun hand at the wrist, and she moved it in a slow sweeping arc. Apprehensively, I followed, eyes panning our surroundings, senses alert. It didn't matter. At the same instant that I saw the flash of a shot from a moored boat, my head exploded.

I was vaguely aware of a voice, but the white pain inside my head was a deterrent to any attempt at consciousness. Fighting through it, I cautiously opened one eye a fraction. I was lying face down on the dock. Janeen was on her back next to me, still unconscious. A few meters away, Terry lay crumpled on her side with her face mostly masked by blood. Squinting through the yellow-gray subconscious haze, I figured Terry was likely dead and myself a close second.

"Is the bitch dead, Barber?"

The Barber bent over Terry and inspected her head, while feeling the pulse at her neck.

"Puede ser—no, there's still a pulse! I guess I need to work on my night shooting. Meant to put it between her eyes, but only put a nice crease in the top of her head. I should finish the bitch off. She's the dangerous one and I don't think we need her anymore." Reaching under his arm he extracted his stiletto from its sheath with an exaggerated, arrogant flair.

"What about these two? I gave the hombre a good whack on the head, but I doubt if he's dead. This other one though, she sure had nice tits. Maybe we could keep her a while."

"Ah, mi Juguete, you make me so jealous that you would think her tits nicer than mine."

Coarse laughter followed that strange comment, and the sense or humor of it eluded me in my dulled state. Through my squinted eyes, I noticed Juguete now moved to stand over Janeen, straddling her. He placed his bare foot onto her chest and began moving it in a circular motion on her breasts. Then he slipped his toes inside the shirt and kicked out, popping several buttons.

"This is not the time for that, compadre, we have work to do yet," the Barber scolded, but his eyes were drawn by Juguete's actions.

Ignoring the Barber, Juguete's offensive foot continued its invasion, and my teeth began to grind. Figuring I had little to lose, I considered how best to make a move. It was apparent there was only the two of them. Juguete held some kind of short-barreled rifle, and I surmised he might have used that to butt-end me in the head from behind. The Barber had holstered his gun and was standing over Terry with stiletto in hand. He was distracted by Juguete and had a look of perverse excitement on his round face.

"You fools!" The third voice caught me by surprise, as I heard footsteps from behind me coming onto the dock. "Get on with the business. You told me you were professionals. Professional bullshit is more like it. Nothing has gone right since I got here. Your mechanic couldn't even sabotage the plane properly. Everything was supposed to be neat and tidy, and this, this is messy. Must I do things myself?" There was something about that voice—something familiar about its smooth, concordant, yet viperous tones.

As he came into my narrow peripheral vision, it was the shock of silvery hair gleaming in the moonlight that spurred my recollection. Tall, slim and attractively well preserved. What the hell was Stephen Saxon, my ex-father-in-law, doing here? Am I hallucinating? It didn't make any sense. Janeen's face was turned my way and I suddenly noticed an unmistakable twitch.

Juguete had no time to react. Janeen's hand shot up and grabbed his crotch in a crushing embrace. He howled and his pop-eyes bulged even further from their sockets. He tried to jump back, but of course this made it worse. Although he slammed down on her arm with his rifle butt, she would not relinquish her vice-grip. He turned his weapon to fire at her.

I rolled into his legs and grabbed for the weapon. There was a gasping screech which seemed to emanate from the Barber as Juguete fell over me, his rifle discharging. Grabbing the gun barrel I rolled with him right off the dock. I managed to get a big gulp of air just before hitting the water. Now we were even. I had him in a bear hug and used my weight to keep him under me. When my hands found his neck it was all but over. My rage knew neither fear, nor quarter. His hands clawed for my face, but could only reach my shoulders. I couldn't see his face, but I felt his jaw muscles contract and bubbles of air finger past my face. My lungs were beginning to burn, giving me the taste sensation of scorched metal when his struggling finally stopped. My feet found bottom and I rose out of the water without relinquishing my death-grip on his neck. I half expected a death-dealing bullet in my back from the Barber, but my need for air overrode any danger.

I stood in waist deep water pinioning his dead form up against a dock pylon with my hands still locked about his neck. Seeing his tongue lolling from its mouth and his eyes bulging grotesquely, I forced my hands to release their grip and let him slip down into the water. I stared, stupefied, at my curled, claw-like fingers, unable to straighten them. Still gulping volumes of air I became aware of a strange, unearthly wailing. Somehow the noise reminded me of Terry, but from another world.

It took all my remaining strength to drag myself back onto the pier. On hands and knees I crawled to where Terry sat with her legs around Janeen, cradling her in her arms. She was rocking Janeen slowly, as a mother with young child, and an unnatural guttural moan escaped her open mouth. Terry's face was blank and ghostly pale in the moonlight.

I had never before experienced such dread. My mouth was salty and tasted like metallic powder. My heart seemed to sink to my loins, which quivered and shuddered. My head swirled beyond dizziness. I reached Janeen to find her chest soaked in blood. There was a strange sensation, warming my cold, sodden trousers and legs. My bladder had released of its own accord. I felt oddly removed from my body. No, this could not be me, it must be someone else, and therefore, this was not happening—probably just a ghastly dream.

Janeen's eyes were open and as I gently touched her face she blinked. Wild hope surged within my breast. Terry's face had become eerily impassive, staring into the river. Carefully peeling back the soaked fabric of her shirt, I found a gaping hole in the right side of her chest, oozing her lifeblood and soul. No, no, this cannot be—this is my Janeen. I put my hand over the offensive wound that it might disappear. Oh God, why hadn't I moved quicker? I wanted to scream and wail as had Terry, but Janeen's eyes then found focus on my face. She managed a weak smile and tried to speak, but it was blood that escaped her mouth rather than words. We sat her more upright that she might be able to speak. Her face was devoid of any color and her breathing was a hollow rattling, like sucking on a straw in an almost empty pop can.

Jenny's lips moved as if to speak, but she grimaced instead. Then falteringly, she said, "Neither one of those pricks would have fathered anymore bastards. Terry made sure of that and… " She tried to suppress a cough, but was only partly successful and blood trickled from the corners of her mouth. "They won't be giving us anymore trouble," Jenny whispered.

Tears streamed down Terry's stony face through the streaks of dried blood. I felt catatonic and was weeping freely.

"L, look at you two. Don't pull that weepy shit. I've been lucky in life and love; loved by the two of you. I'm sorry I haven't always been totally honest with my feelings, but please believe me, that I love you both very much. If I could've married you both I would have, except I'm married to my career, just like you, Terry, my sweet." She paused, and struggled for breath. "I've always thought of you like hard candy—hard, but melts in the mouth." Terry cracked half a smile, and Janeen almost laughed, but for the pain. "Jack, my handsome, wonderfully irrational, sensitive stud. You're such a good man and you don't even know it."

Her whispering colloquy and breathing were becoming more ragged. I realized if we had any chance at all to save her, we'd better move quickly and forcing myself back from the brink of demented despair, I said, "Terry, you have to snap out of it. We've got to get her out of here, and fast. Get that sky-buggy cranked."

Terry looked at me with a, what's-the-use dull stare, so I slapped her—hard. Her hand from behind Janeen came up and something flashed in the moonlight. She stopped in mid-swing, and I recognized the Barber's stiletto. I didn't move, but unflinchingly matched her glare. Janeen seemed to be fading out again. Terry's eyes suddenly softened and she mouthed plaintively, barely audible, "Jenny's dying."

Fighting the crushing anguish, and hoping we had a slim chance, I raised my hand again. "For God's sake, Terry, we've got to try," I pleaded.

Suddenly, it seemed, Terry was back. It was in her eyes; they hardened and somehow blackened. She handed Janeen off to me, and struggling to her feet, bolted down the dock to her plane. Very gently, I scooped Janeen up into my arms. Following Terry, I stepped over a gruesomely disemboweled Barber. I stopped briefly and looked around, for I suddenly remembered Stephen Saxon. Could it really have been him? If so, he was probably long gone now, for he was never one to get his fingers dirty.

Terry had the tarp off in seconds and helped me get Janeen aboard. She untied us and pushed off while I strapped in the unconscious Janeen. As Terry climbed in, I forcibly stopped her to examine her head wound. Pulling back a thick, blood-matted clump of hair, I could see a nasty scalp laceration. Rivulets of dried blood streaked her pretty face and it seemed the hard edges normally around her eyes and mouth were gone, almost hinting at vulnerability. I then did something inexplicable, surprising both of us. I tenderly kissed her wound. In the nearness I could smell her fragrant hair and her sweat mingled with the fresh pungency of blood. And then, and then softly, but briefly, I kissed her lips. She did not resist.

Chapter Two

THE FLYING DUTCHMAN

TERRY TRIED and tried again, but the starter couldn't seem to get more than a half turn out of the prop. We were drifting with the flow toward open water and I was praying we wouldn't get hung up amongst the small flotilla of fishing craft near the shore. I realized suddenly that Janeen was now conscious and trying to say something. As I put my ear close to her lips, she repeated weakly, "Bill, my father, said, 'when she's stubborn, it's no time for ticklin.' Open up the goddam choke."

Dutifully, I relayed this instruction to Terry. We both knew Jenny's father, Wild Bill, as he was nicknamed, had been a helluva bush pilot. Terry shrugged in a what-the-hell kind of manner and opened the choke wide. When she cranked it there was a loud bang, a puff of black smoke, and the prop sprung into some serious revs. The old otter was alive and well.

"Musta been a little crap in there from our friends that I missed. Good ole Jenny, she knows about more than just old bones," Terry hollered over the engine noise, her voice cracking emotionally at the end.

Lifting off we flew high over the smoldering remains of our adobe, unable to see much in the hazy half-moon light. Climbing up beside Terry I suggested we try making it to Talara and take our chances with the authorities there for Janeen's sake. Terry agreed, as we had less than half a tank of fuel and couldn't go much further anyway. Terry produced a canteen of water from under her seat and we each took a brief swig. She suggested I moisten Janeen's mouth, but not to let her drink fully in case of internal injury.

As I went back to Janeen I could feel Terry dropping altitude. Obviously she wanted to stay off any possible radar. We just weren't sure who our friends were anymore. I slid in beside Jenny and cradled her in my arms. Her shallow breathing was not a good sign. I wet my handkerchief and used it to swab her pallid lips and face. Carefully, I dribbled a few drops of water into her mouth. There was considerable blood around her chest wound, but I would have expected even more for such a serious wound. There was nothing to do but pray and hope for a miracle. I stared out the window into the dark for a while. It almost seemed I could see whitecaps nicking our pontoons. It occurred to me that it would be a bizarre ending to die in a head-on collision with a ship.

I'm not sure when I realized it, but as a glorious mid-day sun might be taken away by an unwelcome black cloud, so did my sunshine, Janeen, pass quietly from life. Her shallow breathing had ceased and there was a perceptible coolness gradually pervading her body. There was a blanket on the next seat. Reaching for it, I carefully wrapped Janeen in its tacit warmth and lightly kissed her lips for a last time. I was grateful for the numbness that enveloped me. Raw emotion, animated grief, was somehow not seemly—nor would've it been appreciated by this, this wondrous woman, this heroic heart, this love of my life. I drew her close, cocooning her within my arms and curled my leg protectively over her's. Her face was peaceful—almost smiling, in that classical Madonna manner of hers.

For a considerable time I was unable to react. I was numb, empty. Finally, I forced myself to move, for I knew I must tell Terry. There was the risk of debilitating grief, but I felt she deserved to know.

"Terry, I'm sorry—I truly am lass. I know you love her as much as I, but… "

"I know, Jack. I know," Terry interrupted softly. I looked at her questioningly, as she continued.

"I knew she didn't have a chance. I've seen operatives die of lesser wounds with medical aid. She was tough, though. I applaud you for your efforts, Jack. Funny, I just realized something else too. My long lost woman's insight … Well, let's just say I felt her touch me when she left about half an hour ago."

I was only slightly surprised at her revelation, but more so that she revealed it to me. I was beginning to see many of the redeeming qualities in Terry that must have intrigued Jenny. We sat silently for a time—dealing with grief, I suppose.

"I guess we might as well try for the Ecuador border now," Terry said, in a lifeless, flat tone.

Glancing at the gauges, I was startled to see the fuel gauge bouncing on the big 'E' while a little red dot flashed persistently next to it. "Terry, I, a… " I faltered, while pointing.

"I know, Jack. I'm trying to keep close to the shoreline. I think I saw the shore lights of what could have been Tumbes a few minutes ago. It's pretty inhospitable shoreline near the Ecuador border. If we could successfully get down in Ecuadorean waters, I like our chances a lot better than Peru. So obviously I'm pushing it as far as… "

Her pause was induced by a subtle sputter in the engine. Her reaction was immediate and she gently banked shoreward. My heart should have been in my throat, but in light of all the recent trauma, there was hardly a flicker on my nerve's Richter scale. Terry could sense my ambivalence to our plight. Her cold professionalism was once again beginning to take control, but nonetheless she reached out to say softly, "Jack, Jenny was right, you are a good man. Life doesn't seem as worthwhile right now, but it will be again and… " She was interrupted by a loud sputter and cough from the Otter's engine. The prop slowed, sped up, and then stopped. The sudden silence, save for the rushing air, defined the urgency of our peril.

"Okay, hang on, Jack, we're gonna try and glide down onto the water near shore. If you have any favorite gods to pray to, ask for no rocks and no waves."

With a partly misted headland rapidly coming at us, I could see nothing BUT rocks and crashing waves. It would have to be one hell of a blessing to survive this landing, so pray I did—prayers of desperation, foreign to my lips for years.

We broke through a patch of mist, and incredibly, there it was. I pointed at the narrow channel of semi-quiet water on our left, as Terry was already delicately banking our Otter toward it. With no power she had little control, especially with the strong sea breeze on our tail. She was trying to keep the nose steady and slightly up, but our wings seemed to be fighting each other, threatening to send us into a horizontal death-spin. Suddenly, our nose came up too high and Terry could not control it. The rear rudder of the left pontoon caught a wave and abruptly pitched our nose back down. The front of our pontoons skipped off the water. This slowed us down, but it also turned and tilted us. As the right pontoon touched down again in the chop, I looked out my side in time to see the right wing catch a high wave. Our world then became like a python roller coaster. We cart wheeled crazily and the otter began to break up. There was a jaw-jarring shudder that rocked us violently, followed by the sounds of bending, creaking and ripping metal. Rivets popped and glass broke in a rapid cacophony that I shall never forget. It all climaxed with the crushing rush of suffocating, icy cold, salt-water.

Everything was black, but at least I remained conscious. I knew I was underwater, but wasn't sure which way was up. In panic, I felt around and located where the windshield had been. Unbuckling my seatbelt, I felt for Terry in the cold blackness, but could not even find her seat. Desperate for air, I squeezed out through the window frame and discovered our fuselage was upside-down. Pushing upward, with bursting lungs, I surfaced almost immediately. Thank God the water was only chest deep—sweet, sweet air. The human psyche can be devastated and broken, but the will to live endures.

Blinking the salt and sand from my eyes, I looked about for Terry while fighting the swells to stay upright. Oh God, she must still be in the plane, I realized in panic. I felt sore everywhere, especially that same old shoulder, but had no time to dwell on it.

I could see the tail section had been broken off, as well as the right wing. I plowed through the waves to the gaping tail of the fuselage, thinking that would be the best way to re-enter. Sure enough it was wide open, but mostly submerged. With dread, I plunged back into the darkness. From feel, it seemed that little was left of the interior. I could not even find Janeen's seat or her body as I felt my way. And then at the cockpit entrance something bumped into me. It was Terry. She was still strapped in her dislodged seat. Frantically, I pulled her, seat and all, out the back. It seemed the wave undertow was assisting me, or my strength was superhuman.

Once outside the wreck I recharged my aching lungs and grappled with the seatbelt. I managed to free her without much difficulty, and grasping her under the arms, I pulled her toward shore. Occasionally, my feet would lose bottom, as I struggled against an undertow. My body complained from the excruciating exertion, for my normal energy had long ago been sapped and I was running on pure adrenaline.

I reached a rocky, sandy beach and collapsed with her in my arms. It seemed little breath remained in my lungs, but I knew I must immediately get some into hers. Turning her on her stomach, I forced what water and grit I could from her lungs. She regurgitated sand and seawater and seemed to take a breath, but then stopped again. Tucking her right arm by her side I flipped her over and began mouth to mouth. It seemed she would draw a breath or two and then stop again. I turned her back over and forced more seawater from her. Again, I went back to mouth to mouth and after three or four more puffs she began to breathe on her own, though somewhat shallowly. Thank God, I muttered, for I don't think I could have stood any more misery this day.

Perhaps she would be all right, but there was a nasty goose-egg on her forehead that bothered me. Flopping on my back I shivered from the damp and wind, but was too exhausted to move.

That is until I thought—ahh shite, Jack—the packsack!

I knew Janeen's memory would forever haunt me if I quit now. So shaking with fatigue and cold I went back into the water. I knew it could be my undoing, but what the hell, my life seemed already undone. To my surprise, I found the packsack almost immediately—in fact, I also found Janeen. Both were caught up on the tail section, which was caught up on a jagged rock barely below the water's surface. The manuscript had been well sealed so I simply strapped on the packsack with numb, shaking fingers. In getting to the tail section it had felt as if there was a riptide at play, for it took surprisingly little effort, but near the rock where it deepened, I could feel it tugging at me from the depths. I knew I could never get Janeen's body to shore. In retrospect I should have realized the tide was going out and I might have simply clung to the tail section. But in my fatigued state, I felt I was likely to die from exposure if I stayed, and the manuscript, which was now Janeen's legacy would be lost forever.

With a shivering kiss to Jenny's cold forehead I bade her Godspeed and committed her to the sea. "Thank you for loving me and sharing your life with me. I know and promise I will be the better for it," I whispered, as she slipped away into the indigo deep.

The shoreline was about fifty meters away. I am only an average swimmer, and in my depleted condition, I was afraid the undertow would surely suck me out to sea. The water was probably only about shoulder deep, but I could not possibly get back to shore against the nasty undertow. There was a much larger rock-reef sticking out of the water about twenty meters away and slightly further from shore. I felt my only chance was to take a tangent between the shore and that large rock, hoping to get into a protective shield from the current. Before allowing myself second thoughts, or for the cold to totally debilitate me, I forged back into the chilly brine and swam for my life.

How I did it, in my state, still amazes me. I like to think it was Jenny's spirit which carried me to Herculean effort. I was barely able to grab a jutting crag of the large reef as I fought against the current trying to sweep me away. Along side it the undertow became even stronger as it rushed past, out to sea. With the strength of desperation, I was able to pull myself onto the rock. Barnacles chafed my bare flesh and clawed at my sopping clothes, but I was barely aware of my pain and bloodied flesh. Simply to survive was all that mattered. Indeed, I was fortunate, for in the lee of my reef the water proved to be only waist deep over a sand bar, and the undertow was but a sleepy serpent without fangs. Crawling on to shore upon hands and knees to a breathing, but still unconscious Terry, I collapsed in a comatose state of exhaustion.

When I awoke, it must have been sometime near morning, judging by the slivers of light filtering through the trees on the eastern horizon. I think it was the cold, or perhaps pain that raised me to consciousness. With agonized effort I struggled onto an elbow, and checking Terry, was surprised to find her eyes open. A moment of panic gripped me as I saw a dead, vacant look in those dark brown eyes. I was much relieved when she moved, shivered actually. She was lying on her back, staring straight up with her arms folded and her fists clenched.

"Terry," I rasped. "Terry, are you okay?" She blinked and stared at me blankly. After a few moments she replied with an odd, detached tone to her voice.

"Where are we?"

"On the beach, Terry," I said, realizing she was probably in a state of shock. "Hopefully, in Ecuador."

She still looked at me blankly. "Everything is fuzzy. I, I remember bits and pieces and … oh God, no, Jenny."

She began to shake violently now, so I put my arms around her and held on. We shook and sobbed together in our sadness, shock and cold. It was a long while before either of us settled back down to simple shivers. Dawn is usually the coldest time of day and this was no exception.

Terry seemed to be fading in and out of consciousness and our sodden clothes had us in danger of hypothermia. We had to find somewhere warmer than this damp, windy beach. Lurching like a drunk, I forced my battered and bloodied frame to its feet. Gently at first, and then more forcefully, I managed to coerce Terry up and wrapped an arm around her for support. I do not know for what reason—perhaps Janeen's invisible hand upon my shoulder—but I moved us south along the rocky beach. This was contrary to normal instinct, as Ecuador must lie to the north. Going inland was not an option, for the bush and rocky headlands were too daunting in our condition.

After only a couple of hundred meters I found a small creek trickling to the sea. My thirst was suddenly incredibly acute, and not caring how safe the water might be, I fell to my knees and slurped great handfuls of life's sweet elixir. I was aware of Terry at my side, sipping tentatively. I could not seem to get enough, dehydrated as I was, but suddenly Terry yanked me back. "That's enough, too much not good," she gasped, and slumped over on her side. My body screamed for more, but I realized that she was right.

Shelter—we must find shelter, the body-racking cold reminded me. Looking up the thicket-lined creek bed, I thought perhaps I might be hallucinating in this early light, for there appeared to be a little hut about fifty meters away.

Terry was now on her hands and knees beside the creek in an apparent stupor. Her head hung down with its black hair hanging about it in matted strings. Helping her up, I put my arm around her waist again and we struggled toward the apparition.

Perhaps the good angels of fate had not deserted us after all. It was a rudimentary fisherman's hut, apparently deserted. It had short adobe walls, a frond-thatched roof and crudely cut, planked floorboards inside. Best of all, there was an old discarded alpaca blanket folded in the corner. Other than that, it was completely barren and windowless. In my semi-delirium, I kept thinking, 'Thank you Jenny, thank you Jenny', for I was sure it must have been her guiding hand that led me here.

Caring not what vermin it might still contain, I shook out the large blanket and spread it on the plank floor. Terry was crouched, shivering in the corner, with that blank look still in her eyes.

"Come Terry, please stand. You need to take these sodden clothes off. We need each other's warmth to get better." As I was undoing her shirt buttons with stiff fingers her hand shot up, grabbing mine. "It's alright, Terry—Jenny's here. She understands."

A wee bit of light crept into her dark brown eyes. Slowly, she reached out with trembling fingers and began awkwardly unbuttoning my shirt.

Chapter Three

SENSATION AND SALVATION

AFTER THE shivering stopped, we slept. We must have slept all day, for when I awoke it was dark again. I awoke to a gentle sobbing. Gradually recovering from a comatose state of sleep, the reality of recent events descended over me like a malignant shroud. I shivered, but not from the cold. I pulled Terry close, and stroked her hair as she sobbed into my chest. "Tis okay, lass—tis alright … tears are proper. We have a right to cry."

Terry's face turned up to mine and her hand touched my cheek, feeling the wet warmth of my tears. Strange how emotions are sometimes immediately communal. "Jack, oh Jack, what will we do without her. We can't even fight over her anymore."

I knew Terry must have no knowledge of the plane crash aftermath, so with cracking voice I explained to her how we had escaped the wreckage and I had retrieved the manuscript for Janeen's legacy. We continued to hold each other tight as the sobbing slowly subsided. It was then Terry raised her head, and in a most natural and tender manner kissed away my tears. Without thought or design I in turn kissed away her tears.

Then our lips touched.

It was as if a powder keg of physical emotion had been set off. When our lips touched there was a pause—suspended animation—electric fusion. Then we devoured, devoured each other with a desperate hunger, like animals, wild and ravenous. Our lips mashed together. Our teeth collided. It was an intense, urgent hunger, such as I had never experienced before. All aches and bruises and lacerations vanished. My erection was instantaneous, aching. Terry seemed suddenly possessed. Her sobs had turned to gasps. Tentatively, our hands explored each other's body for the first time.

It was an incredible galvanic reaction, almost causing me to lose control, when her hand reached down and gripped my penis. She gripped it firmly, released it and then gripped it again up and down its length. She seemed to be measuring its breadth and span in a most sensual way. I gripped her buttocks with both hands and let my fingers play the length of their crevice. This elicited louder gasps and groans from her, and she reached around to rake my buttocks with her nails. We tasted each other greedily and fenced with our tongues. She drew one leg up over my groin, allowing full access to explore and manipulate her very wet, most private self. My touch sent immediate convulsions through her, such that she bit down on my tongue and seemed to suck the very breath out of me.

"God, yes … do it now."

With those gasping words she swung fully over my hips and grabbed the base of my penis. She moved the head around the entrance for a long, but pleasurable time, before finally easing downwards. She seemed to need to take control, and I was more than content to let her. I caressed her breasts as they erotically dangled before me, and then ran my hands down her flanks to knead those incredibly firm buttocks. Slowly, with some travail, I was entering her—or rather, she was engulfing me. She leaned further forward and bit my shoulder, whimpering softly. Slowly, slowly we rocked, until finally she had all of me. We rested a bit, savoring the fullness of our oneness. Gently, I rolled her onto her back and took control—and she let me.

It was tender, it was caring—it was beyond imagination. As we approached climax the strokes were long and deep. She raked her stubbled calves up and down my flanks as if urging on a thoroughbred to the finish line. When we erupted, I almost passed out from the intensity, while Terry in her rapturous swoon, emitted soft hiccupping sobs of relief. We did not move or speak for a long time after—nor could we.

Drained physically, emotionally and sexually we slept through the night. It was only the mutual need for fluids and to relieve ourselves that stirred our exhausted bodies to wakefulness at first light.

With some embarrassment Terry immediately looked to clothe herself. Without a word, I wrapped the blanket around her and slipped on my still damp boxers. I was not surprised that something was not the same as last night, but what puzzled me most was the apparent dried blood on the blanket. Examining myself, while doing my duty, there was assuredly dried blood around my groin. My God, I thought, that's why the penetration was so difficult—she was a thirty-year-old virgin. Perhaps it was menstruation, but no—I knew in my heart. The gravity and implications suddenly and inexplicably weighed heavily upon me.

"Terry I … I think we ought to talk about our immediate plans, but I also feel … I mean about last night, I… "

"There's nothing to talk about on that issue," she said between slurped handfuls of water scooped from the creek. "It was a one-time, freak accident. End of story."

I felt tremendous disappointment, as her softness was once again suppressed by that hard edge. "But Terry, Terry darlin, it was no just an accident lass. You were a, a vir… " My words trailed off and her head snapped around.

Her jaw was set and its muscles were flexing as her narrowed eyes bore into me. Then they suddenly widened, as if in surprise.

"If you choose to move, then you choose to die," came chilling words in Spanish, from somewhere behind me.

Terry rose, cautiously, holding the blanket around her, and I turned, very slowly. My guts were churning and I screamed inside, 'NO, not after all we've just been through!' I was surprised to see an old man and two boys. The boys were perhaps twelve years of age and the little old man must have been eighty. They were clothed like simple peasants. Leveled at us was an ancient looking rifle, shaking ever so slightly in the old man's grasp.

"Why are you pointing a gun at us? We are just tourists, we mean no one any harm," Terry said, meekly.

"Tourists! There are no tourists around here. I am no fool," scoffed the old man.

"But we were sailing and wrecked on a reef. We barely survived. Our, our boat sunk," her voice cracked. Terry was good. She sounded scared and she sounded convincing. This was likely the old man's fishing hut and he had been surprised to find us here. His eyes narrowed suspiciously, as he thought it over. The boys looked nervous, ready to bolt.

"Tomas, see what is in the hut. Topa, you look around for anything suspicious. I don't think there are anymore of them. I used to be a professional puma tracker, you know," he chuckled softly. "Now I hunt and fish for fun and food."

He was calming down, relaxing, apparently believing Terry. A trusting soul he and possibly just a wee bit dulled with age. Though his face was creased and his body bent, he retained incredibly long gray-black hair tied in a ponytail. The young boys similarly had strikingly long hair down to their waists, though without the gray or ponytail.

"Big hombre, have you no tongue? What is your story?"

"No hablo Espanol," I said, playing dumb and figuring to let Terry take the lead.

The old man shrugged and the boys soon returned to confirm nothing was unusual—no guns or contraband. He frowned and then smiled a mostly black-toothed grin. "You must be hungry, muchachos," and lowering his vintage weapon, he sent the boys for their packs.

"Venerable and generous friend, could you perhaps point us toward the Ecuador border?" Terry asked, keeping her shy, respectful demeanor.

With a snort of a laugh, he replied, "You are almost standing on it, pretty senorita. You are in my province of El Oro and around the far point is the peurto Huaquillas. On the other side of this creek begins Peru."

Paolo, as he called himself, became our guardian angel. While his grandsons stayed behind to harvest the fishing nets, we trekked upstream to his rusted old pickup truck. It was an hour's drive from there to his little village of Santa Maria near Pasaje.

We met his wife, Consuela, and in their simple, but deliciously warm adobe, we were able to rest and become whole again. We were given clean, rudimentary bandaging for our many cuts and scrapes. Simple, hot, corn tortillas, tunta (dehydrated potatoes), and cuy (guinea pig) have never tasted so good. After our horrific ordeal, such nurturing was a heavenly experience. Consuela's perpetual, coffee-bean-blackened smile, on a face that must have had a crease for every year, was a carbon copy of Paolo's. Also, her hair was richly long and slightly grayed as Paolo's. Inquiring as to their extravagantly long hair they related that they were of the ancient Canaris culture and it was their custom. Consuela said it was in reverence to their ancestral goddess of the sea, *Mamacocha*. Short and weathered, as they both were, certainly lent credence to couples becoming look-a-likes with age.

Time seemed to cease for us, as in our state of mental and physical debilitation several days passed before we regained some equilibrium. Slowly emerging from this enervating fog I could not help but ask of their altruistic nature. They said it was the ancient Canari way and they simply tried to maintain the ways of their ancestors. Paolo and Consuela were an amazingly warm and open couple. A bonding between us seemed to take place that felt a most natural thing. Insisting upon nothing in return, Paolo subsequently drove us to Cuenca, where we were able to catch a domestic flight to Quito. Fortunately, our credit cards had survived the odyssey. We were able to fill Paolo's old clunker with gas, against his protestations. Such kindness could never be repaid, but I silently vowed that someday I would try. The farewell was sadder then I anticipated, but after such travails, it was a great relief to return to the bosom of ostensible civilization.

It was a revelation, or at least a reawakening, that the Paolos and Consuelas could still countervail the Barbers and Huamans of this world. And what is so different about that, for it has ever been thus. Yes, for every de Rais and Tremoilles, there has always been an Alex and Jeanne. Such is the bane and blessing of mankind.

Chapter Four

Epilogue

Once we got to a phone in Cuenca, life suddenly got so much simpler. With considerable trepidation I turned the manuscripts over to the American embassy in Quito, as Terry assured me that was our only logical option. Legal no, but she said it was the only way we might continue to have input and see that Janeen eventually got her due. Terry guaranteed me her agency had the power to do this and I trusted her. Even though she didn't want to admit to our new closeness it was assuredly there under the surface on a slow simmer.

It was not a total surprise when we learned that Stephen Saxon had been indicted on charges of conspiracy to smuggle antiquities and illegal drugs. It explained his presence at the dock during our escape. Terry and I both had wondered if that had been hallucinatory. His dealings were a labyrinth of duplicity and greed. He had Japanese Yakuza connections procuring priceless antiquities by whatever means. They in turn needed to transport their illegal drugs internationally. With his high placed connections he had access to secure government transportation, making all things were possible.

Saxon was able to indulge his passion for priceless antiquities with incredibly arrogant disregard for international legalities. Peru, being a fertile ground of unexcavated ancient cultures, and with a strong, influential Japanese presence, his table was set. Unfortunately, for him, his machinations all began unraveling after the murder of the respected curator, Samuel Gasparojo. It was doubtful that Gasparojo himself was actually involved with this illicit black-market. However, some lesser officials who were involved panicked and ran to the authorities out of fear for their own lives and families. Enough evidence emerged to start a chain reaction of scandalous implications for the various powers, and the demons were defanged. When Americans became implicated someone had to be sacrificed, and why not the chief perpetrator. Stephen Saxon had always been more feared than liked, so with the evidence in place, it was an easy choice for the power brokers.

Another part that came to light was the fact that Saxon had set his *Yakuza* thugs loose on Terry. It was while talking to my ex-wife, Sharyl, at Janeen's memorial service in Calgary that she told me of her father's venomous hatred for Terry. He knew of Sharyl's bisexuality and blamed Terry for deviating his daughter. The bogus gold medallion story I had concocted provided the pretext for him to have the *Yakuza* pay Terry a visit.

The manuscript has since been secretly transported through diplomatic channels to the University of Florida, where specialists are studying it. If anyone can authenticate them, I am told it is the resident expert, Professor Martin Moseley.

The winter winds have whipped the Bay of Aberdeen into surly swells and white froth, as I sit looking out from my condo balcony tumbler of scotch in hand. The skyscape is a dark and brooding swirl of gargoyle-like nebulae, befitting my troubled mood. Both Terry and I have been on R & R, but unfortunately, she is in Florida and I am in Aberdeen. I'm not sure when, or even if, we'll ever see each other again. I can only hope.

I feel as if there is something left undone. Something left unsaid. Certainly the ordeal has permanently scarred both of us, but life goes on. We can only hope to grow as individuals through such adversity. My somber state will surely clear, just as the bonny sun will return to Aberdeen in spring. Sometimes you must lose something to truly come of sage age. It could be innocence, it could be virginity, or it could be love.

Perhaps there is a reason that I found the scripts, for the spell that Alex's text weaves excites my being immeasurably. I feel a strong empathy, a kinship, which is only separated by the vagaries of time. It seems a palpable thing—like an echo in time, an echo of destiny.

It must be the loss of Janeen that has enervated my good sense. I do not believe in reincarnation, or in ghosts of the past, but yet….

Jenny had once said to me, 'To understand our present, we must first unlock the puzzles of our past.'

I cannot see the sun, but I know it is rising. With a practiced flick of the wrist, I drained my scotch.

THE END!

'Man is justified by the greatness of his acts, but woman, through the magnitude of her illusions.'

The Koran

'History is but a parcel of tricks played upon the dead by the living.'

Voltaire

ISBN 142512909-9

9 781425 129095